don't
brake my
heart

# don't brake my heart

## LEONIE MACK

Bedford Square
Publishers

First published in the United Kingdom in 2026 by Bedford Square Publishers Ltd,
London, UK

bedfordsquarepublishers.co.uk
@bedfordsq.publishers



ISBN
978-1-83501-408-0 (Paperback)
978-1-83501-409-7 (eBook)

2 4 6 8 10 9 7 5 3 1

Typeset in 11.75 on 13pt Perpetua
by Avocet Typeset, Bideford, Devon, EX39 2BP
Printed and bound in Great Britain by
CPI Group (UK) Ltd, Croydon CR0 4YY

The manufacturer's authorised representative in the EU for
product safety is Easy Access System Europe, Mustamäe tee 50,
10621 Tallinn, Estonia
gpsr.requests@easproject.com

*To us, the overachieving girls at school, who are now women trying to work out what really matters and whether we can have it all.*

# 7 September, the year before

## Leesa

Some people go out with a bang – they hit that final round number: 50 wins! 100 wins! Break a record. Wild cheering and bike wheels raised in tribute.

I went out flat on my back, in throbbing pain under a grey sky, a stone windmill at the edge of my vision, the striped sails rotating listlessly in a half-hearted salute to my lacklustre career in road cycling. An anticlimax was all I'd earned in ten years of racing.

No records broken – just a bone, I was pretty sure. My left wrist had that stabby pain, my nerves screaming that something was very wrong. The usual twisty pain flared through the rest of me, sharp enough that I didn't want to move, even to check if my arm was still on the correct angle.

Mud spatter had made it inside my mouth, tasting of rotten life forms, moss and iron. Or maybe the iron was blood. Supporters wildly waving cardboard signs at the side of the road had caused a split-second lapse in concentration from the rider in front of me and we'd all gone down. 'Wheel contact' it was called, although 'asphalt contact' felt more appropriate to the burning scrape on my hip.

So this was it. The end. I wouldn't even be able to finish my last race from this position halfway down an irrigation ditch, with only one functioning arm. My final result: 'did not finish'. I could imagine those words on my tombstone.

The sails of the windmill flickered and went blurry and for a second I *wanted* to pass out, to get through this next part unconscious. It was easier than accepting that I'd failed. A cool drip at my temple revealed why my vision was blurred and that was worse. I couldn't *cry* about a stupid sporting career. I had my whole life ahead of me: graduation, internship, a good job with a decent salary.

This sport had chewed me up and spat me out, a muddy, bloody mess in a ditch on the last day of my last race. I never wanted to touch a bike again – didn't want to see the faces of my teammates. Crap, now I was thinking about the others – Bonnie and Doortje, *Lori* – my vision wasn't just blurry, but swimming. I was letting them down.

'Leesa!'

Urgh, that voice. I didn't want to hear it in my moment of self-pity, even if his tone was genuinely alarmed, rather than the usual mocking drawl.

'Leesa!' It was louder now, shocking me into lifting my head. Bad idea. I couldn't pretend I was unconscious any more and it hurt like hell. That, and I made the mistake of looking at him, the golden boy of the men's team, who played juvenile pranks and screwed up spectacularly on occasion but still managed to be universally popular.

Lori's little brother.

His face was closer now, hovering above me. 'The medics are coming. Stay still, ay? We've got you.'

Fingertips under my chin released the helmet strap and I could breathe a little easier. Was this one of his sick jokes? Or was I truly unconscious and my brain was tormenting me with images of the guy who'd once slipped blue food dye into my oatmeal.

'Hang in there, sweetheart.'

*Sweetheart?* I couldn't be entirely conscious. Surely I was imagining him – the gentle fingers at least?

'Colin… Gallagher?'

'That's me,' he said, his voice smooth. 'Shhh.'

This was a prank gone wrong – surely, like the time he'd hidden a Bluetooth speaker in the room I was sharing with Bonnie and played 'Baby Shark' in the middle of the night. He thought this was funny, right? Showing up just when I was crashing out of my life?

'What the *hell* are you doing here?'

# Chapter 1

## Leesa

*Get a good education, a steady job and make your own happiness.* That's what my parents had been telling me since I was old enough to understand the words — in English and Polish, since they'd insisted on speaking both all through my childhood. The education part I'd finally managed after a decade of part-time study around my race schedule, but the other two? A long way off.

Eight months into my transition from women's elite cycling to normal life and I couldn't say it was going well. After two rounds of surgery and physio, my wrist was completely healed, apart from a knobbly purple scar. I couldn't say the same for my spirit — or my bank balance.

I was living in a tiny room in a tiny apartment in Pasadena — and even those precarious developments could all come crashing down in a few weeks when my internship came to an end, shortly followed by my sublet.

When my parents were my age, they'd both qualified as doctors, moved to the US to set up their practice and had a baby on the way. All I had to show for myself at nearly 30 was one competitive — but ultimately demoralising — career and the beginning of another, transitioning from sports into sports marketing, neither of which paid much at the bottom rungs, I had discovered — at least not for women. And while I appreciated I was lucky my mom and dad had helped out with college fees, I still had a student loan the size of their crushing expectations.

Maybe I should have taken their advice and enrolled in

pre-med, but I'd been inspired and wanted to walk my own path – or rather, cycle it, before I'd quit all that once and for all. That inspiration was supposed to serve me well in my internship at Redwin, a prestigious sports marketing agency in LA, but after four months of being dismissed as inexperienced and performing mind-numbing, repetitive tasks for others – not to mention the sad fact that inspiration doesn't pay the bills and neither does an intern's salary – that well was empty too.

My feet were heavy as I arrived at the office one morning at the end of April. Even the trophy wall in the reception area, with framed photos of previous campaigns in professional and grassroots sports – even the campaigns directed at women that usually got me in the chest – couldn't shift the chip on my shoulder.

I was out of cash and would soon be out of time, unless Redwin offered a real job at the end of the internship. So much for being school valedictorian, a bachelor degree summa cum laude from NYU and a masters from Rice – plus the intelligence test results in my medical file that my parents strictly forbade me from ever mentioning outside the family but talked about constantly between themselves.

I had a meeting with the vice president first thing. His assistant had slipped it into my diary two days ago without explanation. It sucked being the bottom feeder who apparently didn't even deserve any hints as to whether it was a hire or fire moment.

If I wasn't offered a job, I might be stuck back at home, taking pity shifts as a medical receptionist at my parents' practice, as though nothing had changed since I was 16 years old. As though my entire sporting career had never existed. Sometimes I thought it might be better if it never had.

Needless to say, I was not inspired, not any more, and I might very soon also be unemployed.

Usually, I waved to the receptionist and glanced hopefully at the trophy wall, but that day I slunk past with little more than a mumble and headed to my desk in the open-plan office. I just had time to knock back an espresso – a skill I'd mastered over months spent in Italy and France during the racing season – before I headed to the VP's office to hear my fate.

Bill Weekes, Executive Vice President and Head of Account Management, was too big a fish to be my direct supervisor, but he held the purse strings for my department and I suspected he had the sadistic streak required to give tiny cogs in his machine sleepless nights, waiting in suspense.

'Leesa!' he boomed unnecessarily, as though my appearance in response to his summons was a surprise. He dragged out the 'ee' in my name, even though I pronounced it like 'Lisa'. It was still a mystery to me why my parents had saddled me with the unusual spelling – a long-winded explanation instead of a first name, as though they wanted me to be special, but ended up with simply 'complicated'. 'Come in, come in. Sit down. Would you like anything? Coffee? I can get Julie to—'

'I'm fine, thanks.' Perhaps I shouldn't have interrupted him, this big cock in the marketing henhouse – no pun intended – but I didn't want to hear him pimp out Julie's coffee-making services. I met his gaze expectantly, which I possibly also shouldn't have done.

'Right then, well, you must be wondering what this meeting is about.'

I held in my sarcastic response with my last hopes that this was a 'hire me' moment and not the opposite.

'You understand, Leesa, salaries are our biggest expense.'

Not my shitty wage, but okay. My chest felt hollow and my head pounded. I understood. Food and housing for me – independence, vindication, purpose – was an expense for him. The all-powerful bottom line was getting ready to slice me off, even though I'd had nothing but good feedback over the past four months.

'We can't hire every intern.'

'I understand.'

He eyed me, as though I'd said something wrong, as though dying inside wasn't allowed in his office. The poor cleaner would have to wipe me off the floor.

'I thought you had a lot of promise.'

Oh crap, now I had to listen to *his* disappointment? I was already panicking about how to tell my parents, who had their own trophy wall for their only child: my school certificates — framed and hanging alongside their medical degrees in Polish — and *one* cycling trophy, the only one they'd deemed an equivalent achievement to my studies, the stylised wave from last year's Great Ocean Road Race.

He wasn't the first person to tell me I wasn't reaching my potential.

I struggled to tune back in as he continued speaking. 'It's a shame, since I would have a project for you, except you're sure to refuse it.'

'What?' I breathed out through pursed lips to slow down my brain. 'I'm not sure what you mean. I'm interested — in anything.'

'That's not what you said when you started here.'

I could barely remember what I'd had for breakfast in this panic state, let alone what I'd said four months ago.

'I wanted to send Morgan, but the event is in July and, as you know——'

'They're getting married,' I finished for him.

'I'm having real trouble finding the right person. Content creation at an important event in Europe in July, weeks away from home in a hotel — it's a hardship assignment.'

I couldn't quite stifle my snort. It sounded like a dream — actual responsibility, performing the work I'd studied for ten years to do. And travel — I didn't even care where. With my non-existent vacation time I'd travelled precisely nowhere since I moved to LA. Plus, the hardship hotel would solve the pressing practical problem of the end of my cheap sublet.

'I'm sure I can do it,' I blurted out.

Bill continued speaking, as though he hadn't heard me. 'It's a hardship for anyone with a family or a partner anyway. You don't have commitments, do you?'

I hated to think of the colour of my face as I shook my head. The whole office must know my social life had been non-existent for… even longer than they thought, actually.

'None at all. I'm completely free in July — June and August too.' *And I really need a job.*

'But, alas, I completely respect your wishes, so I can't ask you to take on this project. It would have been excellent experience for you – working with a major talent in the sport.'

Everything I'd wanted to do since I started my internship.

'With your knowledge and connections, it would have been perfect for you.'

For all the sheets of paper certifying my education and intelligence, I should have been able to work out what Bill Weekes was talking about.

'I said I'd do it – I can do it. Please, I'm sure I can.'

He grinned – the kind of smile the recipient wasn't supposed to share. 'Good, good. I knew you'd come round. Here's a file Morgan put together with some of our previous work with the client.' He pushed a manila folder in my direction and even through the wash of relief, my gut was insisting I'd been played, although understanding was still a luxury Bill obviously thought I didn't deserve. 'I understand you requested not to be put on the PowerFuel account or anything cycling-related, but to be honest, your connection to the community is your greatest asset – the main reason we would consider taking you on long-term.'

A tingle skittered from my neck to my hairline. PowerFuel was a manufacturer of carbohydrate gels for endurance sports, the weird little sachets I slurped hours into a race to keep my metabolism functioning despite burning more nutrients than my body could actually replace – I *had* slurped when I'd been the one on the bike with my body pushed past its limits.

Bill was right, I'd asked to stay off cycling accounts – for a better range of experience, I'd claimed, but mainly because of the tingle that was turning into a stab of memory: failure, pain. That last race had been such a disaster I'd vowed never to get back on a bike and I'd kept to it.

Then I realised what Bill was talking about and my breath deserted me.

PowerFuel – July – Europe. *Shiiit.*

It took me a moment to find my voice. 'You're thinking of sending me to the Tour de France.' The swoop in my stomach wasn't all dread. The Grande Boucle, the three-week race that had started my own love affair with cycling – televised in the waiting room at my parents' practice over a long summer when I was 13. It would break my heart to go back, but the prospect of being there again stole my breath with anticipation.

'"Tour de France",' Bill repeated with a mock French accent that made me grimace inwardly. 'You could be a real asset to the PowerFuel account. Did you ever win anything then?'

'A handful of races,' I managed to answer.

'Pays peanuts, I imagine,' he mused. 'Especially for women.'

I hoped my silence implied enough assent for him to leave the subject.

'But it's an interesting sport. Lovely scenery and the grassroots aspect makes it intriguing indeed.'

He looked up, as though expecting me to say more, but my heart wasn't beating properly and, if I didn't get out of this room soon to emotionally process this development alone, I was going to burst into tears and prove how much I needed the expensive therapy I paid for out of pocket because the crappy insurance I had through this job wouldn't cover it.

'If that's settled, I'll get the contract drawn up and you can discuss the rest with Morgan.'

I stood to leave, but Bill stopped me before I got halfway to the door. 'Don't you have any questions for me?'

Dear God, I was supposed to have questions as well?

'Don't you want to know who the talent is? It might be someone you know. Wouldn't that be a delicious development?'

'Delicious' wasn't exactly how I'd describe anything to do with PowerFuel.

I still said nothing and Bill went on, 'He wasn't our first choice, but he's quite a personality. Not always the most successful, but a crowd favourite – if you can capture the charisma and… play down some of his less redeeming qualities.'

He could have been describing Colin Gallagher, with his 'less redeeming qualities'. 'Big personality' fit, too – bigger even than his quads. Wouldn't that be a cruel joke——

No, I wasn't going to imagine that. Bill meant someone else, someone who hadn't mocked me and pranked me and... I didn't want to think about what had happened in the hospital after my final race – what had *almost* happened. Between me and Colin.

My throat closed. Surely my luck wasn't that rotten?

'But you'll know all about that, I'm sure, since he's on your old team, I understand.'

I groped for the back of the chair I'd just vacated as the enormity of what I'd agreed to washed over me. Even if I clung to the dim possibility that this assignment wasn't about Colin, Bill was making me go back – to everything I'd lost.

'The team is Harper-Stacked?' I hadn't said those sponsor names in months and they felt like an incantation that brought back everything I'd been trying to move on from. My teammates Lori and Doortje, Bonnie and the other riders – we'd been a kind of family, the feeling all the more powerful because we were so different.

The team *was* Lori's family – her dad was the manager and her brother... Her *brother*.

'Harper-Stacked indeed,' Bill continued, lacing his fingers over the bulge at his middle.

My eyelids drifted shut and the room seemed to be spinning. My voice was thin when I finally found it to ask, 'And the talent?'

'In the file,' he said, nodding indulgently at the folder that suddenly seemed to be burning my fingers. 'Have fun, Leesa!'

I lurched out of the room, finally breathing again on the other side. Escaping behind the dividers surrounding my desk, it took me several long, stern words with myself before I could bring myself to open it.

When I did, the truth was so much more frightening than I'd expected – my own reaction in particular.

Of course it was him. Somehow, every time I was struggling, there he was, with his shit-eating grin that couldn't be called anything other than a smirk. Five years on the same team – and that one mortifying moment after my surgery back in September.

The moment I'd looked at him and for the first time felt... *attraction*.

I slammed the folder shut, but it was too late. I could still see the blue of his eyes, the curve of his bottom lip. I could *hear* that low, deep drawl that made everything sound like dirty talk. I thought I'd been at my lowest back in September when I'd last seen him, but this felt like some kind of prank — exactly the kind he'd play on me.

But this was my only chance. Joke or not, I was going back into the cycling world — and all because of Colin Gallagher.

# Chapter 2

## Colin

*'If there's no pounding in ya bollocks, it hasn't been a good day! Keep going, boys! Feel that lactate in your blood!'*

Was it utterly cringeworthy being 25 years old and still having your dad training your sports team? Absolutely. Add in the fact that my dad was an Irish-Australian potty mouth with a fixation on testicles and a sadistic sense of humour and, yeah — sometimes he was enough to make me want to claim an immaculate conception.

Tempted to rip out my radio, I filtered him out instead, the world narrowing to the strip of asphalt in front of me, the cool air flooding my lungs, the sting of power in my body as I hauled myself up the mountain.

I was pretty sure I had lactate up to my eyeballs, but it wasn't exactly something to celebrate from where I was sitting — and occasionally standing — on my bike. I could almost hear the screams as my cells demanded oxygen and my blood turned acidic. I also didn't need my dad to point that out to me.

Another five minutes and I'd be cooked. Dad probably knew that. Maybe he'd push me anyway.

*'Amir, good progress, son. Keep it up. Two hundred metres to go.'*

'Come on, magic mo!' my teammate Amir grunted as he passed me.

I smirked in response, rubbing a thumb across the scruff of bristles on my top lip, soaked with sweat. It had a little more ginger than the sandy blond on my head and it made me look like a baby gunslinger. We'd been ribbing our youngest rider about not being able to grow a beard and this was the result, but at least it was a little thicker than Derek's. He looked like that kid from *Sex Education* – and twice as awkward.

Amir took the position at the front, 'pulling', as we called it. Although my legs were very aware that it was only slipstream and there wasn't any actual pulling involved. I was still fighting gravity with everything I had.

'*Last curve. Great stuff, Derek.*'

Up this high, there was still snow on the ground in June – piles of it, despite the daytime temperature hovering in the 20s. At the beginning of my career, I'd gawk and simp at the sight of the brittle summer snow in the Alps but, like high taxes and cheap beer, I'd got used to the weird stuff about life in Europe, although the socks-and-Birkenstocks thing would always be a step too far.

We were at the iconic Passo dello Stelvio, with its endless switchbacks. 24 km of punishing gradients that Dad probably thought was character-building this early in our training camp. Altitude stole my breath just as effectively as the astonishing views of stony summits and snow-covered rock debris.

But even the Stelvio came to an end eventually, the kiosks and the quaint hotel at the top of the pass swimming in my vision as the gradient finally eased. Pressure lifting, my lungs opened up, my chest expanding as drops of sweat puddled on my handlebars and the numbers on the display of my bike computer finally began to drop.

'*Don't ease off yet!*' Dad cried.

*Fucking oath.* My throat was raw, but I followed orders, pumping harder to pick up speed before the descent, whipping through the milling groups of other cyclists and motorbikers who'd been allowed to stop there for a rest.

With a strangled gulp, I swallowed down the burst of stomach acid making its way up my throat. *Fuck.*

The radio crackled and I bit back a grimace. But all Dad said was, '*Watts are looking good, Colin.*'

My bike computer had already told me that – without the passive-aggressive tone.

Sweeping through one more bend, the air rushed at me suddenly as we hurtled into the downhill, reinflating my lungs after the crush of the high-altitude climb, beginning to fly. Dad was saying something, but I zoned him out as I tracked the hairpins, marked in my mind's eye with angles and trajectories, accompanied by the rapid ticking of my wheel hub.

I zipped ahead of the others. It was my job to be faster, to push the limits. Dad had built the whole team around me, which was why he was such a hardarse. When I screwed up, I screwed up the whole team.

But jacking up the speed on a descent was something I was more than happy to do. It beat battling the asphalt on a climb. Tucking myself down, tight to the frame of my bike, my mind soared with my body.

Lime-green alpine meadows and ancient grey rock, jagged peaks with patches of snow – the world was enormous around me as I harnessed gravity instead of fighting it. I always felt like Magneto on an epic descent – although that was kind of embarrassing to admit and the marketing people would hate that I identified with a villain, even a little.

But I certainly wasn't a hero.

Gravity seemed to be on my side this year. Whipping around curve after curve, my knee a whisper from the road, I didn't need to look at my computer to know I was killing it. I couldn't look at my computer. I needed my eyes on the road, my brain and my instincts all in tune to master the bends.

I let the bike fly through the straights, hanging on for the ride. There would be no winner of this training ride, no pressure to fight. There were no obstacles on the road – I was going too fast to see them if there were. The pulling sensation on my skin and the tenor of the vibrations in the handlebars made me think I'd cracked 90 km an hour. The wind sluicing over my slick body – slick from sweat and from the slippery Lycra of my jersey and bib shorts – drowned out every other sound.

It was a shame to slow down as the road flattened out, but there was another set of bends ahead and, at this speed, I'd shoot right off the edge. Deceleration was like popping out of a wind tunnel as I finessed the brakes. Racing since I was nine years old, I felt ageless, immortal, on these familiar descents – part of the landscape and beyond the reach of the laws of physics. Maybe life would have been easier if I had been.

The crackle of Dad's voice in my earpiece greeted my return to the real world. '*Thank the fucking saints, Colin. That's 20 years of my life I'll never get back. There's no fucking reason to hit 95 ks an hour on a fucking training ride.*'

I eased around the first bend, my skin suddenly cold. Did he know how many years of *my* life *I'd* never get back? But he'd made his point. Only a helmet and a thin layer of material separated me from the cruel road and I'd seen what a crash could do to someone in a split second.

My older sister, Lori, had never been the same after she'd broken her back. She'd recovered physically – because she was such a stubborn shit – but mentally? She wasn't as tough as before. To top it off, she'd got together with Seb Franck, the spineless wonder whose only special talent was mooning over her. Except I kind of missed that bugger, now he'd retired.

We were heading straight down the valley to Bormio, through the gallerie, half-tunnels that protected the road from the steep hillside above. The gradient felt like going over the handlebars, but I knew exactly where my front wheel needed to be. I felt the updraughts and the force of gravity, heard the whistle of the rocks whooshing past, close enough to touch.

I was soaring, ignoring the mumbling in the background over the radio. Then came Dad's voice. '*Did you hear that? It's Leesa Kubicka!*'

*Whoosh*, I went straight down. A split second's misjudgement and I overcorrected, hitting the deck with a metallic clatter and a rip of clothing – and skin. Gravity no longer bowed to me as it scraped me down the road for long enough that the pain kicked in, but I came to a stop eventually, my feet pointing up the hill and my helmet caught in some weeds.

'*Farking hell, Colin!*'

Chest heaving, I stared up at the sky, fluffy little clouds taunting me as the world seemed to be at the wrong angle, trees growing down and physics pulling me up. Blood rushed in my ears and the aftershocks of adrenaline zapped in my arms.

That was the effect Leesa Kubicka had on me.

I slammed my eyes shut and I could picture her, caked in sweat, a smile on her lips and her curly hair rioting when she took off her helmet. Bright, sharp eyes. A divot in her chin – a face I thought I'd never see again, punching the breath out of me when I'd watched her go down in her last race, back in September.

Hearing the screech of car brakes and then footsteps, I wrenched my eyes open to find Dad bending over me. He reached out a hand, but I hauled myself into a sitting position before he could begin his examination. My skin pulled over my elbow and my thigh stung – no big deal. Everything moved as it should.

'Look at the state of your paintwork!' Dad cried, clapping me on the back as though I were a toddler with wind. It smarted – both the wallop between the shoulder blades and his words. After nearly 20 years of training with him, I knew when he said 'paintwork' he meant 'skin', but it got to me more than usual.

Everything seemed to be getting to me, which didn't bode well for the Tour starting in four weeks.

'What was that?' he prompted.

'I got distracted,' I mumbled back.

'No joke! This isn't what I meant when I said we should hurry back to meet your new content manager.'

Whipping off my reflective sports glasses, I squinted up at my dad, slowly putting two and two together. She'd been about to start an internship at a sports marketing agency after acing her studies. Wilhelmina, our team marketing guru, had told me something (I'd mostly ignored) about a partnership with PowerFuel. If Leesa was here…

Leesa was *here*?

Heat rushed up the back of my neck and I swiped a hand over the stupid moustache.

'Let me give you a hand.'

I batted Dad's arm away and rose to my feet, stumbling as I found my balance on the steep slope. I had my bike upright and one leg halfway over the saddle when Dad stopped me.

'Come back in the car. You should get those scratches looked at.'

I hesitated, my hair standing on end as I hoped he couldn't see this restlessness that shadowed me more and more often these days.

'Be a hero another day, Colin.'

Dad was unfortunately right. There was no reason to finish the descent under my own steam, even on the off chance that she'd see me riding in. It was no use trying to impress her. I'd tried that once and it had ended in disaster. Besides, Leesa was too smart — too *everything* — for me and she'd unfortunately seen all the stupid stuff I'd pulled over the years.

Stupid stuff like growing a moustache to rub a teammate's face in his junior position. But, damn it, my heart was pounding and my knees were bouncing in the car as we headed for the hotel. I should have descended on the bike. It would have been quicker.

As well as the power to bend gravity, I had apparently developed a sixth sense as well — my Leesa sense. I heard her voice as soon as I entered the lobby of the hotel. Despite the blood-smeared elbow, the rip in my jersey at the ribs, a day's worth of stale sweat and an idiotic moustache, I still swerved helplessly in her direction.

I was under no illusions about my own attractiveness right now, to say nothing of the fact that she'd always seen through me, but I wanted to see her, even if it was only to work out exactly how much she resented me now, after everything I'd done in September.

She was sitting with Wilhelmina in the dining room. Her back was to me, drawing my eyes to the curve of her neck, an earlobe with a simple gold hoop. Her hair fell to just below her shoulders. A woman's hair had never registered with me before, but Leesa's was something else: springy curls in tight loops, somehow neat and wild at the same time.

And perfect. She was fucking perfect.

Leaning heavily on the wall just outside the dining room, I took long, controlled breaths and tried to talk my stirring body out of its extreme reaction.

'I'm so glad it's you they've sent,' Wil was saying. I gave that statement a hard agree until she continued. 'You remember what he's like.'

Leesa chuckled — a throaty laugh that would have shivered over my skin, if she hadn't been laughing at me. Actually, I still felt that dry laugh in a few places that weren't very comfortable in my bib shorts.

'That's what worried me about taking this assignment,' she said. 'How on earth could I accept responsibility for making *Colin Gallagher* into a sympathetic protagonist? I don't think PowerFuel would approve of the pranks and relentless jokes.'

My shoulders slowly sank.

'But I remember you enjoy a challenge.'

She tucked her hair behind her neck and straightened. 'I sure do.'

'Just don't let him guess that he's your challenge.'

'Oh, God, no! He'd never let up. I'd find lizards in my breakfast and frogs in my bed.'

At least I could inwardly scoff at her lack of imagination. Lizards and frogs? How old did she think I was? Nine? I might have been a green youth with bum fluff on my chin when I'd first met her nearly six years ago, but the age gap between us had closed further every season since. Besides, when I was nine, I'd already graduated to putting food colouring into my sister's toothpaste.

'There are so many star-struck women working in marketing,' Wil continued. 'If they'd sent anyone else, I might have got worried Colin would turn on the charm and end up AWOL in the evening.'

I straightened with a grimace. *One time* that had happened. It had been a nice invitation, and who could blame me when I had to share a twin room with Amir or Nelson for months of the year in shitty hotel rooms without much space between the beds?

My ears were hot, picturing Leesa taking my hand and steering me down the corridor to her room as my heart vaulted in my chest. Wil couldn't know about last year, that I'd come back early to watch her last race and nearly made a fool of myself.

But then Leesa replied, 'There is absolutely no danger of that.' Her tone was steady — amused, even. 'Colin is *not* the person I picture when I hear the word "charming".'

The urge to prove her wrong flickered in my chest.

'That's one pitfall we don't need to worry about. It's so important to safeguard your professionalism in this industry — especially as a woman in sports,' Wil continued, giving Leesa's forearm a squeeze.

My intentions deflated again. She was here to do a job and that was all — to make me look good, which drew a smirk to my lips. There was no need to react personally to anything she said.

But that didn't mean I had to play along.

# Chapter 3

## Leesa

'Let me know if you need *any* help — or if Colin gives you any trouble. I remember what it's like starting out,' Wil said — too kindly, because I was already struggling not to tear up.

'What? Sending emails and making coffee?' I joked, mostly to give me a second to pull myself together.

It was triggering, being back here.

I'd come to this exact hotel on two occasions, with the girls. It was a dreamy chalet, all wooden beams and lacy curtains, nestled in a sloping mountain meadow and surrounded by the peaks of the northwest Dolomites. Every view out of every window was heart-stirring.

But it wasn't me pulling on the tight Lycra skinsuit this time. I didn't even want to touch a bike.

'Yep. I had those days too,' Wil said with a smile. 'You'll need to meet with Tony and the directeur sportif to go over some conditions, but you know all about how things work. Tony was looking forward to catching up.'

That made one of us. I knew he'd be all father-like and comment on how good I looked — likely without meaning it — and I didn't want to hear it. Plus, I couldn't be certain how much he knew about what had happened in September.

That was when I heard it — that voice, coming from right behind me.

'Fancy meetin' you here.'

My throat closed and goosebumps whooshed up my arms.

Here was the guy who'd brought down my entire career – okay, I knew that was unfair, but it was still difficult to swallow the bitterness he triggered in me. Worse was the kernel of confusion – the memory of what had happened after my last race and how I'd felt… something that made no sense.

I tried to turn around, opening my mouth to speak, but only an inarticulate wheeze emerged. Oh, God, it was worse than I'd thought.

Wil came to my rescue. 'Colin! Good, you've come straight to see me. You remember Leesa from the women's team? What a coincidence, she's back with us.'

He swallowed audibly. 'I don't believe in coincidences. Leesa must be back where she belongs.'

His words cut a tear somewhere only he could touch, stirring everything up. Forcing myself to face him, I found those dark blue eyes on me and an open-mouthed half-smile that strongly suggested he was remembering something different about me from what Wil had mentioned.

But, as my eyes dragged themselves to the familiar shape of his mouth, I noticed the bristle of hair above the top lip.

'What is that fluff on your face?' Oops, that probably wasn't the best thing to say the first time I'd seen him after… everything.

He straightened, which only drew my attention to his eye-popping body, lean and strong with muscle definition up the wahoo – cords and ridges down his chest, scars raised on his skin. Whatever his flaws, no one could accuse Colin Gallagher of not taking his fitness seriously. My gaze snagged on the oozing wound on his elbow and then the rip in his jersey, exposing a scrape and a hint of more tight muscle on his abdomen.

'What happened?'

He waved a hand in front of my face. 'Just a little altercation with the road. Nothing Doc Angie can't patch up – unless you want to give me a hand with that?'

Phew, I needed to work up some immunity to him. He was good-looking at first glance, but the shock of his deep voice ramped him up to devastating. At least so much shit emerged from his mouth that I had a chance. A couple of days and I'd be back to busting his balls like before.

Rubbing his fingers thoughtfully over the moustache, a shade redder than his hair, he gave me a world-class pout. 'But don't you like the 'tache? I thought it gives me a certain… je ne sais quoi.' I knew he could actually speak decent French, so he either had a terrible accent or he'd mangled the pronunciation on purpose.

'You look like a serial killer.'

He laughed, propping his hands on his hips. 'Is that a compliment?' he drawled with a wink, ducking his head until he was a little closer – close enough to suck some of the air out of my lungs. 'Who would I be killing at this altitude?'

*My composure.*

'I'll leave you two to get re-acquainted,' Wil said with a smile, hopefully as oblivious to the churning undertones between Colin and me as she appeared.

When she'd left, his smile was back. 'Re-acquainted?' he repeated with a lift of his brows.

'Colin, can you drop the act for a moment. We need to talk.' Without thought, I grabbed his forearm and steered him towards a table.

'What act?' he prompted as he sank into a chair. Palms up, arms wide, he continued, 'What you see is what you get.'

*Fuck my life.*

'You know what I'm talking about.'

'If you mean when I brought you a cake and I asked if we could—'

'I mean it!' I snapped. 'If we have any hope of a good working relationship, I need you to be an adult about this!'

'Because I'm a boy in a man's body who likes making trouble for other people for his own amusement, right?'

There was still a wobble of a smile on his lips, but the accusation in his words struck me in the chest. 'If the shoe fits,' I said defensively.

'How's your arm? No lasting effects? That's a pretty nice scar.'

The concern in his voice made me lose my train of thought.

'I needed some physio, but it's fine now. I know it wasn't really your fault.'

'But you resent me for it anyway,' he said with a nod, as though he wouldn't try to change my mind. He chewed on the inside of his cheek, a gesture I surprised myself by recognising. The action showed up the sharp lines of his jaw. 'We don't have to talk,' he finally said, lounging back into his chair and stretching his long legs out. 'You said enough back then.'

I ripped my gaze away. 'But what happened after—'

'Nothing happened.'

I wasn't sure I agreed with his definition of 'nothing', but I could see how he got there.

'Don't worry. I know the whole thing was my fault. You're here to do a job now. If you promise to insult my moustache and keep me in my place, I'm sure I won't get any more ideas about you and me. I'll try at least.'

He was joking – surely he was joking – but the flutter in my chest didn't care. 'I just think it would be better if no one knows about the...'

'The what?' He paused, working his top lip between his teeth. Damn, I was looking at his mouth again.

'The cake,' I finished in a hurry.

There was a definite twitch of amusement on his lips. 'The slagroomtaart? I thought that was a nice gesture.'

'You're mocking me,' I muttered, annoyed that his teasing was heating my insides.

'Now I am, yeah,' he admitted.

I wasn't sure I'd ever heard that gruff tone in his voice. It had certainly never made me weak-kneed before.

'But I get it. You can be mad at me. Nothing happened. We can forget about it.'

He was lucky if he could. 'Good,' I said, blowing out a breath. 'And I hope you haven't told anyone about...'

'What I asked you?' He shuddered, as though I'd just told him to drink one of those disgusting ketone drinks – or the orange-flavoured PowerFuel gel. 'Why would I? That moment wasn't exactly worthy of my trophy room.' He shot me a broad smile to paste over the awkwardness in his tone.

'I do *not* want to know about your trophy room,' I mumbled, disturbed by the unexpectedly intriguing prospect of appearing in it. If my answer had been different in September... I had to get a grip. I wasn't interested in being a notch on anyone's bedpost and my buzzing mind would never let me get that far anyway.

But when he spoke next, his voice was steady. 'But I get it. Nobody knows I was at the hospital at all. I understand you're not here for me — well, only with professional interest. I can be professional, Lees.'

For better or for worse — undoubtedly for worse — I believed him and ignored the squeeze of intimacy at the way he shortened my name.

'Except maybe when I swear on camera.'

'You're lucky I have great editing skills.'

'I'm looking forward to seeing all your skills.' He gave me another wink.

'Five seconds, Gallagher! You managed five seconds of professional.'

Tugging off his fingerless gloves, he rested his hand on the table next to my forearm, not quite touching, but close enough that the fine hairs on my arm felt him there. 'I was wrong. Insulting my moustache and keeping me in my place still gives me ideas. Maybe you should flatter me instead.'

'Except that you're good enough at flattering yourself,' I quipped, but my voice was thick from the lump in my throat.

'Is that right?' he replied as he stood. But he grimaced, and my gaze flew to his scraped-up skin. Just looking at the patches of angry red road rash made me shudder.

'You should go and get that looked at.'

''Tis but a scratch,' he replied with a warped smile and a wave. He was gone before I'd managed to place the quote. *Monty Python and the Holy Grail?*

# 9 September, the year before

**Leesa**

'Can I come in?'

Just when I'd almost convinced myself I'd been hallucinating on the day of the crash, his voice from the other side of my door gave me enough of a shock that I knocked over the little pot of hospital-issue yoghurt.

'Uh, yeah?' I hurried to right the yoghurt, only belatedly wondering how bad my hair looked after days in bed.

He seemed hesitant, running a hand through his already wild mop of hair. That was new, but I supposed even Colin Gallagher was capable of feeling pity.

'What are you doing here?'

'That's what you said last time you saw me. My sister is on your team, remember?'

'But she's not in this hospital room,' I answered doubtfully. 'How did they even let you in?'

'I told them I was your boyfriend,' he explained with a shrug. 'I, uh, brought you something.'

What fresh hallucination was this? He thrust a gold-foil cardboard box in my direction. Reaching up with both hands, I grimaced when I moved the fingers of my left hand, where the cast came halfway along my palm.

'Hey, easy.' He set the box on the table next to the glob of spilled yoghurt and settled my arm back at my side. 'Go on, have a look,' he said as he rummaged in his pocket.

'Is it going to squirt cream in my face?'

He raised an eyebrow at me and I could have pulled out my own tongue when I listened back to what I'd just said – in front of a known juvenile wannabe comedian with a dirty sense of humour. With a sigh, I carelessly opened the lid to find a little cake. There was cream, but in pretty rosettes with chocolate shavings – not the sort usually used in pranks, unless he was going to shove this in my face.

'Uh, thanks.'

'I heard you like slagroomtaart,' he said as he produced a felt-tip pen and reached for my left arm. He exaggerated the pronunciation of the Dutch cream cake atrociously.

Before I could come out of my stunned stupor to work out whether to stop him, he'd scrawled 'Get Well Soon', and something that was probably supposed to be his name on the purple soft cast. Waiting for the punchline of a joke I hadn't understood yet, I studied him for long enough to notice how much sharper the lines of his face were at 24. He was kind of grown up.

'What?' he asked, making me glance away momentarily with a gulp.

'I'm waiting for the prank. It must be here somewhere.'

'No prank,' he assured me, his gaze steady on mine. 'I just wanted to see how you were before we fly out to Quebec.'

Not sure how else to respond, I waved around the room with my cast arm. 'Not sure what you wanted to see.'

'Anything – everything,' he said. 'You.' The last word seemed to surprise him as well. 'And I wanted to say sorry. I think it's my fault you broke your arm.'

# Chapter 4

## Leesa

Tony wrapped me in a wiry, mint-scented hug the minute I walked into the meeting room the following morning. I hoped he hadn't noticed the enormous bags under my eyes. After rolling around for three hours from 4 a.m. — the unfortunate fault of jetlag — I'd then overslept and missed breakfast. I needed coffee like a… well, like a cyclist halfway through a Sunday ride, but the drive for punctuality my parents had drilled into me was still stronger than the call of caffeine, so I arrived for our meeting a semi-conscious wreck.

My old team manager was a spindly, weathered type with a perpetual salesman's smile and an excess of energy that made younger people look bad, so his hug was less like comforting squishiness and more like a cottonwood tree wrapping its branches around me. But I respected him. He was a real champion for women's cycling — not least because his own daughter stood to gain — and I had missed his crooked pep talks and wonky sense of humour.

'It's a pleasure to see you back so soon!'

He meant it too, which made me feel like bursting into tears. I was supposed to be happy to have left all this behind, but grief and guilt were real. This had been my team, even though it had sometimes felt I'd given more than I'd received in return. I forced a smile I hoped didn't look as watery as it felt, desperately hoping my professionalism would be strong enough for this.

It had used to bother me that my parents — especially my mom

– had never taken the time to understand why I loved cycling but, right now, I was glad she couldn't see me like this.

'Sit down, sit down. Alan will be here in a minute – and Wil. I just wanted to say before we get started that I'm really glad you're here. I wasn't too sure about this arrangement with PowerFuel. Alan will go over the sensitive bits. Colin's not as… solid as he looks and I wouldn't have been able to trust anyone else. But you're one of us.'

The renewed tears pricking my eyes disagreed with him. Quitters weren't part of the team.

'You understand the kind of pressure he's under,' Tony continued.

That dragged my attention off my miserable self. 'What do you mean?'

'He's on form this year. He's got a real chance at the *maillot blanc*, if he can drop the tomfoolery and perform. It's his big chance to step up.'

Tony's Irish-Australian mangling of the French *maillot blanc*, the white jersey for the fastest young rider at the Tour de France, would have amused me if it hadn't made my insides squeeze. That was a lot of pressure to put on Colin the Clown.

'Okay,' I responded thoughtfully, trying to reconcile impishly flirtatious Colin from yesterday afternoon with Tony's expectations of a young lead rider. 'The client has set out in a lot of detail what they want from the coverage, which is basically captivating content with a lot of footage of Colin's butt.'

I nearly choked when Tony's gaze swerved to me in alarm.

'The logo on his shorts,' I said, swallowing a wheeze. 'I meant the logo.'

'Of course ya did,' Tony said with a doubtful smile.

My cheeks were hot, but I prayed Tony wouldn't think I was blushing for any reason other than my verbal faux pas. It was a fact of life as a rider that we were stamped with logos all over our bodies and the butt-sponsor was one of the most visible.

'I just meant I won't need anything hard-hitting. It's supposed to be entertaining.'

'Being entertaining isn't his problem – it's keeping his head down for a win. We have the chance to attract more lucrative sponsorships for next year, but only if he doesn't flip out before he's secured a good finish in the Tour.'

I wanted to clarify what he meant by 'flip out', but that was unfortunately clear, especially after Morgan and I had compiled the challenges-and-pitfalls document for this project, containing a meticulous list of Colin's bad behaviour. After he'd missed out on first in the Australian Nationals this year, he'd stomped onto the team bus and let loose a string of profanities. Of course, the clip had gone viral. His tantrum after a series of mechanicals during his first Paris-Roubaix two years ago had also become legendary – and not in a good way for the sponsors.

It was one of the only times I'd seen a viral video actually censored in order to be shared and 'Colin Gallagher outburst' was now the most common search term featuring his name.

'He puts on a brave face, but he's not tenacious,' Tony continued, his voice surprisingly steady, given he was discussing his own son. 'I've seen his power stats. The boy can do it this year – if he wants to, and that's what worries me. Creating entertainment for a sponsor... I know we have to do this stuff but, if you distract him...'

My hair stood on end as I pictured him sprawling in the chair yesterday, a lazy, teasing grin on his face. Could I distract him as much as he could distract me? Everyone kept saying how well all of this worked out to have me embedded in the team, but I could only see complications, the foremost of which was that I suddenly found him inexplicably attractive. If Bill had known Colin had come to my hospital room pretending to be my boyfriend, he would never have sent me and Tony certainly would be giving me a much sterner lecture right now if he knew everything that had happened that day.

'We all want Colin to do well,' I said diplomatically.

'Except the boy himself,' Tony grumbled under his breath. 'We want him to *win*. He's got by being a larrikin all these years and I know the sponsors love the attention, but he's not Peter Fucking

Pan. He's got to grow up now and take some responsibility. The other riders are working for him and we need to see results. Whatever you post, it can't endanger that.'

With a gulp, I faced the fact that this job was a lot more complex than I'd expected and I was a green intern with more education than expertise. To top it off, I was a quitter who'd never had the psychology to succeed at this sport and I couldn't afford to let that rub off on Colin.

This was all before I considered what was best for my own career, although I wasn't feeling much spark for my future in that moment.

'I understand,' I assured him solemnly.

His face broke into a grin. 'Thanks, pet. You always were one we could rely on.'

I forced a smile, although his words were another blow. Sensible. Reliable. A team rider always sacrificing for someone more talented than me. I should have just become a damn doctor, like my parents.

I'd never had much to do with Alan Hargreaves, the men's DS — *directeur sportif*, and God forbid anyone said 'sports director' instead, even though we were an English-speaking team. I suspected he didn't even recognise me when he came through the conference room doors, his hand extended.

Wil squeezed my arm in greeting and, before I knew what was happening, Alan thrust a piece of paper and a pen at me, *Non-Disclosure Agreement* written in big letters at the top. I glanced up in alarm.

'Has this been agreed with the client? I'm supposed to have access.'

Tony's gentle gaze dimmed. 'You will have access. This is about certain information you can't post. It was a condition of the arrangement.'

Alan picked up where he left off. 'While you're shadowing his preparation and the competition, you'll naturally come across sensitive information, so we've set out here all the things that are off limits: Colin's training stats, FTP, watts and all strategy discussions are strictly embargoed. We don't want the other teams to know how good he's punching right now. They'll suspect, but we want to be the underdogs, keep the pressure off him until he can cope.'

*Cope* was an ominous word.

After signing the rather daunting NDA, I could finally rush to the breakfast room to grab a coffee before the team meeting, where I'd be officially introduced — or re-introduced. But by then my stomach was churning with nerves and the biting Italian coffee jangled straight into my blood.

I'd known some of these guys for years, spending several weeks a year on team training camp together, but it was different now that my career was officially over.

Coming through the doors into the hall in that state of distraction, a nudge to my shoulder made me jump. Turning reflexively, I started again at the image assaulting my eyeballs: miles of pasty skin, lightly freckled, over tight muscle and bone; a tattoo of a compass pointing northwest decorating his body on the left, just below his ribs; soft tracksuit pants that clung precariously to his taut waist; tan lines on both arms that were more clearly demarcated than the North Korean border.

I dropped my gaze, muttering to myself about Colin's inability to put a shirt on.

'There you are. We're all waitin'.' His deep voice was rich and rough, like nougat chocolate, and I was distracted by the scent of him — clean and soapy, like that day in the hospital. He was wearing the branded slides all of the riders wore at the hotel, his feet bare, toes a little crooked.

Nobody has sexy toes. I focused on the toes and not the easy movement of his body, or the way he seemed to set the molecules in the air fizzing. When I'd finally gathered my composure to look at his face, the view of his stupid moustache — even bushier today, I imagined — got rid of the last few sparks.

'I hope you're not waiting for moustaches to become sexy again, because that one is more "little dirtbag" than "Tom Selleck".'

'I still secretly think you like this little dirtbag — moustache,' he added with a wink. 'But it took me four weeks to grow this. I can't shave it off until Derek admits mine is better than his.'

'Why am I not surprised it was for a bet? If you're trying to remind me how juvenile you can be, it's working.'

He grinned, the bright curve of his mouth acting on me like an amphetamine. 'I can be a jerk for a good cause.'

'Sometimes I wonder if that's your calling in life.' And there was my first angle. If I couldn't get him to behave, maybe I could turn him into a loveable idiot at least.

'It isn't enough that Derek sacrifices his own chances of winning for you?' Derek was a support rider, like I had been. Lead riders like Colin used the slipstream of support riders to conserve energy for an attack later in the race.

'Is this a chip on your shoulder?' he said, pretending to pick something up from my upper arm. 'Looks like a big one.'

'Well, thank you for removing it,' I said sweetly in reply.

'The 'tache isn't a competition, you know.' He made that 'pfft' sound that he must have learned from living half the year in France for nearly a decade.

'You just *told* me it's a competition. I might be a bit strung out on coffee and jetlag, but you can't pull that on me.'

'That's rough.' He shoved a hand in the pocket of his tracksuit and sauntered ahead of me, unfortunately giving me an irresistible opportunity to admire the ripples in his back, the glimpses of his tattoos: the Southern Cross and Olympic rings on one forearm; a simple, but fascinating dragon across his shoulders.

'Are all you guys allergic to clothes?'

'I'm not allergic to clothes,' he insisted, shooting me a pout over his shoulder. 'It's doctor's orders. Gotta air the road rash.'

With a flourish worthy of a 1950s Hollywood musical, he gestured to the ugly red patch down his side and my stomach turned.

'You're familiar with road rash, right?'

My gaze snapped back up to find him peering at me with a glint in his eye.

He had the unnerving ability to speak directly into my

bloodstream when he continued, 'I seem to remember a pic from the Vuelta a few years ago. You crossed the finish line with a rip from your ribcage to your thigh – via the back.'

The lump in my throat grew unbearable as I tried to interpret his tone. There was a hitch in his voice. Or perhaps I was just terribly susceptible to it. I had been certain he'd never spared a thought for me during the years we were on the same team – including that year when I'd crashed at the Vuelta.

'What, you never looked *me* up?' he said with another pout.

'I haven't needed to know how to swear like an Australian,' I quipped.

His response was a swagger. 'You *have* looked me up.'

'Colin, I'm using you to create content for my client. Of course I looked you up.'

He bit his lip, sending a jolt through my veins, although hopefully that was just the coffee. 'I kind of like that you want to use me.'

Before I could splutter a response, he disappeared into the conference room, where the DS and coaching staff were waiting to give the day's briefing, and I stumbled in after him, my skin too tight. Everything he said shot straight to my gut – or a little lower – and I had to struggle to pull myself together.

Rather than a sleek, white-painted, glass-panelled space, at this family-run hotel tucked into the middle of nowhere in a place called Lüsen in the back corner of Italy, the wood-panelled conference room looked more like the place where hunters used to meet up to smoke pipes and play cards while plotting each other's deaths.

It still reminded me of the times when I'd sat with the team like this, Bonnie and Doortje next to me, and Lori being Lori – rushing in late. The pressure for results had always clouded our friendships, especially with Lori, who I'd never truly called a friend, but I missed those girls now. I wished I'd made more of our camaraderie.

After the NDA I'd just signed, nothing was clearer to me than the fact that I was no longer on this team. I'd never been on *this* team, but the women's equivalent — 'just' the women. And I'd never made enough of an impact to be remembered for anything — except maybe crashing out of my last race.

Slumping into a seat at the back, I took a few moments just to breathe, feeling the air in my lungs the way I'd been taught to while pushing my body at high intensity. God damn it, there had been a good reason I'd asked to distance myself from cycling in my new job. I had enough to deal with before I even added the adrenaline hit of verbally sparring with Colin.

I paid attention to the opening of the session with only half an ear but, when Alan looked over at me, Colin leaped to his feet.

'Ahhh-hm,' he began, something alarmingly like a smile on his face as he scratched the back of his neck. 'Because she's a friend of my sister's, I thought I'd... introduce our special guest from PowerFuel.'

I peered at him through narrowed eyes. He must have known Lori and I had never been close. After a pointed look from Colin, Amir leaned over the laptop at the side of the room, connected to the projector, and Nelson jumped up to tap off the lights and slowly — way too late — I realised Colin was up to something.

# Chapter 5

## Colin

The way Leesa's eyes widened to the size of a wheel rim was the highlight of my week. I kept my gaze on her as Amir cued the video – not a chore, when she'd gathered her hair in a high, fluffy bun that drew my attention to her neck. Then I cleared my throat to read the script I'd put together.

'Before she was a marketing genius joining us for the Tour, Leesa Magdalena Kubicka – yup, that's her middle name – was herself an elite pro with none other than the Harper-Stacked women. Her best results were a stage win and fifth overall in the Tour of Scandinavia and a very memorable first place at the Great Ocean Road Race in her final season, before she retired at the advanced age of twenty-nine.'

Sending another glance her way, I found the scowl I'd expected.

'We, her biggest fans in the men's team, have put together this video tribute to present the great achievements of our new guest.'

I'd chosen a hip-hop song with a driving beat that burst from the speakers as the images came up on the screen: Leesa in a helmet and sunglasses looking over her shoulder as she stood in the saddle; Leesa at the front of the peloton, her jaw tight with effort; a still from a photoshoot with one hand on her hip and the other resting on the saddle of an aero bike; Leesa grinning and holding an American flag, her arms covered in dirt.

It hadn't been difficult to find videos to cut together. She'd been so good at coming up with entertaining stuff for her social feeds, which was probably why she'd landed a job in marketing. Looking through them all had also been an hour I'd happily spend again. She had these breasts that were so tiny, I wanted to give them extra attention.

She was wearing a light dress today, with a floral print and provocative buttons running down the front. It was a far cry from the skintight Lycra of cycling kit that hinted at every smooth line of her body. I couldn't decide which look I liked more.

I'd picked one video of her and Doortje Stoepker doing some viral dance with bikes instead of dance partners and then some GoPro footage from a tour somewhere in Portugal. She had this way of smiling right to her back teeth that made me want to hold her against me until some of the magic soaked into me. I hadn't seen that smile yet this time. She didn't usually give it to *me*.

Next came a couple of short race videos, one of her and Bonnie Tham clinging to each other, laughing and crying after a race — I didn't even know which race. Then a clip of her stepping onto the podium in front of the palm trees in Geelong, Australian native flowers in hand, after she'd earned that first place last year — when Lori had been sick after a spider bite.

I'd won the men's race and lorded it over my injured sister like a dick, but it had been worth it to see her get some fight back — as well as that ludicrous grin on her face when she'd been texting Seb and thought I hadn't known what she was doing.

Maybe because of Lori's injury, Leesa had been named lead rider, given all the team's support and then she'd brought the trophy home. I wondered how she looked back on that now.

Behind me, the light changed and I turned to watch the moment I'd selected to end the clip: slow-motion footage of Leesa hurtling towards the finish line in Geelong, the street lined with supporters behind the barriers. Her face — usually soft and rounded and prone to smiling — was drawn tight with effort, with *fight*. Her body was bowed over the handlebars, the silver chain she wore bumping against her chest with every pump of the pedals.

As she crossed over in first place, her eyes flew wide and her mouth dropped open and then she threw her fists into the air.

There was no sound with the video, but we could all hear the way she'd hollered in disbelief.

God, there was something about a woman on a bike.

Turning back to my teammates and staff with a grin on my lips, a surge of satisfaction rose in my chest. Yeah, I knew it had been a shitty thing to do to introduce her like this without warning but, while I'd apologised for what happened in September, I hadn't promised to refrain from more pranks. Plus I wanted everyone to know that she wasn't just a marketing executive, or whatever her job title was.

But when my self-satisfied gaze found her once again, my grin vanished. The scowl was gone, replaced with something hollow. With a swipe at her face, she got to her feet and walked woodenly to the front of the room as the applause tapered off.

Her eyes were deep and huge with betrayal and my skin pulled too tight all of a sudden. Nelson clicked on the lights and she flinched. Oh fuck, I'd screwed up – again. I only seemed to screw up when Leesa Magdalena Kubicka was within ten feet of me.

I wanted to shoo everyone out of the room, protect her from view, pull her onto my lap and rock her while I apologised. But apologising now would only make everything worse and she *definitely* wouldn't let me pull her onto my lap.

Taking a deep breath through her nose, she faced the team. 'After that entirely unnecessary introduction, I barely need to say a thing. But I wanted to reassure you all that I hope to have a positive impact on morale, if anything. I won't disrupt your training or preparations for the Tour. I still really just want you guys to do well – even Colin.'

One of the coaches sniggered. Her voice shook and I found myself silently begging her to snipe at me, put me in my place.

'Might need to watch your back, ay, Colin!' called Derek and I flipped him off subtly from waist-height.

'All right, all right,' Dad intervened from where he sat to one side, his arms crossed. 'You've had your fun, Colin. Now leave her in peace while we get back to work.'

She stiffened beside me and, for a moment, I thought she was close to tears. But Leesa could give as good as she got, surely. A protective comment from Dad wouldn't push her over the edge.

But as she pasted a smile onto her face, brushed past me and headed for the sliding doors, there was something about the set of her shoulders that I didn't like. I wished I'd pulled her into my lap — screw the consequences.

Her departure was followed by a chorus of groans. 'For fuck's sake, C!'

'Have you really gone and pissed off the woman in charge of your sponsorship stuff? That takes balls — or stupidity.'

'I put together the highlights of her career,' I said defensively. 'What's so bad about that?' I already knew the answer. I'd aimed and fired my shot. I just hadn't meant to shoot to kill.

I made it to her door that afternoon with my hair still dripping from the shower. Back here again, on the other side of her door to apologise for my shit.

Leaning one hand heavily on the wooden doorframe, I pressed the heel of my other hand to my forehead. Staring at the laminated picture of a furry alpine mammal stuck to the door, I tried to summon the courage to knock. She had the marmot room, a single tucked under the staircase — the wooden staircase. Everything in this place was made of wood. No pun intended.

Amir and I had the chamois room and, if it hadn't been my third time in this hotel, I might have still thought that meant the crotch padding of a pair of cycling shorts and not a horned sort of goat thing.

I eyeballed that cute little creature on her door for long enough that the familiar sense of frustration rose up my throat. Nothing I did was right. Leesa wouldn't want to see me anyway. All she wanted was for me to keep a professional distance and standing in front of her door agonising wasn't exactly professional.

But I wanted to see her — not only to make her listen to an apology she probably didn't want. I wanted to know what nerve I'd touched.

Straightening quickly, I rapped on the door to cut off my overthinking.

'Go away, Colin!'

Despite everything, her words made me chuckle. 'What if it had been Dad – or Wil?' I called back.

'You're not your dad or Wil, so go away!'

Pressing my palm to the door, I brought my forehead close, as though I could feel her through the wood. 'Can we talk?'

'I thought you didn't want to talk.'

At least she had her fight back. 'Yeah. I was an arsewipe this morning. I'm sorry.'

To my surprise, that seemed to work. The door flew open. 'Do you think apologising and calling yourself an asswipe will erase what you did?'

'Nah, but hoped it might make you smile again.'

Not the reaction I expected, she slumped against the doorframe, resting her temple and letting her eyes fall shut.

'You're supposed to be mad at me. Go on.' I lifted my chin and pointed at it.

When she finally spoke again, it wasn't anything like what I'd expected. 'If I punched you, would it get rid of the moustache?'

'I don't think you hate this moustache as much as you say you do. You talk about it all the time.' I ducked my head. 'Just think, without it I might be devastatingly handsome.'

She cracked an eyelid open. '"Might be"? What happened to your self-confidence?'

I laughed, hoping she didn't notice it was choked. 'I didn't think you liked my confidence. Except in—'

'If you say "bed", this door gets slammed in your face.'

'There's my girl.'

She shot me a peeved look.

'I'm sorry. There's my *woman*,' I corrected with a less-than-convincing straight face.

When she rolled her eyes, I knew I was making progress. 'You've made your apology and we've had some obligatory banter. You can go now,' she said.

That response wasn't the one I wanted. 'Do you wanna go for a walk?' I tried out.

'Why?' was her response, but I was just glad it wasn't a straight no.

'It's so fuckin' beautiful around here.' Especially when she was standing in front of me.

'Aren't you supposed to be resting?'

'A walk is restful, isn't it? Therapeutic.'

'Maybe you should just get therapy.'

I might need to if she kept breaking my heart with every word she uttered. But I deserved it, after what I'd pulled over the years.

I crossed my arms. 'You still haven't said no.'

'I noticed that too,' she mumbled. 'Are you planning to lure me into the forest and leave me there?'

'Cross my heart, I'm not. Last time I did that to someone it backfired badly.'

She almost smiled. Just a slight lift of one corner of her mouth, but it felt like a gold medal – and I'd won two of those at Australian Nationals two years ago, so I knew what I was talking about.

'Whether you believe me or not, I just want to talk.'

'I suppose we should discuss how this project for PowerFuel is going to run.'

That wasn't the kind of talking I'd pictured, but if the other option was the door slammed in my face, I'd take it.

'Give me five minutes to change?'

# Chapter 6

**Leesa**

Angry. I was angry with him. Fuming. He'd humiliated me in front of the entire team. It was so much worse than the time he'd replaced a painting in the hotel breakfast room with a photo of me and I hadn't noticed for a week. Or the time he'd somehow managed to put Bubble Wrap under the sheets on my bed.

Colin was an idiot. It wasn't news. But this time not only had it hit harder – deeper, somehow – but he was still able to disarm me with a few jokes and that crooked smile. Although it hadn't been his smile. It was something in his eyes when he peered at me that I'd first noticed only last September, when I'd thought I'd never see him again.

I didn't dare look at him at first, as we dawdled along the gravel path from the hotel across the vivid alpine meadow. As much as it pained me to admit Colin Gallagher was right about anything, a walk had been a good idea and the landscape was so beautiful it was painful.

One of the approaches of altitude training was 'sleep high, train low', so the hotel was nestled in a saddle at over 6,500 feet above sea level. The rays of sunshine were so intense you could almost touch them. Stony Dolomite peaks ranged up on all sides, protecting this isolated valley and the smattering of wooden cabins on the sloping meadows.

The absence of noise felt like a cocoon around my head.

'I missed being in the mountains.' I hadn't meant to say those words aloud, but they were out now. Maybe in a second I'd be admitting I wasn't any happier for quitting cycling, that I wasn't sure I'd made the right decision, but it was too late now. Luckily, Colin stopped me.

'Doesn't America have mountains?'

The question was asked lightly, a reminder that he didn't want to have a heartfelt conversation with me and I was being stupid imagining he might listen, simply because I caught shadows in his eyes sometimes.

I nodded in reply. 'I grew up in Colorado. Oh yes, there are mountains. But I haven't left LA in six months and now it feels weird to think I used to conquer gradients like these on a bike.'

'Six months isn't that long.'

'It's a lifetime,' I mumbled. 'A different me.'

'You're still Leesa Kubicka,' he insisted.

'And you're still Colin Gallagher. Will I have to search my suitcase for a toy snake every night while I'm here? You've even managed to trick your impressionable teammate into growing an ugly moustache.'

'I didn't bring any toy snakes with me,' was all he said at first. 'But fair warning, I might trick you into going on a recovery ride with me.'

He said it with a shrug, his hands stuffed into the pockets of his tracksuit pants and I was annoyed that my stomach flipped as though he'd asked me out on a date, as though I couldn't tell the difference between a date and a dare. I didn't want either.

'I'd be worried you'd leave me behind with only a bivouac bag and a can of beans,' I responded drily. 'I haven't been on a bike outdoors since I broke my arm, so you won't want to take me on a ride anyway. I'll stick to the team car when I need footage.'

'What? You mean you quit cycling altogether and not just pro? You don't even ride a beater down to the shops?'

'Did you miss the part where I moved to LA? I'd rather not be mowed down by a Mack truck before my thirtieth birthday.' I paused to wince. 'God, I sound like my mom.'

'She worries about you?'

'She *disapproves* of my hobby.'

He opened his mouth, but appeared to consider his words for once. 'It wasn't a hobby.'

'Mom always treated it like one,' I said with a shrug. 'Plus, I needed to sell my bikes for the security deposit on my sublet. So, yeah, no more riding.'

He thumped a hand to his chest in mock horror. 'Not your bikes!' Possibly it was real horror.

'They would have been stolen anyway if I'd been sleeping on the street,' I pointed out with a straight face, enjoying his alarmed expression. 'Don't worry, I would have gone begging to my parents before I ended up on Skid Row and they probably would have helped me without a lecture for once, since I've finally done what they've been telling me to do for ten years now: I quit cycling. I'm working on getting a real job, one that might actually pay the bills – one day. No more self-indulgent failure-porn on two wheels.'

It appeared I'd managed to shock Colin Gallagher into silence as he didn't even drawl a teasing retort. I might have preferred one to the stormy look he was giving me.

It wasn't enough to stop me speaking now that I was on a roll. 'It just sucks that my first real job is... *you*.'

I forced a breath into my lungs, not sure if I felt better or worse for having blurted all of that out. Decidedly worse the longer Colin remained silent next to me. He swallowed audibly and, when I glanced at him, he was staring into the distance.

'Yeah, I'm... sorry about that,' he said slowly, his voice gravelly. 'Rough gig.'

'I don't mean it personally,' I clarified in a rush, but the doubtful look he shot me suggested he smelled the platitude.

'It's all right, Leesa. We all know the orange PowerFuel gels taste like cat piss. That should probably be the name of the flavour. And I know what you think of me.'

His words caught me in the chest. I wasn't so certain myself these days. When he walked so pensively beside me, the wind in his hair, I wasn't thinking of him as my young, inane teammate from six years of training camps.

'I didn't want to get involved with the clients in cycling at all,'

I explained, not sure if I wanted to reassure him or simply defend myself. 'But my boss made it pretty clear: this is my only chance to be offered a proper job at the firm.'

His face twitched with a grimace. 'You used to make great stuff for your own social feed.'

I gave a snort, trying not to dwell on the fact that Colin must have looked at my socials. I'd been tempted to take the posts down so many times.

'Why don't you want to keep doing that for cycling teams? You'd be brilliant. You know what I think?' he said suddenly, his combative tone lifting the pressure off my chest. 'I think you're scared you'll want to get back on the bike.'

'Of course I'm scared of that!'

'Then just get back on the bike. You were a work of fucking art on a bike.'

It was his turn to shut *me* up. He shot me a glance that ricocheted down my body and quickly away again.

'Although that dress you had on this morning was nice too.'

A rush of prickles to my hairline felt like some kind of warning. 'Don't overdo it, Colin,' I drawled. 'I kept my stationary bike and tapered training, but my metabolism still hates me and I would not dare to wear a jersey and bib shorts any more.'

He had the guts to look me up and down more thoroughly. 'Maybe you're a little squishier in places.'

'Colin!' I spluttered, flinging my hands up.

He grasped my arm, more gently than I would have expected. 'It's a good thing,' he insisted. 'You were always hot and…'

My brain insisted he was pulling my leg, but my body responded with a full-on flare-up, his words dragging over my skin. The brush of his thumb over my forearm was almost unbearable. His mouth moved as he searched for more words and all I could think about was what he'd do if I lurched in and took the silly moustache for a ride.

'… you still look good enough to… eat.' The sentence went up at the end, punctuated by a wince and everything wound up inside me seemed to burst like heated glass.

'*What* did you say?'

His Adam's apple bobbed. 'Forget it.'

'Did you say I look good enough to *eat*?' I rolled my eyes and poked him for emphasis.

He stared at his feet as he chuckled. 'Yeah. You only have to ask.'

My nerves must have short-circuited because I tripped on a rock. Instead of landing heavily on the ground that was rushing up at me, a wrench on my arm and pressure around my middle halted my fall. He eased me upright, one hand splayed at my waist, his thumb brushing my ribcage, and I couldn't get enough air.

*This is bad. He's the talent. You want a job.*

Trying to give myself a pep talk couldn't quite erase the memory of him apparently offering oral sex. Or perhaps I'd lost the plot entirely and that wasn't what he'd meant. I should not be having sensual thoughts about my talent, the golden boy – emphasis on the *boy* – of my old team.

Then he swallowed heavily and his hand shifted, exerting just enough pressure to turn my insides to liquid. An inch higher and his thumb would stroke the underside of my breast. His jaw clenched tight, he looked as though he was pouring all his energy into resisting exactly that move.

'Christ, you feel good, Lees,' he said, his voice as jagged as cobblestones under a bike wheel. His chest rose and fell with uneven breaths and I was no longer sure what planet I was on, where Colin seemed to be all undone – for me.

He straightened all of a sudden, lifting one hand. For a heartbeat I thought he was going to touch my face, a tender action I would never have expected from him, except he hesitated and said, 'You… Uh, there's a bug in your hair.'

My lungs deflated like a hot-air balloon at the end of the day. This was a familiar routine from Colin, the prankster. 'There is *not*.'

'I'm serious. Do you want me to get it out?'

'And then what? Don't you dare put slime in my hair. If you had any idea how much work these curls are—'

'It's worth it,' he cut me off with an echo of the soft words that had tied me into a pretzel a few minutes ago. But he was failing to stifle a wobbly smile that was unfortunately every bit as charming as Wil had warned me he could be. 'I'm not going to put slime in your hair,' he continued smoothly. 'I'm telling you, there's a grasshopper heading for your ear.'

Just the word 'grasshopper' was enough to induce a full-body shudder.

'I promise I'm not shitting you. I know you don't like insects.'

'Which is why you put a fake beetle in the light fitting of the women's toilets that time in Milan!'

He stifled a snort of laughter. 'That was when I found out you don't like insects.'

'And you proceeded to order a bulk batch of clear insect stickers for every time you saw me afterwards.' I took a deep breath. 'There's no grasshopper. I'll never belie—'

Something skittered near my ear and I shrieked.

# Chapter 7

## Colin

I didn't mean to laugh at her, but she had her face screwed so tight she could have been on the cover of one of the depressing literary masterpieces Amir liked to read. Her curls made freeing the poor insect a strategic operation, especially with Leesa a jittery mess.

But I still had time to appreciate the fact that I had my hands in her hair, the soft, springy curls tickling my skin. A minute ago I'd had my fingers an inch from her breast and the distinct impression she would have let me go higher.

I was screwed. Every course of action would get one of us into trouble. Even if she'd made the sweetest sigh while my hand was teasing both of us, she'd also said it sucked that she had to work with me. Excuse me for having a bit of dignity — a little bit. It had been a close-run thing, not letting the touching go any further.

Now I was wondering if this grasshopper was a lucky creature, since I was allowed to be close to her without the potential to screw anything up.

'Get it off!'

'I'm trying.'

She jumped, narrowly avoiding shoving my nose back into my brain. 'It touched my ear!'

'Easy.' Steadying her with my left hand around the back of her head, I swiped with my right until the poor little creature finally managed to free itself and zing back into the grass. I released a deep breath, reluctantly unwinding her hair from my fingers.

'I promise, there was really a grasshopper and I didn't produce it from my pocket on purpose.'

She popped one eye open.

'In fact,' I continued smoothly, 'I think this makes me your hero.'

She drew back and eyed me. 'I think it makes up for *one* of your previous pranks.'

Six years down the line, it was still true: Leesa Kubicka was way too classy for me. 'Which prank does it make up for? The fake bug in the light fitting was funny – admit it. I think maybe I've compensated for one of the worse ones.'

'What? The cling-wrap incident?'

'*That* was harmless. Like the moustache bet. It's not hurting anyone.'

'Except my eyes,' she mumbled. 'But admit it: you're trying to make Derek feel small.'

That pricked under my skin. It made me uncomfortable to think that was her opinion of me, but it was fair enough. 'I told you it's not a competition, not really. I don't care who has the bushiest.'

'Then why are you making him do it?'

Tension crept up my spine at the prospect of explaining. 'The kid needs a bit of confidence. Yeah, he's my support rider for the Tour, but he's good. I want him to feel like he's good enough to compete with me.'

She didn't respond for a long moment. I glanced from my feet up into her face, awaiting judgement, but she was regarding me warily, as though she might believe me. 'That's… a worthy reason for mangling your faces with those things. As long as Derek realises it's ugly.'

'I tell him every day. But mine is a sexy little dirtbag moustache, so I think I'm rocking it.'

She shot me a doubtful look that was mostly a smile. We'd started walking again at some point after the grasshopper incident, but I hadn't noticed. I could barely see anything when she had her eyes on me.

'I'm not sure "sexy little dirtbag moustache" is on-brand for the client. I still think it'll have to go.'

'All right, but you'll only have one chance to find out if it prickles when you kiss me.'

She rolled her eyes and I should have been relieved we were back on even ground with the fake flirting. 'You need to give up on that joke. We both know you're not going to let me kiss you.'

I strongly disagreed, but I let her think it.

'Do you expect me to believe that all your pranks are for a good cause?'

'I wouldn't exactly say a good cause, but you know how it is. Training, testing, racing, recovering. It's intense. It's gotta stay fun somehow.'

She peered at me as though she knew something I didn't and it gave me goosebumps. 'That's a good point. But what about that sex doll and all the stuff you pulled last year on Seb?'

She was way too sharp. 'The sex doll was funny, but I admit, programming the wrong destination into his bike computer was low. I honestly didn't think he'd get all the way up the mountain.' It was odd thinking back to a time before my sister and Seb had got together, since it felt like their golden wedding anniversary already. 'I was getting vibes from him,' I grumbled. 'I knew he'd be trouble for Lori.'

'You know how badly that backfired, right? That was when she slept with him the first time, after she had to go collect him.'

'Too much information,' I said with a grimace. 'I did apologise to him later. He's practically my brother-in-law now, so he got the last laugh.'

She was quiet beside me for long enough that I could tell she was dropping back into complicated terrain in her busy brain.

I saw my chance. 'I'm sorry for this morning. When I stopped to think about it, I could see it was a shitty thing to do.'

That got her attention. Her eyes were big and a little sad. The squeeze in my throat was back. It wasn't fair that she was hurting – that she'd had to leave the sport we both loved because of the patriarchy and it wasn't fair that there was nothing I could do about it.

'Are you going to try to tell me it was for a good cause?'

The images from the video I'd made flashed in my mind, along with her graphic descriptor for her career: failure-porn. But telling her she should be proud of herself when she was hurting wouldn't be productive and it wasn't my only reason either.

'I overheard you speaking to Wil yesterday,' I admitted, 'about me being your challenge. I... decided to be difficult. This sponsor shit isn't my favourite either.'

'I suppose that's fair.'

'I'm not a... nice pin-up boy. Even without the moustache.'

'You don't have to pretend to be someone else for this gig, Colin.' Her straightforward tone warmed me.

'I thought that's exactly what I had to do. I'm supposed to convince serious people to buy serious gels, right? I need gravitas.'

Her wince was delicate and made me want to smile. 'That might be aiming too high.'

'Great, thanks,' I mumbled with a chuckle.

'Fun content gets the best engagement anyway.'

'I can do fun,' I said emphatically. 'You're the one who might need a nudge in that direction, since you don't like cycling any more.'

'It's not that I don't like—'

I didn't give her a chance to sink back into uncertainty. 'I know what you need!'

'I don't need a moustache – or a tattoo, or something equally ridiculous.'

'Tattoos are not silly, and I thought you already had one? Didn't all the girls get a matching one a few years ago?'

The colour in her cheeks was perfect. 'I didn't.' She didn't say she regretted it, but I heard it anyway.

I jogged ahead a few steps and cut her off on the path, holding up my hand. 'Two things you need, apart from a tattoo, which goes without saying. One: to get back on the bike.'

Before she could argue, I wagged my hand in front of her face and kept going.

'You are music on a bike – art. You're cutting off your arm to spite your face and I want to go on a ride with you.'

'I'm not—'

'Uh-uh,' I cut her off again. 'The second thing you need is—' Fifteen years of pranking my sister and everyone else in range had given me a great feel for a dramatic pause. 'You need to get me back for this morning.'

God, she was cute when she was indignant. After spluttering inarticulately for a moment, she finally said, 'We've just established how your prank backfired – badly – and your solution is for me to just prank you back?'

'Yep.'

'I'm not going to lower myself to your level.'

'Then think up some classy prank that goes with your fancy words.'

Her only response was a wary look that tried to get under my skin, but I was willing to take that as assent.

'Working with you is the only upside of all this sponsor shit,' I continued. 'I want to make it fun – for you too. A little bit of you for a little bit of me. That's fair, right?'

She stared at me as though surprised I wanted to spend time with her. I would have thought, after September, that part was clear.

'Are we good?'

She was too kind to drag out her response. 'We're good,' she said quietly. 'But I have ground rules.'

I gestured magnanimously. 'Please.' Holding my breath, I waited to see how far she trusted me.

'Firstly, no gratuitous flirting on camera. I'm doing a job here.'

'What about non-gratuitous flirting?' I asked with a straight face.

'All flirting is gratuitous,' she insisted.

'I beg to differ, but okay. You didn't say anything about off camera, so I'm fine with that. What are your other conditions?'

She hesitated for a moment and then said, 'Don't push me. I'll think before I say no, but if I say it, I mean it.'

'Yes, ma'am,' I said, so damn impressed by how she calmly and fairly set her boundaries.

'Secondly, you can't use me as an excuse for screwing up your training. Stick to the rules.'

Okay, that wasn't what I'd expected. 'That's no fun,' I pouted. 'You won't screw up my training because I don't have a lot of choice in that, but my free time? What's the harm in a little rule-bending.'

'Then you're on your own. You can't count on me to join in.'

She must have had no idea her words were like a red cape to a bull. 'Fair enough. I won't promise not to try to convince you, though.'

'I suppose I've been warned,' she muttered. 'And, more importantly—' She drew herself up. It seemed I wasn't the only one who could deliver a dramatic pause and she was prettier while she did it. 'No more making fun of my middle name. It's my saint's name and my grandmother would hurt her knees praying for your soul if she knew.'

'Darn, I was going to start calling you Magda, but for the sake of your grandma's knees, I will refrain. A long, complicated name suits you.'

'You should have stopped before that last sentence,' she muttered.

'Not that you're long or... complicated. Maybe a bit complicated. Okay, another sentence too much. But I know what it's like to have an interesting middle name. I suppose I thought it was something we had in common.'

She fought with herself for a whole minute while I tried not to smile. 'You... have an interesting middle name?'

I simply flashed my eyebrows at her. 'You can google it and laugh in private.'

'I'm not going to laugh at your name, especially since that would make me a hypocrite.'

It might have been pushing things, but I slung an arm over her shoulders and leaned on her. She went still, but she didn't tell me to get lost, which I counted as a win. 'You just remember you said that when you laugh. And don't forget to linger over the photo of me winning Nationals two years ago with my jersey ripped to shreds.'

'Why am I not surprised you google yourself?'

'Now I've got you to do that for me.'

She rolled her eyes and shimmied out from under my arm.

'You do know, right,' I began slowly, 'that we're friends now?' I let that sink in for a moment, but I didn't give her time to reply. 'Come on. We should get back. It must be your jetlag bedtime.'

# 9 September, the year before

## Leesa

'Is this some kind of joke? Not everything is about you.'

'You're good at reminding me of that,' he said with a chuckle that was a total mismatch with the look on his face.

I couldn't imagine why he thought he'd caused half of the peloton to come down during my last race.

'I was there,' he said, which explained nothing. 'With the spectators. You didn't see me. I think I distracted some of the others.'

'You think your face is such a distraction?' Oops, maybe he'd think I was flirting with him, from that quip. My throat was a little thick with the realisation that I did understand why people thought he was hot, no matter how much I wished I didn't.

'Look, I just wanted to say sorry and... goodbye — you know?'

I wondered if I was still under the influence of the painkillers, because this Colin seemed way too serious for the guy who'd squeezed my energy gel until it squirted me in the face more than once.

My phone buzzed and I picked it up to see a message from Lori: *Urgh, I should have known my idiot brother was behind this.* She'd sent a picture, a still from the race footage. When I tapped on the picture, a spluttering gasp rose up in my throat. The incident — and Colin's words — were beginning to make sense.

'What the hell is this? Some kind of prank, right?' I turned the phone around to show him.

With a groan, he hung his head, rubbing a hand over his hair.

The still clearly showed Colin standing at the side of the road as the bikes whipped past, holding up a cardboard sign that read: *Go Leesa*.

# Chapter 8

## Leesa

I still wasn't sure how he'd made me agree to be friends. When I woke up from my still very jetlagged sleep, I wasn't even sure what I'd agreed to. Maybe I'd given him the green light to prank me, which was a scary prospect. I certainly remembered he wanted me to prank him back, which would take some thought.

I'd managed some extra internet searches last night and discovered his middle name was Valerio, from the Latin, meaning 'strong' or 'healthy'. I tried not to admit it suited him, or that there was an affinity between us, our families and names that spanned cultures. He'd put that idea in my head, along with his insistence that we were friends.

He'd probably meant a friend with benefits.

I could still remember him as a pimply 19-year-old graduating to the senior team for the first time. Now I had to record every aspect of his existence for a job, while ignoring the little details that were *not* part of it, like the way his hair caught the evening light and glowed reddish. It had a wave in it and needed cutting. He had a surgery scar on his right forearm and I guessed he bit his nails. And I was the only idiot interested in that.

I had two weeks of training camp to amass as much content as I could to drip-feed during the Tour, when I wouldn't have as much access to him. Luckily, the man was disgustingly photogenic, even with a dirtbag moustache. My first few days passed in a blur of hotel breakfasts, training rides and an ice bath under the mountain sun, where Colin and his teammate Jarin Nelson had traded barbed banter about shrivelling private parts that made me want to apologise to my hard drive.

At least it helped temper the inappropriate *interest* I'd suddenly developed. I was relieved I'd never noticed before. I couldn't imagine how mortifying it would have been to moon over him in the breakfast room in front of my teammates.

Doortje would be clutching her stomach with laughter if she could see me now, spending my time watching him through my phone screen, watching him in real life and then going back to my room to watch him on my laptop as I processed and uploaded the content.

On the third day of my assignment, he was spending hours hooked up to various machines, half-naked, to measure his performance on a stationary bike. Lucky for the sponsor, their name was stamped right above his butt and was impossible to miss even when the only things he had on were skintight shorts and a heartrate monitor strapped around his chest.

The testing brought back visceral memories. I'd been pricked and prodded and pushed to my limits too, but not with the intensity that the entire team hovered around Colin. He was a test subject, a science experiment, where the results would ultimately show themselves at the end of the gruelling Tour de France. Except there were too many variables for the team to hope to control — not least their test subject himself, who was still decorated with patches of angry road rash and red scabs, to add to the criss-crossing puckered scars on his knees.

Annoying how scars on a man were intriguing, but mine were something to hide with pantyhose. I hated pantyhose.

'What's the hardest thing about cycling?'

I had been admiring his tight obliques, decorated with the dark compass tattoo and glistening with sweat, and had to rip my gaze from his torso when he asked me the sudden question.

'What?'

His lips twitched in a smile. 'The road!' he ground out, chuckling when I finally realised he was making a joke. 'When are you hitting the road with me, Kubicka?' he asked, his voice gravelly with effort.

'Hopefully never,' I mumbled, keeping my eyes pointedly on my phone.

'You scared?'

Terrified, for a host of reasons, none of which I was going to discuss with him, so I rolled my eyes instead.

'Don't worry, I'll be gentle with you.'

I considered telling him off for flirting with me on camera, but I seemed to have swallowed my tongue. One of the soigneurs, the vital support staff who looked after us, interrupted anyway to take a sample for lactate testing, pricking his ear. Colin didn't even flinch as he kept up a recovery pace on the bike, didn't react to the drop of blood landing on his shoulder, before the soigneur wiped it away.

Lactate testing was pretty gross all round. It measured the point at which overuse of muscles started to turn the blood acidic, making fatigue inevitable – and it felt like hitting a brick wall. I had enough memories of that feeling to last a lifetime and the stakes were so much higher for Colin. If he blew up, so did the chances for the whole team.

I tried not to look at his results, terrified I'd accidentally blurt them out to no one in particular, after I'd signed the NDA, but what glimpses I caught were some incredible numbers. In my head, he was the team clown, often the second-choice lead rider, with some famous blow-ups as well as wins, but it seemed he'd earned the support of the team with hard work as well as raw talent.

Perhaps it was fair enough if he let off steam in his free time, given everything he put into the session. By the end, he had sweat pouring off him, his hair dark and curling. Finally, on the warm-down, he let go of the handlebars and sat up, accepting a water bottle from a soigneur. After taking a long drink, where suddenly my world seemed to shrink to the image of his square jaw and the bob of his Adam's apple, he lifted the bottle and squeezed water onto himself, spraying his face and then his chest, and shaking off like a dog.

Watching him glow, all slippery muscle and stamina, fired up all of my senses. My brain, which usually never shut up, was happily occupied cataloguing every detail of him as I hid behind my work phone, taking footage.

He shot me a sidelong glance. 'Did you get all that?'

Maybe I hadn't been hiding as well as I'd thought. 'Yes,' I squeaked.

'Are you sure? The phone seems to be pointed at the floor.'

I hastily raised it again, giving myself a shake, although that didn't help my temperature, because he looked just as tasty on screen as he did in real life. I had to change the subject before I went up in flames and the soigneur had to sweep my ashes into the trash.

'Want to tell me about your tattoos?' As subject changes went, it was out of the frying pan and into the fire, but I'd said it now and had to keep a straight face as he lifted a brow at me.

The strength coach made a few final adjustments to the computer running the stationary bike and excused himself, gesturing for the soigneur to follow, and suddenly I was a little too alone with Colin, who was a little too unclothed.

'Or… don't tell me. It's up to you.'

'No worries,' he said with half a smile. His bright eyes were locked on me. Keeping up the pedalling through the warm-down programme, he twisted on the bike to stretch his left arm out for the camera. 'This one needs no explanation. The five stars of the Southern Cross for Australia. I got it done when I won the National Under-23 title the first time and added the rings when I got selected for the Olympics.'

No one could accuse him of flirting right now, but it seemed he could say anything and I'd feel it under my skin.

'I didn't manage the win at Nationals this year, but my sister did. She's been through hell recently, so she deserves a bit of glory.'

I wanted to ask about his relationship with Lori, but I was scared of going soft on him and he kept speaking anyway, before I had a chance to press.

Straightening, he gestured to the compass, just below where the heartrate monitor was strapped around his chest. 'The compass pointing northwest for Europe. I mean, from Australia, Europe is northwest on the usual world map projection. This is where my parents come from and where I've spent most of my career.' He looked up suddenly. 'You've been very restrained.'

I had. My feet hadn't moved even an inch in his direction, even while my eyes had slid over his skin. But he couldn't have meant that.

Stopping the video, I said, 'Hmm?' rather stupidly.

'You haven't mentioned my middle name.'

Only about a hundred times in my head. 'I haven't looked it up.'

When he grinned at me, it was all cheek. 'Liar.'

It was completely irrational how that word, spoken in his deep, soft voice, could seep so far into my skin, especially when it was an accusation. When he said it, it felt like praise.

'It's not relevant,' I insisted, hoping he wouldn't read anything into my breathy voice. Lifting my phone, I started recording again, clearing my throat before asking, 'What about the dragon tattoo?'

'You'd better go around the back to get a shot of that artwork,' he said.

I made my way to the other side of the room, where I could record the rear view for my avid audience. 'Are you sure you mean the tattoo?'

It just slipped out before I could judge the wisdom of teasing him. He spluttered a laugh and peered over his shoulder at me, making those butterflies in my stomach flock wildly.

'You can be damn certain this arse is a work of art, d——' He cut himself off. 'Probably shouldn't call you darlin', right? At least not while you're recording.'

'You probably shouldn't say "ass" either.'

'You said it last.'

Lowering my phone with a sigh, I marvelled at how quickly this conversation had spiralled out of control when we'd been left alone together. Maybe there had been a potion in that slagroomtaart back in September, because I'd never been this much of a wreck around him before.

'You still recording, Kubicka?'

'Yes,' I said in such a rush that it emerged an octave too high.

Staring into my phone screen, the first thing I saw was that dragon tattoo, writhing between his shoulder blades, its wings open and bowed as though in pain. Next to it was a tiny drop of blood, spilled when the soigneur had pricked his ear.

My throat thickened, pondering the image, wondering if there was an allegory hidden there. How did he feel about the upcoming trial by endurance? It was three weeks and over 2,000 miles of hurting, endless opportunities to screw up and only a fleeting few for glory.

My heartbeat echoed in my ears as my thoughts raced ahead to July, when he would carry the future of the team up and down mountains and through every battle on the road. Damn it, I cared. This choking anxiety was one of the reasons I'd decided to retire and I feared it could be even worse, given I couldn't do anything but watch and feel frustrated.

'Lees? You all right?'

Shit, there was going to be a lot of footage to delete. I released a long breath and met his gaze. 'Yeah. You?'

'O' course. We all done, or do you wanna know about the dragon? He's called Valerio, by the way.'

'Ha! You named him after yourself?'

He sucked on his bottom lip and I saw sparks behind my eyes. 'I told you, you're a liar, Kubicka.'

There was that praise again.

'I didn't laugh,' I insisted.

'I don't know whether to believe you.'

I held up my phone – a cowardly excuse to cut short the flirting. 'Tell me about the dragon, Colin.'

He considered his words for a moment and I held my breath, hoping for a hint of insight, an indication that my sympathy wasn't irrational.

'I was at the tattoo place,' he eventually said with a shrug and a wry smile. 'I didn't know what to get. My mate said girls love dragons and… you can see the result.'

# Chapter 9

## Colin

Leesa had her work cut out for her, presenting me as a champion. Between Dad's backfiring pep talks over breakfast and the way my brain seemed to fix on capturing the exact blue of her eyes so I'd never forget it, I had restless energy to burn. I never knew if I was going to get away with just teasing her or whether that would be the time I'd crumble and kiss her. It was a knife's edge, but kind of a fun one.

My act of desperation in September, in a panic that she'd leave without… *perceiving* me or some shit had backfired spectacularly and she'd told me clearly enough she wasn't interested. But suddenly, she was *looking* at me and I didn't know what she saw.

If Dad knew how much energy I was expending thinking about her, he'd probably hit me over the head — although he wasn't actually violent. He was just a hardarse who knew more about my lactate threshold than my personality.

I was surprised it had taken Mum this long to leave him. She'd sent me photos of her new apartment in Docklands and I was happy for her. Dad had mentioned so little it was conceivable she hadn't told him, although I doubted it. He probably just didn't care, when the Tour was so close, and he'd hate that *I* did.

The Tour was everything for Dad. Maybe if I hadn't followed in his footsteps and taken up road cycling pro, I might never have seen him. Sometimes it didn't feel fair that both Lori and I ended up chasing *his* dream, especially when Mum understood there was

more to life than the yearly jaunt around France – and more to me
than a set of hamstrings and quadriceps.

Resting, calm and chill, all that Zen shit wasn't going to work
for me when the Tour was a little over three weeks away. I knew
the pressure was bad because I was thinking of heading into Brixen
to the tattoo place – and wondering if Leesa would come with me.
Matching ink. A little 'mine and yours' to commemorate the last
time she screwed with my head.

Maybe I could get a skull and crossbones to remember her by.
I'd been such an idiot in September – and in every conversation
with her since. A skull and crossbones would probably be a good
symbol for her to remember *me* by as well.

It was Tuesday of the second week of camp and we were out
on the road in the valley. I came alive on the twists and turns,
the asphalt opening out under me and the gradients no match for
my current fitness. I could look off into the distance and imagine
never stopping.

Sometimes that thought started to consume me.

'You ever going to take a turn at the front, Derro? Scared your
moustache will blow off?' Thank fuck for the guys on the team.

'If you need a break, old man, just say so,' Derek called back
and I was almost proud of him for the shit-talking.

Leesa was in the team car today, pointing that phone at me
whenever they drew alongside. The phone was starting to annoy
me, but not in the way I'd thought it would. It was more intrusive
than usual, this sponsor arrangement, but I'd been somewhat
prepared for my life to be splashed all over the internet. No, I was
miffed that I couldn't tell what she was thinking as she recorded
me.

Sometimes I imagined she was enjoying herself after all, which
puffed up my chest so much it probably affected respiration. But
I was haunted by memories of her face as she explained how the
assignment had triggered all of her complex feelings about the
sport – *I* triggered her. I hated it.

I had to get her back on the bike. No matter what shit went
down in the pro peloton, cycling was a grassroots sport and

without that, everything was pointless. Even though she'd retired from the elite, she could ride.

It upset me that she'd sold her bikes. I would have bought one, if I'd known.

We pulled off the road for a drinks break in a high meadow, beneath a row of jagged mountain teeth. Leesa climbed out of the car and stretched and my mind was full of her again in a second – wants and needs. She popped my cork just by… *being*. All the weird shit deep inside me bubbled to the surface and I couldn't keep anything in.

I collapsed against the car next to her, peering at her phone as I guzzled my water. The high-altitude sunshine was skinning me alive today and my body was slippery with sweat.

'You know a way to get even better footage?' I asked.

She glanced up at me and that's all it took to make me smile: the little dent in her chin. 'How?'

'A GoPro,' I said with a provoking lift of my brows, 'on your own bike.'

She chuckled, even though I hadn't been joking. 'I'm not going to ride with you guys.'

'You said you weren't scared to get back on a bike.'

'There's a big difference between "getting back on a bike" and a training ride for the Tour de France. I said don't push me.'

'And I found it incredibly sexy when you said it.'

She eyed me doubtfully and crossed her arms, which only drew my gaze to her outfit. She must have had a whole suitcase of these dresses in different colours and patterns – all designed to pull my eyes to the little details of her body that sucked me in.

Today's number had little strings tying the sleeves up, which made me think about undoing them, tugging one shoulder down—

I took a deep breath. 'You could hop up on Nellie's bike right now and have that skirt blow up in your face.'

'I think you must be confusing this one with my other exploding dress.'

Grinning at her, I slid along the car a little closer. 'Which one is the exploding dress? The one with the floof things at the bottom or the one where you could undo the belt and the whole thing would fall off?'

I liked making her jaw hang open so far I could almost hear it creak. 'Firstly, that dress has a button that keeps it closed,' she began after recovering from her strangled cough.

'Way to destroy a guy's fantasy.'

She made that frustrated noise in the back of her throat that I had grown fond of, but ignored the comment. 'And secondly, the one with the floof things – if I have interpreted your questionable description correctly – is a skirt, not a dress.'

'There's a difference?'

'Of course there's a difference! One can be worn by itself and the other needs a blouse for the top half.'

'I think "needs" would be open to interpretation.'

She made the noise again. 'Your imagination is a scary place.'

'But you're in it pretty often – usually in a nice dress that doesn't explode. I like your dresses.'

'I don't think I have one in your size,' she quipped.

When she matched my smile, I was a little worried my *heart* would explode. 'You owe me a prank, Kubicka,' I reminded her. 'I'm waitin'.'

'You can wait a little longer,' she said, her nose in the air. I never wanted to see anything else in my life, with Leesa looking happy in front of me, the majestic Dolomites a dramatic background.

'That's enough for now, Colin! We're not here for the charming company.'

She stiffened at Dad's interruption and I swallowed the many unwise words bubbling up in my chest, instead giving her a lazy salute and heading back to where the others sat, legs sprawled, on a park bench.

'I hope you got some good footage,' I heard Dad say. 'Lots of shots with the logo.'

I slowed my steps so I could hear her reply. 'It's not only about the logo. Maybe you'd have ten minutes for me at some stage so I can show you the approach we want to take? I've spent quite a bit of time analysing successful content from previous Tours and it's not going to look like advertising. I'll be happy to take you through it.'

Damn, I liked her accent when she was being all articulate.

'Sounds good. I remember the dance videos you used to do with Doortje and the girls. Looks like you might have found your feet even though you left us too soon.'

Even before I turned around to confirm, I knew Dad's comments had hit a nerve again.

'You were bloody difficult to replace, you know,' Dad went on, oblivious to her pasted-on smile and fidgeting.

No, Leesa didn't fidget, she just died inside.

'It's a… special team you've built,' she managed.

Grabbing my phone from the holder on my bike, I opened up my DMs, hoping she still had the app installed. I knew she followed me – or she had done, when she'd still been on the team. I remembered the moment a few years ago when I'd received the notification that she'd followed me back.

*Are you going to show ME the approach you want to take? Or am I just the muse?*

When she frowned and fished in her pocket for her personal phone, I sighed with relief. She glanced warily at me as she read the message.

*You're the talent, not a muse. I'll show you everything anyway.*

'Everything' sounded pretty good, especially when she briefly met my gaze. I started typing a response, but she beat me to it.

*I mean all the content and the strategy and everything. Don't get any ideas.*

Too late for that. Despite numerous sets of eyes on me – including my father's – I chuckled at her message. I wanted to respond just to rile her up, to make her feel something, but I knew I was toeing her lines already. And bib shorts were definitely not sexting attire.

*My biggest idea is seeing you enjoying yourself on a bike again.*
*You have strange fantasies.*

I couldn't quite stifle my smile as I responded: *You don't know the half of it.*

I was about to clip my phone back into the holder, but Dad clapped his hands to get us moving and I snatched it up again, thumbing one last quick message.

*I'm sorry about Dad bringing everything up again.*

Her lips thinned, creating little dimples at the corners of her mouth and I shouldn't have been staring at her, but I was. Such an expressive face.

She replied: *Don't be. I can't get upset about every little mention of my career. Stay safe on the descent.*

I caught her eye and exaggerated a 'pfft'.

# Chapter 10

## Colin

She was deep in conversation with Wil when I walked into the dining room the next morning. I didn't know if I would actually have sat with her, but not having the option turned me into a grumpy little boy again and then Dad saw me and I was in for it.

I swerved for the buffet, taking my time to work out my portions with the nutritionist and clap the chef on the shoulder for making the banana waffles that he knew were my favourite. But Dad was cool as a cucumber – a sure sign that something was up – and I wasn't surprised when he waved me over as soon as my plate was ready. As I shuffled to his table, I glanced longingly in the direction of Derek and Nelson, who were watching stupid videos – probably of cats, knowing Nellie – and guffawing.

Actually, these days they could have been videos of Nellie's newborn son Rupert. He'd made me watch a few and I didn't get the appeal. Rupert was this little wrinkly thing that jerked his limbs around and looked so much like an alien I wouldn't have been surprised to hear he'd burst out of his mother's stomach from the front. Except I wouldn't wish that on Nellie's wife.

Urgh, thinking about birth made me shudder. I knew my mum had had two terrible pregnancies with Lori and me and I didn't like to ask for details. Plus, it would have been better for everyone if Nellie had watched his swimmers a little better and had the baby in the off-season.

'Did I miss something between you and Leesa when she was on the team?'

I dropped my fork with a clatter. Dad had barely stopped chewing his muesli to drop that bomb.

'I'm not running a farking dating agency,' he muttered with his mouth full.

'You seemed pretty happy when Lori got together with Seb last year.' Not that Leesa and I were anything like my sister and Seb. Lori might have been ready to move in with someone when she'd been 26, but I was 25 going on 19 – coincidentally, the age I'd been when I'd first met Leesa.

'I wasn't happy. I was *worried* – until Seb proved he only wanted what was best for her,' Dad continued gruffly.

'You mean for her to win races.'

'Of course!' More chewing. 'So, are you together? Or is it just casual?'

'Neither, actually,' I grated out. 'Not that you'll believe me.'

'You've got enough cheek for a second arse! Given the way you're behaving, there's good reason why I won't believe you.'

The heat in my face was betraying me. 'I'm not sleeping with her and I never have.' And given everything that had happened in September, I was fairly certain I never would.

Dad took a long look at me, even putting his spoon down for a moment. Then he released a deep sigh. 'You'd better keep it that way. PowerFuel is shaping up to be one of our major sponsors next year and you getting involved with *anyone* on their payroll is… Jesus, Mary and Joseph. I don't want to think about it.'

As he rubbed a hand over his weathered face, I wondered when he'd started to actually look a little older. 'The Irish Bullet' Tony Gallagher was ageless. He'd been a grizzled, wrinkled 30-year-old when he'd married Mum and 28 years later he was only slightly more grizzled – except when the haggard expression crossed his features as it was doing now. It was the expression that meant he was thinking about the money hustle again.

'You don't have anything to worry about, Dad.' She was way too classy – intelligent, sensitive, thoughtful, *soft*.

'Good, 'cos you should only have one thing on your mind: winning. And that's a nice girl – not the kind you toy with.'

*Gee, thanks, Dad.* He was waiting for me to reply, expecting me to assure him my head was in the game and I was like him: no life outside the sport. Instead, I met his gaze and drawled, 'She's safe. I like big tits, you know.'

Dad cleared his throat. 'Ah, hmm.' He was looking over my shoulder and, with a zap of misgiving, I turned to see what had grabbed his attention.

*Well, shit.*

Leesa stood behind me, a tablet tucked against her chest — obscuring those tiny breasts that were unfortunately — for me — every bit as beautiful as a big set. Her hair was in a loose ponytail today, twirls everywhere. I couldn't tell what she thought of what she must have overheard. Her chin was up and all I could think of was that maybe she *wasn't* safe with me when her throat looked so smooth.

'May I join you?' she asked Dad, not looking at me.

'O' course, child.' Forty years Dad had been out of Ireland and usually he sounded more Australian than Crocodile Dundee, but he was still Irish enough to call a grown woman 'child' — and get away with it.

'I can show you our ideas now, if you have time?'

Taking the seat side-on to both of us, she tapped a few times on the tablet and a branded visual appeared. I was distracted with the hint of something sweet from her shampoo — raspberries? There was a herbal note I couldn't identify and the combination suited her: sweet and complex.

'Our research indicated the most successful social-media content from last year's Tour was humorous. You know, funny statements about daily life with pictures of cyclists or unrelated film footage cut together with an amusing moment with fans — stuff like that.'

'Finally, something Colin might be perfect for!'

I gave Dad a doubtful glance. He was a little too enthusiastic.

'My thoughts exactly,' Leesa beamed. 'And given the placement of the branding and Colin's, uh, assets, the specific focus of our campaign will be...'

She swiped to the next slide and I inhaled a piece of waffle on my gasp. Even when I proceeded to hack up bits of fluffy batter with my hand over my mouth, she pointedly ignored me, turning the tablet in Dad's direction so I had to stretch to see it — to see the action shot of me on the bike wearing *only* my shorts.

'Bike bro memes,' she announced, her voice smooth. Zooming casually with two fingers, right over my butt, she enlarged the photo of me on the screen. I was out of the saddle and peering over my shoulder, which placed my arse up and fully visible, from cheek to crack, glutes covered in shiny blue Lycra, the padding of my shorts with its awkward genital seams clearly visible and no pantyline because we freeball under those fuckers.

But it was the words at the top that had made me choke. In playful white lettering it said, *All guys like the same thing: b_ _ _s.*

'Are you…?'

'Very serious. Why, is there a problem?' she answered me with a smile, swiping to the next picture, where the word was filled in as 'bikes'.

She zoomed in again, a smile playing on her lips. 'Here, where the PowerFuel logo is,' she began, brushing her fingertip just above my arse — in the picture! Although I swore I could almost feel it. 'This grabs attention and then the joke reels them in. I've mocked up a few more.'

When she said 'grabs', I was sure she knew it made firecrackers go off in my head.

'What's this, then?'

I hadn't noticed Derek approaching. He leaned over Leesa's shoulder — far too close, in my opinion — and peered at the screen, swiping back and forth.

'I can think of a few more options — especially for Colin!'

'Oh, I did more,' Leesa said, gifting Derek a bright smile.

She swiped through 'balls', 'butts' and 'beans' to the inevitable 'boobs', at which point she coolly met my gaze with a lift of her brow.

'You know him so well,' Derek complimented with overdone admiration.

'He's teasing you,' I grumbled.

'I am usually aware when someone's teasing me.' She bit her lip over a laugh, her face contorting. It shouldn't have been cute when she was calmly suggesting using me in memes for promotional purposes.

While I was distracted, she lifted her phone and snapped a picture. 'More resources for my Colin memes. I've got a lot of material for social-media *ass*-ets.'

Dad clutched his stomach, cackling along with the boys and the tingling at my hairline was the first clue I had about what was really going on. Zeroing my gaze on Leesa, I studied her expression critically. The longer I stared, the wobblier it got. Dad gave up the ruse entirely, hooting with laughter.

I sat back in my chair and crossed my arms. '*Ass*-ets? I suppose I should be thankful you didn't make a joke about how much I like time trials.'

Nelson howled with laughter, slapping his knee. 'Colin rides big TTs!'

'The Australian TT champion!' Derek added.

'Big TTs, huh?' she repeated, shooting me a provoking look. I was provoked — and enjoying it, although I wished the others weren't here so I could tell her I'd been lying and her tits were the sweetest ones I'd ever seen and I'd imagined in some detail what they might look like if she took off that floaty dress and let me see.

'How were your TTs, when you were racing?' I asked her instead. 'I'm really, really interested in your TTs.'

'My TTs were never impressive enough for you,' she retorted.

Leaning over the table and tipping my face up to hers, I said, 'Well played, Magda. Well played. For a second, I thought you might actually post this on the client accounts.' I snagged the tablet from under her nose. 'I'm going to need a copy of these works of art. I'll give this back to you later.' Along with a few other photos I was going to enjoy taking.

# 9 September, the year before

**Leesa**

'The sign wasn't a prank,' Colin insisted with a groan that caught me in the gut. 'The men's team is flying out to Canada from Amsterdam, so I came to support you guys. To support Lori.'

My bullshit radar was off, since part of me insisted he was telling the truth – the same part that had recently decided, in an inexplicable turn of events, that he was hot.

'To support Lori with a "Go Leesa" sign?' I pushed. 'There was something on the back, right? An insect to scare me? A spider?'

The colour in his cheeks confirmed my suspicion. 'It was your last race,' he said quietly.

'Huh, I was aware of that too!' And Colin Gallagher had had a part in the disaster my last race had turned into.

'Shit,' he said under his breath. 'I tried to apologise. I really didn't mean—'

'It doesn't matter,' I cut him off.

'It does to me! If this is my last chance—' It was his turn to cut himself off.

'Your last chance to prank me?' I finished for him doubtfully.

As though a screen was raised over his face, he shot me a sudden smile, intent and a little bit dark. 'You got it,' he said with a wink.

My gaze dropped to his little pout. My mouth was parched, my heartbeat misbehaving. He'd just admitted to a stupid prank that had gone so very wrong. I should have hated him; one part of me was imagining screaming and pounding on his chest. But another part of me pictured that as a prelude to something like… a kiss, where I could pull his hair and scratch up his back. The way he was looking at me, all heat and intent, made me think about the thin line between enemies and lovers.

God, what was wrong with me? I couldn't reconcile it, Lori's gangly younger brother and this slow, liquid charm he'd turned on me.

I gave a desperate swallow as subtly as I could. As though hitting a final nail into my pride, he licked his lips.

'You know I only pick on you because you're hot.'

This was a new torment. Were these the strange effects of a general anaesthetic? He seemed to be closer all of a sudden and I didn't mind it.

'Do you think we should kiss, Kubicka?'

# Chapter 11

**Leesa**

When the first of my reels hit a new client record, I had to admit there were some advantages to my reluctant return to the cycling world. Morgan had been sceptical when I'd shown them the footage I'd taken. If I hadn't been entirely certain the target audience would soak it up, I wouldn't have pushed to release it. But if there is a truth universally acknowledged among cyclists, it's that tech is like a religion.

I'd flagged Colin down in the car park with the quaint hotel and the mountain landscape in the background and asked him to show me his bike after a training ride. The result was a striking video of a sweaty and rumpled Colin pointing out the different gears and cassettes with his oil-stained hands, all while saying words like 'derailleur' and 'electronic drivetrain' in his lazy, deep voice and casually swearing.

At the end, he'd looked right into the camera and said, 'I can't tell you the exact gear set-up for each stage of the Tour or I'd have to kill you.' Then he'd winked and held a finger to his lips and I could still hear the swooning over the internet — especially from the bike tech nerds — as the clip garnered more and more views.

I'd edited out the part at the end where he'd accused me of drooling over the sleek aero bike with all the latest gear. While it was unfortunately true that I still remembered the feeling of the gear shifters under my fingertips, the ultimate cooperation between engineering, physics and biology, that hadn't been the reason for my open-mouthed staring.

Because no matter how much like an overgrown child he behaved – pulling stunts like walking off with my tablet and coming up with flimsy excuses not to give it back – I couldn't pretend that Colin Gallagher wasn't utterly compelling in just about every situation. Even after I'd overheard him criticising my *boobs*, he'd still made my skin tingle moments later, when he'd looked into my eyes and spoken in his soft drawl.

The clips from the lab with the stationary bike had felt incriminating when I'd finally uploaded them, even though I'd spent an hour editing out the worst parts. I was nervous about what Morgan would say. But riding high on the unequivocal success of my first reel – and the butt prank Colin had swallowed whole – I was in a positive mood as I reported back to my supervisor.

'I think the combination of content for the bike nerds and things with wider appeal is going to have the best outcomes for the client,' I was saying into my laptop.

I was perched cross-legged on the chair in my tiny room, Morgan's face on the screen. On my top half, I wore a nice pale green blouse, but off-screen were my favourite nasty old shorts. The enthusiasm I'd expected from my colleague wasn't forthcoming and the silence stretched for long enough to tease out the prickles at my hairline.

'He's good on camera, at least,' Morgan commented. 'Gallagher doesn't have the best name recognition, according to the latest reports. We have to keep things punchy.'

'He's got form. His name is being mentioned in connection with a top-five spot and I saw his stats——'

Morgan's eyes glazed over and I shook myself inwardly. We were talking about sports *marketing*, not actual sport.

'To be honest, I think PowerFuel got lucky.'

I wanted to reel those words back in when Morgan's gaze flickered to mine with a hint of curiosity.

'They're a manufacturer of energy gels. Only people who are super into sport will buy them,' I continued defensively. Your average punter wouldn't want to hit themselves with a meal's worth of calories in the form of congealed, cat-piss-flavoured carbohydrates.

'What about runners?' Morgan countered. 'They won't care about the biking side of things. We need wider appeal.'

'I've been thinking of doing some coffee-related stuff,' I rushed to say. Coffee was the other religion cyclists subscribed to.

'That's great, but we need to get more personal. Sit him down for an interview. We can use sound bites and then release it as a whole on the YouTube channel at a later stage. You've got some great action shots, but there's no *story*, is there?'

'I suppose not.'

'Like, does he have a girlfriend or a boyfriend?' Morgan asked.

'No,' I answered reflexively, but I choked on my reaction. I *assumed* he didn't have a girlfriend. Wil wouldn't have said that stuff to me on the first day if he did, right? He hadn't had a girlfriend in September.

At least, I thought not. I hadn't actually asked.

'Then why not?' Morgan asked. It took me far too long to realise it was a rhetorical question. 'What drives him to the edge of endurance? Is he really friends with the guys in his team, or are they rivals? We want the Netflix documentary and not the real sport.'

Morgan was right. Remembering Colin strapped to the equipment, the sad dragon on his back, I wanted to know what was under his skin too. I just wasn't certain he would share that stuff – not without extracting a price from me.

'Sports marketing is all about the narrative,' Morgan reminded me.

Green graduate me had not shut up about building narratives for the entirety of my internship, even as my responsibilities never got me within striking range of forming one. But making a narrative about Colin sounded dangerous. Either I took him at face value and presented him to the world as a prankster – in some magical, sympathetic way – or I dug deeper and asked *why* he welcomed new members of the team with ribbing and reverted to superficial flirting with me.

'Good idea,' I grated out, pulling myself together. 'I'll stick to him like glue.'

In a non-literal way. Not like the thoughts that had swum in my head as I'd filmed that tech video.

'Just…' Morgan's hesitation spoke volumes, 'Leesa, I'm the last person to give you a lecture about this.'

Morgan was marrying Maria from Legal in a few weeks, so I guessed what was coming.

'I realise that your… rapport with Colin is the reason this content is so engaging, but this is your first assignment. Don't get so caught up in the story you lose your own priorities.'

'I know him from before,' I admitted. 'Maybe I should have said something, but…' I hadn't realised we'd have so much 'rapport', since our previous acquaintance had mainly consisted of teasing and one disastrous proposition in the hospital.

'I can see how well you know him,' Morgan said with a dry smile. 'But under no circumstances can *you* become the narrative. You've got your own bright future ahead of you.'

Morgan was right. This wasn't about me, even if Colin wanted to make it so. My future was not on a bike; that had to be my past.

After ending the call, I sat back in my chair, my thoughts buzzing with the many things that could go wrong. Getting personal with Colin was not a good idea, especially when I was a quitter and he had to be a winner but, as I tapped my nails nervously on the desk, I had to admit that part of me wanted answers.

I just didn't know what I would do if it turned out he wasn't the complete jerk I'd always assumed him to be.

A knock at the door forced me to shake myself out of it. Expecting Wil – or maybe Tony – I pulled it open with a smile that immediately died when I caught sight of the figure on the threshold. His hair was still dripping from a shower, he had the beginnings of sunburn and he looked ready to collapse.

'Are you okay?'

He just gave me a tired shrug and shoved my tablet into my hands. He paused, his gaze fixed on the device held between us, and then his thumb brushed mine, the lightest whisper of a touch, but unmistakably intentional.

I only wished I knew what his intentions were with me, this

enigmatic star who sometimes seemed to be showing me cracks. In that moment, he reminded me of the skinny 19-year-old with a questionable vocabulary who'd put googly eyes on my croissant on the third day of his first training camp.

He let go of the tablet all of a sudden, making me fumble for it, and he used my distraction to slip past me into the room without being invited. He threw himself onto my bed and lay still for a moment, staring at the wooden slats in the ceiling, one hand resting on his chest and his T-shirt riding up a few inches I should not have taken any notice of.

Unsure what else to do, I closed the door to my room and dropped into the chair by the desk, letting my itchy hands hang between my thighs instead of patting him on the knee or running my fingers through his hair.

'I'm not sure you should be here,' I began, when he remained silent.

'I definitely shouldn't.'

Then he rolled over and went to sleep.

## Colin

Rosemary. That was the herb. Who would have known that the combination of berries and rosemary could be so intoxicating? I was breathing it in from her pillow – finally. Maybe I could just sleep here for the rest of training camp.

'You smell so much better than Nellie,' I mumbled, coming awake a little more and appreciating the stupidity of what I'd just said. Lifting my head, I unstuck my eyes and squinted around the room, hoping I might be lucky and she wasn't there.

But I found her at the desk, working on her laptop.

'Good evening, Sleeping Beauty. Welcome back to the land of the living.'

She was peeved. I suppose she had a right.

Snuggling back down into the pillow, I let my arm hang over the side of the bed as I rummaged for the dregs of consciousness. 'What time is it?'

'You could have set an alarm.'

'If that's the worst you can do, I mustn't be in too much trouble.'

'It's not getting in trouble with me that you have to worry about. What if someone had come looking for you?' she continued.

'They wouldn't look for me here.'

'Well, what if someone had come looking for *me*? I can't exactly hide a whole doofus in this tiny room.'

I didn't mind her calling me a doofus, as long as I was *her* doofus.

But then she went for the jugular. Spinning in the chair, she eyeballed me. 'Colin, is something wrong?'

'Nah,' I replied immediately, throwing my arm over my face.

'Because… I'm serious. We could get into trouble for this.'

With a sigh, I hauled myself upright, blinking back a few stars behind my eyes. The endurance ride today had wiped me, which was concerning in itself. My body's limits felt close enough to touch – or were those limits in my head?

No matter how good it had felt to wake up in her bed, I shouldn't have come here. It wouldn't make it any easier to take Dad's barbed comments that only made me angry these days. I had conked out so completely on her pillow I was still groggy, maybe the best I'd slept in days. Dad would approve of the rest, but not if he discovered how much I'd been struggling in my own bed.

But she wasn't here for me – not in that way. She didn't owe me anything and I shouldn't have barged into her room and monopolised her bed.

I forced myself to my feet with a groan that made her leap up in alarm. A faint smile tugged on my lips as she grasped my arm as though she would catch me if I keeled over.

'It's nice you're so worried about me.'

She dropped my arm. 'Maybe I still have some loyalty to Tony and the team.'

My smile faded. The stupid wish that she'd have some loyalty to *me* made me just as irritated as the mention of my dad. 'Lucky for the team, I'm all right. I just need to eat something.' And stop wanting to sleep in Leesa Kubicka's bed when she obviously didn't want me.

I should have got the message back in September. Only a stubborn idiot like me would still be dreaming.

# Chapter 12

## Leesa

'I'm not creating latte art. I don't do that shit.'

Two seconds into my video in the breakfast room and I was already glad I had decided not to go live after all.

But Colin was — unsurprisingly — a wiz with the espresso machine, tamping the freshly ground coffee with a flourish and setting the filter in the holder with the practised hands of someone who did this every day, multiple times.

Paying careful attention, he pulled the shot with a magnificent film of downy crema and moved on to frothing milk. I caught it all on camera, including his quick smile, which was compelling enough to break hearts all over the internet.

Morgan might have been sceptical of the power of a coffee-based video, but I knew the community better. Bike ride? With a coffee break, please. Which route are we taking today? The one past the cold brew place. Big ride? Yep. Two hours in the café.

If beer was frowned upon in the pro cycling peloton (sometimes with the tongue firmly in the cheek), then coffee was seen as one of the major food groups. During my time riding pro, coffee had gone from being a daily pick-me-up to a metabolic necessity that would preferably be injected directly into my veins — if injections of any sort weren't such a sore point for the Union Cycliste Internationale, the governing body.

'Can I have that one?' I asked, hoping my voice didn't give too much away on the video.

The little glance that was mostly eyelashes had no business

being so sexy, but I was tired from a whole week of studying him in detail and, aside from the stupid moustache, everything he did caught me right in the gut – or a little lower.

'Ask me nicely?'

'Can you make me a coffee nicely?'

'I'll happily make you a coffee, but this one's for Derek.'

The lift of his eyebrows was concerning.

'Speaking of Derek, when are you finally going to shave—?' My footage wobbled as I saw what he'd done with the milk. 'I thought you said no latte art!'

'This isn't latte art. It's latte graffiti.'

I followed him as he walked carefully in Derek's direction and placed the coffee in front of his teammate.

'Get your milk moustache with that one!'

Derek laughed. 'Geez, man! You made me a cock-and-balls coffee? I have to drink that!'

'Swallow it all down, mate.'

'Aw, you're a little boy, Gallagher!' Nelson scrunched up his napkin and lobbed it at Colin. 'A few manners in front of the lady!'

I gave up and stopped the footage, letting my hand drop.

'She's no lady. She spent years on the women's team with my sister, who is even worse than me.'

I didn't even know where to start. 'No one of any gender will be interested in your cock and balls,' I grumbled. 'Plus, I can be a lady *and* a rider.'

His grin kicked me in the shins, as though I'd told him exactly what he wanted to hear. 'Glad you remember the glory days after all,' he quipped and tweaked my ear, brushing his fingers over the three silver studs in the lobe today. 'Speaking of which, it's rest day tomorrow, which means you and I have a date with a bike.'

My reluctant smile was wiped right off my face again. Why was he pushing this? That line I'd drawn under my career was supposed to be thick and black, to protect me from all the disappointment – and that yearning, frustrated part of me that *wanted* to get back on, screw my nice, neat future. But Colin kept rubbing at it until it was blurry.

The worst part was that I could see the mountains when I closed my eyes, feel the wind on my cheeks. I was fighting myself and I couldn't let him guess how torn I was.

'I haven't agreed to anything,' I said warily. 'I don't have any kit.'

'Not an excuse. You're on a training camp. Kit abounds.' His eyes drifted to my collarbone, a little lower, before snapping back up to my face. I imagined his neck glowed a little pink.

'If you're thinking that my boobs are so small I'd fit into men's kit, you can fuck right off.'

I was not prepared for the view of him biting his lip in response. He eyeballed me, his throat bobbing as he swallowed. 'I know how hot you look in a speedsuit, Kubicka.'

My hair stood on end and I was glad of the cheering and wolf whistles from Derek, Nelson and the others at Colin's blatant — too blatant — attempt to butter me up. He was putting on a show to lighten the mood, that was all. I told myself that anyway.

'What about shoes? I'm assuming you can't solve *that* problem by tomorrow? Do they do next-day delivery all the way up here?' I asked, following him back to the coffee machine, which also moved us out of earshot of the others.

'You're assuming I'm not already prepared. We had a deal. You aren't about to back out, are you?'

'I agreed to prank you in return and be... friends.' That sounded better than repeating that I'd agreed to give a little bit of me in return for a little bit of him. 'You haven't exactly upheld your side.'

'What? I've been playing your little performing PowerFuel monkey.'

'Half my footage has been unusable.' I didn't mention that the other half was pure brilliance.

'What more do you want? You'll have to get in line for your pound of flesh. It's one of the demands of the Tour.'

His graphic comment piqued my curiosity and created the perfect opportunity to introduce the subject I'd been hesitating over. 'My supervisor says I need you to sit down for an interview.'

If there'd been a ticking clock in the breakfast room, we would have heard it. Colin's expression was less than impressed.

'That doesn't sound like a fifteen-second viral video,' he finally said. 'I don't think I can be entertaining in long format. I'd run out of rude jokes.'

He was playing a role. He couldn't really believe I didn't see through him, could he?

'It wouldn't be like an interview with a sports journalist. It's for background, for sound bites we can use over the footage I've taken; what drives you — that sort of thing.'

His expression was still notably blank. 'What drives me,' he echoed with a twitch in his jaw. 'Who gives a shit about that?'

A little bit of me for a little bit of him. I should leave him alone. God knows, with his upbringing he had to have his share of hang-ups about the sport and he was right: no one needed to see him bleed. But I felt close to understanding something; maybe there was a misguided urge to help him.

'Colin, if it bothers you—'

'Nah, why would it bother me?' He broke out another smile, that roller blind crashing down over his expression. How many times had I seen that now? 'Not as much as you learning to ride a bike again, anyway.'

Predictably, my pride rose to that one. 'I don't need to go back to training wheels.'

'If you say so.'

The gauntlet had been thrown, even if he hadn't expressed it in words: a bike ride in exchange for an interview. I was feeling reckless, but not ready to throw myself to the wolves just yet.

'I'm not going to post anything you don't want public,' I assured him. 'The sponsors don't own you.'

He laughed, but it was a chuckle so dark I glanced up at him in alarm. 'Don't they?' But he cleared his throat and flashed me a crooked smile obviously designed to cover his wobble. 'But okay, let's do an interview.' He paused, regarding me a little too intently. 'After you've held up your side of the bargain and come with me on a ride tomorrow. You can record whatever you like.

Wouldn't that be a great feature? Learning to love cycling again after the trauma of a pro career.'

'"Trauma" is a pretty strong word,' I said carefully.

'Don't you think it fits?'

'This is about you,' I insisted.

'I want to make it about you *and* me.'

I gritted my teeth against a desperate retort. 'No one wants that.'

'Are you sure?'

There wasn't enough air in this room and, not for the first time, I wished I were still immune to his strange variety of raw charm. A flicker of his amused smile and I snapped out of it, sucking in an enormous overdue breath.

'My supervisor wants me to do an interview. I'm not interrogating you for my own pleasure.'

'That would be a weird kink, but I can think of a lot of other things I'd rather do for pleasure.'

I opened my mouth to tell him off, but he continued.

'Like an epic descent on the bike tomorrow,' he finished. 'You can remember who you really are.'

'I was never the great cyclist you're trying to make me out to be. In case *you've* forgotten, I *quit*!'

That word finally hit home, his expression turning serious — almost hurt. 'You're stronger than that.'

'Reality begs to differ.'

'Reality isn't what's stopping you getting on a bike.' His belligerent tone took me aback, but it was a crack in his usual persona and I wanted to peer inside more than was wise. 'An interview for a bike ride. That's fair, Kubicka.'

'I don't know why you're so set on this—'

He cut me off with his next words, as agitated as he had been before he'd fallen asleep in my bed. 'I'll shave off the moustache as well. You can film it.' He flashed his eyebrows at me once, as though he wanted to end this conversation as badly as I did.

It was just one ride. It didn't mean I'd regress and give up my future for this sport again. Maybe I'd built this up too much in my mind and going on this one ride would prove it wasn't something that would affect the chemistry of my brain and make me miserable. He was right, getting some GoPro footage from a helmet camera was a good idea – as was a shaving video.

'I suppose I can't say no to that,' I answered carefully. 'But the moustache comes off *today*.'

'As you wish,' he said with an expansive nod. 'Here's your coffee.'

I accepted the peace offering for what it was, sharing the moment of relief as neither of us moved. Then I thought to study the froth on top, thankfully finding no evidence of a cock and balls. 'I appreciate you resisting temptation.'

He pouted at me. 'Can't you see the bike wheel?'

I looked again. 'Oh, I think I see it now. Maybe?'

Clapping a hand against his chest, he said, 'Harsh, Kubicka. That's harsh.'

'*You* claimed you don't do latte art and it's kind of fitting that your entire recognisable repertoire consists of cock and balls.'

'I can do butts too, but I didn't want to tempt you.'


'Go on, choose him. I know you're going to.'

Colin had sprung this on me. Before I could film the demise of the moustache, apparently I had to adjudicate in the competition. Now I stood in the corridor outside the room he shared with Amir, facing off against two gangly cyclists with matching lip fluff, no idea how delicate I had to be with their egos. Nellie and Amir were avidly observing.

'Are you suggesting I'm a partial judge?' I accused, delaying the decision for another few moments.

He chuckled, but didn't look at me, simply stood next to Derek with his hands clasped in front of him. 'Yep,' he confirmed.

'Surely the two of you can sort this out without requiring a kindergarten teacher to settle the dispute. I just want them gone. Humanity can thank me later.'

Colin brushed his fingertips thoughtfully over the pale-reddish whiskers and regarded Derek critically.

'It's an important lesson to learn, you know,' Colin declared, 'how to lose with grace.'

'Have you actually learned that?' Nelson asked doubtfully.

'Shut up, Nellie. I'm prepared to demonstrate.' He cleared his throat ponderously, hitched up his pants and then turned to give Derek a thump on the back hard enough to make him stumble. 'Nice 'tache, mate. Well done!' He offered his hand in one of those bro handshakes, since normal handshakes apparently weren't macho enough. 'You can grow a real moustache – a fine one.'

God, he was good. I had whiplash; one minute he was brewing a cock-and-balls coffee and the next he was building genuine rapport with a junior member of the team, although I was pretty sure he didn't mean for anyone to know he was serious.

He grinned, his usual cheeky number. Stretching his arms out wide, he gave a bow. 'You have learned from the master,' he murmured. 'You going to keep yours if mine has to go?' he asked Derek.

I suspected Colin had never looked so uncertain at Derek's age. 'What do you think? Does it look any good?' Derek's gaze darted to me, but Colin grabbed his arm and turned him away, inspecting him critically.

'I think you can rock it.'

I rolled my eyes, making sure Derek caught the action.

'Don't listen to her,' Colin continued with a dismissive flick of his fingers. 'I have no choice, but you keep that 'tache if you want to.'

'I'm a bit worried if the only woman in the room is advising against it,' Derek said with a dry smile. Good man, he was learning not to trust Colin on everything.

'Nah, she secretly loves mine,' Colin insisted, biting his lip and shooting me a wink that zinged rather annoyingly right through the centre of my body. 'She'll be sad to see it go. In fact, I bet she'll stop me before I get the razor near my face. This moustache makes me *irresistible* – right, Lees?'

'Yes,' I said sweetly. 'It's impossible to resist teasing you, when it looks like you smeared peaches and cream on your lip.'

Nelson and Amir hooted with laughter, but Colin stepped closer to me, his gaze never leaving my face, and I couldn't help feeling as though whatever *this* was, it wasn't over yet.

'Peaches and cream, hmm?' he repeated slowly, tugging one lip into his mouth for the briefest moment. 'Sounds delicious.'

My skin went up in flames, culminating at my hairline, as he stood, hesitating expectantly.

'You coming, Kubicka?' He gestured to the door of his room.

'Hmm?'

'Don't you want to record this, for your viewers or continuity or whatever?'

Not really, now that my stomach was twisted in knots and my brain was hanging on an image of his serious eyes that I was certain no one else could see. Or I was fixating on his lips with too much curiosity.

He'd scraped off too many layers of my outer shell to do this right now, but it seemed I didn't have a choice.

# Chapter 13

## Colin

Tugging my shirt over my head one-handedly as soon as I walked into my room wasn't exactly on purpose, but I rolled with it once I'd done it. She was in my room. This had not happened before, except in the couple of fantasies I tried not to indulge in too often.

I teased her about finding me irresistible, but I was well aware her presence here right now meant precisely nothing. The tingling feeling in my chest was wrong. My instincts had always been wrong when it came to Leesa Magdalena Kubicka — as that disaster in September had proved.

But when I turned and she snapped her gaze away a second too late, I couldn't help the suspicion that there *was* something strung tight between us.

It was lucky she'd never worn these dresses on training camp when she was on the team. Twenty-year-old me would not have coped. I might have tried poetry or some shit and then I would have had to live with that embarrassment too.

'I don't know why guys do that, take their shirts off from the neck.' Her voice wavered, which gave me more ideas I shouldn't have had.

'How do you take yours off, then?'

'Wouldn't you like to know?' she answered drily.

'I would, but I meant it as a genuine question,' I replied with a laugh. 'Don't you do the same? I never thought about it before.'

She glanced down at herself, her hands raised as though she were about to tear off her clothes, and I had to turn away, all my hair standing on end. I knew exactly how *I* would undress her. Today's dress had an elasticated ruched bit around her torso that I would tug down until I could tease myself with a hint of her bra. With the other hand, I'd raise the hem and grip her thigh, around the back.

Christ, this was not helping. I rubbed the back of my head vigorously to clear it. She'd already rejected me once, which was fair enough, since she was a commitment gal and I'd never even tried to be in a relationship with someone. It was usually easier just to say goodbye when my life took me out of the country — whichever country I happened to be in that day.

But I'd struggled saying goodbye to her back in September...

'Maybe I cross my arms?'

My gaze snapped back up to her face. Of course my body had raced ahead with this 'taking off clothes' scenario, while she was still working on the intellectual task, but she was pretty when she was thinking hard, her lips pressed together and a dimple between her brows to match the one in her chin.

'I wonder if that's a thing, that men rip their shirts off like you do and women cross their arms. It would make a good short video,' she mused.

'Men ripping their shirts off?'

She laughed, the sound shooting through my brain. 'Exactly. Although it might not be as effective for marketing. No one would remember the sponsor.'

I tried not to take that as a compliment and turned for the bathroom to keep this thing moving. 'At least the PowerFuel followers will have seen me half-naked so much, they're desensitised to it,' I said as I turned on the water until it ran hot.

It was true, she'd filmed me wearing less than the tracksuit bottoms I had on, but something in her body language was setting me off this time, my oversensitive Leesa radar bleeping continually. When I caught sight of her in the mirror, her gaze seemed to be stuck on the dragon tattoo on my back, her expression volatile.

She came closer with hesitant steps. 'Do you need to tidy up the bathroom?'

'I don't leave condoms lying around, if that's what you're worried about,' I said with a snort. 'We're at altitude in the middle of nowhere. Opportunity for that sort of thing is kind of lacking.'

There it was – her vivid eye roll. 'Do you ever think about anything else?'

'Not when you're looking at me like your favourite ice-cream flavour.'

Her eyes flashed. 'I was not!'

I didn't argue with her. 'Should I put my shirt back on?'

'It's fine,' she said, which wasn't the most flattering adjective she could have chosen.

I reached for my razor, dipping it in the hot water in the basin. 'You gonna film any of this or were you really hoping to take the moustache for a test drive before I get rid of it? Are you sure you aren't curious about how it feels?'

'How it feels where?'

I had to shoot out a hand for balance, my throat suddenly thick. My gaze swung to hers, only to find her cheeks pink and a flustered frown on her face.

'I didn't mean—'

'—how it would feel on your thighs if I went down on you?'

She gulped, but I suspected I'd got myself more worked up than I'd got her.

'You seem to think I won't call your bluff,' she said, her expression grave.

My mind went blank as she took a casual step closer. 'What?'

'You're not really offering to kiss me – or anything else.'

'What do you think is going on then?' For once, the brainy Leesa Kubicka had no idea what she was talking about.

'You keep taunting me, but if I stepped up and tried to kiss you right now...'

Ohhh, shit. I could barely breathe when she said stuff like that.

'... you wouldn't let me anyway.'

'I would.' The words tumbled out. She could do whatever the hell she wanted to me. I'd even let her set me on fire the way she was doing now and she wasn't even touching me – except with that gaze. The way she looked at me made me forget my own name.

'I sincerely doubt that, Colin.'

I didn't like the brittle tone in her voice.

'You don't think maybe by teasing you I'm salvaging what little pride I still have after September?'

'I don't know how that makes sense. You caused an accident by teasing me, so you're teasing me more now?'

Hands propped on my hips, I sighed deeply, glancing up at the wooden slats on the ceiling of the bathroom as the guilt – the frustration – washed over me again. 'I was talking about what happened in the hospital, not the accident. You know how sorry I am about the accident.'

'The slagroomtaart apology,' she mumbled. 'I thought you insisted nothing happened.'

'My pride says otherwise now. You turned me down. It's not my favourite memory.'

She kept looking at me, her frown deepening. 'You weren't serious.'

I should let her keep thinking that, rebuild my pride on the flimsy foundation, but instead I blurted out, 'Are you sure? I was… quite disappointed actually.' *Shut up, you idiot.*

She laughed, which didn't make me feel any better. 'Quite disappointed. Okay.'

She'd see through me in another second.

'You know what I think?'

*Here it comes.* I thought she was standing too close. My brain was scrambled and I caught a hint of her perfume or soap or whatever it was – raspberries with herbs, tart and sweet. It was classy as fuck.

But she apparently had no idea what was going on inside me.

'You might be a little attracted to me physically,' she began in a superior tone that was still a turn-on, 'but you don't really want to kiss me. That's why you're making a big deal out of this.'

'I'm not making a big deal out of it.'

Her brows rose with the corners of her mouth and that satisfied smile shot weakness to my knees. 'I'm right. You don't want to kiss me. You didn't deny it.'

Choking when I'd meant to make some kind of verbal response, the various things I might have said got all tangled up and nothing came out. All I knew was that she was wrong. I wanted to kiss her too damn much and maybe that was why—

'Colin, suck up your own stupid pride and remember that you don't want me anyway and—'

I grasped her jaw and lifted it, her lips opening in surprise. She drew in a sweet breath, her eyelids blinking. She'd gone still. She would let me do it, press my mouth to hers, make my point. I'd kind of forgotten what my point was. And I wasn't sure what *she* wanted.

Which was how I managed to stop, my lips a breath from hers.

Her cheeks were soft under my thumb and fingers. I felt the bob of her throat against my knuckles. Blood rushed in my ears as my instincts insisted on closer. Maybe we'd make super-special children or something, because every part of me was firing like a party popper. Except it was probably just her. *She* would have incredible children — if she wanted them — with whoever she settled down with.

Which wouldn't be her man-child ex-teammate, who could barely grow a beard and was tied up with a sport that had burned her.

'Whatever thoughts are coursing around in your brilliant brain, Lees,' I began, my voice so low she seemed to be holding her breath to hear, 'that "I don't want you" theory is one you'll never prove, because it's not true.'

'Then why didn't you do it? You didn't kiss me. You're not usually known for restraint.'

I licked my lips, struggling to interpret this game of chicken. The longer I stayed close to her, the more danger there was that I'd blow it all out of proportion, three weeks before the Tour.

'I don't know what we're arguing about,' I said, my thoughts growing foggy the longer I could feel her in the air I was breathing. 'If *you* don't want to kiss *me*, then I'm not—'

My brain was wiped in an instant as she came closer. She stretched up and I was about to pass out like a sprinter who'd gone

too hard to the finish line. Ahhh, breathing in was marvellous —
especially when it was *her* I was inhaling.

Then breathing was overrated. Who needed air? I had the soft
pressure of her lips on mine. It was everything — too much and not
enough and so fucking tender it socked me right in the gut.

# Chapter 14

## Leesa

I'd called his bluff, wanted to prove his teasing was all empty talk at my expense. Now he would extricate himself gently, give an awkward laugh, make a joke about his irresistible moustache.

That was not what happened.

He was not supposed to lean into the kiss, his body thrumming with restraint, and steal the breath from my mouth. It definitely wasn't supposed to feel this good, but I saw sparks and a fire licked up my spine as I struggled for balance.

The open-mouthed kiss gently consumed me. I clung to his shoulders as he bent his head to come closer – deeper. He didn't use his tongue, as though trying to keep the kiss soft and slow, but the breaths he sucked in through his nose were obscene with longing, the hitch of a groan deep in his chest might as well have been pornographic.

I barely recognised myself, the way I was taken apart by a simple, exploratory kiss. I should have known that nothing about Colin Gallagher was simple.

His hands came up to my ribcage, sliding and fisting in the fabric of my dress. My thoughts were floating out of reach; all I knew was that we needed to keep doing this. The brush of his mouth over mine grew firmer, the drag of his lips becoming familiar, along with the light graze of bristles from his top lip – more subtle than I would have expected.

Time sped up, as though this kiss were four or five dates and, if he undressed me right now, I might even enjoy myself. Instead of feeling overwhelmed by sudden intimacy I hadn't had time to process, he didn't quite give me enough.

When I couldn't stand it any more, I dipped my tongue out and he met the action with a groan in response. Desire ramped up inside me with a whump against my ribcage. If I'd known this was how I'd feel, that maybe my brain wouldn't interrupt with its usual reservations, I might have given him a real answer in September.

What would charming, easy Colin think of that? I was starting to think he was such a good kisser, he might be able to make me forg—

'Phew, I—'

No. My fingers dug into his shoulders to resist when he drew away. *No.* I'd expected him to stop this doomed experiment before it got started, not now, when I was just getting going.

'Leesa.'

There it was, the reluctance in his tone. Damn it, I hated being right. He didn't want to kiss me. For the six years I'd known him, that fact had never bothered me. I'd never questioned it. This was the guy who'd given me a mug that revealed a picture of Rick Astley when filled with a hot beverage. One time he'd swapped my sunscreen for self-tan lotion.

Kissing me until my eyes crossed was not part of the pattern. The biggest mystery was why I'd gone along with it. I'd flicked my tongue into his mouth, for goodness' sake. I usually found that action a little gross, to be honest.

'Do you have an answer to your question?' he asked.

'What question?' I hadn't even got my breath back, let alone my full faculty of speech.

To my horror, I only realised I still had my claws in him when he pried my hands gently from his shoulders. I'd left little red semi-circles on his skin.

'You're very clever, but you don't know everything, especially not about me.'

I didn't know *anything* about him in that moment – or about myself.

'Maybe you'll be more careful next time you test out your

theories.' He spoke with his usual slow drawl, but there was a threat underneath that sizzled over my skin.

But it made me find my voice. 'I'm aware of how little I know. You keep muddying the waters with outrageous statements.'

He shrugged and I was almost convinced he'd shaken everything off – including the kiss that I was nowhere near recovering from – except the set of his mouth was too tight. 'Muddy water, ay? Good description of you and me.'

He turned back to the mirror, flicking on the hot tap to pour in more water, and fetching his razor.

'Are you filming this or not?'

Fumbling for my phone, I lifted the device and set up a shot where I couldn't see myself in the mirror. He threw me a half-hearted devilish look, but there was so much wariness in him, I could barely believe he was the same man who'd teased me constantly for over a week.

The dragon on his back rippled as he lifted his hand to his foamy cheek, as though the creature could move independently. I wished he'd say something silly, but if my banter was gone, it appeared so was his. I caught the sound of my own breath, laboured and unsteady, and tried to calm down so it didn't come out in the video.

But on the surface, there was nothing special about the footage. Seeing him shave in a video would not feel as intimate as standing here while he did it. I wouldn't accidentally zoom in on his lips the way my gaze kept drifting there as he made careful strokes with the razor around his mouth. If viewers were dying to know how smooth his cheeks were now, that was their fault and not because I was imbuing the video with my own suddenly clamorous desire.

In the space of five minutes, he transitioned from a strawberry-blond Henry Cavill from the *Mission: Impossible* era back into Colin Gallagher, as I remembered him from years of training camps. Except he wasn't quite the same. Or perhaps he was and I was seeing him differently, which was a disturbing thought.

'What?' he asked, sending me an uneasy look in the mirror.

As he rinsed off his razor and splashed water on his face, the uncomfortably tight feeling in my lungs returned. He had a lively face, full of nuance. His eyes were soft under half-closed lids. Yeah, I might have admitted he was cute if someone had asked, but this scrunching up every time I looked at him was new and not welcome.

'Did I nick myself somewhere I can't see?' he asked, inspecting his chin thoroughly in the mirror.

Giving myself a shake, I turned off the video. 'It's weird to see... you again.'

'I knew I should have kept the moustache.'

I shook my head, aiming for a dry look and probably failing. 'No, I just... We've known each other a long time.'

His brow lifted. 'We have,' he agreed carefully.

'Remember when you put glue on my hair ties?'

His pained grimace almost made up for what he'd done. 'I didn't know that stuff wouldn't wash out.' He lifted a hand and, for a moment, I wondered if he was going to rub a strand of my hair between his fingers. I didn't like the dip of disappointment in my stomach when he dropped his hand instead. 'It was a shame you had to cut your hair.'

'It grew back.'

'I didn't—' He swallowed and rubbed his hand through his hair. 'I didn't upset you, did I? With that kiss? I don't want to make trouble for you — at least not like that.'

My skin prickled at my own confused reaction to his apology. 'No, I mean— It was my fault, right? But we probably... shouldn't...'

'That's loud and clear,' he replied with a lopsided smile. It was a puzzling smile, dark and yet full of relief. I hadn't imagined the eagerness of his mouth on mine, but he certainly seemed less than keen to take things further.

I'd accused him of not being serious in September, when he'd obliquely opened the topic of... this, *us*. But now, I *wasn't* sure.

I couldn't go back to being the Leesa who didn't know what it was like to kiss him.

'You know, maybe the bike ride together is a bad idea,' I blurted out, the prospect of hours alone with him firing me up.

He drew back and studied me. He was half a foot taller and used every inch of that to look down his nose at me. 'I might have a soft spot when it comes to you, but one kiss isn't getting you out of that bike ride.'

I was wobbly on my legs again. What did he mean, he had a soft spot?

He pointed a finger at me. 'You are getting back on a bike tomorrow, even if you parade past me naked, which you are welcome to do anyway.'

'I didn't kiss you to avoid getting back on a bike,' I insisted.

'I know. You were testing a theory about me and got more than you bargained for.'

My gaze snapped to his, but his eyes were thankfully glinting with humour and not deep with that wariness I didn't know how to process. I lifted my chin. 'Well, you can only dream about seeing me naked.'

'Oh, I'm pretty sure I will,' he said with a breathy laugh. 'Tiny tits and all.'

'Colin!' As I spluttered an inarticulate response, he slipped past me, squeezing my elbow and dropping a quick kiss on my cheek.

He tugged his T-shirt back over his head and I pulled myself together enough to realise I should take the cue to leave. I felt his gaze on my back as I headed for the door.

'Nine o'clock, out front. I'll drop off some kit – and shoes – this afternoon. Nothing is going to stop me getting you on that bike.'

'Are you planning to prank me? It is your turn. Is that why you're so set on this excursion?'

His mouth twitched. 'I suppose it is my turn, after your masterpiece. But nah, don't worry.'

'I wasn't worried.'

His only reply was a lift of his brow.

'I don't know why you care so much.'

He considered his words. 'You tested your theory about me

today. Maybe I want to test some theories about you. That's fair, right?'

'What theories?'

He crossed his arms and the smile that stretched slowly on his face was cocky charm personified and I hoped he had no idea of the effect it had on me. 'You'll have to wait and see.'

# 9 September, the year before

## Leesa

'What did you say?' I spluttered.

Yikes, I'd got caught up in that low scrape of his voice over my senses and forgotten what was going on here for a moment – until he'd said the word 'kiss' and I remembered he was mocking me – he had to be mocking me. I needed oxygen to my brain – fast.

Thankfully, he snapped back so swiftly the air rushed in after him. He was off the bed in a heartbeat, knocking the table as he escaped whatever prank he'd been trying to pull on me, asking for that kiss. The yoghurt teetered again and he lunged for it, sending my phone sliding towards the floor.

Proving his lightning-fast reflexes, he managed to stop that falling, but he ended up sprawled on the bed, frantically propping himself up so he didn't crush me. He smelled pleasant: something soapy and not overly tangy. His breath was on my neck, setting off the nerves in my skin like LED warning lights blinking on all at once.

I should tell him to get off me. Another second and he'd realise his proximity was affecting me, despite... everything about him that I resented. But he got there first, hauling himself up, a concertina scowl on his forehead.

'Here's your ph— *Shit*, you've got yoghurt all over your—'

Hurrying to the wheeled table of equipment in one corner, he banged around for a minute before returning with a roll of toilet paper. But he only succeeded in rubbing the stuff all over my chest, going increasingly pale as he did so.

'*Fuck*,' he muttered under his breath. 'I didn't mean for it to turn out like this.'

What did he mean? He'd made some kind of plan for this meeting? Or was the 'Go Leesa' sign part of an elaborate set-up? I wouldn't have been surprised.

'Is someone filming this or something?'

He reared back. 'No!'

'You can see why I find that hard to believe. You suggested we kiss and now I'm smeared in blueberry yoghurt. If one of the guys pops out with a camera right now, I'll—'

'I meant it!' he blurted out. It took me a second to realise he was talking about the kiss and then a blush seeped up my throat like wildfire. He tugged at his hair with an agitated hand, looking at the door, the ceiling – anywhere but at me. 'I mean, now we're not on the same team any more, I thought we could… y'know.'

Apparently, he wanted a response – or maybe for me to finish that sentence.

When I opened my mouth, the only thing that came out was a gurgled, 'Urgh.'

# Chapter 15

## Colin

She was late. Three minutes late, to be exact – maybe on purpose, except hopefully she didn't know how fidgety I was. I did not have the nerves for a technical descent right now, not when my brain was exploding with possibilities, all of them involving her eyes on me.

I almost wished I'd never found out what it felt like to kiss her. She'd just wanted to call me on my crap and, in response, I'd mauled her in the bathroom. One of these days I'd learn, but I suspected it wouldn't be today.

While I didn't want her to feel like she was under pressure, *I* was under pressure. If she really was content to never ride a bike again… It felt too much like leaving me behind. She kept insisting she'd quit. While I understood why she'd retired from pro, I didn't like how she threw that word around.

I'd got so used to her in those flowery dresses, I wasn't sure what to expect this morning. Instead of the men's team kit, splashed with sponsor logos – which, to be honest, probably would have fitted her fine – I'd ordered her a jersey and bib shorts from a women's brand and got one of the swannies to collect it in town yesterday. I knew her shoe size from several years ago when I'd swapped out her branded slides for velvet granny slippers while she was in the swimming pool.

But I wanted to see her in the stuff I'd picked out, feeling like fucking Prince Charming sending a ball gown to Cinderella. I fiddled with her bike while I was waiting – one of the spares in Nellie's frame size. The crank shafts were probably too long, but I wouldn't be timing her and hopefully she'd be comfortable.

The door of the hotel opened with a creak and I snapped my gaze up from where I was crouched by the rear wheel, a smile and a smart comment on my lips. But the smile died abruptly when I saw who was coming.

Getting slowly to my feet, I waited for him to say something first.

'It's rest day, Colin,' he said instead of a greeting.

'I'm aware of that, Dad.'

'Goin' out hard today will only set you back tomorrow.'

'Also aware of that.'

He paused, studying me with a pained expression. 'I know who you're waiting for and I'm not sure this is a good idea.'

If he knew what 'this' was, then it was more than I did. 'She's doing her job. She's supposed to get footage of me.'

'But what are *you* doing?'

I glanced up at the sky, annoyed that Dad was always so closely on my arse that he could cut through the crap like this. 'Recovery ride. Making sure my muscles don't stiffen up.'

It was true. Even during the hell of the Tour, we couldn't afford to stay entirely off the bike on rest days – not that there were many rest days during the Tour.

'You don't need company for that and she's got plenty of action shots from the training rides over the past week. You should be focusing on your performance.'

Did he think there was *anything* else in my life? 'Are you worried we're sneaking off to fuck on a picnic blanket?' I used the word to get a rise out of him and it worked.

He turned on me, his jaw clenched and his throat working. 'You always think your mum understands you better than I do, but I know what you're doing.' He was going to some effort to keep his voice gentle, but I felt his frustration anyway.

'Enlighten me.'

'You're trying to deal with the pressure. Last year, you could still joke your way through the Tour, knowing it was your first and no one expected much, but this year is different. You're trying to reduce everyone's expectations of you.'

'Even the psychologist didn't come up with that shit, Dad. Leesa has nothing to do with my performance.'

'At the very least, she's a distraction. At worst... you're breaking professional boundaries with someone who's not from the team. To be honest, I don't want to know which it is.'

I gritted my teeth so I didn't let out any of the words that were brewing in me. 'She's an old friend, not a distraction and certainly not anything else.' Lucky I'd always been a good liar.

'Friend,' Dad snorted, making heat prickle up my neck. 'You always had—'

'You have nothing to worry about.' I cut him off. Steam would start coming out of my ears soon and he'd be able to see how much his words were winding me up instead of achieving the opposite. 'None of this is news, Dad. But I will say that Mum's pep talks are less cringe.'

'What does your mother have to do with this?'

'*I* still talk to her every week, even if you don't.' Hinting at their separation was sure to shut him up.

But he came back with a jab I hadn't expected. 'You don't talk to her about Lees—?'

'Hi! Sorry I'm late!'

I looked over at her before I'd thought through the wisdom of that action and the punch to my gut was enough to make me wonder if I'd ever breathe again. She was here for me, wearing the clothes I'd picked out for her – and looking beautiful enough to tear my heart out of my ribcage while she did so.

She'd tucked her hair through the space at the back of her helmet and bound it into a fat, messy plait. As I watched, she slipped the sports sunglasses upside down into the grooves with a practised move. I needed her to see what I saw in this moment: a talented former pro; a smart, strong – spirited – woman.

She paused on the terrace when she caught sight of Dad, before pasting a smile onto her face. 'Morning, Tony.'

'Good morning, Leesa. What a sight, seeing you back in cycling kit, although it doesn't quite look right without our team colours.'

She smoothed a hand along her waist and my eyes followed

the movement helplessly. Did she like the colours I'd chosen?

'It is strange without logos splashed across my boobs,' she said and I stifled a snort.

'I understand you're accompanying Colin on a recovery ride.'

The way her gaze flickered to me suggested she'd picked up on the residual antagonism simmering between Dad and me.

'Leesa hasn't—'

'Yes!' She cut me off before I could explain, which was interesting. 'I can't come to the Alps and not get on a bike.'

Dad grinned at her. 'Right you are! Just make sure he takes it easy. No showing off in front of the lady.'

Her smile in response was amused. 'Don't worry. I'll bring him back safe.'

## Leesa

I couldn't help feeling guilty as Tony went back inside, leaving us alone. Apparently, I was a co-conspirator, now.

'Hey,' was all he said in greeting. It was still enough to make me tongue-tied. 'Thanks for taking the pressure off with Dad.'

I gave an inarticulate shrug. 'It's not like I'm helping you sneak out.' Although it kind of felt that way. His eyes on me, hot and glowing, weren't helping the wild mixture of emotions in my stomach.

He propped his hands on his hips. 'How're you feelin'?'

He knew what a can of worms that question was, the bastard, and my nerves were volatile enough to answer with shocking honesty. 'Beautiful,' I said with a huff.

The kit he'd bought me was worth half a month's intern salary. It was sleek and stylish, ochre-pink with geometric swirls up the side and over one sleeve. The fabric was smooth and light without being slippery. I wasn't a pro any more, as the saggy bits on the back of my thighs proved, but I couldn't deny the way my heart had leaped when I'd seen this jersey — and pounded when I'd pulled it on this morning.

'Good.'

I hadn't noticed him come closer and, now that he was in my space, it was too late to pretend I didn't like him there. For a strung-out second, I thought he was about to plant a kiss right on my lips, but it landed on my cheek instead, feather-light.

My throat was thick. That was two cheek-kisses in two days. What did it mean that we were cheek-kissing these days? Just that he'd lived in southern Europe too long? In Poland, he'd press one to each cheek and an extra for good measure.

'Your dad didn't look too happy,' I said carefully. 'Are you sure this is a good idea?'

'You're not getting out of it.'

'That's not why I asked,' I snapped, taking a deep breath. 'I don't want to be a distraction. You don't have to come with me.' Now that I was all dressed up, getting on that bike – and whatever happened next – was inevitable.

I could see he'd guessed I'd overheard more of his conversation with Tony than had been apparent. His chin came up. 'Leesa, I can't do this without a distraction. The Tour, this sponsor shit – I need to breathe sometimes and despite what you and Dad seem to think, I'm a fucking adult who knows what he needs.'

I blinked at him, seeing those cracks again – rebellion. But it didn't seem to make him weak – the opposite. Maybe Colin was finding his strength. Perhaps this was the narrative, except that I was here too. I didn't belong in the picture.

He stalked to the other bike that was propped up against the railing in the car park, grabbing it by the stem and heading for the road, his shoes crunching on the gravel.

'You want to let off steam with me? Is that what this is?'

The smile he shot me over his shoulder was a more familiar one, but with a reckless slant that was compelling. 'I'd love to. You know I would. But that hasn't worked out so far.'

My cheeks burned as I caught his meaning. 'I meant the banter and the pranks.'

'Sure you did, but that's not what today is about.' With a sigh, he turned back to face me. 'You know there are other reasons to ride a bike than winning the Tour de France?'

'Don't let your dad hear you say that.'

He grinned, the first real, amused one I'd seen that day. 'I'm the only one not allowed to have fun on a bike. But *you*.' He tapped a finger on his chin. 'You didn't quit *fun*, did you? You look so hot up in the saddle. I'd hate to think that a stupid mistake of mine meant you never did it again.'

My mouth dropped open. His words weren't exactly complimentary, especially delivered with that twinkle in his eye, but he'd spoken them slowly, dripping with meaning in his deep voice and my lungs wouldn't work properly. He bit his lip and dipped his gaze.

'I knew that colour would look amazing on you.'

The heat on my chest suggested my skin was turning a similar colour. I didn't know what was going on here, felt more than a little out of control, but it was an unfortunate fact that Colin Gallagher was irresistible – with or without a moustache – when he smiled like that.

While I was thus distracted, he waved a little square GoPro in front of my face before attaching it to the holder on my helmet. 'Because you don't have enough footage of my butt.' He fitted a similar camera onto his own helmet. 'Grab the bike, Kubicka,' he said softly. 'Let's go have some fun.'

With some trepidation, I retrieved the smaller bike from the railing, my hands falling to the saddle and the stem automatically. It was a beautiful piece of equipment, made of lightweight carbon fibre, designed to allow the air to stroke lovingly over the curves. Although this one had electronic shifters, the basic physics of the device was the same as for any child's bicycle, any commuter's city bike – or a pastel-coloured Dutch Tweewieler with a basket of flowers on the front: the force from my legs amplified and converted into motion in a hyper-efficient exchange.

It was also beautiful.

'Are you worried about your broken arm?'

I shook my head. It was mostly true. It wasn't the first time I'd broken a bone, although every other time I'd climbed right back on a bike before I could overthink my recovery.

'Then what are you afraid of?'

'I'm not afraid!'

He paused, the tip of his tongue moving inside his cheek in thought. 'Are you lying to me or to yourself?'

'You,' I blurted out without thinking. I was well aware of my own fear. I'd given up my place in the team – in the sport – and I didn't want to regret that decision. I'd trained obsessively for ten years of my life and ended up with nothing.

I didn't belong anywhere near an elite rider preparing for the race of his life. Tony had been right about that. I should have tried harder to get him to stay away.

'Okay,' Colin said unexpectedly gently. 'What are you going to do about it? Talk to me?'

With a vehement shake of my head, I gave the bike a push, ignoring the shock of memory from the clack of the wheel hub. Arriving at the road, I stared grimly ahead as I grasped the handlebars, sparks of adrenaline firing in flashback.

I should be moving forward into my new life and not back, and yet... Whether to shut Colin up or for another reason I didn't want to admit yet, I had to do this. I swung my leg over the saddle, one foot extending onto my toes as I clicked the cleat on my other shoe into the pedal with muscle memory that was stronger than my muscles themselves.

Colin drew up next to me and mirrored my pose, peering at me curiously. 'You okay?'

I shook my head, but stared resolutely ahead.

'Lees,' he said, his voice dropping low, 'you don't have to—'

'*You* forced my hand, Gallagher. You can't let me off now.'

His hand landed on my back, a reassuring touch that only reminding me of Doortje's friendly slaps, touchy-feely team time among the girls.

'All right,' he muttered. 'Let's go.'

# Chapter 16

## Leesa

This was a terrible idea. It had been nine months since I'd been at peak and I was taking off after one of the biggest stars of the men's elite. My lungs were burning just on the flat, trying to keep up, and knowing this was only a recovery ride for him — and he was most definitely going slow for me — was enough to devastate my pride.

I'd felt strong on a bike at one point, playing with speed, manipulating gravity — or defying it. Today there were tears in my eyes and I only felt my weakness. The mountains were too big to even dream of conquering. I didn't belong up here in the wild landscape that was too powerful to tame with roads and machinery.

It was only a small consolation that the bike still felt like an extension of my body, working to multiply the force of my legs moving the pedals and reacting to every minute adjustment I made to the handlebars — which was lucky, because cycling on alpine roads was not for the faint-hearted.

Our hotel was high up, near the pass, so we were soon heading downhill and I could catch my breath. The road wiggled through meadows in a thousand shades of green, swallowed occasionally by patches of pine forest. Swinging around the switchbacks and technical curves was a dance I hadn't forgotten, using my weight and gravity to keep the bike stable.

Fifteen miles disappeared in what felt like a heartbeat — or 25 km, as I'd learned to call it — leaving behind the sleepy resort town of Luson. Before I knew it, we were catching glimpses of Bressanone, way down below, and the fracturing mountain road had become a divided highway. When Colin pulled to the side to gulp down some water, I could barely believe how far we'd come – and how quickly. Most unbelievable was how much I wanted to keep going.

My first sip of water turned into a guzzle, as I realised how thirsty I was. The front of my lovely new jersey was dark with sweat down the middle.

'How are you doing?' Colin asked.

I answered him the only way I could – with a shrug.

'We… Now we have to get back.'

He meant 'up'. We had to get back *up*.

'You gonna make it?'

Another question I couldn't answer. Cursing inwardly, over and over, I was angry with myself for losing fitness, for using the end of my career as an opportunity to wallow. I would always be a hard worker, but I'd lost sight of everything I might want to work *for*. Now the world was too big for me.

Tucking his bottle back in the holder, Colin gripped his handlebars once more, ready to push off. He sent one more glance in my direction. 'Stay close behind me.'

He meant he'd draft me, use his slipstream to help me get up the hill. It seemed he wasn't even going to tease me. I was too much an object of pity for that, even if it turned out I could still rock the curves on a descent.

The PowerFuel logo stamped on his butt was a familiar sight after the week I'd spent filming him, but feeling his slipstream was so much more powerful than just the sight. He didn't set a high pace and I guessed the climb was long.

That turned out to be an understatement. It was relentless.

With tears in my eyes, it was only stubbornness that kept me going as we rounded the mountain range to the east of Bressanone and headed back up into the high meadows. My lungs burned and I adjusted the gears right down, crawling up the hill.

As we crept higher and higher, the landscape was so awe-inspiring it triggered a splatter of emotions I hadn't allowed myself to feel in nine long months. The climb broke me. Surprisingly, it wasn't my body that went first, as I had put in some hours on a stationary bike to taper safely. It was my heart.

I loved this. All of it. The torture of the climb. The utter silence of the looming mountains, the neon meadows and the stoic pines, rays of sunshine sending a glimmer over everything. The strain on my body and the relief of a flat stretch of road. The cool, clear air to feed my empty lungs and racing metabolism.

All I needed was oxygen, sugar and water. My purpose was to go – to *move*. I loved this so much and Colin had known this would happen. He was a fucking bastard for making me confront it when there was no way I could go back.

The computer on my bike ticked up with the altitude. It wasn't fast, or pretty, but I did it. I made it. Just me and the bike – and a little help from Colin Gallagher.

## Colin

I didn't even need to say 'I told you so' when we pulled off the road for a break in a clearing surrounded by deep green pines with Dolomite peaks ranging above. Her face was the age of the mountains and just as austerely beautiful. She still felt it. I could tell.

'It's beautiful from a car, but it's different when you're out here, part of the landscape,' I commented softly, watching her take it all in, waiting for her to say something as she leaned her bike against a pile of stacked-up firewood.

I didn't expect her to stalk right up to me and give me a shove hard enough to make me stumble backwards.

'Are you satisfied?'

'I was until you shoved me,' I responded cautiously. 'You had fun, right?'

'Huh.'

I straightened when I caught the sheen of moisture in her eyes.

'It's not about *fun*. I used to *live* for this. The past nine months have been *so hard* and now I'm right back where I started – because you decided to toy with me!' She tugged off her helmet and ran a gloved hand over her head, turning her mess of curls into a riot.

'I don't understand.'

'Of course you don't! You're the star! You don't have to choose between cycling and life.'

I cleared my throat pointedly. 'Only because I don't have a choice — and I don't have a life,' I said drily. That took some of the steam out of her. 'I don't understand why you quit!' I continued. 'I know it's shit how little you got paid, but you could have taken another job in the winter like Doortje does, if you're so sad about it.'

She flinched and the guilt shot through me as though I'd hit her. I opened my mouth to blurt out something unconsidered in an attempt to make things better, but she spoke before I had a chance.

'I was always planning on getting another job — a career,' she said, her voice shaking. 'It was only a matter of time. I should have quit earlier, then I might not have been a nearly 30-year-old intern in a shitty job market. I'm not like you. I never had what it takes and now being back, this assignment — it's a nightmare. I should have just become a damn doctor.'

Her meaning was clear enough: I was the nightmare. And I'd rubbed her face in it today. If I needed further proof of how wrong I was for her, I had it.

She plonked down on the grass, as though punctuating her statement, then flopped onto her back, staring up at the sky.

I lowered myself warily down next to her. 'I screwed up, right?' I'd made getting under her skin an art form, but I'd never reached her in the way I truly wanted to.

'Get over yourself, Gallagher,' she murmured. 'Yeah, you screwed up, but the problem was here already and it doesn't have anything to do with you.'

'But I——' I considered my words. She was right. Her life was none of my business — and that was the fact that had always frustrated me.

And it was inconveniently sexy, hearing her call me 'Gallagher' and put me in my place. I stretched out next to her, close enough that the ends of my hair brushed hers. Even being this close felt like a miracle.

'I know you gotta eat, but can't you work *and* ride?'

She glanced at me, her face close with a handful of blades of grass between us. 'You make it sound simple,' she said. 'Try telling that to my parents.'

'They're doctors, right?'

She seemed surprised I knew that. 'Yeah, two young Polish doctors who came to America to embrace running their own practice. But maybe they didn't imagine their American daughter would follow her heart instead of her head and achieve precisely nothing with their academic genes.'

Her tone was bitter, but her words grabbed hold of me somewhere in my chest and pulled. These were different expectations from anything I suffered under – so much harder because she didn't have a finish line, no podium places to aim for. Only a vague definition of success. I would have buckled a long time ago, under those conditions.

'I… like that you followed your heart.' Otherwise, I might never have met her. 'I know you're wildly clever, but your brain isn't the only amazing part of you.'

When I risked a glance at her, she was watching me doubtfully. Fair enough, given the history of our relationship.

'Are you mocking me?'

'No!' I couldn't help laughing, which somewhat undermined my point. 'But there's no law that says you're smart, so you have to get a high-powered job. What if that's not what you want?'

'I spent ten years ruining my psyche with this sport. I have no idea what I want.' She lifted a hand for emphasis, but let it drop again, perilously close to mine.

'I get that.'

I heard the movement of her head on the grass and knew she was watching me. 'Do you? What would you do if you weren't required to bust your balls for three weeks in the hot summer sun?'

Her dry tone made me smile and I took another glance at her, bracing myself for the whump when I caught sight of her, eyes glinting with humour. 'It's not a good idea for me to even think about it.'

'Fucking on a picnic blanket?'

I was so startled, I shot up into sitting position, spluttering some nonsense in my defence. I could unfortunately picture it: Leesa in one of her flowery dresses, up around her waist— I took a deep breath to clear that one before it sharpened into focus. Shaking myself, I managed to drawl, 'With you, sweetheart? I can't say no.'

She rolled her eyes and gave an unconvinced 'pfft'. It was probably for the best.

'You heard me say that?' I asked, trying to remember what else I'd talked about with Dad and whether I'd said anything even more incriminating.

She tugged on my arm and there was no way I'd resist her, so I lay back down. I hadn't consciously intended it, but now my shoulder was brushing hers and her face was even closer.

'I didn't mean to eavesdrop. I'm sorry.'

'It's okay,' I reassured her. 'I was just trying to piss him off. Same with the… you know, the comment about big tits.'

She propped herself up on one elbow with an indignant expression and I couldn't stop my eyes drifting down her body. Big ones were lovely too, but Leesa's tits…

'I am aware I have small breasts,' she said drily. 'To be honest, I'd rather skip the back problems and miss out on starring in your boob fantasies.'

If only she knew.

'If you didn't mean those, what part of me is amazing then? Other than my brain?'

Popping my eyes open, I found her leaning over me, sunshine outlining her silhouette in gold. I could just lift a hand to her face, raise myself up and kiss her. That image shook me just as much as the picnic-blanket fucking.

'Your sense of humour,' I answered.

'The only reason I survived as long as I did in cycling,' she quipped with a smug little smile that killed me.

'Your eyes.' Maybe I hammed it up a little, but my voice came out rough and low.

She poked me in the shoulder. 'Where are you getting these lines? A cheesy action flick with a disappointing romantic subplot?'

'Remind me never to watch a movie with you.'

'Fine by me.'

Her tongue dipped out to brush her lower lip and I wasn't sure if this was teasing or foreplay. I'd woefully misjudged this dynamic in September, but yesterday…

That kiss had not been nothing.

'What part of *me* is most impressive?' It slipped out before I'd thought it through, but I tacked on a cocky smile to hide how desperately I wanted to know if she'd grown some respect for me over the past six years – not that I'd done much to earn it.

Her brows shot up. 'Colin, I had no idea your ego required so much stroking!'

I grinned up at her. 'You can just say my palmarès, if you like,' I joked. I'd had such a cracker of a season, she *should* be impressed with my list of wins.

She tapped that dimpled chin as though considering my suggestion.

'My thighs?' I tried out, punching a fist on one leg.

She leaned over me and my lungs started playing up. What the hell was she doing? She was going to kill me. 'Your sense of humour,' she said softly, tightening up everything inside me.

She thought I was funny? Did that mean the years of pranks might one day be forgiven? Maybe if I admitted—

'And your eyes,' she continued, before straightening with a chuckle.

Ah, shit, I'd been had. She flopped back down beside me as she laughed, clutching her stomach, and it didn't matter if she was making fun of me, that sound was enough to turn me into a knot of wants and needs, none of them helpful. Mostly, I wanted her to keep laughing.

I rolled my head to the side to watch her, both disappointed and strung tight with anticipation when her laughter petered out and she met my gaze. Then she spoke suddenly.

'You know, maybe I needed this.'

'Hmm?'

'Letting it all out, getting back on the bike and having a fucking cry.'

'And a laugh.'

She nodded, probably rubbing bits of grass into her hair.

'Maybe if you give it all some ti—'

'Kiss me.'

I didn't hesitate. Rolling onto my side and up onto an elbow, I dropped my lips to hers with a huff of relief. She opened her mouth, drawing me deeper, and I followed her cue, tangling my fingers in her hair and tightening my hand. A low moan built in her throat and I soaked in the sound through my skin.

Her mouth was like nothing else, hot, consuming and thrumming with enthusiasm – with delight. Her hands came up to slide over my jersey, clutching at me in vain before slipping up to my face, my hair, where she had better purchase.

Keeping up firm strokes of my lips and tongue that heated the kiss past what was bearable, my thumb traced the line of her throat, down further, and I splayed my fingers along her collarbone. I wanted closer, deeper, my body delighted to finally have her beneath me, the background hum of want finally vindicated.

My hand drifted down the soft fabric of her jersey as her chest heaved and my brain emptied of everything except the desire to cover her breast with my palm—

'Colin, stop.'

I rolled off her with a jerk, breathing hard. She squeezed her eyes shut and pressed her hand over them, hard, for a second or two, before sucking in a deep breath and arranging her facial expression. She hopped neatly to her feet and took several steps away. It wasn't exactly food for my ego, seeing her shake off that kiss as though it had been another of my stupid pranks.

We obviously hadn't made as much progress as I'd thought.

'Sorry, I—' She couldn't seem to find the end of that sentence.

'You don't need to apologise.'

'No, it was a bad idea and it got out of hand. Your dad's right.'

I didn't care which bit of my conversation with Dad she was referring to. I stood and crossed my arms. 'Dad is not the one who decides whether I kiss you or not. You are – for your own reasons.'

She shook her head with a sigh. 'There's more than just us in this game. You race in three weeks.'

'I'll do my job in three weeks. You're not going to ruin my performance – unless I pull a muscle during sex.'

She seemed to stumble over that word. 'We shouldn't. I'm a bad influence on you – I'm in a different place in my life.'

That statement shafted me painfully – mostly because I knew she was right, but I hated that she was right. She had *always* been in a different place and she always would be, especially when she went home after the Tour.

'Don't you start with the "get your head in the game" shit,' I mumbled.

She peered at me from under a scrunched brow. 'The world will be watching you this time.'

'Because of you,' I commented.

'Partly,' she agreed. 'But mainly they'll be watching the new guy grow into his talent, writing a few stories of battles and feats of endurance.'

I gritted my teeth against the flare of fight in my stomach. She patted my arm, the action affectionate, but not in the way I wanted from her.

'It's your time now. For better or for worse, mine is over.'

# Chapter 17

**Leesa**

He flinched when I flashed the bright light at him, lifting a hand to shield his eyes.

'Sorry,' I mumbled, trying not to think about the last time I'd apologised to him — for ordering him to kiss me and then changing my mind. Trying not to think about that kiss was like telling myself not to imagine a zebra. I could still feel his hair under my fingertips, his tough, hard body — the panic when my brain fast-forwarded to ripping clothes off and then exploded with doubts.

He hadn't exactly been overcome by romantic urges — I'd ordered him to kiss me. Logic dictated he had to be attracted to me, but was that just an indiscriminate biological function and I was a convenient partner? Did that even matter?

My thoughts interfering with my sex drive was not a new thing and I didn't like my chances of switching it off and sinking into a fantasy on the grass under the summer sun. Colin would probably tease me if he knew the hoops I had to jump through in my head just to make myself comfortable enough to have sex with someone.

The strangest part? I kind of regretted not pushing through my reservations. It might have been worth some emotional discomfort for a heated fuck with Colin while the summits looked on. That way, I might have worked it out of my system, rather than remembering the texture of his lips and the brush of his fingertips along my throat as unfinished business.

The spotlight accented the pale freckles on his skin, creating shadows at his cheekbones, sculpting his mouth. He looked fair against the black background I'd set up using screens and a poster with the client logo on it. He watched me intently, his expression unreadable. The illuminated lines of his face felt more familiar than I expected, not only from the past ten days of seeing him through a camera lens, but from earlier memories. He looked his age that morning, a just-grown-up 25.

When I'd been 25, I'd felt the age of the world. Only later had I realised how much my blithe decisions would affect the rest of my life irreversibly.

'*Get him to turn a little to the left.*' It was early in the morning in LA, but Morgan had insisted on having input while I set up the interview.

Colin dipped his head to peer at my phone, where I'd propped it up on a chair. 'Good morning.'

'*Hey, sweetie,*' Morgan answered with a smile. '*You're doing great.*'

He grinned, leaning his elbows on his knees and lacing his fingers between. 'You're so much nicer to me than Leesa.'

Even though I knew Morgan was supportive, a shiver of unease still snaked up my spine.

'*Whatever she's doing, it's getting results, so I'm all in favour of Leesa being a hardass,*' Morgan said with a chuckle. '*The footage is really something.*'

Was there a hint in Morgan's tone? Colin's gaze slid to me, as though he'd sensed it too. Although I'd been careful to edit out anything too personal, every time I watched the video of Colin shaving, or my GoPro shots from Friday's ride, I worried it was obvious we'd had our tongues down each other's throats off camera.

'*I think you should set up your phone to take a close-up,*' Morgan continued. '*It would be a shame to waste that bone structure on a wide shot.*'

Colin pointed at my phone, peering up at me. 'You never compliment my bone structure. Are you still learning from your supervisor?'

'You have a lovely skull, Colin,' I responded drily.

Morgan guffawed. '*I cannot wait to see this interview, you two. It's looking good, so go get personal!*'

I waved to Morgan and ended the call so I could set up the close shot.

'Morgan's nice,' Colin commented, a smile in his voice.

'I'm lucky they're understanding. They noticed you and I have... rapport.'

'Is that what we have? I was going to say chemistry.'

'We don't want anything to show up in your drugs testing,' I quipped with a straight face, keeping my gaze on the phone in its tripod, rather than on Colin's grin.

'I could get disqualified from the Tour. Traces of Leesa Kubicka in my blood, one of the strongest substances known to sport. For the first time in my life I might be interested in doping.' I hoped he didn't know how his words rippled through me when he spoke in that low, smooth tone.

'Except I doubt it would be performance-enhancing,' I managed to warn him.

'I dunno. It could be.'

I couldn't be certain what he meant by 'it', but my mind immediately returned to that moment on Friday, his hand tugging at my hair and his body pressing me into the ground. If someone had told me a week ago that I'd be rolling in the grass with Colin Gallagher and it would be the single hottest moment of my life, I would have laughed them out of town.

Taking a deep breath, I started the phone recording and settled in the chair by the camera. Colin fidgeted, rubbing his hands together.

'Got your scalpel ready?'

'This is an interview, not a flaying.'

He met my gaze with amusement. 'What do you want me to say? PowerFuel gives me wings?'

I ignored him. 'Why do you think you've had such good form this year?'

'I'm just getting better with age,' he responded flippantly. 'Like expensive whisky.'

'I'm not asking for secrets,' I said with a sigh. I'd tried to warm him up gently, but the worry was returning – worry that I'd screw this up, because of this inconvenient *chemistry* between us.

'Then the answer is: I don't know. We've always had great training personalised on data. If I knew how to do this every year, I would have done it before.'

I recognised the edge to his voice.

'Sorry,' he said, shooting me a quick glance. 'I'm doing shit. You want some motivational crap, right?'

I couldn't tear my eyes off him, wondering if this darkness had always been there and how people didn't seem to notice it – how I'd never noticed it.

'What keeps you going when it hurts?' The question wasn't planned, but I couldn't stop it from tumbling out.

'Stubbornness,' he answered, eyeballing the camera as though he couldn't bring himself to look at me. 'Pride. Spite, occasionally. Spite is a powerful motivator.'

'You want to beat the others?'

He chuckled. 'No, I want to prove people wrong.' That sounded like the Colin I knew. I wanted to ask who he wanted to prove himself to, but I had a strong suspicion and the team would never want me to splash the truth of his relationship with his father across the internet.

'There are easier ways to do that,' I commented.

'Maybe,' he agreed with a smile. 'But winning is the best way. You know the feeling.'

The hairs on the back of my neck stood up and I bet he could tell. Denying it would be pointless, so I ignored him instead. 'What about the team? How do you feel when Derek's out in front of you, pushing to his limits to protect you?'

His playfulness disappeared in an instant. 'You know, sometimes the scrappy fight is easier than the smart game. The end of a stage, you're alone and you go on instinct and give it whatever you have left. But at the beginning you have to hold back. I'm not good at holding back. The guys protect me from myself sometimes too.'

'That's insightful.'

He glanced at me with a hint of surprise – and doubt. 'Cycling is all about knowing your limits – and how and when to push them. I fight for the win for myself, but I'm disciplined for the team, because their hard work only gets recognised through mine. It's not… a choice really.'

He might not have thought he could produce 'motivational crap', but this stuff would be amazing as a voice over for action footage. Maybe I wouldn't show the grimace of discomfort that accompanied his words, as though he'd be more comfortable if the team weren't behind him.

'Can you win the Tour?'

He scowled at me, too sharp not to realise I'd thrown him in at the deep end with that question. 'How am I supposed to answer that?'

'With the truth?' I suggested with mock innocence.

Leaning forward, he held his hand over the camera. 'To be perfectly honest, for you and not for this sponsor, no, I don't think I can win the Tour.'

That shocked me into silence. Colin talked such big talk, I'd never expected him to admit to weakness.

He chuckled. 'You told me to tell the truth.'

'Yeah, but I didn't think you *would*!'

'Lees, I don't want to lie to you. Maybe *you're* the one who should have been worried about this interview.'

'Oh, I *was* worried about this interview.'

'I'm trying to behave.'

Goosebumps rose on my skin. If the client's followers reacted to him the way I did, this stuff would be gold.

'Anything's possible,' he commented, slowly and clearly for the cameras.

'Even Colin Gallagher growing up,' I added in a mumble.

'Maybe not that.'

Morgan's insistence that I needed to get a romantic angle in this interview hung over me. I already felt tingly, as though I was digging too deep and might hit an old unexploded bomb that would take me out, but I forced myself to ask.

'What about your personal life?'

'What personal life?' he responded with a wink, not missing a beat. 'I eat, sleep, train and race.'

Instead of responding, I just lifted my brow and gave him a prompting look.

He surprised me by bursting out laughing. 'Yeah, that's what I tell Dad.'

'Wouldn't your dad want you to settle down with a nice girl?' I couldn't help the cynicism that crept into my voice.

'I don't like nice girls.'

I hoped he couldn't see how that sentence sank in my stomach.

'Except you,' he added, melted chocolate in his voice. 'I like you, although I'm not convinced you're a nice girl.'

Christ, the effect those words had on me. My throat was so thick I couldn't swallow.

He looked away with a hitch of a groan. 'Leesa, you're killing me.'

That only seemed fair, given the messed-up state of me. I took a deep breath and said, 'I *am* a nice girl.'

His smile was dangerously tender. 'I know y'are, but I like you anyway and sometimes I think maybe there's another side to you.'

'There's not,' I said flatly.

He leaned even closer, ruining the shot, but I couldn't move to adjust it – or turn it off. 'What if you didn't think about what you *should* do for a moment. If you just *did*.'

'I don't... operate that way.'

'You used to. You can have a good finish in a race by using your head, following the plan. But getting a win takes instinct, gut reaction, a feeling in your skin. It's an art.'

I suspected he knew he was painting a powerful picture in my mind – of the day I'd crossed the line in first near Colin's home city in Australia. He'd been there that day. The memory struck me as somehow new. He'd been there, watching with Tony – watching me take one of the biggest wins of my career.

The way he was staring at me, intently, no hint of a smile, made my lungs tight, as though I needed something more to breathe again.

'Sometimes your gut tells you something is right,' he said, his voice a low ripple through my sinew. 'And you've got to listen.'

He moved slowly, but my brain refused to process anything until it was too late. He grasped my wrist and tugged. I didn't resist, letting him draw me onto his lap. I waited for him to kiss me, but he lifted his face to my hair and inhaled deeply.

'You feel right,' he murmured, setting off sparks over my skin. Then he turned my face slowly to his, fingertips in my hair, and brought his mouth to mine.

Unlike the soft exploration of the kiss in his bathroom and the push and pull of Friday's make-out session, this kiss was like a shot of strong liquor – searing, powerful. He held me still and kissed me so hard there was no time to think about anything except the hot urgency of his mouth, the plunge of his tongue.

His chest heaved under the hand I shot out for balance and a hitched rumble from the back of his throat shivered through me. I turned as best I could to kiss him back, my fingers slipping over his jersey. His hand dipped under my dress, gripping my thigh hard enough to make me gasp.

'Leesa,' he said with a pained groan.

He obviously wanted to say more, but I was tired of my noisy brain, of doing what I *should*, so I cut him off with another kiss, this one greedy. He clutched at me, flipping my skirt up by accident, but neither of us cared.

I wanted to crawl up his body, straddle him, blow his mind. The poor man was wearing bib shorts, so I knew he was on the same page from the swelling bump in his lap. The certainty of his arousal flooded me with relief and then smug satisfaction when he shifted me for more friction, grunting like an animal.

Perhaps because I could feel the hot hardness of it so starkly against my thigh, I was suddenly burningly curious to see his cock – to touch him there. He'd made so many jokes about this simmering sexual awareness between us, at least I knew he wouldn't feel embarrassed to get it out.

I dragged my mouth from his to slide it down his neck, darting out my tongue and making him jolt. A distant tingle in the back of my mind warned me about being too aggressive, but I managed to shove it away again, sliding my mouth up to his jaw and whispering in his ear, 'Don't say anything. Let's just go to my room.'

He drew back to look at me and I stilled, bracing myself for him to speak anyway and throw me off completely, ruining what could be my only chance for hot, meaningless sex with a guy who lit me up like a bonfire.

But this was Colin Gallagher and he was thankfully on board with meaningless sex. He licked his bottom lip and nodded, dumping me off his lap as he reached over to switch off the camera that I'd completely forgotten about. I flushed to the roots of my hair at the thought of what had been recorded on there, but Colin grinned at me, his eyes a little wild, then he shepherded me bodily out of the room with his hands on my waist, pushing me ahead of him so I nearly tripped.

I hadn't locked my door – I kept forgetting in this remote hotel with only the team staying – and Colin didn't hesitate to shove me inside, close the door and then press me back into it, his hands locking mine against the wood near my head, our fingers tangling.

He hesitated for an instant, long enough for me to taste his breath and memorise his heavy-lidded gaze. I was burning to be touched, would probably be afraid of myself if I'd been thinking straight. Even though I strained towards him, he kept my hands clamped against the door, a kick of a smile suggesting he enjoyed my squirming.

'You sure about this, Kubicka?'

'Yes!' I needed him to hurry. My thoughts were pleasantly muddled by the scent of his skin, the pressure of his hands in mine, but there was always a distant bell that could clang and drag me back into overthinking. 'Please, now!'

His brow rose, but then he came mercifully closer, drawling an inch from my lips, 'Anything for you.'

# 9 September, the year before

**Leesa**

'I'm in a hospital gown covered in yoghurt and you're suggesting we *have sex?*'

His throat worked in a convulsive swallow. 'Not *now*.'

'Clearly.' My voice came out on a squeak. He'd assured me – with uncharacteristic vehemence – that this wasn't a prank, but I was still certain this couldn't actually be happening.

'Take it easy, Kubicka,' he said drily in response. 'You're not going to vomit, are you?'

'What? No.'

His laugh was deep and chesty. 'I wasn't going to ask you to marry me. I just thought we could have a… good time, that's all.'

Apparently, I needn't have worried about *his* pride. 'I don't…' *Have a good time?* Luckily, I cut myself off before I could finish that sentence. 'I'm more of a… relationship gal.' Yikes, that made me sound like real fun. But since when did I care what Colin thought of me? 'Too much thinking makes that… sort of thing…'

'I should just go,' he responded – predictably – with a tight smile, getting to his feet. 'I didn't mean to make a dick out of myself. Of course this is just… I don't know. Old times or something.'

Old times had not been like this between us.

'I'm…' He sighed and peered at me again from under his lashes and *whump*, the strength of my reaction to those baby blues got my heart racing again. 'I'll see you… I mean, good luck.'

Lifting a hand in a wordless farewell, he reached for the handle of my hospital-room door and turned it. Time seemed to spool forward too quickly – the yawning future without cycling, without any Gallaghers. Flashes of memory – from today and years earlier – played behind my eyes and this moment seemed to detach from time and create its own life.

And then he was gone.

# Chapter 18

## Colin

My heartrate was out of control, adrenaline spiking so high my vision was blurring – which was a damn shame because I had never seen anything as beautiful as Leesa, eyes glazed, open for me, wanting me. Just over two weeks until the Tour and she was going to kill me.

Vindication was a heady part of the cocktail of emotions mixing in my chest. Six years, all leading to this moment. As I closed my mouth over hers, soaking up her whimper of relief, wallowing in the press of her body against mine, it had been worth the wait – a thousand times over.

I hadn't expected her to burst over me with longing, but she was restless, wound up, and all we'd done was kiss.

'These dresses drive me wild,' I murmured against her mouth as my hand skimmed up her thigh, the filmy material under my fingers. 'If you had worn these on training camps, I might have misbehaved earlier – at least alone in the shower.'

Dropping my lips to her neck, I pressed open-mouthed kisses down to her sternum, to the neckline of the dress.

'Quick,' she said on a hitched sigh, her chest heaving.

With one more unhurried kiss that found the subtle swell of one breast, I gathered the hem of her dress and worked it up around her waist, her ribcage and over her head.

I was unprepared for the sight of her in her underwear. The little bra thing she wore was all lace and the stuff of fantasies. Her knickers were no-nonsense cotton, but that was so *Leesa* the stripes were an unbearable turn-on. I could see she wasn't entirely comfortable getting naked, although she still grabbed me and dragged me back for another kiss.

Her posture brought her words from September back in a sudden strike of memory. *Too much thinking...* I nearly laughed at the realisation of how well I understood that now. On Friday, her sudden about-face.

The rush now.

She fumbled with the zip of my jersey and I let her peel it off me – one little fantasy I wasn't going to abstain from. A second later, my bibs were around my waist and she was working on the shorts. I thought about stopping her, worried my very eager cock bobbing in her face straight away might not be the smoothest introduction, but then it was too late.

Heat rushed up my chest, waiting for the verdict. It usually did the job well, but dicks were kind of weird appendages and it was the first time she was appraising mine. She paused for a heartbeat, long enough for a squeeze in my chest, but then she licked her lips and took it in her hand.

'Flaming hell, Leesa,' I yelped, bracing myself against the door as she gripped me gently, her fingers the softest torture, turning my knees to jelly. With a little hum, she tightened her grip and explored the full length of it, sending sparks racing down my spine.

The floor was a live current and I was one step closer to keeling over in fatal ecstasy. Maybe I was already dead, her touch on my dick felt so good. Except, I couldn't die yet. I'd only just discovered my main purpose in life was to give Leesa Kubicka an orgasm she'd still be feeling next year.

'Babe,' I managed to choke out. 'Hey.' I had to dislodge her hand with mine, but when I kissed her again, holding her arse to pull her against me, she didn't complain. The noises from the back of her throat would give me horny dreams for months.

My muddled brain took a few critical seconds trying to work out how to get her bra off, but she wouldn't wait, pushing down her undies and shimmying out of them before tugging me close around my waist.

All rational thought left my head at the feeling of her skin warm against mine. I wanted closer, tighter pressure and friction and the way she dropped her head back against the door when I pressed her into it spurred me on. Either she curled a thigh around me or I yanked it up — I wasn't sure — but then my cock slipped up between her legs and I choked on a gasp.

She was hot and soft and wetter than my filthiest imaginings, squirming against me. I wanted to stay here forever, but the heat in my spine, the electricity in my veins would be too much — sooner rather than later, I feared, given how worked up we were.

'I should get a condom,' I ground out. I hoped I still had a few in the pocket of my toiletry bag. I didn't need them as often as everyone thought. I struggled to dislodge her arms, which brought a smile to my lips, remembering the way I'd wound her up during the interview about not always doing what she should.

'You don't need it,' she murmured, her voice thick. 'I'm on birth control.'

We both knew I got tested for everything all the time, but I paused. I hadn't had sex without a condom in a long time.

'It's fine,' she said, a waver in her voice. 'Or just use a condom. That's a better idea.' A cloud crept over her eyes and her throat bobbed.

'What is it?'

'Nothing.' She moved her arms in a way that suggested she wanted to cross them over her sweet little lace bra-thing.

'Hey,' I began, lifting a hand to her hair.

'Look, it's totally fine. I haven't... done this since my last medical in the team, so do whatever you want.'

'Your last medical?' I repeated before I'd thought it through. 'What's that, like, a year ago? More?'

She straightened, her tight expression so familiar to me. It should have been strange that she was delivering one of her disapproving frowns right now, but I'd spent a lot of time thinking about her over the years and her beautiful, private skin was only the final piece of a puzzle I knew well.

'I didn't think you'd want my full sexual history,' she grumbled.

'Maybe I should— This is—' She squeezed her eyes shut. 'Damn it, Colin. For a second, I actually thought I could do this.'

## Leesa

Stupid, stupid, stupid. Now that my brain had come back online, I wasn't sure how I had got this far: mostly naked with Colin Gallagher. My bralette was ludicrously difficult to take off, a fact I was almost thankful for now, and he was still wearing his socks, which somehow made things worse.

God, I knew how awkward I was in these situations. To try this with *him*! It might have been the most undignified moment of my life – and that was even before I started blabbering an explanation.

'I just… I struggle with this. There are so many variables. You can't know… what I like. And then if I don't like…' I swiped my underwear off the floor, heat rushing up my chest. The residual throb of arousal between my legs was uncomfortable as I slipped into them. I couldn't help thinking about how his cock had pressed up along the sensitive centre.

I couldn't bear to look at him, to confirm the strange ache of disappointment at how this had ended – this interlude and also the unexpected friendship we'd struck up. I didn't like how stricken I was at the thought of losing that easy banter that had got us to this point.

*Shit.*

'Leesa, I don't care if it's been a decade since you last had sex, although it's good to know.'

'It hasn't been a decade,' I bit out. 'And I realise you don't care, but I do – I mean, I'm careful about being comfortable with my partner. I just… this is complex and I—' I gave up. I didn't want to have to defend myself. 'You don't want this.'

'I don't think you really know what I want,' came his reply after a long pause.

I looked up at him without thinking. Bad idea. He was watching me intently with half a crooked smile, as though nothing I'd said fazed him.

'What… do you want?'

His smile grew rueful and, if I hadn't been deep in the torture of my own awkwardness, that expression would have dug right under my skin. 'You,' he answered immediately, a catch in his voice. 'Just you, Leesa Kubicka.'

Those were some of the only words that were capable of cutting through my haze. 'What?'

'Why do you think I came to watch your last race in September? I've thought about this *a lot*.'

I groped for the headboard and sat down. Colin sat carefully next to me, not close enough to touch, but close enough that I felt… *together*.

'I'm sorry—'

'Don't,' he said, cutting me off before I'd even got the words out. 'Don't be sorry. Kissing you is… like a bucket-list item or something.'

I bit my lip, assailed by warmth at his words, even though my thoughts were still tied in knots at the idea that what happened in September hadn't been a prank at all. 'You can tick me off now?'

'No!' He nudged me with his shoulder, the skin-on-skin contact so much *more* than our usual playful touches. 'I just meant I won't regret anything. No matter what happens, I'd rather have touched you than not.'

'No matter what happens,' I repeated, my voice weak. 'That's where I get stuck.'

'I get it.'

I could almost believe he did get it — get *me*. That was a stupid notion. In which universe did it make sense that Colin Gallagher understood the wild landscape of my brain?

'Does it help to talk about it?'

'No!' I answered immediately, which seemed to amuse him. 'I think, once we get talking… that's it. I can't switch it off any more.'

'Why do you have to switch off? I don't really like the idea of you lying back and thinking of other things.'

'You'd want my head consumed with *you* while we have sex?'

He was smiling again, which boggled my mind. Bracing his elbows on his knees, still almost completely naked, his posture was so easy, as though all we were doing was watching a movie together.

'I wouldn't want you thinking about anyone else,' he said.

'So cocky,' I scoffed, which only made him smile wider. 'I know it's my problem, but I've always needed to sink into some kind of fantasy to…'

'To get off?' He peered at me, his gaze full of curiosity and blessedly free of judgement.

'It's weird, and I always hate the first time and so I've never bothered with one-time partners.'

He didn't say anything for a long time, but I couldn't look at him. When he finally spoke, the roughness in his voice surprised me. 'That's actually kind of hot, Kubicka. Fuck, I would love to know what fantasies run through your brain.'

My hair stood on end, unable to shy away from his honesty. My mouth was dry and I was dismayed to feel the flare of desire over my skin once more. That was not supposed to happen.

'I bet you don't tell anyone though, right?'

'Right,' I rushed to agree before he got any ideas.

'It's not weird,' he said gently. 'Or if it is, it doesn't matter. I like it. It's you.'

*I like you. I want you. I would love to know what fantasies run through your brain.*

I chewed on a nail, trying to stop those words wrapping around me and changing me. Maybe it was the fact that we weren't discussing a committed relationship that made this conversation bearable. There was no pressure to interrogate our feelings, align our goals, make spurious promises.

After the Tour, Colin would continue his gruelling training and racing schedule and I would pursue my lacklustre career. There was no right or wrong in this moment, no life-changing decisions.

It was just Colin, who could sit comfortably next to me with his dick out without a worry, who was apparently so keen on my body that he didn't mind the complex puzzle of my brain. *I want you.*

'You really didn't mean it when you told your dad you prefer big boobs?'

He grinned at me. 'I said it because the opposite is true.'

'You like small ones?'

'I like *yours*. That lace thing you're wearing, I want to *rip* it.'

The way those words flared through me. I wasn't sure if he was doing it on purpose, painting a picture for me, but it stoked that fantasy cortex of my brain as I imagined him doing it, the backs of his fingers on my skin.

'In real life, I'd probably need scissors,' he commented with a dry smile.

I gave him a light shove on the arm. 'That is not hot.'

'Burst the fantasy, did I?'

I made the mistake of meeting his bright gaze.

'You can imagine it though, right?' He dropped his voice and I suspected he was doing it on purpose now. 'I'd rip it right down the middle. Then I'd tell you to straddle me and put those sweet tits in my face.'

I knew he heard my sharp intake of breath.

'You know what, Kubicka? I think I can keep your mind busy while I fuck you.'

Or he could just fry my brain with his dirty mouth.

'Can I try?'

I didn't need to think about the answer. 'Yes.'

# Chapter 19

**Leesa**

'Why is this thing so hard to get off?'

He'd managed to get my bralette over one shoulder, but I was stuck with my arms above my head while he tried to dislodge it on the other side.

I couldn't remember the last time I'd giggled during foreplay. If I hadn't discovered that Colin had apparently lusted after me for a while, if we hadn't had two weeks of banter and innuendo behind us, I might have drowned in discomfort, but the combination of deep, drawled dirty talk and candid humour had so far kept me calm.

'Although,' he said and leaned back to skim his gaze down my body, 'this has possibilities.' He stared at my boobs – my 'sweet tits' as I might have to call them from now on – biting his lip.

'I'm going to get a cramp.'

'I'd better get you free then.' Sliding his hand up my side, he managed to shift the material over my other shoulder and off. 'You need to get comfortable.'

Comfortable wasn't exactly what I felt with his hands casually grasping my ribcage. Worked up, out of my mind, burning hot would be better ways to describe the state of me. When he dropped to his knees in front of me, my lungs were suddenly inadequate. My heaving breath angled my aching breasts up.

'That's it,' he praised with a rumbling groan. 'Give me those cute little nipples. These are the prettiest tits I've ever seen. Gonna suck on them like a fucking lollipop.'

I started to ask myself why I should find his muttered profanities so hot, but he scraped his tongue, hard, over my left nipple and delight showered over me. My eyelids drooped and my head fell back as I clutched at his head, his wavy hair soft under my fingers.

His breath was scalding on my skin, his lips and tongue slow and deliberate. When he closed his mouth tightly around the nipple, my eyes flew open again on a gasp. I needed to see him doing what he'd threatened. Muffled moans told me how much he was enjoying this and he curled his tongue around the nipple and sucked, triggering shot after shot of endorphins, my nerve endings overwhelmed in the best possible way.

As he moved to the other side, his hand stroked along my inner thigh. I had a flash of memory from before, the hot skin of his cock in my hand, between my legs. I was almost afraid of how good it had felt.

'Open up for me, sweetheart. I want to feel how hot you are for me.'

His cocky tone made me want to roll my eyes, but he wasn't wrong. 'A natural physical response to an attractive person,' I said, aiming for a superior tone, but failing spectacularly, my heaving chest giving me away completely.

He just shot me a grin from under his lashes. 'I knew you found me attractive. You can say what you want, but this' – his thumb stroked over my underwear – 'is all for me. Because I'm gonna fuck you like in your favourite fantasies.'

'You've got to stop saying that,' I complained.

'You like it too much?'

'Yes,' I admitted on a groan.

'You'll like it even more when it's my cock right here.'

I hadn't even noticed him moving my knickers to the side and his thumb pushed up through the soft folds and then he worked it partway in, making me gasp.

'Please.'

'I love it when you beg.' He urged me up to slide my underwear down and I didn't care any more that I was completely naked and he still had his socks on. All I cared about was his thick, hard cock, standing at full attention again. 'Up on the bed, babe,' he said, tapping my thigh, and I hopped back without question.

I couldn't take my eyes off his erection as he crawled up over me. I didn't have a large sample to judge, but his seemed rather pretty as well, uncircumcised, straight and pale and I kept thinking about licking it, wondering how it would taste, what his skin would feel like on my tongue.

His voice interrupted my thoughts, his tone amused. 'Go on, Leesa.'

'Hmm?'

'Not too much, because I'm getting ready to blow, but go for it.' He gripped the base and gave it a little pressure, which he seemed to enjoy.

I blushed furiously, wondering how I could have been so transparent.

'Or you can just keep imagining it,' he said with a crooked smile. 'I know I will.'

His baiting worked. I scooted down the bed between his legs, propped myself up and took the swollen head straight into my mouth.

Salty. Smooth. Hot. Mmm.

He jerked in my mouth. 'Jesus Christ!'

I swirled my tongue, flicking it and then taking him further in. His hands fell to the headboard and I tumbled onto my elbows as he went deeper with a choked grunt. But he pulled out again with a gasp.

'How was that?' he asked through panting breaths as I shuffled back up to the pillows, his fingers drifting to my knee and urging my leg up. 'I knew you weren't a nice girl.'

'I *am* a nice girl,' I insisted with a smile, even as he pressed his weight over me, his cock brushing my thigh. Holding him in the cradle of my legs was its own thrill, my impressions of him from the past two weeks swimming in my memory: sweat dripping off his body; drops of blood; the darkness that crept into his eyes; the sad dragon.

'Maybe you are a nice girl,' he allowed. 'You sucked my dick like a fucking angel and I'm going to see that in my dreams when I'm an old man waiting to die.'

The vivid images he drew with his words took me aback. Imagining him thinking of me while he was dying made my thoughts and feelings swirl together in a mess.

'Still with me, Lees?' he asked, his voice rasping as he smoothed his thumb between my legs, along the slippery furrow, stirring me up, making my blood pound, my thoughts consumed by what I wanted him to do to me. The tip of his thumb nudged gently – far too gently – at my clit and I could barely breathe. 'Doing okay?' This time I caught the amusement in his tone.

'Yep,' I managed to reply, grabbing a handful of his hair. 'Just preparing my Henry Cavill fantasy.' I had no such thing. The way I had to separate my thoughts and feelings during sex was more abstract than that. But the stupid comment had the desired effect.

'You're going to have Colin Gallagher fantasies from today,' he promised roughly.

I just raised a brow and he growled at me, his mouth slamming down onto mine, his tongue hungry and insistent.

I was much less self-conscious when he propped one elbow by my head and reached down with his other hand to guide his cock to where I wanted it. There was a moment of sharp pressure, the most compelling friction, and I couldn't contain a gasp.

Then he was there, in my body, lodged deep and tight, his face buried in my neck.

I wrapped my arms around him, the fingers of one hand tangled in his hair. My stomach dipped, questions flooding my mind as I wondered how I had allowed him this close.

But his lips closed around my ear and then he murmured, 'You're gonna ruin me. Fucking perfect around my cock.'

### Colin

My brain had never had to work so hard in bed, but I was having fun. She got a sort of shadow in her eyes when she was going off course. I was getting the hang of bringing her back, though.

She felt so good: the way she softened to take me; how she bowed her body, giving me the perfect angle; the noises she made, as though my dick were the exact thing she'd been missing. It was getting difficult to stay focused on her pleasure when mine was skyrocketing.

I wasn't going to last as long as I would have liked, not when it was this good, when it was *her*. She'd better let me have another go, or I'd be more of a mess than before we tried this.

I was in trouble when she lifted her knee higher and I sank so deep my vision blurred. She hooked her leg around me, as though she needed me closer, didn't want to let go, and I gave her what she wanted – I'd give her anything she wanted. Grinding up into her, I hit an angle that turned her into a panting mess.

'Ungh, ahhh, yes!'

I couldn't articulate anything except a grunt, sharp intense pleasure rolling down my spine at the friction, as though we were made for this – for each other. The pressure only built as I drew out and sank back in, filling her slowly. The urge to let loose and fuck rose powerfully in me – to let out the build-up of steam. But she had to stay with me. I needed her here, melting, drowning, coming apart on the molecular level, the way I was.

Her hands skimmed down my back to my arse, gripping and pulling me, notching me tight against her and I was climbing out of my skin, brain and body floating on separate planes as I struggled to process the reality of this gorgeous woman demanding I fuck her.

'Good,' she whispered on a panting breath. 'Mmmngh, *Colin*!'

I pushed it again, the sound of my name on her lips tipping me over into the animal part of my nervous system. We found a rhythm – jerky and slow, each thrust tearing apart my seams.

'Please tell me you're close,' I whispered in her ear as the sparks gathered at the base of my spine.

'Mmhmm,' she replied, her eyes closed.

'I'm going to get you there, baby,' I blurted out. 'You're so fucking beautiful right now.' Her only answer was a whimper, but the way she moved under me, I was getting her back. 'I'm nowhere near finished with the things I want to do to you – the ways I want to fuck you, sweetheart.'

'Yes.'

The way satisfaction swelled in my chest was almost unbearable. My gorgeous, clever woman. Her busy mind was just as sexy as her body and if she wanted fantasies, I'd give her fantasies.

'I want you to sit on my cock and get yourself off while I play with your tits – in front of a mirror.'

A gratifying gasp.

I lowered my voice to a growl. 'I want to fuck you into the mattress – over the edge of the bed. On a picnic blanket with the mountains all around and you on your hands and knees, a pretty dress up around your waist.'

'*Yes.* Harder.'

*Ohhh, shit.* Two words from her and I was done for. Lightning zipped up my spine. Fumbling for her knee, I pushed her leg down so I could pump harder, deeper – wilder. The slap of her body against mine was necessary for my existence. Her increasingly hoarse cries were food and water.

She was nearly there, but I wasn't gonna— *Oh, fuck.*

Just as my panic rose along with the looming orgasm, she threw her head back and seized around me, thrashing and gasping and breaking in the most spectacular climax I could have imagined and I only wished I could have enjoyed it for more than the second I had before I shattered too, jerking wildly as I went off inside her, on and on, until I was utterly drained and actually a little embarrassed by how hard I'd come.

I had expected sex with Leesa Kubicka to be the best of my life but, God, I was broken – done for. And I had no idea what to do about it.

# Chapter 20

## Leesa

I was pleasantly groggy for a moment or two, but my stupid brain snapped quickly back into action, preparing for the next awkward moment in this theatre piece. He was heavy, still wedged inside me, which was becoming uncomfortable in the oversensitive aftermath of my orgasm.

Had we even finished the interview? I imagined getting dressed again – trying not to look at his cock – and heading back to the meeting room, settling in our chairs and continuing to ask and answer questions as though he hadn't just had me raw and naked underneath him while he fucked like a wild thing.

Perhaps I had had a little more involvement than that sounded, but the image of him completely overcome above me would show up behind my eyelids for a long time to come.

'You okay?'

I realised I had my eyes squeezed shut and forced them open, wary of what I'd find. He was peering at me with his head inclined, a faint smile on his lips and the most earnest expression I'd ever seen on his face. He looked several years younger all of a sudden, reminding me he was just 25 now and he'd been only 19 the first time we'd met.

I couldn't decide if that was strange. I wasn't sure we should have done this. I realised this moment had been brewing since September, when he'd clumsily broached the subject, but we'd crossed the line now. I'd had sex with Colin Gallagher, tangled up with enough feelings to give me a hernia. I couldn't go back and change it.

He shifted, finally slipping out. I must have winced, because he whispered an apology and feathered a kiss over my cheek, smoothing my hair back from my face.

His smile faded. 'You're not okay? It's all right, Lees. Just talk to me.'

Heat rose to my cheeks. I wasn't sure I *could* talk about what had just happened – not coherently anyway.

I lifted a hand to my forehead, as though testing for a fever. 'I don't know if that was a good idea. You could get into trouble.'

'What Dad doesn't know won't hurt him.' He flopped onto the bed beside me, peering at me from under his lashes and shooting me a signature light smile.

Of course we would have to keep this a secret, but wasn't that proof that sleeping together would cause more complications?

'Don't beat yourself up,' he said gently, his fingers moving in my hair. The touch was dangerously soothing. 'It was kind of inevitable, given how long I've been admiring you.'

Wow, I'd forgotten that bizarre part of the bizarre past half-hour. I rolled onto my side to stare at him. 'You're not serious.'

'I'm not lying,' he insisted.

'But——' It didn't make any sense. 'Why did you keep putting fake insects under my door?'

He shrugged. 'Little boys and their crushes. It was better than you not looking at me at all. Hell, I tried something that wasn't a prank to get your attention that last race and you didn't even see me.'

I sat up, staring down at him, sprawled naked on my bed, the compass tattooed on his side pointing at his heart. 'The sign really wasn't a prank. There was nothing on the other side?' I wasn't sure if I was touched or disturbed that he'd tried to earnestly say goodbye to me and it had backfired so spectacularly.

He hesitated before answering my question and I didn't know what to think any more. 'It did have something on the other side,' he admitted.

I gave him a shove. 'That is possibly the most juvenile thing you've ever done, making a distraction out of yourself.'

'More juvenile than when I told you before the Tour Down Under that Australians expect to be greeted with "g'day, mate" and you went around saying it to everyone?'

'That was embarrassing.'

'It was gold. But you can't tell me my pranks didn't work, when I'm lying here staring at your tits, fuck-drunk and mind-blown.'

He knew staying stuff like that got a rise out of me, but despite the renewed prickle over my skin, his words also made me question the wisdom of our actions afresh.

'Colin, if you struggle at the Tour because of me...' I remembered well last year, Lori's chaotic season as she and Seb danced around each other. Not that this was headed in the same direction, but that made it worse.

Colin had a gruelling few weeks ahead of him. When I glanced at him, his expression was unexpectedly sober, which was something of a relief. The volatility in him worried me.

'It was sex, Lees. Great sex, but I'm not going to lose my form because we screwed. You really are hung up about this.'

I suddenly felt cold — and naked. Of course I was hung up about this. He'd told me my overthinking didn't bother him, although perhaps I shouldn't have believed anything he said when we were nearly naked and groping each other. I'd even let his confession about having a crush on me mean something, when it obviously didn't to him. I wasn't the only person he'd been attracted to over the past six years and I certainly wouldn't be the only one in future.

But some part of me was sad and hurt and small, a crash to earth after I'd surprised myself by soaring with him this afternoon.

I slipped my feet over the side of the bed and looked around for my underwear. 'Okay, but from now on, you have to focus. The whole team is relying on you and my client is too. The content is great, but results speak louder than all of that.'

Glancing at him as I tugged my bralette over my head and tried to forget everything he'd done to me that afternoon, I found him staring grimly at the wooden ceiling.

'All right, coach,' he muttered.

'Maybe now we've…'

'Fucked,' he supplied for me with a dry look.

'Yeah, maybe now things will be easier. We've blown off the tension.'

'We've blown something all right,' he drawled, but he wasn't smiling. 'It's going to take a bit more to get you out of my system, Kubicka,' he continued with a deep sigh. 'But don't worry. I know what's important and I won't screw it up.'

## Colin

She was in my head – my bloodstream. I'd thought it had been bad before, but after seeing her naked, feeling her *everywhere*, I could no longer see anything else when she was in the room.

Breakfast the day after was tough. I kept imagining Dad was watching me, that he could tell I'd slept with her, since my heart seemed to beat differently this morning. I avoided him by sitting with Nellie and Amir, but that meant pretending to be interested in the latest photos of Nellie's son. He'd already inflicted them on me, but Amir loved babies and wanted the full commentary.

I didn't understand why Nellie's wife kept sending him so many photos when we were going home soon and he'd see them in the flesh but, apparently, he didn't want to miss any of the little milestones and he found it difficult to be away.

I was trying to think of something to say about the video of his wife playing with the baby's toes, when the door opened and there she was and my vocabulary shrank to something similar to Rupert's.

She wasn't wearing one of her dresses, thank fuck, but she looked bad enough – good enough – in denim shorts and a fitted T-shirt with a sports brand across the chest. My brain filled in what was underneath and I could almost feel her skin under my hands.

'… even Colin said he's getting cuter.'

It took me far too long to realise they were waiting for a response from me. I tore my gaze from her to stare, unseeing, at Nellie's phone. I had to blink for several moments before the picture came into focus: a goofy baby grin that looked like he'd just farted.

Amir shared a look with Nellie.

'I don't know what's wrong with Colin,' Amir said thoughtfully, as though I weren't sitting right there with them.

My ears were so hot they were probably steaming more than my oatmeal. I kept my eyes off her, but I could *feel* her to the side at the breakfast buffet and the way my teammates were looking at me, they knew what was going through my head.

I held my breath, waiting for them to say something, to tell me off for sleeping with the woman from marketing – what a stereotypical thing for Colin Gallagher to do.

But Amir simply said, 'I can't believe he doesn't like babies.'

Nelson grinned at me, his eyes bright. 'Maybe he will when he grows up.'

Scowling at him, I struggled to think of a comeback. Nellie was only two years older than me – Lori's age. 'Not all of us age as quickly as you.'

Hiding behind a sip of coffee, I sensed Leesa moving into my peripheral vision and, when my eyes were drawn there, I found her glancing back at me. That was all it took for my lungs to seize up.

But she winced and sent a guilty glance to where Wil was eating with Dad and the logistics manager. I couldn't bring myself to regret what had happened, even if it brought complications for both of us but, for her sake, I could make sure no one found out.

For her sake, I could pretend it had never happened – or at least try. We had two more days of training camp and then her work with me wouldn't be so… close. Her nightmare job might get a little easier.

As I was heading for my room, Dad stopped me, breaking my reverie, and drew me into the hallway. That was enough for my stomach to sink. It wasn't easy to read his expression – he always had a gruff smile on his face, especially for bad news – but I couldn't think of anything he'd have to say that I wanted to hear.

'I spoke to your mum this morning.'

I might have interpreted that as a good sign but, given how stringently he'd avoided any contact with her recently, this wouldn't be comfortable for anyone. A few years ago, I would have desperately wanted them to work things out but, as I spent more time with Mum alone, I'd started to see the strain she was under trying to reach him and I didn't want that for her any more.

I also realised that Dad had got worse as I'd got better – at cycling. I couldn't deny my success was down to his unrelenting pursuit of improvements, in my body and in my head, but he refused to see the costs and I was too chicken to stand up to him.

'I didn't realise she was already here in Europe,' Dad continued.

'I'm spending the week with her in Treviglio after the camp,' I explained. 'Nonno hasn't been well.'

'Oh, she didn't mention that. I was talking to her about the Tour, since last year was... so awkward.'

The only thing that had been awkward last year was the fact that their relationship was over, but no one was saying it out loud. At least Mum was in touch with reality, if Dad was still ignoring what had happened.

'It's almost impossible to arrange accommodation for her in the team hotel and I thought it would be better...'

'Did you tell Mum she couldn't come to watch the Tour? Dad!'

'She's seen you race so many times.' I thought he was going to say something else, but he stopped. I understood what he meant: I was too old to be upset by this development. If I complained, I'd be the weak little youngster he seemed to think I still was.

'You can give me all the reasons you want, but I know you just don't want her around, now that she's left you. You don't want me listening to her.'

'She doesn't understand your—'

'*You* don't understand everything either, you know!'

Before I could blurt out anything more incriminating – about my state of mind or my encounter with Leesa – I brushed past him in the direction of the staircase, my mood turned sour. As I passed the door to the breakfast room, I almost wasn't surprised when I glanced inside to find Leesa, standing just inside the door, frozen. She probably hadn't wanted to disturb us.

Great. The day just got even more dysfunctional.

# Chapter 21

## Leesa

'I transcribed the interview as well, so you can search for the time stamp on any quote you want to isolate. I've put a few in bold that I thought were particularly good.'

Even presenting online, I felt certain my colleagues could all tell exactly why the time stamps on the interview footage didn't quite make sense. They all knew I'd cut out provocative questions – and answers – and three entire minutes of Colin and me making out while I sat in his lap.

It had taken me too long to realise the phone automatically saved to the cloud and the incriminating footage had sat there overnight, on the work server, before I'd frantically snipped and pressed 'Delete'. Okay, I'd emailed myself a copy before I pressed 'Delete' and watched it back again at least three times on my private phone.

I hadn't expected that of myself. The video should have felt tawdry and mortifying. I had starred in my own soft porn with the lead rider of the cycling team. At one point there was even a flash of my stripey pink knickers as Colin's hand had ventured up my dress.

But I hadn't felt dirty or guilty watching it. I'd been engrossed, fascinated by the stark lines of Colin's face as he'd kissed me desperately. There were fewer glimpses of my face, but what I saw was a looser, freer me and she was damn sexy.

*'Initial feedback from the client has been very positive,'* Morgan said. I was glad of their presence on the call with Bill.

'*It's good work,*' the big boss said gruffly — or maybe he'd just been vaping again. '*I just have one question. The folder marked "Valerio for Magda"? I was looking through your content in preparation for the meeting and I can't imagine why none of those… assets have appeared in your campaign planning.*'

Heat rushed up my chest and I groped for my mouse to open up the folder, panic making the hair on the back of my neck stand on end.

'*Erm, I haven't seen that one,*' Morgan stalled.

I clicked through frantically, telling myself it couldn't be the kissing video, but terrified nonetheless.

'Valerio for… Magda,' I repeated rather stupidly as I searched for the folder on the server. 'Uh, I suspect this is Colin playing a joke, as usual,' I said through gritted teeth.

Double-clicking on the folder, I was confronted with an entire screen of thumbnails, all photos of Colin in front of the bathroom mirror, making various poses. Christ. If Bill hadn't been the one to find these, I might have laughed. As it was, I wanted to throttle him for his long-shot prank that had paid off big time.

'I'm so sorry,' I mumbled. 'He got hold of the tablet, but I'll make sure it doesn't happen again.'

To my shock, Bill laughed, clutching his stomach and then stopping on a cough. '*You didn't direct these?*'

'No, of course not.' I only took footage of him with his hand on my ass, not — I tipped my head to peer at one of the thumbnails more closely — pictures of him balancing a water bottle on his head. Not that anyone would care what he had on his head when he was shirtless, his shorts hanging off his hips.

'*I thought you might have had hidden depths, Leesa,*' Bill replied, as though disappointed I *hadn't* been the one in the bathroom with him. God, I couldn't get this right. '*Maybe you should ask if we can use them.*'

I wasn't sure if it would serve Colin right if we published these photos or whether he'd revel in it and a tiny, embarrassing part of me wished he'd taken them for my eyes only.

'*Leesa* definitely *has hidden depths,*' Morgan commented,

thankfully in a light tone, but I nonetheless got the message. They'd worked out I was a little too close to the talent.

At least the camp was over tomorrow and I had 12 days to recover. I never would have thought a training camp where I wasn't actually training would be so hard on my lungs and my body.

Some unexpected places on my body.

'*Thanks for your time, Bill. We'll keep you apprised of our progress.*'

I wasn't sure if Morgan could read my thoughts or if they were just keen to get off the call. Either way, I ended the meeting a little too enthusiastically and slumped against my desk, my head in my hands.

One more day. And then he'd focus on the Tour and leave me alone. He had to and I would *not* be sad about that. I would not wonder about his relationship with his dad or how his apparent family drama was affecting his psyche. I would not picture him on my bed — not even sleeping peacefully — or in front of me on a bike in the wildly beautiful Dolomites.

I tabbed back to the folder of photos, clicking through them one by one. He still had the little redhead thing above his top lip, looking particularly ridiculous when he pouted for the camera. It felt like such a long time ago. It would be very strange when I didn't see him next week.

Except I would be looking at his face every day as I assembled social-media assets. *Ass*-ets. Damn it, Colin Gallagher had utterly ruined me. But maybe at least partly in a good way.

'Why didn't you bring me here sooner? I've been in Italy for more than two weeks and I haven't eaten a single slice of pizza!'

I had come down to Bressanone with Wil for a 'business lunch' — an excuse to chat away from the chaos of packing up a whole cycling team from an isolated mountain hotel. After more than two weeks at altitude, I was disoriented to see so many people, so many bricks and flagstones. It was a crash landing in the real world.

Wil smiled over her artichoke pizza. 'We're not exactly in Naples. Pizza isn't a local specialty. When we first started coming here five years ago, this was the only place that served pizza, but now every hotel does. Brixen is turning Italian,' she said, using the German name for the town.

I'd spent a few hours in Bressanone before, but I'd forgotten how pretty it was, the bright rendered buildings in yellow and ochre, the narrow cobbled streets, the endless church spires, all framed by a mountain panorama.

'I don't remember this restaurant from the time I was here on training camp,' I commented, biting into my own slice of mushroom pizza. It had a thick fluffy base, drizzled with olive oil.

'We don't bring the riders, Leesa,' Wil said with a grin, gesturing with her pizza for emphasis. 'So, tell me how it's all going.'

I chewed while I considered my answer. 'My boss is happy with my work — and so is the client. That's the most important thing really, for my hopes of getting a permanent job. Now I just need Colin to win a stage or two and it'll be a dream project.'

'Yes, well,' Wil said with a wince, 'we all hope he can pull it out of the hat when the Tour starts. But I meant for you. Have you enjoyed being back with the team?'

I hesitated for a moment too long and Wil gave my hand a quick squeeze.

'I know it can't have been easy to come back.'

I sighed. 'You're right. I wanted to move on.' The final two words echoed in my mind along with flashes of memory of the time I'd spent with Colin over the past two weeks.

Wil put down her pizza and wiped her fingers slowly on a napkin. 'I ask you because I have a lot of connections in various teams. If it doesn't work out with Redwin — or if you have a change of heart about working for them — I'm sure I'd be able to get you placed somewhere.'

The ripple of possibilities was pleasant, especially after the angst of the past six months, wondering if Redwin would employ me, if I was good enough.

'You probably want to stay in the States to be near your family, but I wanted to have it said, so there it is.'

Sure, my parents wanted me closer to home, but they'd prefer I took whatever job would lead to success the fastest – and they probably wouldn't count working for a cycling team as a great success, when Redwin had worked with sponsors for the Superbowl and the NHL. If I *had* to do something frivolous like sports marketing, at least let it be for a team with a lot of money behind it.

'Whatever you do,' Wil continued, leaning closer, 'don't sell yourself short. You might not have all that much experience, but the right employer will appreciate your potential – and so should you.'

I gave her a weak smile. 'Thanks, Wil. But first, I'm actually looking forward to the Tour, which I didn't expect. I wish I could stay and watch the women afterwards.' Maybe if I ended up unemployed, I could, I thought bleakly.

'You're young,' Wil said with a chuckle. 'You still enjoy the madness. I have to deal with Tony and his anxiety. I think it would have made his life a lot easier if he hadn't been so successful at bringing his children into the sport. You'll see Lori at the start.'

Two weeks ago, I would have been dreading seeing her, jealous that she was still racing – actually winning – while I was trying to claw my way out of the sport. But now that I'd let myself remember life with the team, sharing the anxiety and the boredom, the grumbles and the high points with the others, I wouldn't mind so much seeing her.

Except that I suspected Lori would now remind me of her brother.

When we finished eating, we made our way back in the direction of the blue-and-yellow fairytale cathedral, all intricate details and baroque swirls, but a familiar figure down a back street caught my eye just before we crossed the square – a figure I'd been staring at for two-and-a-half weeks straight.

'Just a second, Wil,' I said, stopping her with a hand on her arm, then I dashed off before I lost sight of him. Whatever he was doing in Brixen alone, I suspected it would be trouble.

Following him down a narrow street behind the cathedral, past the gate of the church cloister and terraced buildings in pale blue and pink and yellow, I caught up with him by a low wooden door, his hand reaching for the handle.

'Colin!'

He snatched his hand back, confirming my suspicions that he was up to no good.

'What are you——?' My gaze snagged on the subtle plaque by the door: Norbert Gasser, Tattoo Studio. 'You can't get a tattoo two weeks before the Tour de France!' I hissed.

He shrugged. 'Just a little one. It's fine. It'll heal over by then.'

'If it doesn't get infected and kill you!'

'Take it easy, Kubicka,' he crooned, a hand slipping around my waist – a natural touch that spoke to something deep inside me. 'I have to do this. I'll take good care of the wound. It'll be just like racing with road rash and we've all done that.'

'Not on purpose!' I wanted to shove him away, but I didn't quite manage it, my hand gripping his T-shirt instead. 'You don't *have to* do anything. You could just plan some artwork for later. Your Dad will kill you.' *My* parents certainly would.

Of course he ignored me. 'You should come in with me. I might need a hand to hold. You can make sure Norbert sticks to the hygiene rules.'

'Norbert Gasser? Is that really his name?'

'He's a great guy – a real artist.'

'You've been here before?'

He nodded.

'For all of them?'

'Just one.'

I couldn't help but ask. 'The dragon?'

He shook his head. 'The compass.'

That was all he had to say for me to remember him sprawled on my bed, his hair mussed.

'Leesa? Are you coming back with me?'

I turned to find Wil approaching hesitantly. My face was hot, wondering how much she'd seen.

'I've just convinced Leesa to get the tattoo she's been planning for years.'

I froze, ready to sock Colin in the guts, although preferably without witnesses. He nudged me in the back, an unsubtle plea to go along with him.

'I'll bring her back. She doesn't want anything big, so we won't be long.'

'Uh, okay then,' Wil said, her expression doubtful. I pasted on a smile, which seemed to be enough for her. 'See you later.'

Remaining frozen until Wil disappeared around the corner, I whirled on Colin. 'What did you say that for?'

'It's a great cover story. You got the tattoo, not me.'

'Except that I won't have an actual tattoo!'

He shrugged, trying not to smile. 'You just say it's somewhere under your clothes that no one can see. Easy.' He seemed to like the idea of that. 'Or you could really get a tattoo.'

He wasn't serious, but my skin prickled at my hairline as I remembered all the girls in the team getting matching tattoos and me, watching, unable to take the plunge without at least a month of thinking time – then spending two years regretting my decision.

'You know you want one. You could take the appointment.'

'You are a menace,' I grated out.

'But I'm good, right? Are you going to save me?'

The way his words so often wedged deep, I was in a lot of trouble. 'Let's just go inside.'

# 15 June, three years ago

## Leesa

I showed up to the press conference before the women's Tour de Suisse with eyes like sandpaper and a body that believed it was one in the morning – local time in Denver, where I'd just flown in from. No one would have any questions for me anyway. They only wanted to talk to Lori.

I only hoped I stayed mostly out of the shot. I'd swiped on some eye make-up but, given my barely five hours of uncomfortable sleep last night, I couldn't say whether I'd achieved Taylor Swift or Amy Winehouse. My hair was an oily mess, but I couldn't wash it because I hadn't had time for it to dry. A blow-dryer always resulted in spongy frizz instead of the complex curls I had to work hard to maintain.

As I hoped, the questions passed me by and my job was simply to make sure Lori didn't look as though she had no friends – not that we were friends exactly. It was more begrudging respect between us, which I'd learned not to analyse.

I would never understand these Gallaghers.

Speaking of Gallaghers, I thought for a moment it was just my scratchy eyes, but a blink and a rub proved I wasn't imagining it: there was Colin, lounging against the back wall with his usual laid-back stoop. The men's race was ongoing and he really should have been resting before today's stage. His gaze flickered over me and away again quickly, making me worried I had something on my face.

'A question for Leesa Kubicka!'

*Huh?* I blinked wildly to try to switch my brain on as the reporter continued speaking.

'I understand you competed in the Unbound gravel race in the United States last week and were awarded the "mud prize". Can you tell us about that?'

'I'm sorry, what?' My brain was racing ahead of my sluggish body. 'I mean, I was at Unbound, yes.' The scrappy fight of gravel racing had always brought me alive. 'But I'm not sure what prize you're talking about.'

'Oh.' The reporter glanced down at her phone. 'It just says here: "Leesa crossed the line with her face and body totally caked in mud, earning the coveted 'mud prize'."'

'Where is that?' My media training – from the team and also from the marketing degree I was slowly completing – deserted me.

'It's on your Wikipedia page,' the reporter admitted sheepishly.

'Oh, I—' Another *huh?* was all my brain could manage at first. Then, in my peripheral vision, I noticed Colin shifting against the wall and, when I glanced at him, he was looking right at me, his tongue tucked into his cheek as he visibly swallowed a laugh.

I should have known. He wouldn't have been here without someone to humiliate and, as usual, it was me. I'd been proud of finishing that notoriously tough race, but he'd made it all about the mud, the childish idiot.

'I think someone thought it would be funny to update my Wikipedia page with something that doesn't exist,' I managed to reply, sparing Colin only a brief, sharp glance.

The reporter gave an awkward laugh. 'Sounds like you had a big fan watching your race.'

A fan? *Yeah, right.*

# Chapter 22

### Leesa

The tattoo studio didn't have the grim torture-chamber aesthetic I'd expected. The walls were white with a bold black pattern of interlocking swirls. I glimpsed a rounded retro desk and a curving floor lamp.

The artist himself appeared as soon as we walked through the door. A big guy, he had a full beard – bushier than anything Colin was capable of growing – a neck full of tattoos and several solid silver rings on his fingers. The thick nose ring was little more than an aside to the rest of his appearance.

'Colin,' he said gruffly, a smile somewhere under the beard.

Colin was folded into an enormous, muscly hug, the clap to his back more effective than chiropractic adjustment, while I watched on in dismay, reassuring myself that it wasn't my turn next to find myself under those hands.

I was wrong.

The man turned to me. I truly hoped I'd correctly interpreted his expression as a smile, because his eyes were a little wild as he pressed me in a hug. 'Velcome. You must be a friend of Colin.'

'This is Leesa. She might take my appointment, if she can get up the courage.'

Shooting Colin an *'I'm going to kill you!'* look that I hoped contained the threat to end our friendship, I ignored his quelling hand gesture that only wound me up more.

'Vould you like to come through?' Norbert asked. He rolled

up his sleeves as though he were about to beat someone up – or perform surgery. Tingles shot to my hairline.

Colin turned to me and lifted his eyebrows. The question was clear: '*You or me?*'

'You know I can't— Without thinking about this—'

Norbert laughed heartily. 'A first-timer? Let's see what she's made of.'

A petite older woman with a tousled bob poked her head into the studio from an adjoining room. 'Ciao, Colin!'

He greeted her with a kiss on the cheek that reminded me of how much of his life he must have spent in Europe. She was introduced as Olga and I was distracted, admiring the elegant barbed wire on her upper arm as she greeted me, until she asked, 'Are you Colin's girlfriend?'

I straightened. 'No.'

Olga pouted. 'Aw, I'd hoped you might be here for matching tattoos. Little hearts.' She patted Colin's cheek, which had turned ruddy Irish, like his father's.

'Your first crush, Bua?' Norbert asked with a grin.

I opened my mouth to remind them that I was standing *right here*, but a photo on the wall snagged my attention. It was a black-and-white shot of a woman, naked as far as I could tell, and turned away from the camera, the sensitive parts hidden in shadow. The light accented the folds and curves at her waist. One of her hands – nails manicured into short points – was tucked under her arm and a few strands of hair fell down her back.

Inked onto her side in colour – the only colour in the photo – was a pair of flared wildflowers, their stalks bowed, with round, textured leaves emerging from a cover of snow at her waist. The image was striking, all the more so because it was on her body – it was part of her body.

Feeling pressure on my shoulder, I was almost surprised to find Colin still in the room, his arm now draped casually over me.

Norbert approached as well, gesturing to the photo. 'This is my friend Silvia, with the Alpenglöckchen, spring flowers in the mountains where she walks.'

Something in his tone made me wonder if Silvia was a little more than a friend.

'Would you like to see more flower designs?'

Instead of flowers, my mind produced the image of Colin's bare chest, the dark, delicate ink of the compass pointing northeast towards Europe – or his heart.

I couldn't keep the words in. 'I know what I want.'

The arm over my shoulders tightened. 'Leesa…'

'*You* brought me here,' I pointed out, shrugging off his arm. 'What did you think would happen?'

'I didn't think I'd fall the rest of the way in love with you.'

I had to force a choppy breath into my lungs. Drawled in his usual cheeky tone, I knew better than to take his words seriously, but they still seized my heart and squeezed. There was no happy ending here, but this moment belonged to whatever it was that drew us together.

'It doesn't hurt too much,' he reassured me.

'I'm not worried. I was a cyclist, remember?'

'I won't forget. What are you going to get?'

I followed Norbert's beckoning to a curtained-off reclining chair with gleaming equipment set neatly in drawers and on racks.

'I'm not telling,' I answered Colin over my shoulder, enjoying his hitched groan of disappointment.

'At least tell me where.'

'Nope!'

The curtain swished closed behind me and I took a deep breath. It felt good accepting that maybe I didn't have to be a nice girl all the time. I couldn't know – or rationalise – everything. I was prepared to get this wrong and screw the consequences – today, at least.

'What's your favourite number?' Colin called from the other side of the curtain, making me wonder at the change of topic.

'Nine,' I answered without needing to think about it, while Norbert took up a sketch pad and an enormous folder of designs.

'Really? It's one of my recent favourites too,' Colin replied.

'Is it because I came ninth in last year's Tour that you like that number so much?'

I'd forgotten he came ninth last year. I'd spent most of the men's Tour on training camp, trying to stop Lori moping about her troubles with her boyfriend.

'No. It's been my favourite number since school,' I replied. 'It's the base-minus-one in our number system and can be used to solve all sorts of math problems. When you add all the digits of any multiple of nine, you get another multiple of—'

'You lost me, but it's fuckin' sexy when you talk about multiples,' Colin drawled. I suspected he was trying to distract me from any lingering nerves, but I was quite bright with anticipation, despite the wicked-looking stainless-steel implements spread around the room.

'What's your favourite number then? Sixty-nine?' I teased, wondering when he was going to tell me what this was about.

'That's my second favourite.'

Wow, if he could bottle and sell that voice, he'd have a record-breaking following on OnlyFans, if he ever wanted to stop racing. 'What's your favourite, then?'

He didn't hesitate. 'Number one, of course.'

## Colin

Fuck, it hurt.

I deserved the pain today, tricking Leesa into getting a tattoo, letting her think she'd saved me from the same fate, even though I'd had no intention of leaving here without new ink.

But, truthfully, I was a wimp with tattoos. The road could rip my skin open, I could push my muscles until I had bushfires raging in my legs, even my broken collarbone hadn't reduced me to tears, but the needle spiking my skin over and over again turned me into a whining, bleating weakling and it was a good thing she was behind a curtain and couldn't see me right now. Norbert had turned on some heavy rock music and she couldn't hear me either – thankfully.

'Zitto, ragazzo. Tutto va bene,' Olga crooned, one of her hands gentle on my back as the other held the gun steady.

For the fiftieth time, I glanced at the curtain, wishing I knew what was going on in there. It was her first tattoo and I'd got her there, even though it had taken some well-meaning subterfuge.

'Ungh,' I grunted as Olga started up again after a brief pause.

'The boy is growing up?' she asked with a smile in her voice. I had no idea what language Olga spoke natively, but she'd switched back to Italian once Leesa was out of the room.

'Apparently not,' I said, my voice high as I struggled to lie still. 'That needle still freaks me out,' I added in English.

She chuckled and I hoped her hand was steady. 'I meant you found a girl.'

That assumption tightened up everything that wasn't already tense inside me. 'I found her, but that doesn't mean I can keep her. She's just here for her job.'

'She's not *here* for her job, is she?'

A twinge of something powerful in my chest. 'No, but she's not here for me. It's fair enough.' But I wanted to be here for her.

The sound of voices carried through the curtain, but my thoughts were dim and I couldn't work out what they were saying. A moment later, the curtain drew aside and there she stood, a bright smile on her face that punched the air out of my lungs – a smile that quickly faded when she saw me.

'Colin!' I felt like the luckiest man in the world when she said my name, even in that disbelieving tone. 'You told me if I got a tattoo, I'd stop *you* from getting one!'

'Yeah, well,' I managed through a grimace, 'I lied.'

'It's small,' Olga assured her, looking up from her work. 'It will heal quickly.'

'What is——?' The way she cut off her sentence with a strangled sound suggested she'd seen it. She didn't have to be quite so horrified.

'Relax, Kubicka,' I grumbled. 'It's my number for the Tour this year. Nine for the team and one for my rider number.' At least it was a convenient coincidence. 'Did you think I'd tattooed your favourite number on my arse?'

Her spluttered response would have been more satisfying if I'd been telling the whole truth.

'I can't believe you got a number tattooed on your ass two weeks before the Tour de France,' she said, her voice high.

'It'll make me faster. I promise.' I shot her a smile. 'And it's not quite my arse, as you can see.' It was right at the top of the slope of my butt. All Olga had had to do was pull my shorts down a bit.

'I am taking no responsibility for this,' Leesa said, scrunching her hair at her temples as though she were about to pull out a handful – because of me.

'Of course it's nothing to do with you,' I lied as smoothly as I could.

As Olga finished up her work, the next few weeks yawned before me and I struggled to stay still. I'd made the tattoo appointment in a moment of restlessness, the team, my dad, my fixation on Leesa Kubicka all too much.

It didn't take a genius – like her – to work out that she wouldn't be happy to know she was affecting my head, but I didn't know what to do about it. I couldn't seem to stay away from her – I didn't *want* to. After the Tour, she'd be gone from my life – maybe this time for good.

I'd already said goodbye to her once and it had been so awful I hadn't known what to say.

She was quiet, her arms crossed, as I drove the team car back to the hotel in the golden light of the early evening. I had to confess – only to myself – that my fresh tattoo was uncomfortable when I sat in the driver's seat. I had a feeling I'd regret this one one day.

'Are you going to tell me what tattoo you got? Or did you chicken?'

'I did not chicken,' she answered with her chin in the air.

'Of course you didn't.' It was a miracle I could say anything, my lungs were so tight. 'Can I see it?'

'It's covered under a dressing.'

I was dying to know.

'What time are you going tomorrow morning?' I forced myself to ask.

'First thing. I have an early train.'

*Can I sleep in your bed tonight?*

'Where are you staying until the Tour?' *Want to come and stay with my mum and grandfather?*

'I'm spending a week in Poland and then arriving in Strasbourg a few days before the team presentation.'

'Your family in Poland?'

'Babcia – my grandmother. She won't understand that I have to work, but I couldn't come back to Europe and not visit.'

'I'm visiting my nonno,' I told her with a quick grin that she warily returned. 'He doesn't live too far from here. Do you speak Polish with your family?'

She nodded. Of course, Leesa would be effortlessly bilingual. 'But it's funny: in Poland, I'm an American and in the States I'm Polish.'

'Tell me something in Polish?'

She eyed me. 'What should I say? Hello? Sorry? Thank you? You could just download a language app.'

'If I ever meet your grandmother, I will.'

She stilled, her brow dipping, and I berated myself for the stupid things I blurted out when she was next to me. But then she spoke: 'Co ma piernik do wiatraka.' Her tone was even, the consonants precise and delicate.

'Let me guess, you're calling me an idiot?'

That earned me a reluctant chuckle. 'No. "What does gingerbread have to do with a windmill?"'

'Is that a brain teaser? Am I supposed to answer it?'

'It's rhetorical, but you could answer in Italian,' she prompted, shooting me a sidelong glance I wanted to bottle and store for months.

'Hai voluto la bicicletta? E adesso pedala!' I answered, exaggerating the variations in tone and pinching my fingers together in the famous Italian hand gesture.

Finally. A genuine smile. 'I only caught the bicycle part.'

'"You wanted the bicycle, now pedal,"' I translated.

'Sounds like a judgement on my life,' she muttered with a rueful laugh. 'But I like it better than "You made your bed, now lie in it".'

We fell silent. I had a hundred things I could have asked her, but most of them led somewhere we shouldn't go.

The drive was over more quickly than the distance suggested — either that or my thoughts had tied me up in so many knots that I hadn't been paying attention. I pulled up on the gravel outside the hotel and set the park brake, but I didn't move to get out of the car.

Neither did she.

# Chapter 23

## Leesa

This could be the last moment I had alone with him. I couldn't just walk away without saying *something*.

He'd parked the car at the far end of the row of team vehicles, facing towards the meadow. Our backs were to the hotel. The last time we'd been alone like this, we'd ended up on my bed.

'Um,' I began inauspiciously.

He peered at me, the look in his eyes somehow pained. The energy coming off him was compelling — and concerning. I was picturing his sad dragon once more, the dark expressions that crossed his face occasionally — his tightness with his father.

'Is it this stuff with your parents that's bothering you? I'm sorry I overheard.'

He released a long breath and let his head fall back onto the seat. 'We've all got shit with our parents, right?' His gaze snapped back to mine, heavy with something I couldn't interpret. 'But yeah, I suppose. Some of it. I see Nellie all gaga for Ramila and obsessed with the baby and then there's Mum and Dad, 28 years of marriage and they don't even talk — except to argue about me.'

The vulnerability in his voice shocked me, not because it was there — I'd been catching glimpses of it for weeks — but because he'd voiced it, with me.

'It isn't fair the way Tony treats you differently.'

'I don't need you to defend me, Kubicka,' he responded with a chuckle. Apparently today was not the day for him to confront that vulnerability. 'But thank you. It's sweet.'

'I just think maybe you should sort this stuff out before the Tour. Talking about it might be more productive than getting a tattoo.'

He gave an odd huff and stared out of the windscreen for a long moment. 'You my psychologist now?'

No one in my life had ever made me this itchy with frustration. 'You can't go through life as though nothing can touch you. At some point, you have to own up to feeling something and deal with the consequences!'

He still wouldn't look at me, but his jaw was working. 'You don't know what you're talking about.'

That hurt. It probably shouldn't have, but the accusation that I didn't know him well hit me too hard. 'I can see something's bothering you. You can't hide it.'

So suddenly I flinched back in surprise, he turned to face me, propping one arm on the steering wheel. 'Leesa, how's this for what's bothering me? The woman I've had a childish crush on for six years finally had sex with me and it was so good I don't fucking know what to do with myself.'

My brain seized up, goosebumps racing to my hairline. I must admit, gratification was the first emotion that gripped me. A crush. A fling. They weren't big words. He was using me to avoid his real-life struggles – again.

He kept speaking, his chest rising and falling rapidly, as my conviction slowly crumbled. 'I've always been an idiot when it comes to you. I know it means fuck all. I'm not like Nellie. I only ever learned how to race and to train and everything else has been a series of mistakes. Everything I do hurts you, but right now I'm struggling to think about anything else *but* you.'

I could only react on instinct. Fisting a hand in his hair, I hauled him close and kissed him, open-mouthed, zero to everything in a single second. He was with me instantly, no hesitation, his lips dragging against mine, his tongue in my mouth.

It seemed once we'd started kissing, it was difficult to stop. As he pressed closer, bracing himself against my seat so he could kiss me harder, a bolt of memory intruded on the heated moment:

Colin in the breakfast room of some crappy hotel in Ghent years ago, snatching the last banana right from under my nose on the morning of a race, flashing his eyes at me. He would have been 20 or 21 — such a baby. It was so strange to think that was the same man who was now groaning from deep in his chest and kissing me as though his life depended on it — as though winning the Tour de France depended on it.

I wasn't sure what to do with the knowledge that he'd had a crush on me but, on the other hand, everything was getting a little hazy — other than the feeling of his mouth on mine.

He broke the kiss and I sucked in a much-needed breath. 'Are you sure we should——? Ohhhhhh.'

He'd opened his mouth on my neck, breathing kisses along my throat, and my brain turned the consistency of oatmeal.

'This dress is one of my favourites,' he said, his voice ghosting over my skin as he dropped his head further. My dress had a low, square neckline, ruched at the bodice, and when he said things like that, I imagined grabbing the elastic and dragging it down for him.

His hands still gripping the seat on either side of me, he opened his mouth on the skin below my collarbone, swiping with his tongue. 'You wearing one of those little bra things with this? I'm never going to recover from that lace.'

'You'll have to see.' My voice was mostly breath, but I was oddly proud of myself for getting the words out.

He drew back and peered at me doubtfully. 'You playing with me, Kubicka?'

'Yes.'

The smile that stretched on his face was giddy and wicked and utterly irresistible. 'C'mere.'

I could hardly recognise myself when I let him urge me up and over the centre console. His hands curling around the backs of my thighs, he settled my knees on either side of him and slid the hem of my skirt up. As he reached around to grip my backside, a sudden stab of pain ripped over my skin and I gasped.

'Whoa, sweetheart.' He dropped his hands in an instant and lifted them to my face instead. 'What's up?'

'Tattoo,' I said through gritted teeth as the pain ebbed. The wound from the ink gun was clean and protected under a dressing and it was only the residual sensitivity of the spot that had set me off.

'Shit, I'm sorry,' he hissed sympathetically, massaging the back of my head in soothing circles. 'It's on your thigh?'

I nodded, the pain receding enough for me to miss his touch on my body, although his fingers in my hair were heavenly in another way. 'It's okay. It doesn't hurt any more.'

'Good,' he murmured, dropping a hand to the back of my knee, a sensitive spot that made me gasp and flinch, but then he soothed me with his palm sliding casually up the back of my thigh to tease the elastic of my underwear.

'A thigh tattoo is *hot*.'

His mouth was on mine again, searching and slow, then desperate. His legs were solid beneath me, the fabric of his jeans tormenting my inner thighs.

'Pull down your top for me.'

It hadn't even occurred to me that we were visible through the windscreen and it made me pause, shooting a furtive glance over my shoulder.

'Quick, Lees. Show me those tits and let me get you off. I know you're achin' for me. I'll take care of you before anyone sees.'

Part of me thought Colin's voice should be illegal, since it seemed to burn my rational brain to toast, but mostly I wanted to rub his words over my skin, soak them into my body and take them home with me.

I felt the urgency in his tone, the feeling stronger than the lingering uncertainty at the back of my mind. I couldn't imagine slipping past the swannies and the rest of the support staff (and dodging Wil and Tony) to sneak him into my room. This was happening here.

Dragging down my loose neckline, I went straight ahead and popped open the little clasp at the front of my bra. It was forest-green lace — one of my favourites — but that day it was simply convenient.

'Christ!' His hands clutched my ribcage, urging me up so he could take a nipple in his mouth. Working a hand up between my legs, he made a sound almost like a whimper as his finger slipped into my underwear.

The gentle pressure of his fingertip set off sparks behind my eyes. I needed so much more, even when he worked it in up to the first knuckle. Twisting, desperate for more, I forced his finger in another inch, but it still wasn't enough, especially if this was the last time we were together.

When I fumbled for his waistband, he quickly took over, popping the button and working the fly over his straining cock. Getting my underwear off was more difficult and I hit my head on the roof of the car before I made any progress.

'Ow!'

Slipping a leg into the footwell, I kneed him in the thigh and he yelped.

'Shit,' I said through gritted teeth.

Meeting my gaze with an amused twist of a smile, he steadied me while I wrenched off my underwear, then he shimmied his jeans a few inches down.

'You're keen,' he drawled, dipping his head to catch my gaze, which had snagged on the straight jut of his cock, standing up ready.

'Shut up,' I grumbled, climbing back into his lap.

Despite the confined space, the questionable privacy and the teasing, I surprised myself by being entirely on board with this, no distractions necessary. It was a relief when he grasped his cock and lined up and I could take him inside me, the friction everything I needed.

All the breath seeped out of me and I gasped the next inhale as he shifted under me. I didn't have much experience of being on top but that didn't seem to matter, as he hissed and moaned at everything I did, his right hand tight on my ass and his left bowing my back so he could suck on my nipple.

I rode him, dragging his cock against me until my vision blurred, winding him up until he was panting and cursing. He nudged me back and tugged my knees up and then he was setting the rhythm. My position, braced against the steering wheel, amplified the pressure of his strokes until I was tearing apart.

'You ever fucked in a car before, Kubicka?'

I didn't know how he was still capable of speech, but his words made everything clench tight. I shook my head, unable to catch my breath as he seemed to go deeper each time.

'This is a good enough fantasy just how it is, huh?'

'Yes,' I managed on a moan, part answer, part exclamation.

His cock slipped out from the vigorous movements and he frantically pushed it down, working it back in.

'You look like my filthiest dreams, tits out, letting me fuck you against the steering wheel.' He gave a grunt, his eyelids at half-mast as he gazed at me. 'So fucking beautiful with your hair a mess and your legs spread for me.'

I was ready to fly, moving like a wild thing, desperate for more, for harder, drowning in the gratification of him surging against me, right where I needed it.

I tried to tell him how good it felt, but all I could manage was a choked inarticulate burble. My thoughts spun out, nothing connected in my brain. I was reaching for something, weeping with how close it was.

'Come on, sweetheart,' I dimly heard Colin crooning. 'You were made for this. Feel it. Feel what you do to me.' There was strain in his voice – in his body. His hand closed in my hair, harder than I expected, and the pleasure-pain counterpoint struck me in the chest and sucked me under.

I heard my own gasps as though from outside my body, thrashing as the pressure snapped and gratification washed in afterward. I registered a rip and a choked curse from Colin and then he was holding me down in his lap with a grip that would leave marks as he finished with a jerk and a long groan.

I fumbled for balance and my hand slipped, the loud blare of the horn slicing through the moment.

'Shit!' Someone definitely would have heard it.

I scrambled off him, narrowly missing the important bits, and dived straight for the door handle and fresh air. The way my heart was pounding reminded me of the brand-new tattoo. Right now I didn't even mind if it made me think of him for the rest of my life.

Wobbly on my feet, I clung to the car and straightened while I tried to pull myself together – and I caught sight of a door opening over at the hotel.

'Quick, get dressed!' I said urgently to Colin, who was already in the process of tugging up his jeans. I managed the snap on my bra and rearranged my neckline. It seemed to take him far too long to put himself away, long enough for me to see Tony emerge with a wave – and for me to develop a blush more radiant than nuclear waste.

Colin stumbled out after me, nearly knocking me into the next car. After apologising and steadying me with a light touch to my waist, he murmured, 'Lees, the back of your dress is ripped.'

I hadn't noticed the extra ventilation, given the fact that other parts of me were also very well ventilated right now. Jerking my gaze back to the car, I realised in alarm that there was one more detail I'd forgotten.

'My underwear!' I mumbled urgently.

He dived back in, rummaging wildly.

'Where have you two been? One last publicity stunt?'

Hauling himself out of the car and hitting his head for good measure, Colin came to stand just behind me as a billow of wind swept across the meadow – and the skin of my back through the gaping rip. With an accidental shove that made me stumble, Colin pinched the ripped seam closed.

'I finally convinced Leesa to get the tattoo she'd always wanted.'

Tony's gaze snapped to me. 'Is that true? I hope he didn't talk you into anything that you'll regret.'

'Definitely not,' I insisted. 'I just got a little cardiogram symbol – a heartbeat. It's true, I'd always wanted to get it and the studio was really nice.'

Perhaps I'd said too much, because Tony's prodigious wrinkles got wrinklier as he looked from me to Colin. 'I'm glad Colin wasn't leading you astray.'

'Not at all,' I insisted, unconvincingly, if the nudge from Colin was anything to go by.

'We'd better… go inside and… help.'

I'd expected Colin to be a better liar, but his stilted words did the job and he ushered me ahead of him, hiding my ripped dress from view. I could feel Tony's eyes on us and wasn't sure I wanted to know what he was thinking.

'Here are your undies,' Colin said, coming close enough to speak softly into my ear. He slipped the cotton into my hand as we reached the corridor heading to my room. It was blessedly empty.

'Thanks.'

'I'm sorry I ruined your dress,' he mumbled, letting go of the edges so the floral material sagged around my waist. 'And I'm sorry I manipulated you into getting a tattoo, although I like the sound of the heartbeat.'

'Don't listen to your dad.'

His brow lifted. 'Is that professional advice?'

'No.' It was very personal.

Nostrils flaring, he kept his gaze on the rural watercolour on the wall over my shoulder as he spoke. 'You're too clever not to have noticed Dad and me aren't exactly a dream team, but he's not always wrong.' He tucked his hands into his armpits. 'He told you not to let me manipulate you. I said you were saving *me* from getting a tattoo, which was a lie. It was manipulation.'

'But he's not always *right* either, is he?' I pushed.

'God, no.'

Like my mom wasn't always right about me. But I couldn't help hearing her in my head, all these years after I'd moved out of home. Colin had never even moved out. He still heard Tony in the flesh.

'He needs to listen to you too,' I insisted. 'Then maybe you wouldn't have needed that tattoo. You wouldn't need to hide behind me.'

His response showed me I hadn't made my point – or he hadn't accepted it anyway. 'The tattoo is the least bad thing I could have done. I have to take my kicks where I can get 'em.' His forced laugh made me wonder if he included me in these 'kicks'. 'Plus,' he added, giving me a look that shot concern up my spine, 'I do stupid things when you're leaving.'

I knew he was talking about September, but the implication that he… *cared* clashed with everything else he was trying to make me believe.

'I'm…' *Not leaving* would be a lie. 'I'll see you in less than two weeks.'

He just flashed his eyebrows at me, as though I'd proved a theory he hadn't voiced. If he was waiting for me to fall in a lovesick heap at his feet, he'd be waiting another lifetime. As strange as it was to admit I felt… something here, I wasn't that stupid.

'With a nice, healed tattoo,' he added with a twitch of a smile. 'But you know how wild it gets during the Tour.'

I nodded, wondering if this was the part where he let me down gently. 'No more stolen moments in cars.'

His smile faded. 'Too many people around during the Tour.' His voice was gravelly with discomfort.

But I got the message. This was it. We'd had our fun. We had work to do now.

He glanced down at me, his playful expression back. 'Thanks for the orgasms, Kubicka. You're shit-hot in bed, overthinking and all.'

I tried to ignore the stutter of my heartbeat when he brushed a thumb under my chin. So much tenderness I didn't know what to do with.

I forced out a response. 'I'll see you at the team presentation. Say hi to your nonno for me.'

'Give Babcia a kiss on the cheek.'

'She requires three — on each cheek.'

'That's hardcore.' He slipped his arms around my waist and dragged me in for a hug that was far too quick and still seemed to tilt the earth. 'Take it easy.' Pressing a kiss to the top of my head that interfered with the electrical signals through my whole body, he drew away with a mock salute.

'You too,' I called after him. 'I mean it! And take proper care of that tattoo!'

After turning to place a warning finger over his lips, he disappeared through the doors back into the reception area – some kind of goodbye.

Gathering the edges of the accidental ventilation in my dress, I hotfooted it to my room and spent ten minutes trying to take the thing off. The damage meant I couldn't get enough tension in the zip to pull it down and I nearly dislocated my elbows trying, before I gave up and ripped an even bigger hole.

Perching on my bed in my bra and a fresh pair of underwear, I finally let my overactive brain sink its teeth into what had just happened – in the tattoo studio, the car and, more concerningly, in my heart.

I wanted him to spread his wings – his sad dragon wings. With me, he'd only stamped another number on his butt. I was off course, but he couldn't afford to be. Somehow I had to stop thinking that my heart would be beating for him while he raced.

# 24 June this year

**9.40 p.m.**

Me: My Zia just made ravioli and I can't eat it, so I thought I'd send you a picture.

Kubicka: You thought you'd torture me with a picture so I share your suffering, you mean. That looks incredible.

Me: Doesn't your babcia cook?

Kubicka: Of course she does, but I'm too kind to send you a photo of the pierogi she made me when I arrived. Now I've been here a few days, she's out of energy and won't let me help, so we're back to broth.

Me: Broth sounds very *Oliver Twist*. And no, I have not read that book, but I bet you have.

Kubicka: I'm not really into Dickens.

Me: Not the way you're into me.

Kubicka: …

Me: It's funny how our female relatives show love by cooking.

Kubicka: My mum doesn't. Food is fuel and love is a tiny bit of time carved out of her busy day to criticise my life choices.

Me: That's rough. But I'll raise you, food is fuel and love is giving up everything and every moment in life to criticise me.

Kubicka: I recognise Tony.

Me: I knew you were smart.

# Chapter 24

## Colin

*'Can you see the top of the Tourmalet? You're 300 m from the finish line. Andreu is behind you — with fresh legs. You've been pushing 400 watts for minutes. Tell me what happens. What do you see?'*

I saw the same thing every time I closed my eyes these days: Leesa in a pretty dress, giving me a wry smile over that little dent in her chin. But for the benefit of Vickers, the psychologist on the other end of this video call, I cleared my throat and answered, 'I don't see anything except the finish. I don't feel anything. I just get over the line — ahead of Andreu.'

Oops, I knew that last part wasn't what he wanted to hear.

*'That's good,'* he said so gently I wanted to punch him from several countries away. *'Just remember what the other cyclists do is up to them. You just visualise yourself. It's okay to feel something too, just know that you're stronger than the pain and the effort and you can get over that line.'*

A grunt of assent was all I could muster.

*'All right, Colin. I'll see you in Strasbourg. Until then: rest. Tony asked me to remind you, since he's not there to look after you himself.'*

'I'm resting,' I insisted. 'It's a fucking idyll.' Turning my phone, I showed Vickers the rolling Italian hillside and the actual babbling brook providing a clichéd soundtrack outside my nonno's place. When I turned it back to face me, the image of my face was framed in the cosy rustic view of the old stone house with ancient wooden beams.

It didn't change the fact that the place I most wanted to be right now was somewhere in Poland. I'd looked it up and plotted a route: 12 hours and lots of highway tolls and construction sites. If she was in the north, that was another 500 km. It was a big place.

'*Do you... need to talk about anything else?*'

'Nah, mate,' I said, leaning back in the old wicker chair and propping an arm behind my head. I wasn't about to tell him that Dad's concern for my rest was actually a passive-aggressive comment about Mum via the team psychologist and I definitely wasn't going to talk about the tearing, burning, cut-up sensation that came over me every time I remembered Leesa was heading back to the States after the Tour.

They were not helpful visualisations, when I got caught up imagining her taking my face in her hands before a stage, telling me I could win it and that she'd be there at the end. It wasn't her job to sort out my messed-up head, but I recognised the spiral I was sinking into.

I just didn't want to pull myself out, if it meant I had to stop thinking about her.

I sat down with Nonno after the call with the psych, but I was rusty with the Tressette cards and the weird local version of the game he'd taught me when I was younger — as rusty as I was at speaking Italian. He wasn't very mobile and I was supposed to be resting, which was so wholesome it made me want to text Leesa again.

If Mum had had her way, we'd have lived somewhere around here during the season, but Dad had settled us in France, near the Pyrenees — another of the many things they must have disagreed about. As if it wasn't clear enough: Gallaghers rode bikes, we didn't manage healthy relationships.

Even though I considered myself close to Mum, even that relationship functioned — if it could be called functioning — because we went running together in the off-season. Of the two of them, Dad was more touchy-feely, but at least Mum was interested in more than my performance.

All of which was why I was caught out that evening at aperitivo on the porch with Mum – well, Mum had an aperitivo and mine was soda water with lime – when she asked, 'Colin, are you going to talk to me?'

I sat up in surprise, dropping my feet down from where I'd propped them on another chair and shooting her a wary glance. Mum was tall and thin and strong and her resilience was something I hoped I'd inherited.

She didn't usually want to 'talk'.

'About what?' I asked doubtfully.

'You've been so quiet all week.' Her measured look made the tips of my ears heat. 'Is it the problems between your father and me? I know we probably didn't handle it well and it's you and Lori I most feel for—'

'I'm not upset about that,' I said, resisting a frustrated sigh. 'I mean, it's shit, but I can see how you both might be happier in the long run.'

'Do you know how Lori's taking it? She doesn't… speak to me much.' There was a world of regret in her tone that I didn't really want to address right now. I also wasn't sure I wanted to admit that I *had* spoken to Lori last week. We'd just mumbled some mutual commiserations about how our parents seemed to have regressed into children giving each other the silent treatment, but that was more than I would have expected from my sister. She'd gone soft, since falling for Seb.

'Lori deals with this stuff how she always does: with stubbornness. She's stubbornly making a healthy relationship, despite our inspirational family history.'

Maybe I shouldn't have leaned into the sarcasm, because Mum looked stricken. 'Me separating from your father is no reflection on you.'

'Maybe not, but it doesn't encourage me to try out commitment myself.' Unless a miracle occurred and Leesa Kubicka stood before me in a white dress. I'd run as fast as I could to the altar, which was a rather disturbing thought.

'Well, that's for the best.'

Pressing the heels of my hands into my eyes, I grumbled,

'Thanks so much for confirming that I'm not relationship material, Mum.'

She leaned forward and brushed her hand lightly over my cheek, the way she'd done when I was young. I wondered if she realised how important those little caresses had been for my mental health.

'It's not about being relationship material. You have other priorities right now. I'd hate to see you take on too much and not succeed at any of it.'

Because a good result at the Tour de France was so similar to a committed relationship – both came with pressure for success.

'Colin, I can see it's bothering you this year. Is it because you're a favourite?'

My only answer was a gulp.

'Listen to me, no one's expectations matter except your own.'

That earned a snort in response. 'I know a lot of sports psychology is crap, but that takes the cake. Dad has spent half his life preparing for this. He's brought in a team of amazing support riders. He's trying to sign a major sponsor to fill the hole in next year's budget and that sponsor has been stuck with *me* as their talent. If I screw up—' I didn't even want to finish that sentence.

'Has something your father said upset you?'

'No,' I insisted immediately, leaning my neck on the back of the chair and staring up at the sky. 'He's a tough old codger, but that's nothing new. I wouldn't have got here without him.'

'But?'

'But nothing. He's my coach, as well as the team manager. He's supposed to criticise me and, if I occasionally take it personally, that's my fault. Also nothing new.'

She sighed somewhat dramatically. 'I wish I'd never let him coach you two. First he turned Lori against me and now this. He's your *father*, Colin. If he's made you feel unloved—'

'He just shows his love in a weird way,' I mumbled, thinking of that text-message exchange with Leesa yesterday. Swapping stories about our European extended family, our difficult parents, had made me feel closer to someone 1,000 km away than anyone currently in this country. 'But seriously, Mum, I don't need a pep talk.'

'All right,' she acquiesced reluctantly. 'I'm glad I was imagining things anyway. After Lori last season…'

'Imagining what things?' I asked, taking a sip of my soda water and gazing out at the distant hills over the river.

'Oh, the restlessness, all the time spent on your phone. I thought you might have got distracted with a girl.'

Damn the bits of Irish in my complexion. I didn't want to admit anything, because what was the point, when Leesa would be gone again in a few weeks? But I suspected it would be pointless to deny it.

'You aren't… distracted by a girl, are you?' The pained tone was back.

'What difference would it make?' Something was expanding in my chest, threatening to tumble out of my mouth in a confession Mum didn't want to hear. My stupid heart. It wanted acknowledgement, affirmation, something to feed these feelings that I shouldn't even have — feelings I would take with me into the Tour, che sarà and all that.

'Is it serious?'

'Why are you asking? Because you'd bribe her to stay away from me?' I hated when my own jokes bit me in the arse. I'd tell Leesa to take the money and run.

'Who is it? How have you even had time?'

'I haven't,' I said, trying to calm her down — trying to calm myself down. 'There's no one.'

'You're still so young. At your age, these things grow out of proportion.'

She didn't have to be right, on top of everything else. 'I said there was no one,' I insisted through gritted teeth.

'If you're not ready, love can… twist and consume you and you have too much ahead of you to let that happen.'

'What do you know about that?'

'Don't turn this on me. I *was* young once.'

I knew a little of her history, although not much, I realised. 'And you loved Dad once too? Or did you have another grand love affair in your twenties?'

'I know I'm not the best person to give you advice,' she began, her voice shaking, 'but commitment at your age always comes at a cost. You need to live your life first.'

And Leesa needed to live hers.

'I know that. I'm not Lori.' Although before last year, I wouldn't have imagined my sister could commit to a life-changing relationship.

'Of course not. You're the man. You'd make your partner compromise for you and your career. I was so afraid Lori would give it all up for love last year. I'm still worried it will come to that in the future.'

She didn't know how her words were landing with me; they felt like a hundred needles, pricking me with conviction. I couldn't live with myself if I made Leesa give something up, but the thought of letting her go forever made my lungs seize up.

It was September all over again, when I'd given in to the urge to spill some feelings and caused more pain than I'd ever imagined. I still had that stupid cardboard sign at home, the one that had indirectly caused her broken arm. If she ever saw the back... I should have tossed it a long time ago.

'I've taken on board your advice,' I said lightly to Mum. 'You guys raised us to compete and I respect that,' I continued, although it made me think of Leesa and her intelligence and her struggles with success and failure. Her parents would be horrified if she tossed in her job, her ambitions, to follow a cyclist around Europe.

Mum leaned her head on my shoulder. 'You've grown up a lot over the past two years.'

'I've been an adult for seven, Mum,' I grumbled.

'Yes, but...' She wisely didn't finish that sentence. 'No matter what your father wants for you, *I* believe you're ready to win.'

No matter how many times I'd talked the big talk — even the number one tattooed on my arse — I had to admit I wasn't sure I could hang onto that dream. Here were some home truths I could never admit to Mum *or* Dad. But maybe Leesa would have understood.

'The adrenaline will see me over the line on the first stage, and each of the 21 stages after that,' I assured Mum.

# 28 March, four years ago

## Leesa

We rolled over the finish line of the roughest of races on a miserable day with a groan in unison. I'd punctured; Doortje had skidded out while trying to avoid street furniture and Lori had been left with no team support for her doomed late attack.

It was a day to forget, to wash away in the Flanders gloom.

Our DS Alf gave us commiserating hugs as he ushered us to the warm-down bikes, protected from the drizzle by an awning. I was longing for a shower, but I had to stay warm in the horrible weather until then.

'What the fuck?' Lori was on her warm-down bike already, but she wasn't pedalling. 'Someone put a Chris Hemsworth sticker on my bike.'

'Is it supposed to warm you up?' Doortje suggested with a laugh as she peered at the bike set up for her. 'Ha! I've got Scarlett Johansson! Top choice.'

On the other bikes we found Harry Styles, Orlando Bloom and Idris Elba and I was kind of disappointed when one of the other girls got the Paul Rudd sticker. The swannies had obviously been busy preparing to cheer us up on our ignoble return to the team bus.

'Who've you got, Leesa?' Doortje called out as I approached the bike with my specs, set up at the end of the line.

I peeked at the stem and that warmth of anticipation dissipated in an instant. 'Hmm,' I began, glancing around for a hidden camera, but not seeing anything. Whether this was being recorded or not, I suspected who was behind this and it wasn't the swannies.

Did he think I was an easy target? Last time the men's and women's teams had been in the same city, he'd frozen all of our toothbrushes in clumps of ice while we were racing, but this felt... personal.

'What?' Lori prompted.

Just as I was getting up on the bike, I caught a hint of movement at the door of the bus. He *was* watching, the jackass.

Straightening as my legs started spinning through the warm-down, I raised my voice as I said with as much carelessness as I could muster, 'I have the unmatched Hollywood legend... Steve Buscemi.'

# Chapter 25

## Leesa

'*Babcia says you've been working too much — in the evenings too!*'

There wasn't a lot else to do in the evening in my grandma's hometown. It was a pretty place with cobbled streets and baroque architecture, a leafy pedestrianised square, the rynek, in the centre and a historic manor house with extensive grounds. But Babcia usually dozed on the sofa from about 8 o'clock and the number of people I knew in this town corresponded to the number of vowels in its name: Pszczyna.

On the few occasions I'd taken some time out to go walking or take Babcia to the supermarket for kohlrabi, I'd been assailed by the intense desire to get on a bike and explore the hills and lakes I glimpsed from the car.

I blamed Colin Gallagher for that. I also blamed him for my tossing and turning most nights, vacillating between obsessive questions about his feelings for me and what they meant (my conclusion? Absolutely nothing) and visions of him crashing and mangling his body during some cruel stage of the Tour.

Sometimes I wished I'd never seen past his big talk.

'*Overtime shouldn't be an expectation*,' Mom continued on the video call, speaking in English — her professional language. '*If they get the idea they can walk all over you, they will.*'

Keeping true feelings from parents had probably been easier before the advent of FaceTime. It took a lot of effort to resist rolling my eyes. Mom wanted me to work hard, but not too hard. She wanted me to make a success of my career, but assumed I could do it on my own terms, without sacrificing anything, just because I was her daughter.

'They're not walking all over me,' I insisted. 'I'm enjoying it – my work.' I was especially enjoying combing through all my footage of Colin and reliving the past three weeks with my skin prickling and my heart beating a strange rhythm.

'*Well, that's something, at least. Are they going to make your contract permanent?*'

Mom hadn't got the memo that nothing was really permanent for my generation. 'I don't know, but the client has been really happy with what I'm producing and my supervisor has been letting me do a lot more myself.'

I hated to admit that Colin had been right, but being back in the world of cycling had unlocked something inside me. I knew what I was doing – for the first time since my time on the team had come to an ignoble end in September.

It was strange how my brain had switched the emphasis of my memories. I seemed to remember *more* about Colin, now I knew him better. Except, I didn't really *know* him. I'd only seen hints, put together a few pieces of the puzzle.

'*And what are you going to do if they don't hire you? You have résumés out, I'm assuming? What about the professors at your school? You need to cultivate your network, especially in this creative sector.*'

The way she said 'creative sector' sounded as though she meant 'trash pile'. I couldn't admit that I had been too busy staring at images of Colin to actually send out any Plan B job applications. I couldn't see past the Tour.

'I'll get on it.' I swiped my hair off my sticky back. I wasn't sure how I would have coped with an LA summer when these Polish hills were bad enough. My hair was in a permanent state of frizz.

'*I took a look at this account you're working on.*'

*Ohhh, no.* 'You're not really the target market, Mom.'

'*I can see that,*' she said emphatically. '*I must admit I didn't realise you had to be so entertaining.*'

She meant 'vacuous' or 'frivolous', I could feel it. I struggled against a blush, thinking of the reel featuring Colin licking

PowerFuel gel off his finger with a silly, suggestive gaze.

I stilled, struggling to keep the doubt off my face. 'The memes and funny stuff tend to get more traction.'

*'I can see how that would work. Your own Instagram account had some interesting moments too. It's certainly not… what I expected, żabka.'*

It might seem strange, as the word meant 'frog', but when Mom called me 'żabka' in that soft tone, it was a rare glimpse into her true self. She even sounded a little impressed.

'Did you just discover Instagram, Mamusia?' I teased her with the endearment that usually made her smile and give me a hug.

*'We made an account for the practice a year ago,'* she replied indignantly. *'And we didn't even need help from our millennial daughter.'*

I gave her a withering smile and resisted the retort that I was only *just* a millennial. Usually I found the rueful disappointment with life from my generation intensely relatable, but just then I was too sensitive to the fact that Colin was most definitely Gen Z and still managed to have some stars in his eyes and some weird vocabulary. Sometimes he felt a lot younger than me, and other times…

Other times he shot me cocky smiles and made me blush and then it didn't matter so much that he was nearly five years younger.

*'I don't know where you got your sense of humour from, but you got it. I can see you in your work and…'*

Unexpected tears pricked behind my eyes. 'I can only have got it from you and Tatuś.'

*'Or maybe you're inspired,'* Mom said softly.

I hoped the heat in my cheeks wasn't visible as my brain veered right back to Colin.

*'That rider you're filming… What an accent! I think it's very effective.'*

My throat closed as heat whooshed up my chest. 'Effective' was one way to describe it, how he could make me forget my own name just by shooting me a lazy smile.

*'Handsome too.'*

I choked, hurrying to change the subject. 'It's actually been really good returning to cycling. I missed it.'

*'Of course you did. You were very good at it.'*

I blinked, certain I'd misheard the casual remark. How many times had I wished she'd acknowledge that, and now it was too late.

Swallowing my consternation, I asked, 'Are you just saying that because I finally did the sensible thing and got a real job? At least, I'm trying,' I added with a grumble.

'*Perhaps*,' she admitted. '*I never understood your passion, but I haven't been happy to see you without it these past months.*'

Her statement made all my struggles real. The past ten months had been difficult. I'd been trying not to acknowledge how low I'd felt, blamed it on my broken wrist or the lack of endorphins and serotonin after quitting elite sport. But it was more than that.

I heard Colin's voice in my head again, telling me I'd forgotten who I was; I felt the wind on my face as we weaved through the mountains that perfect day on training camp. My medals were stored rather unceremoniously in a moving box at my parents' place and only the stylised wave from the Great Ocean Road Race was on display.

Maybe I'd never had a chance at the big wins, but I'd been part of it.

Tears stung behind my eyes — something that had threatened numerous times over the past week and I couldn't even blame my hormonal cycle. The urge to cry usually hit me when I remembered Colin's casual admission that he'd crushed on me for years — that he admired me for following my heart. That confession had slowly reordered something inside me, as though the shape of my life was changing.

I'd never questioned my path before. After racing was supposed to come real life, but what if real life didn't look the same for me as it had for my parents? Wil's offer to help me find a job lurked in the back of my mind, but staying in Europe felt like too big a decision — too close to Colin and the past — too *risky*.

'I'm looking forward to following the team for the Tour de France,' I managed to respond.

'*It does seem very exciting.*'

I peered at Mom. 'You sound more interested than when I was riding.'

She gave a slow sigh. '*When you were riding, żabka, I was beside myself with worry. Your poor father had to spoon-feed me beetroot soup to keep my strength up during these longer tours.*'

'*It's true!*' My dad's face appeared in the side of the shot, salt-and-pepper hair and a broad, good-natured face.

'Hi, Dad,' I said with a wry smile, wondering how long he'd been lurking – and wincing when I remembered Mom had said Colin was handsome.

'*I didn't understand it. I still don't,*' Mom continued. '*I just knew there was a chance you'd crash – more than a chance over the course of your career.*'

A tear fell and I couldn't stop it. 'You know, I really wish you'd dealt with that and supported me.'

'*Hey, kwiatuszku,*' Dad crooned, calling me his little flower as he leaned closer to the phone, so the screen was filled with his big nose.

I had to chuckle through my tears, feeling like a train wreck, but in an unexpectedly positive way, like this would mean I could get back on the right track, once I'd suffered through the painful bit.

'Sorry, I'm okay,' I said – my automatic response to Mom's stricken look, even if it was only in the background of Dad's enormous head. Her back was straight and her face drawn. I swiped at my cheeks and sniffed. 'You're right. The last few months have been tough.'

At least that was the reason I was sticking to for this emotional breakdown. It had nothing to do with the imminent strain of the Tour, watching Colin write his destiny – while I considered my own. I should check if my tattoo was infected. Maybe I had a fever.

'*You're tough too,*' Dad said – a platitude but an effective one nonetheless.

I smiled weakly at him. 'Actually, I thought about riding again – amateur. I might just get back on for training and do a few races in the fall.'

'*In LA?*' Mom exclaimed. '*You'll lose your limbs! Or your head! A truck will squash you!*'

Dad muttered something to her in Polish, too quietly for me to catch it, and patted her hand. '*We'll come and see you.*'

The melting feeling in my chest was back. 'Thanks, Tatuś.'

'*Now we're starting to hand the practice over to Dr Bachchan, we'll have more time,*' Mom added.

'*If you want us there, even if we have to shut the practice, we'll come,*' Dad corrected with a pointed glance at Mom.

I thought of Colin and his dysfunctional parents, combined with this gesture from Dad – too late, but still appreciated – and I didn't think I was going to be able to keep this down. I hiccoughed and had to press my knuckles to my mouth in a last-ditch attempt to pull myself together.

'*What is it, Leeska?*' Dad asked, using the made-up Polish diminutive of my name.

'Nothing, I'm good.'

'*If you're—*'

'I should probably go,' I mumbled. 'Babcia is obviously keeping you updated anyway and you can keep tabs on the PowerFuel Instagram account.'

I tried not to cringe at the thought of all the content I had yet to post – including the very thorough tour of Colin's tattoos.

'Bye! Cześć! Ciao!' I tapped to end the call, hoping I'd timed my shoulder droop so they didn't see it. Slumping forward, my elbows on my knees, I blew out a long breath and swiped a curl away from my face.

'Już, już, moja maleńka,' a rough voice crooned behind me.

There was pressure on my back and then a soft stroke down my arm. Babcia shuffled around the sofa and sat next to me, taking my hand and chafing it between her gnarled ones. If she hadn't shrunk to the size of a gnome, I would have rested my head on her spindly shoulder.

'Boys always cause troubles.'

My throat closed and I eyed her. I had a feeling she would be able to tell if I lied to her. I was a terrible liar in Polish anyway.

'This boy especially,' I whispered in reply.

'Big troubles, big love,' she said with half a smile.

I shook my head. We were talking about *Colin Gallagher*. I did not love him. I barely tolerated him most of the time. He'd tried to tell me his love language was fake insects and glue in my hair.

*His love language…*

'No, Babcia…' I trailed off. 'It's not love.'

# Chapter 26

**Leesa**

The cobbled squares and canal-side lanes of Strasbourg were heaving for the start of the Tour. Kids in child-size yellow jerseys trailed after their parents in checked bucket hats handed out by the salami manufacturer – oh sorry, it was saucisson in France. The carnival feeling extended to the colourful buildings of the old part of town, with planters of yellow flowers on the sills.

The quaint city on the border with Germany was the scene for the first three stages: an individual time trial to start, then two hilly stages, the second of which would take the riders to the next stop on the tour.

The Harper-Stacked support team descended on a town nearby called Obernai, a cute little place of half-timbered houses with wooden shutters. The enormous team buses looked monstrously orange in the car park of the gabled brick hotel and the visceral memories they brought back hit me like a grand piano.

Last year, I was the one guzzling hydration gels in the back of the bus after a race, covered in dust and sweat – and occasionally my own pee. The haze of stress and overstimulation were things I didn't miss, but it was impossible not to get caught up in the excitement again.

Each of my teaser videos garnered more engagement than the last and the CEO of PowerFuel himself sought me out when he came to see Tony, shaking my hand and telling me how glad he was to have me on board.

For the first time I allowed myself to really imagine that I'd be offered a permanent job at Redwin after this. The uncertainty could finally be over and I'd have a clear path into the future. I only hoped I didn't get this gig again next year.

Only a small part of me imagined Colin and I might have a two-week affair every year from now on, our stars aligning for the short window before the Tour, but mostly I was concerned with the effect I was having on him, splitting his focus and leading him astray.

I was determined to keep my distance now the real test was only days away.

It was Thursday, the day before the team presentation, when the riders arrived, along with a flock of hangers-on, sponsors and media and fans, all keen to take their piece of the riders. I might have been jealous of my teammate Lori's results when we were racing together, but I'd never envied her the media circus and it was even wilder for the men.

I set up in the hotel foyer, responding to emails while also staying close to help Wil if necessary — and yes, to watch out for Colin, even though I had no intention of greeting him with anything other than a distant wave. But Colin wasn't the first Gallagher I saw.

'Leesa!'

Looking up from my tablet with a start, I was stunned to see Lori barrelling towards me. For someone who wasn't particularly tall, Lori filled every room she entered, elbows out, her loud voice carrying. I had always been a little in awe of her.

Scrambling to my feet, I managed to catch her in a hug. The only times I remembered hugging Lori Gallagher were when she'd won. She had never been very touchy-feely — or particularly friendly.

'You have no idea how good it is to see you!'

'Hi,' I managed inadequately, suddenly struck by the echoes of her brother in her features. Lori's hair was darker, her freckles too. But the crooked smirk must have been a family trademark and her blue eyes were the exact shade of Colin's.

'You don't believe me,' she accused.

'Not really?' I admitted.

Lori barked a laugh and slapped me on the shoulder. 'You see why I missed you!'

I was still a little mystified.

'Bonnie had to pick up the slack with the snarky comments this year.'

A pang accompanied her words — for the time when I'd been one of them, in the ugly orange-and-blue kit, stamped with sponsor names, punching out the kilometres for too little pay, unless one of us won something big.

'It certainly wouldn't be the women's team without the sarcasm,' I quipped flippantly.

'And it wouldn't be the men's team without my idiot brother. Has he been a lot of trouble? I know he was always horrible to you—'

'No,' I insisted quickly. 'He's been fine.'

She eyed me, making my skin bloom with discomfort and words I could not under any circumstances actually say rose in my throat: *I slept with your brother and it was mind-altering, life-changing, erotic fantasy sex!*

Sex, which had apparently given me the ability to exaggerate wildly in my own head.

'You're a miracle worker, making Colin look mostly normal. You deserve a prize.'

I tried for a laugh, but it came out like a choke, attracting too much attention from Lori.

'He did something, right?' she said with a sigh. 'He went too far? Is that why Dad's been on his case?'

There were more sparks under my skin at hearing Colin was still having trouble with his father. 'No, I'm serious. We... cleared the air. I kind of understand him now.'

'That makes one of us,' Lori mumbled cautiously.

'Tony needs to get off his back. I think he's doing more harm than good.'

'Leesa K, defending my brother. I never thought I would see the day.'

My face was hot. I hoped – in vain, I knew, given my pale skin – that the temperature didn't show in my cheeks.

'Is there… God, what am I even asking?' Lori's brow travelled lower and lower as she watched me. 'Shit, you… and Colin?'

'It's nothing. You know Colin.'

'I thought I did,' she said, her jaw sagging open. 'I mean, I thought I knew *you*. Holy fuck, you slept with my brother? After everything he did to you?' She'd thankfully dropped her voice or we would have had the entire floor staring at us. I was worried enough about the walls having ears – or at least people hiding behind the large indoor plant in the corner.

'It didn't mean anything and now that it's the Tour, we're staying away from each other. Please don't tell your—'

Before I could finish my sentence, the doors swished open and Colin, Amir and Derek spilled into the room, dragging suitcases and shoving each other in a juvenile display of affection. Everything inside me went still. The weeks on training camp washed over me: every drawled observation, every cheeky look – every touch.

He was across the room, but I felt him as though *he* were next to me instead of his sister. My hair stood on end; all of my nerves suddenly flicked on.

He grinned at something Derek said, the lopsided smile that wasn't from his heart. His wavy hair was a mess from the humid day. His shoulders were as expansive as I remembered, but hunched today. I thought of Valerio the dragon on his back and a hundred desires rose up – mainly the desire to touch him, anywhere.

Lori was saying something. 'Uh, is this some Romeo and Juliet shit, because I'm not…'

I didn't hear the rest, because Colin caught sight of me and smiled – properly this time – and I lost my faculties. Breathing thankfully returned first, a giant inhale that was a few heartbeats late. I hoped he couldn't tell I wanted to launch myself at him, wrap myself around him like an aggressive octopus and talk to him all night until the sun came up tomorrow morning.

He seemed startled to see Lori next to me, but he headed towards us, only for Derek to call him back, draping an arm around his shoulders. The doors opened again to reveal Jarin Nelson pushing an enormous baby buggy, his dark-haired wife next to him.

'Aw, you brought him, Nellie,' Colin drawled, peering warily at the buggy. He reluctantly allowed Amir to drag him closer. 'He doesn't look much like his picture. Ramila, on the other hand...' He shot Nellie's wife a smile. 'Congratulations!'

'Thanks, Colin,' she replied.

'You, um, sure got busy quickly after you got married.'

Lori gave an amused snort.

'I mean...' Colin gave up with an inarticulate grunt, his neck flushed. 'He's... little.'

'You don't know anything about kids, do you, Gallagher?' Amir asked.

He scratched the back of his neck. 'I know how you make 'em.'

More laughter, which Colin joined in with this time, his throat bobbing.

'Can I hold him?' Amir asked. When Nellie nodded, Amir carefully scooped the little body out of his buggy and cradled him close, cooing and making faces at the baby. 'I love kids,' he said. 'They smell good.'

'Not all the time, they don't! Phewhiff!' Nellie disagreed emphatically. 'Lucky he's cute.'

Amir turned to Colin. 'Are you going to hold him?'

'Nah, mate. I'm good. Well done, Nellie! Your swimmers got there.' He clapped Nellie on the shoulder.

'Go on, you can hold him,' Nellie replied with a perplexed smile. 'He's not that fragile any more and you're not allergic.'

Colin released an uneasy breath. 'I suppose not.'

'I would not trust my brother with a baby,' Lori said to me with a wince. 'Lucky there's no chance of producing one any time soon.'

I wasn't sure if she meant *she* wouldn't produce one soon or Colin wouldn't. Both probably. There was no reason for my throat to constrict or my mixed-up mind to bring *me* into this. I wanted kids – at least I'd always assumed I did. I'd never thought about it beyond soft-focus images of a vague future when I'd hit all my other goals. But I'd never had anyone to imagine as that soft-focus partner in those unimaginative pictures.

And then Amir slipped the baby into Colin's big scarred hands and the soft focus sharpened dangerously — especially dangerously because Colin was obviously uncomfortable. He was just 25. Nellie wasn't much older, but Colin wasn't cut from the same cloth. He was too bright and restless to settle down.

He had to juggle the boy to get him comfortably into the crook of his arm and then the baby fussed, turning his head and flinging his arms. Colin ducked to stare at him, brushing a thumb over the little red cheek.

Then a twitch of a smile touched his lips and no matter how hard I tried to stop my heart changing, it did. So much for keeping my distance.

# Chapter 27

## Colin

*Don't look at Leesa.* Don't *look at her! Under no circumstances—*

My dad could tell you self-discipline wasn't my strong point. I barely resisted. Maybe I'd felt her gaze or maybe I just had no self-control when it came to Leesa Magdalena Kubicka. Whatever the reason, when I glanced up and found her staring right back at me, the ripple of gratification became a full-on wave.

Did she want kids?

I didn't know why I was wondering. I'd never ask her to her face and even if she admitted she wanted a family, it wouldn't be with me. She'd be looking for some solid, stable guy – who actually liked kids. Although this little guy wasn't as weird as I'd expected. He might look like an alien, but he felt pleasantly squishy.

Maybe one day…

'What's all thi——? Ah, g'day, Ramila.' Dad cut himself off to greet Nellie's wife with a kiss on the cheek. 'Lovely to see you. Congratulations on the little nipper.'

'Thanks, Tony,' she replied indulgently.

He studied me, but I had no desire to return his gaze. I shifted the baby carefully and managed to plonk him back into Nellie's arms before any harm came to him – or Dad had a chance to make the comment I could feel brewing.

'Well, boys, don't stand around in the lobby all day. You can at least get out of the way while the swannies move the mattresses in.'

This was a pretty nice hotel compared with some of the questionable establishments we stayed at year after year, but sleep was critical during the Tour, as evidenced by the truck transporting eight ergonomic mattresses all around France, one for each Harper-Stacked rider.

On camp, we suffered through sweat testing and endurance training but during the Tour we were pampered, aside from the gruelling hours spent on the road.

As the guys dispersed, I drifted across the lobby, helpless to move in any other direction except towards *her*. She kept her eyes off me until my toes were in her line of sight, but I could see how much it was costing her. When she finally looked up, her expression was waxy and pinched – and Lori was smirking at me in a less-than-subtle hint that she knew what was going on here. That made one of us.

'G'day, Magda. Monster,' I added as an afterthought, using my childhood nickname for my sister as I draped an arm over her shoulders. She was nearly two years older, but when she was being a hardarse, that age gap felt like ten years and on the rare occasions when she showed her vulnerability, it was no gap at all.

'Valerio,' Leesa deadpanned in reply, a small smile on her lips.

Without questioning my actions, I draped an arm around her as well and squeezed both of them. I wanted to wind a finger in her springy curls, turn that dry smile into a happy one. I felt as though I'd spent the past two weeks as a slab of stone, but one touch from her and I was a person again.

It was definitely the stress talking.

'Why do I feel like the third wheel?' Lori asked, a pained expression on her face. 'What happened to the staying away thing?' she asked Leesa in a stage whisper that I was obviously supposed to hear.

Lori extricated herself, but I leaned heavily on Leesa – in a companionable, friendly manner. 'I'm staying away,' I insisted brazenly.

'Urgh, this is weird, bronads,' Lori commented.

'You don't get to say that,' I countered, reluctantly dropping my arm. 'I shared a fucking bedroom with your boyfriend for half the season last year. I haven't recovered yet.'

'Is that your excuse? I didn't think it was contagious.'

'What's contagious? Falling——?' I cut myself off just in time, although the look Lori shot me suggested she had her suspicions about what I'd been about to say.

Leesa's voice, low and amused, smoothed over the conversation. 'Oh, how I missed the dulcet tones of the Gallagher siblings bickering.'

'Just watch out,' Lori grumbled. 'He's probably slipped a cockroach into your pocket.'

Leesa's gaze snapped up in alarm as her hands dipped into her pockets in a panic.

'It's down your shirt,' I admitted sheepishly.

With an abortive shriek, she slapped at the back of her neck, tugging at the neckline of her pretty blouse. I grasped her forearms gently and tugged.

'I'm joking.'

'You bastard!' Her eyes flashed and her chest was heaving and wow, I'd missed her. Just two weeks and it had been two weeks too long. I wanted to kiss her; just a light peck would take the edge off.

I heard footsteps and then the voice of Lori's boyfriend Seb. He'd retired at the end of the season last year, but was back to help out the support staff for the Tour – and probably to catch a few days with Lori. 'Do we need to separate them?' he asked.

'Pretty sure Leesa can take care of herself and I've got no interest in protecting Colin, but we don't want Dad to find them in such a compromising position.'

I was rather enjoying the compromising position, the familiar scent of her reaching my nostrils and her skin under my fingers. The shot of endorphins was better than a post-race massage. But Leesa drew away, swiping my hand off her arm when I couldn't seem to release her.

'Maybe you can make yourself useful and take a photo of us,' Lori interrupted my thorough study.

'Uh, 'course.' I tore my gaze away, accepting Lori's phone from her.

Looking at the image on the screen as I lined up the shot, I saw so much in Leesa's face. The colour in her cheeks and the way her eyes flickered to me told me a hundred little things that still weren't enough.

'Make sure you don't cut me out of the photo, little bro peep,' Lori said drily, crossing her arms.

Leesa snorted a laugh, bumping Lori companionably and I snapped a photo that made me smile crookedly. I'd have to beg Lori for it later.

I rummaged in my pocket for my phone and handed it to Seb. 'Take a photo of the three of us?'

Lori must have known it was a pretext to get a nice photo with Leesa, but I didn't care. In a month, all I'd have of her was this photo and memories of this moment. Her forehead was *right there*. I could drop my chin and press a kiss there and release all this wild stuff inside me that had been churning since I saw her again – since I said goodbye in September, or maybe even earlier.

'Molly! Frankie! There y'are!'

I straightened, dropping my arm from Leesa's shoulders with a start at the sound of Dad's voice, calling Lori and Seb using his nicknames for them. It was only me he called by my real first name.

'You all coming for lunch?' he asked.

I wanted to grab Leesa by that pretty blouse and drag her with me, but she'd only think I was hiding behind her again to take the pressure off with Dad. Instead I leaned close just as she was about to go.

'Can we talk later?'

Her eyes were wide and wary. 'I'm not sure that's—'

It wasn't 'no'. 'After dinner? Your room?'

Her gaze clouded, as though her thoughts were heading in the same direction as mine and she wasn't certain about it. I didn't expect we'd have sex, although part of me hoped, but I still wanted time alone with her before everything crashed down around me.

'Okay,' she murmured, gesturing that I should go.

*

It took her critical seconds to come to the door when I knocked that night. I scanned the hallway urgently as I waited, panicking that one of the swannies would come by and tell on me to Dad – and then panicking that she wouldn't open up.

But when she did, I drew back in surprise. She was doubled over at the waist, hair over her head, water dripping from the ends of the curls onto the floor.

'Sorry, I washed my hair and I can't blow-dry it or I just get frizz. It's a curl thing. Come in,' she said from under her hair, scrunching it with a towel as she straightened.

She was wearing thin cotton pyjamas, splattered with water, at once so domestic and so incredibly sexy. I wanted to take the towel from her and rub it gently over her hair – then take off all her clothes and give her an orgasm.

'How's it going?' she asked, pulling her hair to one side so she could peer at me, obviously no idea of the storm raging in my chest.

I snagged one sodden curl. 'Better now.'

She watched me warily. 'How was lunch? I would like to have been a fly on the wall for a Gallagher family lunch.'

'You should have come,' I blurted out, which only made her eyes wider. I shoved my hands in my pockets and leaned on the back of her door. 'It's interesting these days with Seb around. Dad likes him, which is weird, because Seb stood up to him for Lori last year. Lori could always get away with more than I could.' I choked off my words, wondering why I'd added that last bit. 'What about you? Did you miss me?' Grasping her around the waist, I pressed my lips to her jaw, soaking up her sigh.

'Colin—'

'I missed you,' I murmured, covering the reticence I didn't like between us with a fraction of the truth. As her body sagged against mine, everything else fell away.

'Colin, we—'

I dipped my head to her neck, using my lips to nip at her throat. Her squeak didn't discourage me, especially not when her thighs opened an inch in response to my exploring hands on the curve of her arse. Her fingers curled around the back of my neck. I was dying to know if she was as ready for me as I was for her – up and eager in less than a minute with this woman.

She opened her lips to draw in a shaky breath, chest heaving, but she managed to say it, the truth I'd been shoving out of my head.

'We aren't supposed to be doing this.'

# 1 February, 18 months ago

## Leesa

For all my attempts to visualise this moment over the years, it didn't feel anything like what I'd expected when I let go of the handlebars and lifted both fists above my head in victory – my first World Tour victory. My *only* World Tour victory, most likely.

Shaking, every muscle and organ screaming and overworked, I doubled over, dropping sweat and tears – and my sunglasses – onto the ground as the oxygen returning to my brain finally cleared my vision and I came aware of the other riders crossing the line after me. Someone barrelled into me, pulling me up by the shoulders and enfolding me in a hug. It was Bonnie, my teammate, and the one who'd pulled hard to make this possible for me.

'You little ripper! You did it!'

Life seemed to wind up at speed as I gripped her jersey and blubbered, snorting hot tears. Doortje piled on and soon I was surrounded by all the girls, the ones I would gladly share my prize money with, and all of these feelings.

Needing a moment, I stumbled to the other side of the bus, leaning against the garish orange paint job and dropping my head back, my helmet limp in my hand. There was too much to process. I was the same person as the one who'd started the race, not really believing a win was possible, but putting myself through it anyway. I wasn't sure if that fact was disappointing. I'd worked so hard only to find that one win wasn't a miracle cure for my entire life. It wasn't much more than a moment, over in a blink of an eye.

With thoughts like this, I definitely didn't have the mindset of a winner.

'I think these are yours, Kubicka.'

Snapping my eyes open, I didn't need the visual to confirm who stood in front of me. The voice had been enough. Colin held out my sunglasses, his other hand stuffed in the pocket of his shorts. He would race tomorrow. I wasn't sure why he was here watching the women. Maybe his dad forced him to, for the PR.

'Thanks,' I muttered, taking the glasses from him. He didn't make any move to walk away, even when I glanced at him in confusion.

'Can I get an autograph?'

Straightening, I eyed him. 'You don't even have anything for me to sign.'

Producing a permanent marker from his pocket, he spun it from hand to hand. 'How about my butt?'

Throwing an arm into the air, I groaned. 'Oh, grow up, Colin!'

As I stalked back to the others, I heard him say behind me, 'Not my butt. My arm? Sign my arm. Or my shirt!'

# Chapter 28

**Leesa**

My legs were wobbly, my breath couldn't seem to fill my lungs, but I was grateful for the cold drip of my hair onto my shoulder to force a little perspective into my heated brain. One touch and I was on fire. Regardless of the poor timing, indulging this intense attraction was surely a bad idea anyway. I didn't want to be so addicted to him. I was supposed to be sorting my life out.

'I thought you said we should talk,' I managed to say around my thick throat.

But I still couldn't step away when he peered at me from under his lashes. I would see those blue eyes and that cocky smile in my dreams for the rest of my life. If he'd grabbed me, pressed me against the door and started things up again, I wouldn't have stopped him.

Instead, he eased away as though it pained him, adjusting his tracksuit bottoms. At least one of us was able to take an effective breath. He collapsed onto my single bed, propping his elbows on his knees.

'Sorry.' He rubbed his eyes. 'It's all getting to me.' Right. This was about blowing off pressure and nothing more. Colin didn't do 'more' and I had to remember that. His leg was bouncing – a move that reminded me more of Lori than her brother.

I sank down next to him, tucking my hands in my lap. 'It wasn't like this last year?'

'*You* weren't here last year,' he replied, shooting me a smile that didn't reduce my dismay at his words. 'But, nah, it was different.

It was my first year as the lead rider. It was all "softly, softly". Ninth was more than anyone expected of me, but this year… I'm all grown up,' he drawled slowly.

'You're still very young for a lead rider, Colin,' I reminded him.

I'd always thought it was an advantage of cycling, that unlike competitors in other sports, riders tended to get better as they got older, to a critical point some time in their early thirties. But maybe it would have been better for me to peak in my twenties like in other sports and then retire gracefully, rather than quitting right when I might have been getting good.

'A young hothead. It's all true, what the pundits say about me. I don't know if I'm going to crash and burn or actually bring the results Dad needs.' He glanced at me. 'Don't worry, I don't need a pep talk from you. I've had enough of those from everyone else.'

'Did the tattoo heal at least?'

He caught my gaze and held it. We weren't touching, but it felt as though we were. 'Yeah, no worries. It's nice and smooth. How about yours? All okay?' *Can I see it?* The question danced in his eyes.

I nodded, a smile pulling at my lips. 'I really like it.'

'I did one thing well then. Two things, all up,' he added with a wink.

Heat rushed up my chest. 'Colin, stop. I admit you were very good for my sexual self-awareness, but you don't have to flirt with me all the time. I just wanted to check how you were holding up.'

'I'm not flirting with you, Kubicka,' he insisted. 'You just understand me better than anyone else right now and I like it – a bit too much.' He sighed – an enormous breath, full of frustration – and rubbed a hand over his head, mussing his hair.

I did understand – how alone he felt. It was dangerous how much I wanted to tinker around in his heart and see what blossomed.

'Leesa,' he said on a groan, 'you can't look at me like that if we're not supposed to be kissing any more.'

His hand curled around my nape and sparks skittered along my skin, gathering in the sensitive places he'd awakened with his hands and his lips.

'I don't know,' I said, my brain stalling. 'Maybe we should… one last time.'

His hand tightened. 'What don't you know? Whether you want me?'

I shook my head with a huff. 'We both know I do.' I lifted my chin. 'I don't know what's best. On Saturday you have to—' I broke off with a squeak when he hopped to his feet and leaned over me, dropping his hands to the bed on either side of me.

'It's not Saturday yet,' he said smoothly, his gaze dropping to my neck. He walked his hands backwards and I tumbled onto my elbows. He loomed above me, not touching yet, but I could feel him everywhere – in the air surrounding me.

'What if this—?'

'Overthink it later,' he murmured. 'Right now, I need you.'

I flopped onto my back, my lungs tight. His words shivered over my skin, but it wasn't only with desire. 'Need' wasn't a pretty word. It was dependent and unhealthy and a pretty good description of the way I felt about him too.

'Just kiss me, Kubicka.'

I didn't hesitate, slinging an arm around his neck and dragging him down for a panting, open-mouthed kiss.

He tumbled into my body as I wrapped myself around him. I felt more than heard the hitched grunt from deep in his throat as he took two fistfuls of my wet hair, tugging just enough to sting lightly.

My vision blurred as he ground into me, absolutely no doubt of how much he wanted me from the hard pressure and the wild sweep of his tongue into my mouth.

'Up!' he said suddenly, rising to haul me to my feet. Undressing me with rough, urgent hands, I was naked in a matter of seconds, his hands curling around my ribs. 'Why are you so fucking beautiful?' The words seemed to pain him, but they made my nipples pebble and my skin burst to life. 'Where's this tattoo?'

With a laugh bubbling in my chest, I turned to show him my right thigh, now adorned with a jagged black electrocardiogram, a heartbeat — for life, for sport. Maybe for him, because I was an idiot. But when he crouched down to feather a soft kiss over the image, it didn't feel like such a stupid thing to have ink on my body that would remind me of Colin Gallagher.

His hand slid up the back of my thigh to my waist as he stood, his other hand drifting to his pants as though the pressure was unbearable — at least, that's how I felt.

'I want to fuck you for hours, Lees,' he said, his lips brushing my cheek. 'But I can't stand it. This might be embarrassingly quick.'

I just nodded, my speech too dull to reply with words, and dragged his hand down to my bottom, lower. When his finger dipped between my legs, I didn't recognise the needy sound I made.

'Christ,' Colin groaned, swallowing loudly. His fingertip traced the swollen line from the sensitive nub to the tender lower end and I had to cling to him heavily, gasping and trying not to thrash as the sensations slammed through me. 'This is so sweet,' he mumbled through gritted teeth. 'You want me to fuck it?'

'Yes!' That word fell easily from my lips.

'All right,' he soothed. With strong hands he turned me around and marched me forward. I was too startled to question what he was doing, until I caught sight of us — of myself — in the mirror on the back of the hotel-room door. My skin was flushed, my nipples points, and Colin's hands on me were proprietary and thrilling. My footsteps stalled, but he urged me ahead, even when I stumbled.

Picking up one of my hands, he pressed it into the mirror and ran his other hand down my flank. 'Have you done it this way before?' he asked, his voice even.

I shook my head.

'Do you want to?'

This time I nodded.

'Good. Hold on.' That was all the warning I got before he shoved down his tracksuit bottoms and underwear and then he was hitching up my hips and sliding his cock between my legs. The slow penetration was exquisite, thick friction and overwhelming pressure, his heavy breaths on the back of my neck, his arm rigid around my waist, fingers splayed.

The choked sound he made was exactly how I felt when he settled in deep. My fingers on the mirror slipped, my palm sweaty. I groped for purchase when he gave a jerky thrust and I had to push back to avoid tumbling face-first into the mirror.

'That's it,' he grunted. 'You feel way too good. I'm not gonna last.'

All I could do in response was pant and gasp and prop another hand onto the mirror as he started to move in earnest.

The next time he spoke, it was into my ear, his voice a velvet whisper. 'Eyes open, Lees. Watch us.'

I hadn't even realised I'd closed them and when I blinked them open, it was to find the most devastatingly wonderful image, so much hotter than anything my brain could have conjured. I was braced heavily on the mirror, my hair wild and falling over my shoulders, hips tilted and back bowed, absorbing the force of Colin's body behind me, his cock buried deep.

My own face loomed in my vision, heavy-lidded, pleasure-drunk but loose and gratified and bright. And Colin was right behind me, slowly falling apart, his expression tight with restraint and desire. He nuzzled my neck, sending tingles shooting down my spine straight to where he was moving inside me. Then he moaned and sank his teeth into my shoulder, the rough urgency setting all my whole body on fire until I was a melting mess of nerve endings.

'I can't—' I gasped for breath. 'Ohhh, I can't take it. Too much!' There was a rising tide in my chest, consuming me.

'Yes, you can. Come on, baby.'

With one hand he delicately teased my clit and with the other, he pushed down between my shoulder blades, making my hands slide lower on the mirror. The combination set me on fire.

On a wave of relief, the flames licked through my body, eating up my skin and consuming my brain and I wasn't even sure I existed for a moment, until Colin's hands bit into my hips, his cock jerking once more powerfully inside me, sending another little swell of gratification as he finished.

His forehead fell to my shoulder as he panted and my gaze was glued to the mirror in front of us, the image of my wobbly-kneed, slowly melting naked body and his fully clothed one behind. He pried his fingers loose from my hips; the white marks faded only slowly.

When he pulled out, the trickle down my thigh made everything seem a little too real — mainly my own thoughts and feelings, an embarrassing flash of the memory of Colin holding a baby. *Do* not *go there*. He had races to win and I had my own success to build — away from cycling.

'Are you… feeling better now?' I asked, barely recognising my own breathy voice.

His gaze snapped up to mine, doubtful and a little dark. My half-hearted smile faded.

'I… um… guess not,' I mumbled, struggling to switch my brain back on to interpret the way he was studying me. He seemed… angry somehow, although I couldn't imagine why. He'd wanted to blow off steam one more time, so that's what we'd done — what I'd offered, so he couldn't even feel guilty about that. Perhaps the quick and desperate act in front of the mirror hadn't felt significant enough to be a farewell to our physical relationship, but this wasn't supposed to be 'significant'.

I blushed as he tugged up his tracksuit bottoms and tucked himself back in. There was colour in his cheeks too. Swiping my pyjamas off the floor, I turned away and slipped into them as quickly as I could. My body felt like rubber, languid and boneless.

'You need to go to sleep, Kubicka?' The amusement in his voice was a relief, but I couldn't quite remember why.

'Talk… We need… distance.'

The covers seemed to move back by themselves, and then I was tumbling into the welcoming softness.

'I don't know that talking is a good idea, sweetheart.'

I struggled against sleep so I could respond, although I didn't know how to answer.

His words stopped me anyway. 'I'll see you for the team presentation tomorrow.'

Gentle pressure on my forehead — maybe from his lips.

# Chapter 29

## Colin

I would hate it if the last time I ever had sex with Leesa was a quick go from behind against her hotel-room door, after which she fell asleep almost instantly. But I was supposed to be letting her go. I'd been thinking with my dick and now I had the unfamiliar flavour of regret on my tongue and a crowd of thoughts clamouring for my attention when I needed to be focused.

She was all business during the team presentation on Friday evening. She didn't need much more content than a quick shot of me — showing the PowerFuel logo on my shorts — but she stood with Wil and the rest of the team. The worst part was how she smiled: bright and open and with none of this churning uncertainty that had me in its grip.

The immature crush had been so much simpler than whatever this was.

I winked at her and slapped my arse and tried to ruffle her up — nothing had changed after all. I wished I'd packed a few fake insects in my bag. I'd spent the evening after that faintly embarrassing sex racking my brain for more stunts I could pull to get everything back on stable ground.

Dad would cark it if he knew how distracted I was, the day before the opening time trial of the Tour de France. Leesa would be watching too. I wasn't sure how I felt about that. Sure, she was classy and businesslike and wore pretty dresses with little flowers on them, but I remembered her in cycling kit, coated in mud.

Maybe *that* Leesa would watch me cross the line victorious and *feel* something.

I was an idiot for wanting her to when she'd tried to leave all this behind.

I was sharing a room with Derek, who was thankfully such a gasbag that he didn't notice me sinking into something like panic. I slept so poorly on Friday night before the opening stage, I had to rip off my smart watch, so I didn't have to explain my stats to Dad, although the fact that I'd taken it off would alert him anyway.

All the stupid psychology sessions I'd bluffed my way through, pretending everything was apples. I wondered what would have happened if I'd actually told the therapist everything. The only answer I got from the darkened ceiling overnight was that it was too late to wonder about that now.

She was watching me at breakfast, although she tried not to let me catch her. The thought that this was the end – the beginning of the Tour, but the end of Leesa's interest in me – wouldn't leave me alone.

Dad's final pep talk — *Keep your pants on and don't lose it on the descent!* — washed over me without sticking and I shoved on a pair of headphones in an attempt to shut out everything else while I waited for my turn on the starting ramp.

I had a love-hate relationship with Individual Time Trials – and everything else in my life right now apparently. Today's was short, only 35 km. Tomorrow, I'd have to save my strength for the end of the mammoth 195 km route, but today I could belt it out. The course was mostly flat and Derek and I had done a recce of the whole thing yesterday. The biggest danger was misjudging a sharp turn after the descent back into Strasbourg.

But it was 35 km where I couldn't afford even a second of distraction. Sometimes it was easier to slog it through five hours of low-pressure racing than minutes where every second counted.

There were cameras everywhere. They were already painting the white jersey on me. Next year I would no longer be eligible for the young rider classification. Dad would have to live with himself if I didn't cut it as a real champion. There was only one guarantee in this sport: I wouldn't always win. Dad didn't want to admit that, but I had to.

I tossed my phone from hand to hand restlessly. I would be one of the last to start, as a race favourite. The wait was like a physical pressure on my chest. The electronic beats pounding in my ears didn't help.

A clamour among the swannies caught my attention and they told me Derek had burned up the route, shooting unexpectedly to second place. There was a good chance I wouldn't beat his time. That thought twinged a little, knowing that Derek would sacrifice his own chances of success for me for the rest of the Tour.

But when he made it back to the bus, dripping with sweat from the baking sunshine and concentrated effort, I was so fucking proud of him.

'I'll be drafting you one day,' I said as I clapped him on the back. 'When I'm an old man,' I added.

'Never, then?' Derek quipped. 'Don't tell me my chances of success are reliant on you growing up,' he said with a mock groan.

I chuckled, but his words struck me. Every minute of the past hour had felt like a year of my life. I must be a wizened geezer by now. Too young for Leesa and now suddenly too old.

The helmet was slippery in my hands as I stood to make my way to the start. Time-trial helmets were smooth and heavy, hiding our faces behind a round visor and making us look like actors in a tacky sci-fi production, but if they shaved a few seconds off, the sacrifice of looking like a dork was just about worth it.

My heart thudded loudly in my chest as I accepted my bike and rolled it to the starting line, at the top of a yellow ramp, the years of my life devoted to this sport hanging off me like invisible sinkers.

Throwing my leg over the frame, I clicked in one shoe and then the next, once the assistant had a firm hold of my saddle. Head down, I stared at the road ahead of me, suddenly imagining it as my own future: empty and entirely up to me.

Empty, because Leesa wouldn't be in it.

My instincts triggered by the starter beep, I launched my bike down the ramp and into the race.

The route I'd practised – in real life and in video reconnaissance footage – over and over again, whipped by in a blur of supporters and within a few minutes, I'd left the cobbled old town of Strasbourg behind, the canal glinting in the late afternoon sunlight.

The course wasn't so short that I could let loose right from the beginning, so I settled into the rhythm that lived in my blood – pedalling, breath, metabolism all pushed in a fine balance. My awareness narrowed to the road, the air on my chin, forces of gravity and momentum. Keeping a loose grip on the time-trial handlebars, my elbows in the rests, the tucked body position was second nature after the hours – years – of practice. About 40 minutes of intense concentration in nearly 30-degree heat and I'd have completed the first stage of this year's Tour.

Without other riders around me, no drafting or the power of the peloton to propel me along, I was exposed – racing against myself. But the odd sense of having a blank slate intrigued me as I flew around a curve through fields of tall wheat, swaying in the breeze under an expansive sky. There was something to learn here, a step I'd been fumbling to take ever since Dad formally made me lead rider.

Before any of these half-formed ideas could solidify in my mind, Alan's voice crackled in my ear. '*Thirty seconds down, C.*'

Thirty seconds! It might as well have been a year. Shit, I had to get my head in the game.

The shot of panic was useful, adrenaline giving my muscles a boost as I hurtled through the next colourful little village, past the pastel-pink chateau with its red roof dotted with windows and two turrets.

'*Twenty-three seconds*' was Alan's update at the next time checkpoint. It wasn't disastrous, but the burn was making its way up my body and drips of sweat blurred my vision. My heartrate was all over the place – or my brain was. I risked a glance at my bike computer to see my power output well above what I was aiming for on this course. At least that explained the sting in my lungs.

Forcing myself to slow down took all of my concentration. My focus spun in and out and all my hours spent on this route went out the window as I reacted purely on instinct.

'*Thirty-one seconds,*' came Alan's voice once again.

I was about three-quarters through – maybe? Too little time to finish well. Now it was about mitigating the damage. There was a point somewhere up ahead where I could go all out. I'd tested myself against this route. But I couldn't quite remember where.

My bike gave a sudden jerk and I wrenched on the handlebars, breaking position for a split second while I regained my balance, veering to one side. The front wheel must have found a stone. It rattled me, but when I shook the sweat from my eyes and resumed my bent posture over the bike, the relief that I wasn't sprawled on the road, covered in cuts and grazes, gave me a much-needed moment of clarity.

'*Twenty-eight seconds, C. Bring her home. Nice and steady.*'

*Fuck*. Gritting my teeth, I pushed harder. So much for a blank beginning, for writing my own future. I'd never be the cool leader Dad wanted. Frustration rising in my blood along with the lactate, I knew I was going too hard even without looking at my power monitor. Alan said something, but I tuned him out.

I hit the final descent hard, belatedly remembering the sharp turn just before the finish. I made it, but barely, unclipping one foot in a panic when the bike tipped. I got away with a quick tap on the asphalt to steady myself and then I was going again, but I'd hear about that stupidity from Dad later, I was certain.

Hurtling over the line, there were white sparks at the edge of my vision, my stomach heaved and I seemed to have forgotten where the brakes were, ploughing into an unfortunate group of photographers and nearly going over my own handlebars.

Then I was staring at the cobblestones in close-up, as strung out as ever. I didn't even want to know what time I'd managed. I wanted to just ride off into the sunset – for once, not with Leesa, since I didn't want to face her just now. I didn't want to face anyone.

Especially not Dad, but of course it was Dad's face that filled my vision first.

'What was that, son?'

Even the gentle way he called me 'son' didn't soften the hard lump in my chest. I allowed him to haul me into a sitting position and accepted the drink bottle he handed me, guzzling the fluid without questioning what it was.

'The first half was bloody awful, but then someone lit a fire under you and you're lucky you didn't end up toast!'

'Not toasted yet,' I muttered.

'You gave me a heart attack, boy! Keep it steady next time, 'kay? Your body's there, but your head? That exploded today.'

I didn't need him to tell me that. 'Is Derek still on the podium?'

Dad shook his head.

'Fuck!' The word failed to make me feel better.

'Jansen and Hellier both had a cracking day,' Dad explained gently. 'He'll get fifth or sixth. A great result for the youngster.'

I nodded. It would have to be the day's small consolation.

'Don't you want to know how you did?'

'Not really,' I mumbled in reply.

Dad looked at me doubtfully. 'You finished 18 seconds down.'

That I'd made up 13 seconds after the final time check was a surprise that rippled under my skin, but it didn't change the fact that I'd busted my way through the first stage with my balls instead of my head.

'The times were close, so that unfortunately puts you in fifteenth, but the time itself you'll get back. You can definitely get it back. We've got our strategy and the team around you. Tomorrow, the real fight starts.'

The fight to keep Colin Gallagher from screwing up his big chance.

One of the swannies helped Dad haul me to my feet. My blood was fizzing and I could already taste the adrenaline crash that awaited me. It was the same artificial cherry flavour as the PowerFuel recovery supplement the swannie pressed into my hand.

After glancing at the logo of the nutrition company, I looked up wildly, realising Leesa was probably somewhere nearby and for the first time hoping her eyes *weren't* on me.

But it was even worse than that. When I finally found her standing with the support staff, she had her phone raised and appeared to be filming me. And I, Colin Valerio Gallagher, followed my stupid, first impulse and raised my middle finger.

# Chapter 30

**Leesa**

I don't know what I'd expected. Colin was never going to rush straight to my side after hurtling over the finish line. A sweaty, desperate post-race kiss probably wasn't as romantic as Lori and Seb had made it look last year anyway.

Besides, I didn't want him to kiss me in full view of a thousand spectators and at least 50 cameras. But a big part of me still wished he'd done it. So much for whatever I'd had going on with Colin Gallagher. It seemed he was back to ruining my work, if that extended middle finger was anything to go by.

Colin would make headlines today, although not for ideal reasons. He'd ridden a dumpster fire of a time trial. How often had the women's trainer drilled into us that a time trial was about consistency and carefully managing our limits? Colin had been all over the place and then worked himself into the ground at the end, although I bet the fans would love him for it. The fact that he'd come off his bike in vaguely amusing circumstances after the finish only added to the viral potential of his performance.

If he wasn't going to come and give me a cheeky kiss — or even a cheeky grin — then I'd decided I might as well get some footage out of it, lining up the shot, trying not to notice the trickle of sweat down his throat as he guzzled from a drink bottle. With his hair dripping and mussed, his chest still heaving, every contour of lean muscle on display under his time-trial skinsuit, he was a sponsor's dream — a sexy dream.

When he'd accepted a recovery gel and lifted it to his mouth,

I could almost believe we'd planned the moment with PowerFuel in mind, even though I was all too aware of the fact that I hadn't spoken to him since Thursday night, when I'd passed out almost immediately after he'd fucked me against the mirror.

I was trying not to overthink that encounter, although it grew more difficult the longer he ignored me.

At least flipping me the bird was a useful reminder that although he might have lusted after me for years, he wouldn't let anyone pin him down. After all the unbearable winking and being charming, I had assumed we were back to our barbed banter, but whatever that was in his expression, it wasn't good.

As he sauntered in my direction, I stopped the video and lowered my phone warily.

'Not exactly a performance your client will be happy with,' he grumbled.

'There's a… narrative in there somewhere,' I replied, my forehead tight as I studied his reaction. 'When I edit out your eloquent hand gesture.'

He didn't laugh. 'A narrative. I suppose that's what I am to you.'

The disappointment in his tone punched me in the stomach. 'But today was… phenomenal. The second half anyway.'

There was a hint of the open smile I realised with a pang that I missed. 'Half a phenomenal performance. Good luck making your narrative. It's what you're here for and you're so fucking talented you'll make me look good no matter what you really think.'

My skin tingled with unease as I tried and failed to interpret his meaning. Whatever he felt he didn't want me to see and that hurt too, even though I should have known better.

'At least you know how good I am in bed.'

I was almost happy to see the cocky smile back, except I wasn't sure about the reminder that this thing between us had always been casual. This was *Colin Gallagher*. He hadn't even managed to be serious about the opening stage of the Tour de France.

'I'm glad that comforts you while you're busting your balls in the saddle.'

That made him laugh and he swiped away a drip of sweat. 'A shame I can't have you to make me feel better at the end of the day.'

I couldn't tell if he was teasing me. His tone suggested so, but I hated to think he was so flippant about everything we'd shared.

He lifted a hand to my head and I was alarmed by how much I wanted the curl of his fingers around my nape, fisting in my hair. But the flash of a camera made me flinch and I came back to myself like crashing to the pavement. He couldn't kiss me — not in public.

When I jerked away, there was a spark of something in his eyes, but I couldn't have said what it meant. And then he was gone, more quickly than I would have thought him capable of after half a phenomenal performance.

The peloton and its entourage of brightly coloured buses, team cars, motorbikes, ambulances and the caravane publicitaire, the bizarre parade floats with saucisson and supermarket brands tossing out samples, made its way across the top of the French hexagon over the first week of the Tour.

In contrast to the smiling fans wearing polka-dot T-shirts or costumes and waving cardboard signs, amused by the bizarre vehicles shaped like fruit and vegetables or cheese or the laughing cow, the mood in the team bus was tense. Like that rebellious kid in class at junior high, Colin did just enough over the first week to stay within striking distance of the top ten without actually making it there.

I posted clips and photos from the training camp, each one gaining more traction than the last, but my content from the Tour itself was lacklustre and it showed in the engagement stats. Perhaps it simply wasn't possible to top the video I'd cut together of Colin shaving his moustache, but I suspected it was because he wasn't oozing his easy charm as he usually did. The only clip from the Tour that had made any impact was a three-second flash of him lounging in an ice bath and giving the camera a wink.

Sunday was a hilly stage through Brittany, ending on the outskirts of the mediaeval town of Guérande. With our enormous team buses parked around the ancient city wall, we kind of ruined the aesthetic of the quaint little place with bunting strung across the top of the narrow lanes and pastel shopfronts like the cover of a book.

We'd even lucked out with one of the only 15 sunny days in Brittany every year. Actually, I wasn't sure of that statistic. It did rain a lot here, but 15 days might be as spurious as the pseudo-science factoid that people are within three feet of a spider at all times. At least I hoped that was spurious.

The sun was wreaking havoc with the riders, though, the team car busy distributing more bottles to the swannies placed along the route with their musettes, the string bags the riders grabbed to refuel without stopping.

Because I noticed every little damn thing about Colin, I knew he had peeling sunburn on the back of his neck and if he stripped off, I'd see the outline of his skinsuit as though he were still wearing it, just with a pale-skinned, naked man printed on it, which would incidentally be the best birthday present in the entire world for Colin Gallagher.

Except, I wouldn't be around when he turned 26.

Hilly stages were flat enough that even the riders who weren't climbing specialists had a chance at the win but mountainous enough that a bunch sprint at the end was unlikely. These types of stages used to haunt me with their uncertainty. Instinct, quick reactions and risk-taking were often rewarded and none of those had ever been my strong point.

'God, I love a hilly stage.'

Of course Lori did. I'd hitched a lift into Guérande from our hotel with her and Seb and then we'd made our way to the team bus to watch the coverage. After 20 minutes in the car with Lori and her boyfriend, the day before they had to separate for Lori to prepare for the Tour de France Femmes, I felt like a third wheel and was trying to ignore the casual affection that seemed so easy between them — and Lori's collection of nicknames for him, from 'Frankie' to 'Loonie' to 'baby', which I suspected she didn't realise she was saying.

Maybe I was trying to forget how Colin had called me 'baby'. I wasn't sure I liked it. I didn't think I'd ever let anyone else call me that. But Colin...

That man was the exception to every rule.

'I bet you that Colin can't keep it in.'

I jerked my head up from where I'd been scrolling absently through the PowerFuel feed on my phone to find that Lori had been talking to me. She was sitting one row in front of me in the swivelling seats. The TV coverage was on a screen behind the driver's seat, the riders rolling out of the city at a leisurely pace in a neutralised start.

The helicopter footage sent visceral memories over my skin: handlebar tape under my palms; Lori behind me, getting in the zone while Bonnie and I enjoyed the calm before the storm. Later in the race, we'd give it everything to lend Lori extra speed while she bided her time for an attack.

That was Colin's job today and I finally realised what Lori had meant with 'can't keep it in'. Of course she hadn't meant anything to do with his sex life. She probably preferred to imagine he didn't have one, which must have taken an enormous effort, given his boundless swagger.

'I think the strategy for today is to stay in the peloton, mark the other contenders,' I replied. *Don't do anything stupid*, had been the DS's words. 'Except I'm not supposed to tell anyone that. I signed an NDA,' I continued ruefully.

'Don't worry. I'm safe,' Lori said with an amused smile. 'I bet between Colin and me and that last crash, you were happy to see the back of Harper-Stacked.'

I'd always assumed Lori was the embodiment of the team: a winner, happy to sacrifice everything. But in that self-deprecating comment, I understood she'd simply been dealing with the pressure her way.

'I was pretty down after the crash,' I began, 'but it still hurt to leave. You're lucky you still have the team. I didn't get on a bike at all for a while, I was so upset.' Until Colin had forced me back on and reminded me there was more to the sport than winning – an unexpectedly mature lesson.

To my surprise, Lori nodded grimly. 'That's relatable. I'm glad we didn't entirely kill your love of the sport, especially last year when I was a jerk.' Her outburst at the Paris-Roubaix came to mind, when she'd dislocated her shoulder and taken out her frustration on her bike — and the rest of the team.

'I know you had rotten luck last year. I was there. And it was kind of nice to see you had a human side.'

She snorted in amusement. 'I had to learn I wasn't infallible. Sometimes I think Colin's the other side of the coin,' she mused.

'How?'

'He puts so much pressure on himself for others and he doesn't even realise that's what makes him a leader. I'm not painting him as a saint — not by a long shot. But he'd do anything for those guys — for Dad, even though I know their relationship isn't the best. He's got his fucking heart on his sleeve.'

I wrinkled my nose. 'If his heart is kind of shaped like his dick, then maybe.'

She laughed, clapping me on the shoulder. 'He thinks he's such a big guy. But what he says and what he does are two different things. I thought you might have worked that out.'

I was too struck by her statement to respond and she continued without waiting for me to find my words.

'He plays the impulsive delinquent, but Colin grew up years ago. He just hasn't noticed yet — hasn't accepted it.'

I had to remind myself firmly she wasn't talking about his feelings — his attitude to relationships. All this stuff was getting mixed up in my mind, as though the next two weeks would make all the difference to his future — and mine.

'If he's all grown up, then he needs to stick to the strategy today,' I said lightly, hoping to change the subject. 'He needs a quiet ride in the peloton, saving his strength for the mountains.'

So, of course the impulsive delinquent was in the first breakaway, following Nellie when he jumped onto the wheel of an attacking rider from another team. We all held our breath as the gap between the breakaway and the peloton widened to five seconds, then ten, then twenty.

The rest of the contenders for the general classification, the overall win, remained safely in the peloton, assuming the superior power of the large group of cyclists would reel in the breakaway later in the day. It was the most likely outcome.

'Farking hell, boy! He'll be the bloomin' death of me! What does he think he's doing?' I heard Tony before I saw him, coming up the steps into the bus, his eyes on the TV screen.

I knew Tony was never allowed on team radio and I now had first-hand experience of why. I studied Tony as he sat glued to the footage I could barely make myself watch, remembering all of Colin's comments, how he'd make a joke rather than admit he was afraid of disappointing his dad.

Tears were gathering behind my eyes and I did not like this at all. Was he just acting out, or had he considered this move, even though it was not the strategy for the day?

'I told you!' Lori said, pointing wildly at the screen. 'Baby brother can't keep it in.'

My anxiety levels only built as the stage wore on and the breakaway remained out in front. Tony's grumbling had quieted as though he'd at least accepted that this would be good publicity, even if Colin was wrecked tomorrow. I should have been posting more content, but I couldn't bring myself to do it and the followers would be more interested in clips of the race right now anyway.

His place in the breakaway meant a lot of coverage of the sponsors on the jersey — and a body that felt far too familiar to me. Hunched over the bike, the cords of muscle in his calves and forearms standing out in high contrast, he was like music in motion, pushing it up the climbs and sweeping down the descents with precision.

I heard over the radio when he managed to accept a musette from one of the swannies along the route, but in the breakaway there was never much time to sit back and rest, so he guzzled calories whenever he could, his body slowly depleting its reserves as he kept pumping through the long kilometres.

With 30 km to go, the peloton started picking up speed, the other teams eager to catch the tiring breakaway. Nellie dropped back, exhausted after hours of lending his slipstream to Colin. Two of the other riders couldn't take the speed either, leaving only three in the breakaway and forcing Colin to take his turn at the front.

The chances weren't good, but no matter how many times I told myself that, my heart leaped and I imagined him doing it, finishing on the podium and proving everyone wrong.

The gap between the peloton and the breakaway ticked downwards along with the kilometres. Two minutes, then 80 seconds, 40, 20. The three riders out front were working hard, shooting along the country roads at 30 miles per hour. Colin's heart rate was sky-high, setting off all the monitoring equipment.

The race footage was astonishing as the riders approached Guérande, the twisting, curving peloton moving across the haphazard grid of coastal ponds where sea salt crystallised to be harvested, the water a mirror for the afternoon sky and the low rays of the sun.

'Come on,' I muttered through gritted teeth, still horrified but now unable to look away, annoyed when the footage switched back to the peloton.

The salt flats disappeared, replaced by red-roofed houses on the outskirts of the town. After navigating a tight turn, the breakaway powered into the curve along the mediaeval city wall, followed by the peloton, mere seconds behind them.

I toppled out of the bus behind Lori and Seb and we all rushed for the finish line. Seb had the footage running on his phone and I stumbled on the cobblestones, my gaze locked on the small screen. He held out an arm for me and I took it without even thanking him.

I couldn't breathe. The image was striking: Colin and the other two in the foreground with the platoon of riders storming at them in the background. My fingernails digging into my palms, I was wound up so tight, I wondered when I would break. The commentator's voice grew impassioned as the gap persisted. Any second now—

My phone rang.

The annoying buzz drew my frustrated gaze and I would have silenced it and ignored it, except I caught sight of the name 'Bill Weekes' and then I froze. When the big boss called, one didn't refuse it.

Letting go of Seb, I connected the call. My gaze strayed back to the view of the race, a shot from above showing three vulnerable figures pedalling for their lives, the commentator's voice tinny over the small speaker.

'Hi there, Bill. What can I do for you?'

'Leesa! How're you doing? Is now a good time?'

I opened my mouth to say no, it really wasn't, but he continued as though the question had been rhetorical.

'I wanted to catch you personally before I send this email.'

Those were some of the only words capable of slicing through my distracted haze. The sounds of the admin and support staff milling around the finish line dimmed to background noise. 'An email?'

'Yes, in light of the recent stats on the PowerFuel account – and a rather glowing endorsement I received—'

*Can they hang on for the last 300 m? A heroic effort from the breakaway today. Nearly 150 km alone, draining all of their reserves. To be caught on the finish line? It would be heartbreaking. But it hasn't happened yet. They're still out front!*

The commentator's tone had reached fever pitch. Lori grabbed my arm and tugged me with her as she found a spot with a view of the finish line and there they were, Colin and the other two, small specks in the distance. Just a few more yards—

Bill's voice was still in my ear. 'I'll be sending you a new two-year contract. I'm pleased to offer you the second pay grade already, in recognition of everything you've done on this project.'

Contract! A pay rise. I struggled to register everything Bill was saying. There was a sense of relief there, vindication, but also—

Colin was 50 feet from the finish line when it happened. One moment he was up out of his saddle, baring his teeth and throwing everything into a sprint, and the next the peloton swarmed and I lost him from view.

Seb was holding his phone limply, the TV commentary still running.

'*No! At the very last second! That must feel like being run over by a freight train! The peloton absolutely flattened Gallagher, Arnim and Keller. Jonah swallowed by the whale and just as epic. That is bitter! So very bitter. It looks like Archambault might have been the first over the line, followed by De Jong, but it's going to take a minute to disentangle that finish. What does this mean for Gallagher's GC chances? What do you think? Fifth or sixth today? But with no time advantage over the peloton and he's gotta be running close to zero right now. We love to see these battles, but he's run himself dry before we've even reached the mountain stages.*'

I fumbled for something to hold onto and found the cool metal of a barrier with some sponsor's name blazoned on it.

'Leesa?' Bill prompted, his voice suddenly sounding an ocean away.

'Um, that's wonderful news.' My voice was all breath and I hoped he interpreted that as excitement.

I was supposed to be excited. I could finally tell my parents I had a real job – and start properly paying off my degrees. I could get a lease on my own place, invite friends around – I could *have* friends who weren't teammates or colleagues. I could have a relationship that wasn't disrupted by distance or training or psychology.

A relationship that wasn't with Colin Gallagher.

I scanned the chaos at the finish line, men and bikes scattered, groaning and cheers, hugs and confusion. I couldn't find Colin and Bill kept talking in my ear.

'I'm glad to hear you'll be accepting. Now, I'm pushed for time, but I wanted to make sure I spoke to you in person rather than a big fat contract just showing up in your inbox. Take your time to read and then sign on the dotted line – I mean, the online document signing procedure – and send it back when you're ready. I'll let you get back to it. Keep up the good work!'

The 'good work' of tearing myself in two because of one rider who meant too much to me. The person who made me question what I wanted, even though he had no right. This was a moment

I'd waited months for, but my mind was in so many places at once, I was struggling to care.

I somehow managed to respond to Bill as I ended the call. 'Uh, thanks. Bye.'

The commentator's words had merged into a buzz as I let the phone fall from my ear. I saw Tony first, grabbing a swannie and gesturing wildly towards a light pole off to one side. At the base of the pole, my gaze found him.

Colin was slumped, half-sprawled on a traffic island, legs akimbo, one gloved hand lying limp between his thighs. His jersey was unzipped to his belly button to reveal the strap of the heartrate monitor – and the dramatic hollow of his diaphragm as his breath heaved. His skin was shiny with sweat, the sun glinting off every sharp furrow.

But the most arresting sight was his face: eyes closed, jaw clamped, the dusty outline on his cheeks from where his sunglasses had sat. It was a look of defeat that I felt in my lungs – in my gut, my *heart*.

Two swannies were with him now, getting recovery fluids into him as he only half-heartedly participated. Draping his arms over their shoulders, the assistants hauled him to his feet, his wobbly legs unsteady. He looked like 207 km – that was 130 miles.

But the swannies were dragging him into the media area, where a crowd of cameras was waiting for him to talk about how he lost the stage. My stomach lurched and I had to press my knuckles to my mouth to suppress the nausea – and the tears.

God, I hated this. *What have you done, Colin?*

I wasn't only talking about the stage.

# Chapter 31

## Colin

I wasn't sure what I regretted most and who I wanted to see least: Dad, the guys or Leesa. No, actually I still wanted to see Leesa, even though it might feel like bleeding. She'd want answers and I didn't have any.

Why did I join the breakaway? *I was feelin' trigger-happy and thinking about that dress of yours with the split up one leg.*

Why did I flip her off in Strasbourg and give her a wink from the ice bath instead of just smiling like a normal person? *Because I'm annoyed you're leaving me and I'm annoyed that I'm annoyed.*

Was I okay? *No idea. Probably not.*

I shoved in a pair of earbuds and zoned out while Chris, one of the longest-serving swannies and an old friend of my dad's, gave my tortured legs a thorough massage. I felt like a diva to be ignoring him, but he must have seen it all before, because he didn't look at my face, just calmly rubbed at my seizing muscles.

I was nobody's hero today.

Whenever my eyes opened a crack, I saw my phone, where it sat on the bedside table, and then I'd start wondering if she'd texted me. Eventually, I couldn't stand it and snatched the device up, only to find that I had no messages. Zero.

I shouldn't have been surprised. Dad would chew me out in person and nobody else was interested in the day I'd had. Even the combativity award for the most attacking rider of the day had gone to one of the other guys in the breakaway.

Since I was messed up anyway, nothing stopped me from

punching out a provoking message: *How's your narrative?*

I leaned my head back against the wall with a thunk and tried to tell myself I wasn't waiting for her reply.

'What's upset you more? The Tour? Or the girl?'

Tempted to pretend I hadn't heard Chris, I eventually sighed and popped out my earbuds. I wanted to talk about Leesa. I *always* wanted to talk about her.

'Don't tell Dad,' I began, which made Chris chuckle.

'The girl, right? She's finally given you the time of day?'

'Just barely,' I said with unexpected heat in my chest. 'It's more than I deserve.'

'I'd say, after everything you did to her over the years.'

And over the past month…

There was a knock at the door, which was disappointing, just when I'd been warming up to the idea of letting my thoughts about Leesa gush out. I assumed it was Dad, which sent another pang of guilt squeezing in my gut.

'Are you decent?'

My sister. Huh.

I checked the tiny towel keeping the important bits covered. 'Mostly. Come on in.'

She burst into the room as she always did, as though a herd of stallions were chasing her. 'Look, bro-nut, I've got to go, but get your shit together, for fuck's sake!'

Chris backed away, hands raised. 'I'd rather not be in the crossfire.'

'Get out while you still can,' I drawled, rolling my eyes at him.

'If you don't want a lecture, then start behaving like a functional adult.' Her voice was even and there was even a little catch that reminded me of how Mum told me off — as though it pained her too.

'I'm trying,' I admitted. 'I'm not good under pressure.'

She crossed her arms and looked at the ceiling. 'Nobody's good with pressure — well, except me. I love it. But that's not what I meant. I'm talking about Leesa.'

'What about Leesa?' I grumbled. 'You can't exactly get up on your high horse about a relationship after what you put Seb through last year.'

'I did not *put him through* anything. You, on the other hand…'

She was still annoyed with me for the pranks I pulled on her boyfriend when he was new on the team. I'd felt the vibes between her and Seb right from the beginning and it was my way of testing his mettle, if he was going to go a round with my sister, but I understood she hadn't been happy about my interference – and I had gone too far on occasion.

'I just know how unsettling it is to… wonder if someone really likes you.' She looked faintly embarrassed. 'Just reel her in or let her go and then get on with the fucking Tour. I can't stand it.'

'Because the Tour de France is all about putting my sister out of her misery.'

'*You're* a misery.'

'And I'm pretty sure Leesa shares your opinion, so you can let the subject drop. The only *reeling* going on here will be her social-media clips of me being some kind of tragic figure in this race with a sponsor logo shining out of my fucking arse.'

At least that made her fall silent for long enough to take a breath. 'It's worse than I thought,' she commented eventually.

I laughed. 'You hadn't worked that out yet? I'm a disaster this year and she's going to witness it all and then go home to her new life congratulating herself on getting the hell out of cycling – and away from me.'

Lori considered her words for a long time – another surprise as my big sister was usually an impulsive force of nature. 'I think I know Leesa a little better than you do—'

I snorted before she'd even finished her sentence. 'I doubt it. I've been taking note of every little thing she does every time the teams were together for the past six years. I know that she hates peanut butter and likes those classical art memes. She can't blow-dry her hair because of the curls, she wishes she spoke Polish better and I'm pretty sure I'm the only person in the world who's seen her tattoo all healed up.'

God, it felt good to say that stuff.

Lori's eyes were wide. 'Farking hell, Colin. What happened to you?'

'Nothing,' I insisted lightly. 'Nothing new, at any rate. I met her on the 29th of November five-and-a-half years ago. The only thing that's changed is I now know touching her feels even better than I imagined, which is saying something.'

'All right, you can shut up now. This is… *a lot* worse than I thought.'

'You're getting the idea,' I said with a tight smile. 'She's going back home after the Tour. Last time I said goodbye to her I ended up breaking her wrist.' The sarcasm hadn't quite left me yet.

'Maybe…' Lori's brow knit. 'What if…?'

I sighed. 'You think I haven't run these scenarios? The one certainty is that she *hasn't* been crushing on me all this time, so that's that.'

She straightened her shoulders. 'Come on. You're a Gallagher. It's not over 'til you see the finish line and some other guy's crossed it.'

That metaphor made me grind my teeth. Would there be some other guy in Leesa's future? Someone else who could get her out of her own head during sex? That might have been my biggest win where she was concerned, that and maybe getting her back on the bike. I'd wasted far too much time making her life difficult because I was allergic to my own feelings.

Another knock at the door startled us both and Lori bounded to open it before I'd even had time to triple-check my loin-towel. Normal people probably didn't have these discussions almost naked, but then normal people didn't cycle over 3,000 km in three weeks, with all the accompanying Vaseline and discomfort.

I gave myself a quick rearrange and then a choked cough revealed the full extent of my indignity.

'G'day, Lees,' I drawled. 'You here to chew me out too? Doesn't a guy get a break?'

'No, I just wanted to check on you, and…'

Forgetting my burning cheeks for a moment, my gaze snapped up to find her expression wary. 'What is it?'

'It's nothing… not to do with you, but I got some good news today.' Her face wasn't screaming good news, but I had to pay attention to her words and not her gorgeous features.

'You gonna tell me what?' I hoped it was the fulfilment of everything she'd ever wanted — as long as that included me. It didn't matter so much that the stage had gone wrong today, that I'd tried to be a hero and ended up a failure.

'I've got to go,' Lori said apologetically, wrapping her arms around me for a quick squeeze that I appreciated more than I'd ever tell her. Waving as she backed out through the door, she closed it behind her with a snick.

Leesa came closer and I imagined slipping my arms around her waist, resting my head against her sternum while her fingers slid into my hair.

But what she said threw a bucket of cold water over me. 'I got the job,' she blurted out. 'The big boss called me and now it's all official. I have the contract in my inbox. For two years, at a higher pay grade than I expected. I finally have a job.'

It was difficult to keep my smile pasted on my face as my stomach sank. This felt an awful lot like that finish line, the moment I had to buck up and accept that this wasn't going to be my race — just when I was starting to realise how much I wanted to win.

'That's… You know you deserve it, Magda.'

She flicked a dry gaze at me and then gave me a nudge with her elbow, just a gentle blow to my side that still caught me in the chest. 'It's such a relief, to have an offer after…'

'After *me*?' I shouldn't have blurted that out, but there it was.

Colour rose in her cheeks. 'That wasn't what I was thinking, but I suppose so. I mean, this project is what got me the job. It's worked out so much better than I expected.'

For one of us. My stomach was churning worse than it had at the finish line, full of acid and disappointment. 'So, you're just… that's it.'

Her brow knit as though I'd been speaking another language, rather than just choking on half-sentences. 'There's still the rest of the Tour,' she said warily.

'The rest of the fucking Tour,' I muttered, the yawning emptiness opening before me again.

'I thought you might be happy for me.'

Usually I liked her tart tone, but today I was scraped raw, my organs on the outside, and I couldn't take it. 'Happy? That you're leaving me? Casually moving on before you've even left the country? Before I've finished this bloody race!'

'Colin…'

'Don't "Colin" me like I'm your little brother.'

'Then stop acting like one!'

'I have *not* been acting like your brother.'

'Oh, come on, Colin. You're going to make this about sex?'

'Of course it's not about sex. It's about how you're in my head and nothing I do seems to get you out!'

The way she flinched, I might as well have punched her – and guilt spiked through me as though I had. She hadn't done anything wrong and I didn't want her to think she had. It was me who had raced ahead, got attached when there was no way forward for us. I felt 19 years old again, no hope of the woman with the gorgeous smile ever looking at me as anything other than a cheeky kid.

'Are you blaming me for your performance? I never wanted this! I wish you could have stayed that immature *dickhead* to me instead of this…' She obviously couldn't find any other words. Because I *was* an immature dickhead.

I wiped a hand over my eyes. Even the base of my palm hurt after the day on the road. Now my chest was squeezing too and I had to find enough pride to let her go with dignity. In my head, I'd known she'd never truly be mine, but my heart was stubborn and contrary.

I raced with my heart. Maybe that's why nothing was working.

'I know I never had any real chance with you, but cut me a bit of slack for taking this badly. I didn't want to say goodbye to you the first time and I did something stupid enough to physically hurt you, but the second time? It's gonna kill me, Lees. Forgive me for not being fucking happy!'

The room was so quiet I heard the air whistling into her lungs on a choppy gasp. 'You can't... put this on me. I'm trying to work out my life and I can't—'

Christ, her eyes were shining with tears.

'I know you can't,' I tried to reassure her. 'I'm not asking you to—'

'I don't want to be responsible for your races,' she choked out, swiping at her cheeks as a few tears fell. I was desperate to touch her, but I didn't trust myself. 'It's an impossible choice. I want you to do well. You deserve it—'

'Nah,' I cut her off with a shake of my head. 'Don't make excuses for me. Go and... take over the marketing world. You don't owe this dickhead anything.'

'*Colin—*'

If she said another word, I was going to fall to pieces right in front of her – wearing nothing but the tiniest towel known to man.

'Congratulations,' I said with as much earnestness as I'd ever pretended. 'I hope you celebrate your good news. I need to get some rest.' Not that it would help much. I was going to be dead on the bike tomorrow after my stupidity today.

*Racing with my heart.* What an idiot.

Her gaze remained on me for long enough that my skin prickled. 'I am going to miss you.'

Bloody hell. 'Get out o' here, sweetheart.'

Then she delivered the body blow. 'I still think you can do it.'

'That makes one of us,' I mumbled.

When she opened the door to walk away from me, she startled and I noticed with a groan that Dad was standing there, his fist raised to knock.

'What is this, a revolving door of disapproval? Can I at least get dressed or do I have to have my pride flayed again in the nuddy?'

But as Leesa disappeared down the corridor, not even looking back to find me staring forlornly after her, I was so numb I was pretty well prepared for the chewing out Dad was sure to give me. I could hold the lecture all by myself: I was supposed to be a leader; these juvenile shenanigans for attention were all right when I *was* juvenile, but now I had to suck it up and take his orders. I shouldn't forget the classic: *This is the biggest race of your career, boy.* I could already hear it in Dad's crackly voice.

Waiting for him to start with the castigation, all I could think about was that I didn't have a whole lot to race for now.

# 29 November, six years ago

## Colin

I wasn't in St Kilda any more.

There were certain similarities: the coarse sand, palm trees, skyscrapers in the distance and the sounds of an amusement park nearby. But this wasn't home. Everyone around me was speaking Spanish and they were all strangers — even the blokes strolling ahead of me, laughing and joking.

My new teammates. The guys who only knew me as the manager's son. All older, tougher — you could see it in their stringy muscles and weathered faces. I could see their scepticism too: I was a kid, just 19, promoted too early from the youth development squad.

Maybe they were right, but Dad had warned me to show no fear.

Far from the 40 degrees of a sweltering Melbourne, Malaga basked in a mild 13. Perfect cycling weather for a winter training camp, but honestly a bit cold for a walk on the beach. I should never have taken my shoes off.

A wolf whistle from one of the guys drew my attention away from the wide Mediterranean.

'Nice one, Gallagher!'

Although I glanced up expectantly, no one had been talking to me. Lars Fiske, a Swedish rider who'd been one of Dad's early signings, was grinning at my sister, who was tossing a ball from hand to hand by a volleyball net stuck haphazardly in the sand. She raised her middle finger in reply.

Some of the guys joined in with the volleyball game, while the others sprawled on the sand, chatting about the off-season – family, friends in common. I wavered in indecision, my feet freezing, as neither group invited me to join them.

*Show no fear.*

'Hey, you new?'

I whirled around and *whump*!

Wow.

I couldn't stop blinking as my eyes worked overtime: soft blue eyes; curved lips that looked as though an artist had painted them; a doubtful smile, full of good humour; a riot of curls glowing with the sunset – and a little dent in her chin.

She was looking at me expectantly. Oh, right, she'd said something. I was supposed to say something back. Except every single word had fallen out of my head apart from one: *beautiful*.

'What?' she prompted.

Fuck, I'd said that aloud. Clearing my throat with a choked cough, I gestured wildly out to sea. 'Evening,' I added. 'Beautiful evening. For fooling around on the beach—'

Her eyes widened.

'Fooling around with a volleyball and a bunch of mates.'

'Sure is,' she said in a soft American accent, her smile crinkling.

She was laughing at me, but I didn't care. It was still a smile. I claimed it, matched it, grinning at her while the stars blinked on one by one in the sky behind her and I fell a bit in love in an instant.

Her head tipped towards me and I leaned closer, drawn helplessly. 'It's just…' She gave a little shrug and I held my breath, waiting to hear what she'd say. 'You're standing on my sweater.'

# Chapter 32

**Leesa**

All I managed to do after stumbling out of his room was to hunch under the shower for 40 minutes and then collapse into bed without eating dinner. I didn't keep track of how much of that time I was leaking tears. I'd cried before — over much more meaningful things than some guy who'd made me feel special in bed. I'd fractured four ribs in a crash once. That had hurt more — a bit more, anyway.

I wanted to go home — back to the States, back to my parents' place. Anywhere but here, seeing Colin everywhere I looked. My head was such a mess I was very glad I wasn't the one lining up for a stage of the Tour de France and I felt wobbly every time I thought of him getting out on the road.

But I was also so *mad* at him I was worried it would start to show in my work. How dare he suggest his feelings for me went beyond sex and then calmly ask me to leave the room! Talk about some weird back-handed compliment. He was a silver-tongued, juvenile heartbreaker.

And he was going to break *my* heart.

Lori saw it in me when she said goodbye the next morning — I was certain. But she didn't say anything, she just wrapped me in a hug and told me Colin was an idiot. Maybe he was, but I kind of wanted him to be *my* idiot.

There was a passionate part of me that wanted to hang over the barriers and holler for him, wear a talisman for luck — get another tattoo. God, if he knew about that, he'd grow an even bigger head. But I'd lived ten years of sacrifice and failure in my own career. My brain pulled me up and told me I'd hate myself when I was 30-whatever with nothing to show for myself but an unhealthy obsession with Colin Gallagher – who might well have passed me over by then, no matter what he'd not quite said last night.

I'd noticed the major glaring omission from our discussion: any hint of a future relationship. He'd been all selfish and needy about his feelings, but he'd put me in an impossible position. It would be so much easier if I could convince myself he was a jerk who'd led me on.

I avoided him – or he avoided me – for the rest day on Monday. It was bad enough I had to look at his face – with and without the moustache – all day every day for my job. I wasn't ready to see him in real life after whatever we'd tried to say to each other in his room. Even on the morning of the next stage, an epic day in the mountains, I went down to breakfast late so I wouldn't have to see him.

I must have looked as bad as I felt when I finally emerged from the hotel with my suitcase, because Wil steered me away from the bus to a team car driven by Chris, one of the swannies.

'Do you want to talk about it?' she asked out of the side of her mouth after we'd taken our seats in the back.

'There's nothing to talk about,' I mumbled, hiding behind my work phone – legitimately, honest. I'd scheduled the next PowerFuel video to go out in the early engagement window and I had to double-check everything had worked as planned. It wouldn't be the first time a post got swallowed up by Mark Zuckerberg's pet shark.

But the video was there, Colin's big, gorgeous face filling the little screen – and every last one of my obsessive thoughts. I knew how his throat bobbed when he spoke lazily in his deep voice, how his wry smile covered up the times he was secretly being earnest.

I could say his words in the video along with him, hear them in his slow voice: *'You want some motivational crap, right?'* I didn't need to watch it again, but something made me do it anyway. Masochism probably.

I knew what came next. I'd asked him what kept him going when it hurt and he'd answered: '*Stubbornness. Pride.*'

Morgan's suggestion of a close-up camera had been ingenious and I had two angles of his face, a permanent record of the few minutes before he changed the way I thought about myself. I should never have given him that power.

'Is it going to be a problem? For you at work?' Wil asked.

'I don't know,' I answered with a grimace. I thought of my shiny new contract and the fact that Bill Weekes might find out that I'd slept with the talent. I hadn't even signed it yet and Colin had tarnished even that achievement, the inspirational bastard.

He'd cut me in two and I didn't know how to put myself back together. I almost wished he'd been a bad influence and asked me to stay. At least then I could have thrown away my life for love.

*Ohhh, shit. I did not just think that.*

Now was not the time to remember his rasping tone as he'd insisted my departure was going to kill him. Such melodramatic hyperbole. But he hadn't even given me the option of staying, which showed that under all the stuff I'd started to fall in love with, he was still an emotionally illiterate dickhead.

A dickhead who was letting this tension between us affect his performance.

When we arrived at the windswept mountaintop where today's stage would finish, I was confronted by the more immediate problem: Colin still had the rest of the Tour to survive — and so did I.

## Colin

All my life, I'd found distractions — more often created them — to keep my mind off the blinding pressure of expectations everyone had for my sporting career. I'd never imagined that racing the Tour de France could be a decent distraction for something else that was upsetting me even more than the prospect of failure. I would never have imagined there'd be a day when I wouldn't want to see Leesa Kubicka.

Dad's dressing-down after the ill-fated breakaway hadn't been as awful as I'd expected, probably because I'd only been half-listening as the rest of my brain tried to process the fact that Leesa was able to blissfully anticipate moving on from me.

He'd told me all the usual stuff: the lead rider had to stick to strategy; save your strength; hold your nerve; blah blah blah. I knew what he truly wanted to say: don't be such a bloody idiot. He didn't need to say it, since I had that bit covered. No one wanted me to be a hero.

I had the legs of a 70-year-old when we lined up for the first mountain stage on the winding roads of the Pyrenees, a thought that amused me, considering I apparently had the brain of a 12-year-old. Nellie certainly babysat me in the peloton as though I were five. He probably regretted listening to me when I told him to go for the breakaway. It wasn't the first terrible idea I'd had.

As the day wore on, I thought of just following my front wheel off into the distance so I'd never have to cross the finish line and walk past her, feeling the furtive glances she thought I didn't notice. I noticed *everything*. She should have known that by now.

I didn't even know what I should do to defuse the situation, when I'd probably say the wrong thing and set it all on fire again. I should stay well away from her, even when I was pulled in two, part of me wanting to talk everything through with her and part of me hurting too much to contemplate it, when she'd be gone again in a few short weeks.

My disappointment about her contract didn't make sense. I'd never expected anything different. But then I'd never expected her to want to be close to me at all. I should have quit while I was ahead, even though that 'Q' word gave me hives. Too many years of sports psychology and I was imagining I could train enough to make her stay.

There was something in that sports psychology idea though. I couldn't quite put my finger on it – probably something to do with the haze in my brain as my muscles produced some serious watts on a hardcore climb. Everything hurt; my recovery had been insufficient. But I didn't mind the pain. It numbed everything else.

I heaved myself up the summit finish at Hautacam to the blur of colourful supporters and the taste of sweat, and crossed the line in sixth place – somehow my best finish of the Tour, although far from impressive. Looking at the guys around me, I suspected I'd made up a bit of time for the General Classification and the white jersey.

Fine. It would make Dad happy.

I had a camera shoved in my face with the logo of an Australian TV channel. Surely they were sick of me drawling nothing in particular in the aftermath of a lukewarm performance. The highest-placed Australian and I couldn't inspire a toddler on a balance bike right now.

To think I'd had the guts to try to inspire Leesa. I didn't have a bloody thing to offer her.

I almost wished I'd raced poorly that day rather than having to accept the back-slapping and cheers from my teammates for the rest of the evening. Turned out I was top ten after that punishing climb. I just wished I knew what Leesa was feeling.

Which was why I found myself swerving away from the others the next morning at breakfast to plonk into the seat opposite Wil.

'Is she okay?' I blurted out.

Wil gave me a doubtful look. 'If you have to ask me that, I'm guessing you did something you need to make up for.'

I ignored her comment. 'Did she sign the contract?' It wouldn't make much difference, since I would force her to pick up the pen myself if she didn't sign, but my brain was snagging on thoughts about crossing the finish line of our relationship. We weren't there yet.

'Shouldn't you be asking her this?'

'I don't think she wants to see me. I was a bit too… blunt when she told me about the contract.'

'You mean you made this all about you instead of about her?'

Wil patted me on the hand in a motherly gesture. 'I'm keeping an eye on her, don't worry. You need to focus.'

'If one more person tells me to focus, I'm going to—' I wisely cut myself off. 'I'm well aware prioritising anything other than the Tour de France right now would make me a bloody idiot.'

A low cough behind me made me jump and I turned and jumped again when I saw her. Christ, she was too beautiful to sneak up on me like that, wearing the kit I'd bought for her at the training camp, looking like every wet dream I'd had when I was 19.

I opened my mouth, but I couldn't speak, as though I had verbal constipation. The way my belly was churning did make me wonder if loving someone was a bit like a stomach bug. With heartburn. Or maybe I just needed to see the team doctor and take a bit of everything to get me through this one moment of looking at Leesa and *not* telling her how she made me feel.

'Um, I was hoping to talk to Wil, if you're done.'

I reared up to standing, stumbling because my nervous system wasn't responding adequately to my commands. It had been like this since the moment I'd first seen her, only it seemed to be getting worse.

*I fucking love you, Kubicka.*

The words stayed down, but they dug an enormous hole in my psyche and I wasn't sure I'd ever get them out again.

'Going for a ride?' I asked.

She nodded warily. 'You know these mountains… Old times' sake. Just an hour or— Before today's stage.'

Full sentences were not on the menu for either of us.

A wolf whistle from the other side of the room was the only thing that could tear my gaze from her.

'Lookin' hawt, Leesa!' Derek called out, with Amir giving her two thumbs up.

I snapped into action, ushering Leesa into my seat with light pressure on her shoulder. Even that small touch lit a fire in me as I purposefully obscured her from their view. 'Don't let Derek get a crush on you,' I mumbled through clenched teeth.

I deserved the spiky look she gave me. I had to let her go live her best life without me. It might be easier if she thought I was a jerk.

Snatching my coffee cup off the table, I gave her a mock salute with it, ignoring the drop of espresso that smeared on my forehead, and stalked away from the table.

# Chapter 33

**Leesa**

'I'm going to have to add "therapist" to my job title, aren't I?'

I tore my gaze from Colin's retreating figure to find Wil studying me with a wry smile. 'What? Why?'

'First Colin is here to talk to me about you, now you're here to talk to me about *him*.' She waved her hand in a circular gesture.

'He was?' My voice came out an octave higher than normal and heat flared in my cheeks as I pictured him agonising about our argument, still thinking of me. But, of course, he wasn't. He'd been so rude to me just now. 'I mean, I'm not here to talk to you about him,' I reminded myself. Morgan had left to get married and I missed talking through my work with someone else. 'I was looking for a marketing pro, not a couples therapist.' I winced at the last two words. Colin and I had never been a couple.

'I thought everything was going great at Redwin.'

'It's not that – I mean, it is going great.'

'New contract all signed?' Wil was wearing a dry smile that I couldn't interpret. 'I wondered whether you might look around for more options, something in cycling maybe.'

The poorly veiled hint caught me in the gut. Lifting my chin, I asked her, 'Would you? As a woman in sports, if you were in my position? Would you turn down a job offer from a prestigious agency?'

Wil's smile faded. 'No,' she answered. 'At least not without an equally amazing alternative offer.'

'Which isn't going to be forthcoming in the next week.'

I thought the topic was done, but Wil continued. 'Now I understand why Colin was asking.'

Maybe I'd picked up a bit of sunburn over the past few days of hanging around the team bus and the finish line, because my skin was hot and tingly. 'Who knows why Colin does anything?'

'He was upset, although I know that boy doesn't show his emotions well.'

I knew she was right. 'I didn't upset him. At least, I didn't mean to,' I said with a sigh.

She studied me for long enough that the sunburn feeling flared up my chest. 'After so many years of pining for you, he probably doesn't know what to do with himself now.'

Everything inside me went still. *A childish crush.* Those had been Colin's words. He hadn't been *pining for me.* He'd been pranking me and seeing other women casually for so many years.

'He hasn't had any trouble knowing what to do with himself up until now,' I commented, resisting a twitch in my face that felt like imminent tears. 'I thought you said he liked to sweet-talk all the social-media assistants.'

Wil gave a pained smile. 'Only because he couldn't have you. I think you've always been the only one who could break his heart.'

My vision tunnelled. 'I am not breaking his heart,' I insisted, but the words came out stilted and breathy. I wanted to slap my hands on the table and yell, '*He broke* mine!' Instead, I propped myself up with my elbow on the table and swallowed. 'I really don't think so. He never said… anything.'

Just that I wasn't supposed to be in his head. Colin wasn't flowery with his words, but he usually meant them. He'd said he'd missed me when we were apart. Sure, he said everything with a glint in his eye, but if I'd really hurt him, his heart and not just his pride—

Surely not. Colin was invincible — at least he pretended he was.

Lori's words came back to me: *Colin grew up years ago. He just hasn't noticed yet. He puts pressure on himself. What Colin says and what Colin does are two different things.*

When my eyelids sank closed, I could almost see a younger, leaner version of his face – staring at me in the fading light of a Malaga sunset – and something in me shifted.

I'd hurt him – during the biggest race of his career. He was such a professional that he was mostly keeping it together, but he thought I'd rejected him, that stupid hero, when he'd never given me anything *to* reject.

The first tear broke free and I swiped it hurriedly away. 'What difference does it even make what either of us feels?'

Wil's wince was relatable. 'It is a very... delicate time.'

I remembered what I'd overheard when I'd first warily approached the table. His first priority had to be the Tour. After that, I wasn't sure what could even change. We lived on different continents and I'd only just found my feet in my new career. But even though a long-distance relationship had to be difficult, I imagined those obstacles weren't insurmountable – if he was interested in... surmounting them with me.

He'd probably joke it was a complicated sex position, I thought with a rather hysterical snort of laughter. Swiping at my nose, I discovered more tears on my cheeks and there was no point in hiding them.

'This truly isn't what I wanted to talk to you about.' I straightened, trying to channel the sought-after professional I was.

Wil nodded. 'I'm sorry for bringing it up. It's your business. You're a marvellous marketing exec and not only a... Well, I just feel a little personally involved, given how long I've known you two.'

'It's okay,' I insisted. 'I am personally involved in this team. It's a fact. But that's a good thing.' I squeezed her arm and she pressed her hand over mine. 'You all helped me find my spark again and I want to keep that going.'

The way I was almost brave enough to try to keep things going with Colin too, despite the obstacles – *if* Wil was right. *If* his gigantic pride would ever let him admit he wanted to. It was a big if.

*

The second stage in the Pyrenees was tense, the whole team beginning to realise we had something to lose, now Colin was in the top ten. Watching the coverage, I felt the familiar pull as the grey rock and the mountain meadows filled the screen – for both my childhood excursions in Colorado and my time in the saddle.

This time I was also remembering a more recent ride – in the valley in Italy on training camp, where I'd looked up into the sky with Colin by my side, almost touching. The day's stage would finish on the formidable Col du Tourmalet, forcing the riders to suffer up 20 km of constant altitude gain, some stretches at a ten per cent gradient, where gravity dug its claws into you.

Lori and I had done this climb last year in the Tour de France Femmes and I was still shocked I'd lived through it. I'd cracked about halfway up, clicking my gears right down and inching up to the finish at a fraction of the power I was usually capable of, but I'd pulled Lori for most of the race, giving her slipstream so she had fresher legs for the monster climb.

Unlike the dramatic switchbacks of some other mountain passes, so much of the Tourmalet was long and straight that I'd managed to see Lori attacking, a small speck well ahead of me, but it had made my suffering worthwhile.

Today it was the men's turn – Colin's turn. The mountain stages were a chance to separate the good riders from the truly great ones and I knew Colin had all the potential to be the latter – if he could work out how to reach it.

*Potential…* There was that word again. I suspected it haunted him as much as it haunted me, but I wanted him to make this race his own somehow so he wasn't just suffering for his dad's sake.

There was no space for all the team buses, so we bundled into cars and one van to drive up to the finish, every available screen running the footage. I was glad Tony had let Edgar, the logistics manager, drive, because he couldn't take his eyes off his phone.

I was surprised how much time I spent glued to my own device, especially given the enormous landscape out of the window. The road to the pass wiggled through a neon-green valley that bordered on the rock and scree of the summits just above, five, six, seven of them. Being up here had always felt like touching the sun to me.

On the other side of the pass, the road was steeper — meaner — and would set the scene for the final battle of the day, although the peloton still had two other climbs to conquer before they arrived at the finale.

A throng of team and support staff milled on the opposite side of the hill from the finish line. A white marquee had been set up for the post-race protocol, including drugs testing and media. The yellow podium stamped with logos was under construction, the place where the current holders of the jerseys — yellow, green, polka-dot and white — would be presented at the end of the day.

It had already been 25 degrees this morning in Pau when we'd set out and the lower stretches of the race had been sweltering, but the col itself was a refreshing 18 degrees — 65 degrees as everyone in America except my parents would call it. Tugging a team-branded cap on to ward off the high-altitude sun, I hunched in the back of the van with Wil, watching the progress of the stage on her laptop.

A breakaway had formed, but no one expected them to hold out against the peloton. The big group was unsettled on the narrow roads and switchbacks, several teams jostling for control of the speed.

'He's marking him, the bugger!' Tony said grimly. 'What does he want with Colin? He's only one position down.'

I quickly saw what he meant. The former Italian champion Gaetano Maggioli — also Lori's ex-boyfriend — appeared to be shadowing Colin, although Nellie was doing a brave job getting between them.

'He's expecting an attack on your home roads,' Edgar mused.

'Then he knows more than we do,' Tony said with a humourless laugh.

Tony and Colin lived in Lourdes, in the foothills of the French Pyrenees, for half of the year and Colin would have trained on these roads day after day for years, but the ascents were extreme and while he was competent in the mountains, he was stronger on the hilly stages.

On the screen, the peloton was tipping over the edge of the Col du Soulor, half-man, half-bike, like cyborg lemmings dropping into the descent. The pace soared, spreading the riders out as the average speed rose over 50 miles per hour, two or three shooting out even faster in a risky attempt to catch the breakaway on the descent.

If Colin had been one of them, I wouldn't have been able to watch, but he was still caught behind the pesky Maggioli, now isolated from Nellie, Amir and the others. I breathed out again when they managed the right turn safely and reached the end of the long descent. Now was the inexorable rise towards the Tourmalet, the climb that would expose the true condition of every rider in the bunch.

They raced through the final feed zone of the day, groping for musettes and stocking up on bidons, the water bottles that were as much an icon of the Tour de France as they were an environmental challenge.

But the pace picked up as soon as the riders were clear of the feed zone. The teams with a strong contender meant business, thinning out the bunch even on the lower stretches of the climb as the weaker riders were forced to drop back when they couldn't keep up.

Colin was looking untroubled so far in the few glimpses the coverage gave us. They swept through the quaint ski town of Pierrefitte-Nestalas and then there was only up.

The caw of a bird making dives in the alpine updraughts drew my gaze and I took a deep breath, gathering all of my hopes for Colin to finish well today, and that was the moment it happened.

A swerve; a slip; the slightest touch of wheel on wheel and the diminished peloton toppled like dominoes.

# Chapter 34

## Colin

Flat on my back staring up at the blue sky, it was impossible not to accept that some things in life were out of my control. If your life was supposed to flash before your eyes a second before death, then a crash was like an entire lifespan passing in the space of a few seconds: disorientation, pain, confusion, more pain, grief – acceptance.

For several throbbing heartbeats, I thought that was it, that was me done for this year. I was a flash in the pan – exactly what I'd always feared I was. The end of Dad's dreams – and Leesa's assignment.

I wasn't dead – there was too much pain for that. But the way my blood was rushing to my head did not feel good. Oh wait, I was upside down. The pure discomfort of my position made me shuffle until gravity felt more normal. Then I closed my eyes…

And snapped them open again a moment later. Something was unfinished. The Tour – yes, of course, the Tour. That wasn't over until I dragged my arse over the line in Paris – or got whisked away in an ambulance. The thought of abandoning brought a sour taste to my mouth.

But that wasn't all that was unfinished. I thought of that cardboard sign from September that I'd shoved in the back of my wardrobe at home in Lourdes, my half-hearted and utterly inadequate attempt to show Leesa why I'd always singled her out. I'd done such a poor job of it she still thought I'd been pulling a prank.

I didn't deserve her grace after everything that I'd done, but I wanted it – I wanted the chance to work for it.

That's when the jumbled thoughts from the past few days – and weeks – finally coalesced into something I could understand: sports psychology; growing up; Leesa – *Leesa*. I was aware I didn't deal well with things I couldn't control in my life, like a crash in the Pyrenees, my parents' dysfunctional relationship – or Leesa returning home to the States.

But there were some things I *could* control.

The same wispy white cloud still hovered high above me in the sky. Only a few seconds had passed, but the fire in me had started burning again – maybe even a new flame, brighter and stronger than before.

I would not abandon the race until a doctor told me to – and I would not give up on a relationship with Leesa until I'd made up for my years of shitty pranks and told her exactly how I felt.

But first, somehow, I had to get up.

### Leesa

'*A crash! Something's brought down several riders in the peloton!*' The commentator had little to add to the scene of carnage developing on the screen. I'd watched hundreds of crashes like this in my time – I'd been in a couple and had the knobbly scars on my knees and elbows to prove it – but I'd never had my lungs constrict and my vision fog with panic.

I grasped Wil's arm and leaned close to the laptop as though that would help me find Colin in the mêlée – help him come away from it unscathed. A crumpled heap of bikes and humans was scattered across the narrow road, a couple had tumbled a few feet down the slope. Unable to stop quickly enough, riders ploughed into the midst and spilled over the top of each other.

'This coverage is a pile of shit. Show us the fucking riders!' Tony groped for his phone to call the DS in the team car, his hand shaking. 'Do we know where everyone is? Can you get to them?' Mashing the screen with trembling fingers, he put the call on loudspeaker and let the phone clatter to the bench seat of the van.

'*Stand by, Tony,*' came Alan's steady voice from the team car. '*We're not far away, but there's a lot of traffic.*'

The screen showed splashes of colour moving among a mess of metal as riders scrambled to untangle their bikes. I scanned the footage desperately, but I didn't have a hope of finding that particular orange helmet in the sea of riders.

Some appeared largely unaffected, hefting their bikes to pick their way through the carnage, but it was quickly clear there were so many riders affected that they'd stop and wait, a quirky honour rule of pro cycling that wasn't written or enforced, but everyone generally respected.

Motorbikes with first aiders were already on the scene and my heart crept higher in my throat with each second that passed not knowing where he was or if he was hurt. There were even a couple of bikes sticking out of the bushes like discarded shopping carts. Riders were on the ground, bodies strewn across a bizarre battlefield.

Then Nellie's voice sounded over the team radio and made everything worse. '*The neutral medic's with Colin, but we need help here!*'

My nose stung so sharply I had to shove the ball of my hand to my face and my vision swam again. Sagging heavily against the passenger seat, I rubbed the raised scar on my knee as though that would help me hear some better news. I tried to tell myself it wouldn't be the first time he'd crashed – I'd crashed over and over again during my career.

But I'd rarely needed a medic.

'Alan!' Tony yelled into the phone.

'*We're on our way. It's bumper-to-bumper.*' Then, over the team radio, '*Can you give us any more information, Nellie? Any other injuries? Damage?*'

It was Amir who answered. '*We managed to pull him back onto the road and if his language is anything to go by, he'll live, but he's in some pain – to say the least. His bike's a mess.*'

The footage picked up a close-up of Colin and I couldn't contain a yelp. The left side of his face was smeared with blood, a wound above his eyebrow still profuse. He was holding his arm, a powerful grimace on his face. He appeared to be shivering.

I couldn't breathe for the unexpected *pain* of seeing him like that, when he was supposed to be the larger-than-life leader who couldn't keep down his own powerful personality.

'*I think we're looking at wheel contact for the origin of the crash,*' the commentator explained, but I didn't care any more how it had started, I only cared about how Colin was feeling.

'Does he need an ambulance?' Tony's voice was approaching a shriek. If he hadn't had the health and fitness of an ox, I might have been worried about him having a heart attack, the veins in his temples were bulging so severely. 'Where's Angie?' Tony barked into the phone, asking about the team doctor, who was in the car with the DS. 'I want Angie to check him!'

Alan's voice came over the radio again. '*Colin, Angie's on her way. Hang in there.*'

Tony muttered something under his breath about a concussion that made my hair stand on end. He looked a thousand years old, rather than his usual weathered hundred.

I had the unexpected urge to go and stand next to him for comfort, bump shoulders. Tony wasn't perfect; he'd probably been a rotten father at times. But I could see the genuine fear, the worry in him and I knew what that felt like.

I suspected I knew exactly what it felt like to love Colin Gallagher: frustrating and intense.

Tony swallowed audibly and turned halfway to me. 'Do you want to talk to him? We could patch through the radio. I think he'd respond well to that. He's always responded well to you.'

Except when I'd told him I was leaving and he'd pushed me away – and I'd been stupid enough to let him do it.

His words from that evening in Guérande came back to me with a stab of remorse: *It's gonna kill me.* I wanted to get on a bike and race to him, grab his face in my hands and tell him he meant so much to me, he'd scrambled all of my priorities. It was clear that was the last thing that would help him right now, but only my hands clamped to the edge of my seat in the van kept me where I was.

'I'm not sure he'd respond well to me right now,' I said weakly.

Tony's grumble came from deep in his chest.

'I'm sorry. I should never have let any of this happen.'

'No, you shouldn't have,' Tony agreed flatly. 'Neither of you. But the damage is done now.'

'The peloton's getting going again,' Edgar interrupted warily, pointing at the screen.

Tony's attention was off me in an instant. 'Like hell they are! Someone put a stop to that! The boy's still on the ground!'

As though turning its nose up at Tony, the coverage showed Colin bending his legs tentatively and then wobbling to his feet. Swiping something out of his eyes – blood and sweat, I imagined – he bent his head to allow the neutral medic to dab at the wound on his face.

'*Well, he's up and walking, but the question is: where to? Back on a bike or into an ambulance. With the looks of those abrasions, I wouldn't like to guess which. What a huge disappointment for Harper-Stacked – and Gallagher himself. Such a big rider, great to watch.*'

My stomach twisted with a lurch of disappointment for him, but seeing him flash a smile at the neutral medic also flooded me with relief. I had wanted him to do well, but mostly I just wanted to be able to wrap my arms around him again soon.

My gaze was glued to the screen, curious about the way he was holding himself, surprised he didn't look angry and frustrated. His hand rose to his chest and the radio crackled on.

'*Tell Dad not to have a heart attack. Nothing's broken.*'

Colin's voice always got under my skin, but in that moment, it dug right to my heart, his deep, slow drawl with a hint of humour so *Colin Gallagher* that I could have cried. Wait, I *was* crying. Wil's soothing hand on my back was a tiny bit embarrassing.

'*Just let me get patched up—— Argh, fuck, that hurts!*'

The footage moved back to the peloton, slowly accelerating away from the scene of the crash, leaving Tony bouncing in his seat. 'He's not going to get back on a bike, is he? Someone tell me what's going on!'

My breath left my lungs one more time when the coverage switched back to Colin, swinging his leg over a bike saddle and clicking his helmet back on.

'Bloomin' 'eck! The devil fucking take that boy. What is he doing?'

Apparently, this wasn't over yet. The *Tour*. That's what wasn't over. But as I stared at his image on the screen, his head up, shoulders back in that cocky Colin Gallagher pose he'd developed some time around his 21st birthday, I couldn't help thinking this meant my time with him wasn't over either.

*'Bensaïd has handed his bike over to Gallagher. He's not too far behind the bunch but, with those injuries, I don't fancy his chances of making the time cut. This is the Tourmalet and he's still a long way from the finish line, but wow — he's going to attempt it.'*

He looked a little wobbly as he took off, blood smeared down his arm below the hastily applied dressing. As the footage followed his tentative first few metres, I noticed — along with the rest of the world — that his jersey had split down the back. Valerio the dragon was eyeballing the camera, apologising for nothing, daring the world to underestimate him.

And further down, where the rip reached nearly to the top of his thigh, was the number 91.

*'Would you look at that? Gallagher seems to have lost one of his numbers in the crash, but he has a spare,'* the commentator said with a chuckle.

'Is that a tattoo?' Tony's voice was high. 'When did he get that? Farking hell. That boy can't help making headlines for all the weirdest reasons.'

Whether it was on purpose or not, Tony glanced at me with those words and heat rushed up my chest. I should keep quiet, stare at my shoes, not rock the boat. I was a woman in sports, always having to prove I belonged. But looking at Colin and remembering the day we'd got those tattoos made me unexpectedly stubborn. And proud.

'He's *your* son, Tony,' I said lightly. 'What did you expect?'

He regarded me, his expression drawing in. 'That's what I'm worried about, child.'

# Chapter 35

### Colin

The Col du Tourmalet had it in for me. The road was so long and straight, poking its tongue out at me as I slogged it up, throwing in a few switchbacks every now and again to steal my breath and make my muscles burn.

Today, it wasn't only my muscles. My arm was blowing up, which made me a little wobbly with concern. Angie had taken a look while I cruised alongside the team car, but there wasn't a lot she could say for certain without an ultrasound or an X-ray. It was up to me to decide how this stage played out.

I'd fucked around for ten stages like a hurt little boy and now the only chance I had to make something of this Tour was to get to the top of this vindictive mountain while I was losing blood.

Lucky I knew something about the motivating properties of spite. I'd explained it at length to the one person who made me want to take my life more seriously. I wondered what she was thinking now.

She was something so bloody special and I had a lot of making up to do. I just had to… get to… the top.

'Still with us, C?'

Nellie's words snapped me out of a glazed pause in my thoughts. I was clinging to his wheel, letting him take the friction of the air instead of me. Without him, I wasn't sure I'd make it. I wasn't sure I'd make it anyway.

A sting in my side accompanied that thought. My jersey was in shreds, which would be bloody embarrassing later, watching footage of me with half an arse-cheek on show. But, for now, it was just a little extra ventilation from the cool mountain air over my sweat-soaked skin.

The drips onto my handlebars were pink and profuse and my breath was tight. I wasn't sure what shape I'd be in when the adrenaline faded.

That was when I realised I was also starving. Bloody rookie error, forgetting to keep up my carbohydrate intake. We burned through about 8,000 calories on a day like today – I'd probably need more after the shock of the crash.

Fumbling in the pockets at my lower back, I found skin and loose Lycra – and a stinging graze that made me grit my teeth harder. Not only were my pockets empty, they were no longer pockets.

'*Uh, C?*' Alan's voice came over the radio. '*You done something to your heartrate monitor or are these readings accurate?*'

My throat was dry.

'*You're not bonking on us, are ya? Come on, mate. Someone get him a gel!*'

Groping for the bidon on my frame, I guzzled some water, waiting for the spots at the edges of my vision to recede. Blinking furiously, I started when someone waved a little sachet of energy gel at me and I snatched it with relief, squeezing it down in one go, even though it was the cat-piss flavour.

'Thanks,' I growled, still no idea who'd handed it to me. 'How much longer?' I knew every summit around here, every curve and incline, but it was all a blur of green and blue and pain, throbbing through me at unexpected moments.

'At this rate? Half an hour?' came Nellie's answer.

'Shit!' I could still read between the lines of his answer. I was losing time faster than I was losing blood. The white jersey was getting farther and farther away, even as the finish line inched closer.

I'd finish this for my pride, but it would be better for all of us if I could finish it a little faster. Taking a deep breath through my nose, I picked up a bit of speed, rocking on my bike to get my thigh muscles to pull.

'You haven't given up yet then?'

'Not yet,' I shot back, ignoring the gentle goading in Derek's tone.

'What do you think, Nellie? Will she be waiting at the finish line?'

The strike of endorphins through my nervous system was an instant response. Leesa… Her skin, her hair, that smirk she made when she was verbally sparring with me.

'I reckon so,' Nellie replied, not subtle at all. 'She seems to like him, although to be perfectly honest, I have no idea why.'

'I know what you're doing,' I grumbled.

'Yeah, because it's working,' Nellie said with laughter in his voice. 'I thought she was a bit too clever to fall for you, but you must be more of a catch than I realised.'

'Of course she's fucking clever! She's got an IQ higher than my heartrate right now and that's saying something.'

Nellie grinned. 'Gallagher finally found someone, but he's too much of a wuss to tell her how he feels.'

'Fuck off.'

'Maybe it's his vocabulary that's lacking, rather than his courage!' I heard from Derek, up ahead. I was surprised to see him still hanging around to help me limp to the finish.

'You fuckwit, Sabel! Get back to the front! If I can't finish this fucking race, then you have to. Grow some balls to go with your piss-poor excuse for a moustache!'

Derek just grinned at me. With a mock salute and a, 'See ya later, old man!' that got lost in the wind, he accelerated ahead before he could hear my approving grunt.

'You call that "mentoring" the new guy?' Nellie asked.

'Yup, I'm the bloody leader of this team!' My laugh was cut off by a groan of pain. 'Shut up now. We've got an appointment with the Col du Tourmalet.' Where Leesa might be waiting.

I fumbled for the button to activate the radio. 'Is Leesa listening?'

The shitty day washed over me. I probably wouldn't have asked that question if I hadn't been quite so cooked, but I was too tired for embarrassment.

'*I dunno, C,*' came Alan's voice in a soothing tone. '*Just get home safe now. She might be at the finish line.*' Along with blessed rest and complex carbohydrates.

The road was lined with spectators blowing horns, cheering and yelling and shaking all kinds of objects at me as I struggled up every metre of altitude gain. A bunch of guys in polka-dot shirts and Cochonou bucket hats gave me a Mexican wave. Cheering rang in my ears as all the spectators waved and clapped and celebrated my progress, even at grandma speed.

I wasn't a prize today. I was just a guy letting his team help him so I could fight another day.

It wasn't far now. Keeling over was no longer an option. I could keep pedalling after death – I was certain of that. Something yellow swam in my vision and it took me too long to realise it was the scaffolding of the finish line, still so… far… away at the top of a nasty ascent.

Leesa might not even be there. It was her right. I'd been a dick to her almost from the moment we'd met. But if she was…

I started to imagine her, just up ahead. She might sit in the car with me while we made our way back down to the hotel, holding my hand across the bench seat.

Had I ever held her hand? Linked my fingers with hers as though we were one organism instead of two, like those jellyfish that were actually a whole colony of jellyfish and not just one animal. Except it would just be me and Leesa, not lots of us. Given the way my vision was blurring, there might be two of her by the time I saw her – and not much left of me.

It was impossible to tell what was the crash and what was just the Tourmalet, but I felt as though I'd just donated a kidney – and maybe a lung. And still the finish line just seemed to get farther and farther away. But I wouldn't stop.

I was writing my narrative – the start of it anyway – the way I wanted to go on. Sometimes my heart ruled my head, but that didn't have to be a bad thing. My heart was getting me up the Tourmalet today. This was my race – *my* life.

I just wanted Leesa to appear and give me another chance – to make things different. Because I wanted her in my life more than anything. Miserable and in pain and drained of everything except the steel in my spine, I just wanted the chance to show her I'd grown up.

# Chapter 36

**Leesa**

The finish area was a crush of bikes and bodies, media crew and support staff and heaving, exhausted riders. Squeezing through the crowd, I kept my desperate gaze on the tall figure of Chris, the swannie, up ahead, pushing people out of the way as he barrelled towards the finish line.

My cheeks were cold with tears. I'd barely been able to watch Colin drag himself up the mountain. Right now I just had to get to him, make sure he was all right and then kiss him and *shake* him for a stunt that had taken years off my life — and inspired so much pride and heat and admiration I didn't know what to do with it.

Chris parted the crowd just in time for me to see him with his head bowed over the handlebars, up out of the saddle, pushing once, twice, and toppling over the finish line, unclipping a foot to catch himself.

God, he'd done it. I only hoped it hadn't cost him too much.

He fell right onto his ass when he dismounted, leaving Nellie to grab the bikes while Chris dragged Colin to one side. He glugged down a recovery drink and then most of a bidon, scrunching his face up with pain as his body slowly wound down.

I stared at him, taking in all the familiar lines of his face, the freckles that only showed up when he was bathed in sweat. I didn't know what I was going to do when I couldn't see his face every day. That was the thought that propelled me forward, even though I didn't know what was best for either of us — or if he even wanted to see me.

'Colin.'

His gaze snapped up. Despite his exhaustion, he straightened, lifting a shaking hand to my hair as I crashed to my knees in front of him.

'*Colin*.'

I finally had his face in my hands, his name on my lips and tears streaming down my face.

'Shhh,' he responded, a smile tugging at his lips. 'C'mere, Kubicka,' he rasped, curling his hand into my hair and pulling me closer.

This was my kiss at the finish line, aching and fearful, tender, sweeping and heady. His breath on my lips was choppy, his hand stayed tight on my head, holding me where I was as he used all his remaining energy to keep his mouth on mine, sharing adrenaline, endorphins – that moment in time that was only ours and would always be ours.

No matter what happened, how much this hurt when I left, I was glad I loved him – right now.

It couldn't last. He probably shouldn't have used his last energy for a kiss anyway and when he drew away with a groan, blinking as though he was trying not to black out, I felt faintly guilty.

He opened his mouth to speak, mumbling groggy words that were not what I expected. 'Have we ever held hands?'

Flashes from the past few weeks rose in my mind, but not one where we'd done that. 'I don't think so.'

I was about to ask him why he wanted to know, offer to hold his hand, but he continued, 'Like those jellyfish, the ones that are made up of different creatures holding hands.'

Perhaps he wasn't entirely conscious. 'A siphonophore?' I clarified, peering at him in concern. 'They don't exactly hold hands.'

His eyelids drifted closed and he leaned back on the barrier behind him. 'You're so fucking clever. That's exactly what I mean.'

'Colin, why are you talking about jellyfish?'

He didn't answer, but Chris spoke, interrupting whatever the moment had been. 'We should get him to a hospital.'

*

My fingernails were bitten-down stubs and I'd only been able to swallow two bites of dinner. Amir, who'd grabbed another bike and just managed to finish within the time cut, Derek, Nellie and the others had all been subdued as they tried to eat as well.

Now I was pacing my room, wondering who I should call to find answers and peering out of my window – not at the darkened silhouettes of the mountains but at the street, waiting for a team car to return either with or without Colin.

When a vehicle finally pulled up, I pressed my nose to the pane, fogging the glass as I tried to identify who was getting out. I needn't have worried. I'd have recognised those shoulders anywhere.

He was walking. No sign of a bandage – or a cast. He was back at the hotel – surrounded by Angie and the medical staff, but he was back.

My vision blurred for a moment with relief. But it didn't mean he was still in the Tour.

I would be heartbroken for him if he had to abandon and I would have been crossing everything for him if I'd been as superstitious as the average cyclist. But my parents were doctors and would be horrified at me crossing any body part for a medical outcome, so all I could do was prepare myself to be heartbroken *with* him, if that's the answer he'd gotten.

Snatching up my phone to send him a message, the screen flashed up before I'd even unlocked it. A message from Colin, but all he sent was: *Sorry.*

My stomach flipped as my negative brain immediately assumed he was out of the race.

*What are you sorry for?*

Biting my lip as I read over the message, I wanted to rush down the corridor to the room he was sharing with Amir to make sure he didn't misunderstand, but I didn't want to disturb the doctors and realistically, he was probably butt-naked again by now.

His reply arrived mercifully quickly: *Everything.*

*Are you finally apologising for all the insects?*

*Don't eat the cornflakes tomorrow.*

I grinned, even though nobody could see me except maybe the five spiders that were within three feet of me at any one time, now relieved we seemed to back in Banterville, our home town. I didn't know what to do with a serious Colin.

I wasn't sure what to write back. Asking him how he was sounded trite by text.

*Can you please tell me you were impressed today, Magda?*

In Banterville, I suspected a joke would pep him up more effectively than the truth of my nail-biting.

*Just a sec. I'm bidding on your race-worn.*

The fan auction of today's ripped and stained jersey would probably go higher than my annual salary.

His reply came immediately: *Stop making me laugh. It hurts.*

After more hesitation, the dots coming and going a few times, he wrote: *You can have the race-worn. Put it under your pillow when you sleep.*

That sounded more like the Colin I knew.

*I'm glad you're mostly conscious now. For a moment there, I thought you wanted to retrain as a marine biologist.*

*The jellyfish thing is kind of hard to explain by text.*

*I figured as much. Shouldn't you be listening to the doctors or something?*

*They're whispering about me in the corner.*

The shot of nerves was cold when I thought about the medical advice from the team doctors.

*I'm bored actually. Wanna come keep me company?*

There was no way I could say no to that casual invitation, but I strung him along for a moment. *I'm not entertaining you already?*

*Just get in here.*

*Will I be mentally scarred by the sight of you?*

*You weren't before. I'm waiting!*

*So bossy!*

I wouldn't let him guess that I skipped down the corridor, but I slowed my steps when I saw Tony standing outside, speaking to Alan. They looked up – guiltily, if I had to judge – when they saw me.

'He, uh, asked to see me,' I volunteered before anyone asked.

'O' course he did,' Tony said, his smile tightening.

'What? Have they finished the tests? Have they found anything?'

Tony hesitated, which wasn't good.

'What?'

'The scan didn't show a clear break, but there could be bruising or a hairline fracture in the lower arm. We're just not sure it's best if he continues with the Tour. It was a heavy crash.'

I'd seen the replay. Tony wasn't wrong.

'I thought something had gone wrong with the two of ya,' Tony added, his eyes a little wild.

Giving half a nod in a non-answer, I just said, 'Nothing was ever "right", but I seem to be here anyway.'

He just studied me in response, for long enough to seed prickles at my hairline. 'You goin' in? You might want to prepare yourself.'

'I'm familiar with the amount of nudity in this sport,' I responded wryly, but Tony didn't smile.

'I meant his face.'

With a gulp and a tense nod, I stepped cautiously inside – stopping short when I caught sight of him sprawled shirtless on the bed. There was an ugly lump slowly turning purple above his left eye, one part dressed with gauze and medical tape. He had cuts and scratches everywhere I looked, which really was everywhere, because my eyes were drawn to all the familiar bits of his body.

'You summoned me,' I said.

His face brightened in an instant as he turned to me. I searched his expression for some gentle mocking, finding none, which was disconcerting.

He snagged my T-shirt and tugged until I was closer. 'My best idea all day.' There was a lightness in his tone, as though he truly meant what he said. Maybe we weren't in Banterville after all.

'What's up with you?'

He looked away with a self-deprecating chuckle. 'A few things became clear when I was flat on my back on the mountain today,' he explained, his voice gravelly. 'We've known each other a long time, haven't we?'

'We have.' I wasn't sure what else to say in reply. 'A lot of years of pranks.'

I wasn't sure I'd ever seen that smile before. It was playful, yes, but also... vulnerable? 'Did you hate it? Hate me?'

That he seemed to expect an answer put me off balance. 'I never hated you. Some of your pranks went too far.'

'Fair,' he said, crossing his arms.

'Some of them were funny,' I admitted without really meaning to. 'At least they are with hindsight. Why? Are you giving it all up?'

'I thought about it.' Peering at me, a smile grew on his face. 'But the truth is, I like pranking you.'

Heat rose to my cheeks.

'And I think maybe if you trust me, you'll like me pranking you too.'

'Trust is a big word,' I blurted out, my lungs suddenly tight. It was just as big as the word that seemed to be growing roots in my feelings about him – maybe even bigger.

'I know,' he said softly. 'It's just that I don't want to prank anyone *but* you, Kubicka.'

I couldn't say anything in reply, my thoughts swimming, too much hope and confusion and dismay.

'I'm just giving you fair warning,' he said, peering at me with half a smile that suggested he had some idea of the stricken feelings creating a cocktail in my chest.

'Avoid the cornflakes tomorrow. I remember,' I squeaked, trying to find even ground between us.

'And don't forget to check your socks,' he added in a whisper.

Tony and Alan had slipped into the room and Colin glanced at them before beckoning me even closer and lifting his hand, holding it a foot above the bed.

'Jellyfish,' was all he said at first, shaking his hand at me.

While I wasn't certain about the metaphor, it was clear what he wanted. I opened my fingers and pressed my palm to his.

His rough, warm hand closed around mine, strong fingers, thick knuckles, a callus or two. After a few heartbeats where he studied our hands as intently as I did, he jimmied his fingers between mine.

My breath stalled as the raw intimacy of the gesture crept over me. Even when he'd held me and got in my head during sex, I hadn't felt this close to him.

Feeling his eyes on me, I met his gaze for a quick smile and then he shifted, taking a deep breath and clearing his throat to catch Tony's attention. His dad's eyes fell immediately to our joined hands, but his only reaction was a quick lift of his brow.

'I appreciate your concerns, but this is my Tour and I want to start tomorrow. I have no interest in running myself into the ground. I'll abandon if and when I need to. But I'm lining up tomorrow morning – and hopefully every morning until Paris. We're not done yet.'

# Chapter 37

## Colin

A little bit of pressure — from myself — was a good motivator. I had half of the Tour still ahead of me, if I was lucky and my injuries didn't fight back. Ten stages until Paris — to show Leesa I would do anything to keep her in my life and try to make up for all the weird stunts I'd pulled before I started believing we could really be together.

It should have felt like a distraction, planning ways to convince Leesa we had to stay together after the Tour, but my two goals coalesced seamlessly into everything I was fighting for. Both would show her what I was made of, that I was serious about my life and her place in it, regardless of whether I brought home any silverware.

Although it would be a fuck of a lot easier if I did win something. I reckoned she'd like it too.

I had to improvise on the first morning. My body creaked and groaned as I hauled myself out of bed, but the compression bandage on my arm appeared to have done a good job and I didn't notice any swelling. My reflection in the mirror startled me. I was black and blue as though I'd been in a bar brawl — not just my face, but all over my torso dark spots were coming up. But I had too much to achieve that day to linger, so I slung on tracksuit pants and a loose T-shirt and padded down to the breakfast room in my slides.

Thankfully I'd beaten almost everyone else up, so all I had to do was take aside a member of hotel staff to enact the first stage of my plan.

When Leesa emerged through the doors an hour later, I stood and approached her with a smile, slipping my hand into hers. She peered questioningly up at me, but I was determined to do all of this perfectly, so she'd have no doubts left by the time I told her everything.

'I'm sorry for the sock thing,' I said softly into her hair as I pressed a whisper of a kiss there.

She scowled. 'That is the worst kind of prank: a prank that's not actually a prank.' Of course I hadn't put anything in her socks, but I knew just mentioning the possibility would have had her checking every pair.

I let go of her hand. 'Enjoy your breakfast.'

Still glancing warily at me, she headed for the buffet and I held my breath, waiting to see if my plan would actually work. When she went straight for the little container of cornflakes, a stubborn look on her face, I couldn't stifle my grin.

I saw the exact moment the little object plopped into her bowl. It would have been impossible to miss, because she yelped, dropping the container to the table with a thud. A hand on her chest, she peered at me again with narrowed eyes.

But when she picked through the flakes to fish out the object, she studied it curiously. It was a wrapped local chocolate – les Pyrénéens, little bite-sized bars of filled dark chocolate – with six legs, two feelers and some beetle wings drawn onto it with permanent marker.

My first goal of the day – making Leesa smile at me – achieved, I went to find the chief mechanic to bend him into my service for the most important part of my plan, which would take some time – hopefully not so much that I missed my shot and she left for America before I could sort it out. I also called our cleaner back home in Lourdes and requested a favour. There was an embarrassing object in the back of my cupboard I needed her to post to our hotel in Paris in preparation for the moment I would place my pride on the line for a chance to make it all real with Leesa.

Only then did I turn my attention to the mammoth climbs that awaited me on stage 12. It was a miserable stage – not the weather, because the July sun was still sending its cruel rays to peel up the back of my neck, but the relentless pace of the peloton made no allowances for my recovery.

I was two minutes down on the white jersey, back in 16th place overall. It was a miracle it wasn't more, but two minutes was probably insurmountable at this point, unless I had great luck – or the others had rotten luck.

The aim for the day was just to survive. Amir and Nellie stayed close in support, but I'd insisted we send Derek out and the kid had a great time in the breakaway, although he was caught again with 10 k to go. Staying with the peloton to the end lost me another 30 seconds on GC and I had to spend another hour letting Angie test everything under the sun, but I was cleared to continue, which was enough for now.

One day at a time...

I got some supplies shipped to the hotel in Gap for the rest day that I was holding out for, so I had to improvise again on the morning of stage 13. Waiting until Leesa was in the breakfast room, I prepared my prank and then strode in, stretching out my time at the buffet as long as I could without arousing suspicion and then sashaying past where she was sitting with Wil.

I was afraid for a moment she wouldn't bite, but then Wil called after me, 'Uh, you've got a... something on your back.' She stood and plucked off the sticky note, inclining her head to read it. 'It says: "Hug me". I didn't know you needed a hug. Come here!'

With an inward groan, I submitted to a hug from Wil, but Leesa laughed at me over her coffee cup as I leaned down to squeeze our diminutive marketing officer. Mission sort of accomplished.

Two hilly stages and a flat one rounded off the time until the rest day, with views of the fantasy-castle city of Carcassonne and glimpses of the Med. I still didn't trust my body very far, but the strange thing about endurance was that the harder the race got, the stronger I felt. The grazes were healing and I imagined they would heal up tougher than before – kind of like my heart.

When we piled into the hotel in Gap at the end of stage 15, I was so upbeat Amir was grumpy with me, although he still hung around to see what was in the box of supplies I'd ordered for my win-Leesa-back-and-maybe-also-a-stage-of-the-Tour-de-France plan.

For the rest day, after our recovery ride, I pulled on my brand-new T-shirt and a pair of shorts and went down to lunch with my chest puffed out like a male duck. I had a lot of practice with swagger that came in handy that day as I wore the shirt with pride, waiting to see how she'd react.

## Leesa

I knew something was up as soon as I walked into the dining room for lunch – not only because Colin had already pranked me with nice things nearly every morning, but also because my gaze was drawn straight to him and he was obviously holding something in.

He sat up straight when I saw him and I froze, my mouth swinging open. A flush of embarrassment rose up my chest when I saw what was printed on his T-shirt, but it was already mixed with a shot of gratification. I hadn't seen that photo in months. I looked rather good with my mouth open in a shout of triumph, one hand above my head in a fist as I crossed the line on my bike in Geelong.

But it wasn't quite the angle I remembered from the press shot published after I won the Great Ocean Road Race. It was slightly to one side, as though—

When my gaze snapped up to his, I found him looking at me as earnestly as he ever had, brows raised. He gave me a little nod which I took to mean that what I was thinking was correct: he'd taken that picture himself. The flush over my skin became something else entirely.

After lunch, he dragged me into the paved streets of the town, ringed by forested slopes and rocky peaks. With the yellow and ochre render on the houses and the colourful shutters, Gap had a Mediterranean flair, even though it was tucked in the mountains. There were a couple of really nice patisseries where Colin demanded I share my treats and proceeded to devour half of my

French custard tart. Then he was so guilty he blew a small fortune on handmade chocolates and thrust them at me.

He took my hand occasionally, his face a study in casual that I didn't quite believe, but I wouldn't dare make a comment in case he let go. Arriving back at the hotel, he stopped me before we entered the foyer.

'Tomorrow or the next day,' he began, thrumming with familiar energy, 'I'm going to go for it. Not just a nice, safe attack 20 k from the finish line. I have to go early if I'm going to make up serious time. It could backfire.'

My hair stood on end and I nodded, not entirely sure why he was telling me, but understanding something on a non-verbal level from the way he took my other hand as well, threading his fingers restlessly into mine.

'Will you scrape me off the road if I don't make it?' His eyes glinted with humour and I'd never had any chance of resisting the sparks he sent racing over my skin – and under it.

'Do you mean physically or mentally?' I asked.

'Maybe both.'

'I think you're looking forward to it,' I mused, drawing a grin from him.

'What, the scraping? Yeah, you can put me back together any day.'

I nudged him with my shoulder, since he had both of my hands and I couldn't poke him. 'You know what I mean.'

He gave a thoughtful nod. 'Yeah, I am. Maybe it's the underdog thing, but yeah. Maybe it's your eyes.'

That earned him a stronger shove. 'It's your character, not my eyes.'

'I dunno,' he disagreed with a cheeky smile. Then he hesitated before peering at me uncertainly and saying, 'Just don't go anywhere, okay?'

I stilled. Where would I go when I was following the Tour for my *job*? Did he mean don't go back home? That was something I had not prepared a response to.

'I mean after the Tour,' he rushed on. 'No, I mean— Don't go without saying—' He blanched and seemed to reconsider. 'Don't go without letting me say—'

'Goodbye?' I prompted when he seemed incapable of finishing the sentence. Given the sour taste of that word, I understood why he didn't want to.

'I hope not,' he said under his breath. Grasping my hands more tightly, he managed to say, 'I've got some ideas I want to run by you.'

'Uh, okay.' I didn't know what to make of his heavy hints that could be anything from glue in my hair to jellyfish holding hands – or my wildest idea: that he wanted to carve a place for me in his life.

He looked relieved and lifted a hand into my hair, tugging me gruffly to him for a hug. I fisted the back of his shirt and held on, soaking in the warmth of his body and the mineral scent of him, the dynamism in his muscles and the push and pull of the way he held me.

'You feel good,' he said in a gravelly tone.

Then Amir's voice interrupted. 'Is that some kind of slow dance and I can't hear the music?'

Damn this constant audience. I eased back at the disapproving rumble in Colin's chest. Tipping my face up, I eyeballed him and whispered, 'Go make your mark on the Tour.' Then I pressed a quick, light kiss to his lips and slipped inside.

# Chapter 38

## Colin

The Alpe d'Huez was legendary with good reason. The site of the first ever mountaintop finish in the Tour's history, the road was an epic 21 switchbacks and over a kilometre of climbing. We crawled up there like centipedes with the deep valley behind us and thousands of supporters encroaching on the riders.

A steep drop-off on one side of the road tumbled into a rocky gorge and, above us, the endless grey peaks took shape more clearly with each metre of gruelling altitude gain, patches of snow like polka-dots on the vast landscape.

Crunching up the 15th hairpin, I cut through the crowd of deafening fans spilling onto the road in their excitement, caught up in the adrenaline of our struggle. On the Alpe d'Huez, it truly was a fight.

If the Tourmalet was one long torture device, the Alpe d'Huez was 21 punches in the face – well, in the stomach or the balls would be more accurate – with a punishing gradient.

I was all alone. Derek had held on until the first two hairpins, but then it had been adios. A guy from another team had stuck with me for another three, but he was gone now too. Up ahead, I caught the occasional flashes of Gaetano Maggioli's arse and if that wasn't a powerful motivator to overtake him, I didn't know what would be.

'*De Jong's taken the stage, C,*' I heard Alan's voice in my ear. Even though I'd known I had no chance to catch him, the cold dip of disappointment in my gut made me wobbly for a few metres before

I swallowed it down. The news hurt, but it wouldn't stop me. The win wasn't the only thing I was racing for.

'How much… time… have I made up?' I managed to ask. It was tempting to ease off the effort, click down a few gears and cruise up more comfortably but, if I was gaining time, then I'd push it.

'*Listen to your body*,' Alan warned me, but then he answered my question. '*Gretsch has lost time in the minutes. If you can keep it up, you'll jump a few places.*'

I could definitely hang on for that. Thinking of Leesa's sweet little kiss last night, I set to it. I rolled over the line fifth, but the surge of lactate and adrenaline and endorphins, particularly the endorphins from seeing Leesa whistling with her fingers in her mouth, felt entirely life-giving. The jump from 13th place overall up to 10th didn't hurt either.

Spite, I thought, glancing at Leesa again as I wobbled towards a warm-down bike. Today was for spite. Tomorrow could be for stubbornness. I already knew I was going to go again, maybe even earlier than I had today. There were only two mountain stages left and I was going to attack one of them, then hold on for Paris.

At the evening strategy briefing, I lounged in a chair with a kind of artificial calm that wouldn't have fooled Leesa. But when Dad opened the briefing, his words seemed to electrify all of my nerve endings with anticipation — of chaos, of a well-fought battle, of *excitement*.

'Well, boys, there's a big change forecast in the weather overnight. We've got ourselves some fog rolling in.'

Bring on tomorrow.

I'd been saving this particular merchandise for a special occasion, but stubbornness had decided that today was special, so I made sure I was downstairs early again and kept watch for her.

My phone buzzed with a message and I pulled it out of my pocket to give the screen a cursory glance before returning to my vigil, except my gaze snagged on the device when I saw who the message was from: Fergie, the chief mechanic.

*I've found it. You're lucky it was still with us, as it's retired from service. The wheels are a lost cause, but I've found the rest of it and we're putting it together, like you asked me to. Let me know if we should proceed.*

Of course we would proceed. This was my big chance, my 'actions-speak-louder-than-words', because it was clear from that doomed conversation in Gap that I was shit with words. I was typing an enthusiastic reply to Fergie and nearly missed her appearing on the stairs. Giving up on the message for now, I hot-footed it to the breakfast room and hovered by the buffet, waiting for her to approach.

Just as I'd hoped, she made a beeline for the coffee machine, so I enacted my plan and then sidled away, feeling her sharp look between my shoulder blades and turning back to watch the results when I thought it was safe.

Her hair was mussed this morning, which only made me think about all the ways I'd dishevelled her over the past few weeks. Her cheeks were ruddy and I guessed even the support team got a bit strung out during the Tour. She grabbed the nearest coffee cup and I closed my fist in glee to see this playing out exactly as I'd planned.

She shoved it beneath the coffee machine, but then stilled, drew back, then ducked to peer at the mug. She turned to eyeball me as though in slow motion.

'What's this?'

'Your new favourite mug.'

'Please tell me it's not Rick Astley this time,' she said, waiting for the heat-sensitive picture to appear and failing to disguise the amusement in her tone.

'You liked the Rick Astley mug,' I accused tentatively.

'It's a nasty song to have in your head,' she insisted. 'But I still have it.' Her admission was enough to power me for several kilometres – uphill – today.

'This one's better. It's got a pun on it. You like puns, right?'

'Who doesn't like puns?'

She pretended she wasn't holding her breath, but she totally was. When the picture came up, she didn't quite grant me the chuckle I'd been after.

'Erm, that is a very weird picture of your face stuck onto a piece of bacon.'

When she put it like that, it wasn't a very good joke. Swiping the mug to tamp down my panic, I pointed to the text. '"Don't go bacon my heart" – see there? And it's a different song to get in your head.'

'I get it, Colin,' she said. But she smiled indulgently and pressed another little kiss to my mouth and that was my day saved.

I thought maybe she was starting to get what I was doing. Spite had got me a long way. Stubbornness would win today – whatever place I managed. And at the end of the Tour, I would gather my pride to lay everything on the line for her – for us.

## Leesa

We all had the sense that this was the day that things would change.

All the riders lined up at the start, the GC leader in the yellow jersey right at the front in the middle, flanked by the leaders of the mountain and sprint classifications in the polka-dot jersey and the green jersey, as well as the holder of the white jersey, the fastest rider under 26. Behind them was the usual chaos of 200-odd bicycles, minus the 30 who'd already pulled out.

But I only saw one.

I wasn't ready for this – these feelings. He surely wasn't either. But whatever he'd done to me couldn't easily be undone. Most likely we were headed for heartbreak whenever this thing fell apart. Right now, though, we were both on the same piece of the earth and I wanted to remember this for the rest of my life.

He leaned casually on his bike frame, one powerful leg propped on the pedal. The Southern Cross tattoo with the Olympic rings was visible on his forearm next to a raised, speckled scab from the crash. I felt as though his face had changed over the past two weeks.

But the same cheeky smile formed on his lips when he caught sight of me. He gestured to his thigh and then mimed a beating heart – as though he knew that tattoo would always remind me of this time. Then he blew me a kiss and nothing could have stopped me blowing one back.

'It's all right!' he called over the top of the clank of bicycles and the excited murmurs of the crowd. 'You'll be there at the end regardless of what happens, right?'

You bet I would. I gave him a soft nod, but then stretched onto my toes, holding a hand near my mouth to amplify my words. 'But it would be better if you won!'

His grin was wide and infectious and so damn charming I should have used it for marketing and not kept it to myself, but that one was not going on the grid. With one more wave, he turned for the start line, head down, eyes up.

He was heading into this moment with everything he had, forging his own path.

The first half of the race was wild, with a gruelling climb almost as soon as they headed out. At over 6,000 feet of altitude, there was snow in places in a bizarre juxtaposition with the weathered and sunburned cyclists. A group of riders attacked early, but when the fourth-place rider joined them, the peloton reeled the group back in.

Watching the footage of the epic descent on the other side as the team bus lumbered in the direction of the finish line, I held my breath. I wouldn't put it past Colin to attack. It took a certain daredevil spirit to attack on such a steep descent, where every curve was technical – and dangerous. Colin had the head – and the heart – for it. But the restless peloton thundered down together, not letting anyone break free.

In the jagged hills that followed, the fog descended, as though an overenthusiastic TV exec had thought smoke machines would heighten the drama of the event, when in reality it meant that the viewers didn't have much chance of understanding what was going on. Trying to keep track of all the riders was a nightmare that caused Tony another square inch of baldness.

The lights of the neutral support motorbikes blinded the cameras, turning the riders into blurred chunks of colour. The mountains were interminable, even if we couldn't see them from where the bus was now parked at La Toussuire, a ski area nestled in an alpine meadow that was usually neon-green but today was green-grey.

The peloton curled its way towards us, passing the Col du Lautaret, the infamous Col du Galibier, Col du Télégraphe, long and arduous ascents followed by an epic descent that grew more dangerous with the reduced visibility, until the riders burst out of the fog in the next valley.

'There's a break! Someone's gone! Who is it?' Tony was shaking a finger at the screen. 'Did he make it?'

Three riders had made it clear of the peloton on the descent and were accelerating away, throwing their energy into an attack to see if it would last as far as the finish line. Colin would be with them, surely.

'*Gerritsen, Mackelden and Den Otter,*' the commentator managed eventually and Tony collapsed back into his seat. Colin was still in the peloton as they swept down, down, 6,000 feet down. Next came the ascent to the Col de la Croix-de-Fer, 30 km of relentless climbing – and waiting to see if Colin would give chase.

The peloton pushed the speed at the beginning of the climb, dropping rider after rider and slowly closing the gap on the breakaway. Then they were sucked up into the veil of fog, the coverage eerily quiet as even the spectators struggled to see what was going on a few feet from their faces. The bunch looked ghostly, all shadow and movement.

'*Nellie's cooked and Derek got dropped,*' we heard Alan report over the radio. That meant fewer riders to support an attack, when Colin chose his moment.

Through some miracle, I found him on the screen, out to one side, his orange helmet showing up against the dim background – and he was up out of the saddle.

I stood out of my seat. 'There! This is it! He's going! Oh, my God, he's going. He's going to attack!'

His movements, up and down, a little side to side as he used all of his weight to propel his bike forward, were almost hypnotic on the screen, his body elegant and powerful, but I could see his chest heaving, his cheeks blooming red with exhaustion.

Now we waited to see if he could create a gap away from the peloton – and then if he could catch the breakaway.

No one went with him, which was the worst. Taking turns to shield each other from the air resistance always felt a little better than struggling up alone. But Colin didn't hesitate or stop. He didn't even bother to look behind him. He was all in – the way he was with everything that truly meant something to him.

The camera followed him as he battled the climb and the fog, pushing 10 m of distance between himself and the peloton, then 20. His stats would be going haywire: power and heartrate shooting high. But he kept it up, push after push, using his weight on the pedals.

*'It's a stunning attack from Gallagher, all on his own – the sort of thing we see from him on his brilliant days. No one else dared. If he pulls this off, it would be legendary, but surely the peloton won't let him get away, not when he's still within striking distance of the young rider classification. It's clear now what he wants and after that crash in the Pyrenees, he's got some guts to still be going for it.'*

I couldn't have written better marketing copy myself.

*'But surely he won't make it all the way, not from here.'*

The commentator was probably right. Colin could be proud of an attack like that regardless of the outcome, especially since he caught the breakaway just before the top of the pass. There were 50 km to go and two more climbs. I wasn't sure how I was supposed to survive it.

# Chapter 39

## Colin

I'd come too far to stop now, even though I could taste metal in my mouth and my stomach was threatening to eject its contents all over the road. I would see the endless grey bitumen in a foggy haze in my dreams tonight. Maybe I wouldn't be able to stop, my legs might lock and I'd keep going until my blood poisoned my lungs and that was it: game over.

But in a few minutes… just a few minutes, Leesa might put her arms around me again. I knew this was the last climb, but I also knew the last climb always felt three times as long as the rest of the stage.

*Steady, breathe…*

There was only Den Otter with me now; the other two from the breakaway had fallen back, exhausted. The Dutchman was looking worse for wear – although I knew I was too. But I had more pride. I was certain of that. My pride always flared when I was knocked down, when I was low and frustrated and a little bit desperate.

And when I thought of Leesa putting her hand in mine, despite my years of acting up, growing up so I could meet her in a place where we were level – like the top of this fucking mountain – I was more than a little desperate to get there.

Alan's voice came over the radio, vibrating with a restless quality that was odd for him. *'1 km, C. You're doing it. They can't catch you now. The peloton is too far behind. You're knocking it out of the park. Steady as she goes. Don't blow up now!'*

The fog was a kind of embrace as the seconds ticked by, accompanied by Alan's updates on my progress towards the blessed end of this torture. I should have been looking at my instruments. We had tested exactly how long I could keep up these levels of power, but I was running on instinct, feeling my own limits.

This was my heart on the line. Win or lose, I would show Leesa what I was made of, what I would throw into a relationship with her. I would goddamn *make* it possible to stay together.

'*500 m!*' came Alan's voice, high-pitched with excitement now.

I heard Leesa's voice in my head: *It would be better if you won!*

The road was lined with spectators jostling for a good view behind the barriers, cheering and whistling as they got their show: two escapees on their way to defeating the peloton, about to fight it out for the stage win, because second place wasn't even close to a consolation.

Hyper-aware of Den Otter, clinging to my wheel now, I decided this stage was *mine*. Not for Dad – or Mum – or PowerFuel or any other sponsor. For the guys, yes, because without them I wouldn't be here, grabbing this moment by the balls. But *my* name was going to be on the record today.

I felt my opponent about to try, a slight change in the fog between us, but I was quicker, jolting my body right back up to maximum. My lungs burned. I felt as though someone had turned me inside-out and my organs were hanging off my skin. But none of that mattered. It didn't matter that I could barely see through the encroaching blackness at the edges of my vision.

The finish line was just ahead. Three more seconds – the longest of my life. The road was clear before me. Den Otter couldn't catch me. The line was hazy and jagged in my brain, but I raised my arms over my head and bellowed from somewhere deep inside me.

Stage 16: Colin Valerio Gallagher, Harper-Stacked. My first stage win. My first *everything* – with Leesa watching. I was never going to let her go.

The first thing I did, before I even stopped rolling, was clap Julian den Otter on the back. He'd had an epic day and we would face each other again without a doubt. The second thing was scan the crowd for the one face I wanted to see, finding her easily, as she was rushing through the mêlée as though I'd just survived a hostage situation, not simply a stage of the Tour de France.

I managed to get my feet down to catch her, hauling her tight against me as the bike clattered, forgotten, to the ground. With a whump, everything in me settled. No more restlessness.

Her hands gripping my face, she made a sound suspiciously like a sob and then her mouth was on mine, tight and urgent. One hand on the back of her head, I deepened the kiss to scalding, setting off all the sparks we'd always had and feeding the flame inside me that was just for her.

There was no way I wasn't saying it. I took a moment to marvel that this was happening, that she was peering up at me, tear-stained cheeks and the chin dimple I adored, then with one more gentle, soothing kiss, I looked her in the eye and said the words that had lived in me for a lot longer than I'd ever admitted. 'I love you, Lees.'

Those gorgeous eyes widened. 'You… what?'

It wasn't the most flattering response, but her arms tightened around my neck.

'Shhh,' I managed gently. 'I know, it hasn't been straightforward between us and I screwed up a lot, but I've loved you for such a long time. I loved you before I knew what that meant, let alone what to do with it. Yeah, maybe at the beginning, I didn't know you well, but these past few weeks… You're so real to me now and I love you so much more than I—' My voice gave out and I had to blink away the spots in my vision.

'Hey.' It was her turn to soothe me, wrapping her arms around my chest and holding me up as Chris rushed to help me stumble to the team area. He pressed a recovery drink into my hand and I guzzled it greedily and demanded another with a flick of my hand.

I stayed standing for another half a second before my legs gave out and Leesa had to ease me to the ground.

'Take it easy, champ,' she said with a smile I could hear in her voice. 'I'm not going anywhere. You've got time to tell me all about it later.' She smoothed my hair off my forehead and I leaned my head on her shoulder with a groan.

'You are going somewhere – after Paris.'

Her sigh was eloquent. 'We can try to make it work. Maybe I can look for work in Eur—'

I shook my head, vehemently enough that it hurt and I had to squeeze my eyes shut for a moment. 'No.'

'No?' I loved that doubtful tone.

A smile touched my lips. 'I will not accept you making sacrifices just because my life is a circus. I've started looking for a place in California for the off-season.'

That stole the wind right from her lungs. She gawked at me, another expression to add to my favourites. 'You *what*? What does Tony think of this?'

'It's not his life,' I said with a shrug. 'It's mine and I want you in it. I just won a fucking stage of the Tour de France, but the thing I really want? More than all of this?'

I clutched her shoulders while I let the dramatic pause have its effect.

'I want to make you happy. I want to hold you and ground you, treasure that clever brain of yours and sometimes make it shut up so you can just enjoy life. I want to be wherever you are as much as I possibly can. I'm yours, Leesa,' I said emphatically. 'I always have been and unless you tell me to fuck off, I always will be.'

### Leesa

My brain had well and truly checked out for the evening. No thoughts for the cameras pointed right at us, sniffing out a story even more thrilling than Colin taking the stage win despite his awful crash less than a week ago. I wasn't even worried about stealing the limelight when, really, the news should be him and not… us.

I didn't care about anything except the words spilling out of him, raw and untainted by his usual bravado, the words I understood now he'd been working up to all week. He loved me

– enough that he was willing to upend his own life so I didn't have to sacrifice mine. There was no 'Let's try this out long-distance.' No, that wasn't Colin Gallagher's style.

He loved me and that meant all in. That meant for real – through thick and thin – because that's the person he was, the person I'd only seen clearly for the first time five weeks ago on training camp, although I'd caught glimpses over the years.

'I told you it was just a crush,' he continued, 'but it was always more than that. I never thought you'd see anything in me. First I was too young and then I was… an idiot.'

It was difficult to believe that, under everything he'd said and done, he'd always been hiding this depth of feeling, but I also couldn't doubt him, not today – not after everything he'd planned and executed over the past few days. Thinking of the years he'd lived with unrequited feelings for me, there was only one way I could respond – with my own surprising truth.

'You know what?' I began, my lungs tight with the words ready to pour out.

'What?'

'I love that idiot – so much.' With the words out, the truth of them only seemed to sharpen. My journey to that declaration had been longer, but I'd fallen in just as deep.

The disbelieving smile that formed on his face felt like a mirror and his breath hitched, which probably wasn't good for him right now.

'You're still with me, right?' I grasped his face in my hands – dusty, smeared with sweat and tanned from his helmet straps. 'Don't keel over now. I've got a long future I want to live with you.'

'You won't get rid of me that easily,' he mumbled. 'And I'll remember that you said you want to live with me.' His arms came up and tugged me closer.

'I have to tell you,' I whispered in his ear, 'I'm not a very tidy person.'

'I can handle that, Kubicka. Now tell me again.' He lifted his chin to prompt me.

'What? I love you?'

'That's the one,' he said with a smile, stretching up for a kiss that was soft and slow.

'None of that now! We need to get him recovered and ready for the podium protocol! My boy! On the podium! You beaut, he did it!'

Instead of listening to his dad and drawing away, Colin's hand came up to hold me where I was. 'Screw the podium. Leesa Kubicka is in love with me. I officially win *everything*.'

I pushed at him. 'Go! You've worked so hard for this.'

His arm snaked around my waist. 'I've worked harder for *this*.'

Smiling down at him, I nodded. 'I know that now. But I want to see my idiot on the podium!'

Then Tony's shrill voice added some of the only words capable of knocking some sense back into Colin: 'In white! He did it! He made up two-and-a-half minutes with that mad effort. He'll be on the podium in *white*!'

# Chapter 40

## Colin

For the first time in my life, I understood and appreciated that the final stage of the Tour wasn't contested like the others. It had never made sense to me that the general classification riders would cruise into Paris together, so no time was made or lost. But today, I needed the gentle journey to come to terms with what I'd achieved – and the affirmation of the crowds on the Champs-Élysées to make it all real.

No more rolling my eyes at sports psychology; I'd proven it was possible. The Tour hadn't played out the way Dad and Alan had planned, but that was part of the experience – the part I relished most. With 3,000 km in my muscles and victory in my blood, it was the freedom I'd fought for – to discover my own motivations and priorities – that had made the biggest difference.

I was rolling into Paris a different person, someone who didn't have to play a part – except maybe for a joke.

Derek, Amir and Nellie were close by, Derek's grin growing wild as he took in the throngs of fans lining the iconic avenue of limestone buildings, plane trees and a century of cycling glory. I would never deserve their support and sacrifices, but I was so glad to have them, to share this moment with them, after everything we'd been through together.

Pedalling with no hands, I raised my arms above my head to whip up the crowd, enjoying the privilege this jersey gave me to demand cheering and wolf whistles.

'Gallagheeer!'

A fan held a sheet spray painted with my name and a stylised kangaroo and I sent him a thumbs up as I passed. My favourite was an enormous piece of cardboard with the block letters 'Gallaghers' and sketches of me *and* Lori. I tossed the fan my bidon for that.

Approaching the finish line under the yellow arch, my lungs were tight but not with the usual strain I felt this close to the end of a race. My throat was clogged with two months – or 25 years – of emotions. In the team area would be my dad *and* mum, this time brought together by something I'd done, rather than torn apart. And Leesa would be there too, waiting for me. For *me*.

She'd be wearing the beetle pendant I'd slipped into her hood yesterday, making her shriek when she found it – but then her eyes lit up at the gift. She was aware of my flaws and knew how to deal with them. When I'd sent her fake spam emails from the 'Colin Gallagher Appreciation Club', which thankfully didn't exist, she'd signed me up for the real newsletter of the Saskatchewan Moustache and Beard Association. But somehow, she'd still agreed to come along on this wild ride with me and I would never take that for granted, would always be desperate to see her.

I was particularly desperate to see her today, for my biggest prank ever – and a long-overdue confession about what I'd done back in September last year. I'd presented her with a helmet this morning before we set off, with the promise that she'd get the rest of her gift after today's stage. Maybe the suspense wasn't all that kind, but I wanted her feeling the drama with me today and she'd proven she was a good sport. She had to be, considering everything I wanted for our future.

With a bruised ulna, scabs and scratches, legs like overcooked mutton and a pounding heart, I finished the Tour de France – and rolled into the rest of my life.

After we wiggled through the finish area to the team bus, the boys fell on me, oblivious to the fact that just about every place on my body hurt somehow. Nellie rubbed my hair into a mess. Amir squeezed until he reshaped my ribcage. Derek's shrill cry in my ear as he slung an arm over me just about burst an eardrum. But I grabbed them back, laughed and crushed them in hugs.

'You're not gonna get all emotional on us, are ya?' Derek asked, looking suddenly alarmed.

'Save it for your old woman,' Nellie advised with a grin.

'Go right ahead and get emotional,' Amir contradicted both of them. 'I'll tease you about it for the rest of your career.'

I gave him a slap on the back that was more a shove. 'It's a pleasure to share the prize money with you lot' was what I said in the end. I could have said more – with a lot more feeling – but there was someone else I wanted to celebrate with and I'd just caught sight of her, hanging back behind my parents, who were barrelling this way.

'Gimme a sec,' I said, darting out of Dad's path with the skill of a soccer player. Her eyes widened to see me heading for her, but she shouldn't have been surprised. I obviously had some work still to do, proving my commitment – which shouldn't be a problem, since I had the sign from September, ready to show her.

I scooped her up before she had a chance to say anything. Her arms clinging to my neck and her hitched giggle of happiness were the final pieces I'd needed for the enormity of the moment to settle in my chest. There were definitely cameras on us, but I didn't mind, as long as it wasn't *her* interrupting this moment with that PowerFuel phone. I didn't mind if the world saw how far gone in love I was with this woman.

One kiss became three, growing softer, more intense with every second. She stayed with me, her mouth clinging just as much as her arms, and I knew holding the heavy glass trophy on the podium later wouldn't feel as good as this.

'Come on, son! There'll be time for smooching later.'

I groaned when Dad's words made Leesa pull back with a guilty – but very cute – blush. Dad probably wanted me to sign autographs, wave for the cameras, do the publicity work that kept the financial gears oiled.

But instead of pushing me towards the waiting media, he wrapped me in a fierce hug, holding on with both arms. 'You raced a belter, son,' he said. Was his voice shaking? 'Taught your old dad a thing or two. I'm happy to see you succeed but, my

God, I'm impressed by your fight, even if you don't.'

I blinked at him, not quite sure what to do with this new phase of our relationship, but looking forward to finding out. Maybe one day he'd even come to terms with the fact that I was going to spend my off-seasons in the US as long as Leesa was there.

Mum kissed my cheek and threw her arms around me. 'You'll always have this day, Colin,' she said softly into my ear. 'It's not your father's or mine. It's yours. You did it.'

'You'll be telling me I can win yellow, next,' I said with a grin but shook my head to warn her, when she appeared about to say just that.

Her gaze darted to Leesa and back. 'Looks serious,' she commented.

I dropped my voice. 'She'll be your daughter-in-law one day,' I said as casually as I could, ignoring the way Mum gaped in shock.

Untangling myself from my parents, I went straight back to Leesa, grasping both of her hands.

'If everyone can just chill out, I need a moment with Kubicka.'

She eyed me warily.

'Don't worry. It's good,' I said, a grin stretching off my face that didn't seem to reassure her. 'Come with me.'

## Leesa

'If you're trying to prank me, I'm not sure this is the time,' I said with a laugh as Colin dragged me around the back of the team bus. There were no cameras around here, which had possibilities. I slid my fingers between his. 'But if you brought me here to make out, that's a great idea.'

'Ahem.'

There might not have been any cameras, but we weren't alone. I belatedly noticed Doug Ferguson, the chief mechanic, watching us expectantly, holding a gleaming aero bike by the saddle.

It had beautiful paintwork – graduating colours in orange and blue for the team, with white and pink added for a sunset effect. How I'd loved that look when Harper-Stacked had unveiled it for the women last year. I approached with a smile, stroking the top bar fondly. I could immediately tell this bike was my size.

I shot Colin a grateful look. 'You got Doug to tell you my measurements.'

He shrugged and dipped his head to one side. 'Not exactly. Look closer.'

Tracing my fingers along the bar, I brushed the remnant of an old sticker just behind the stem, in the place where our names were printed for transport. The rest of the bike was polished and glossy, but this sticker, peeled off on one end, had been left there. I thought of that Steve Buscemi sticker years ago, one of the many memories that I was beginning to treasure. But this old sticker wasn't a photo. It was the few remaining letters of the name of the person who had piloted this bike.

It read, '—bicka.'

This wasn't a prank. It was a gift. A bike, yes, but more than that. *My* bike... I shoved my hand to my mouth as my vision swam with tears. He was giving me back this part of myself I'd thrown out when it hurt too much. But I was stronger now, with a future full of possibilities. I could get back on this bike and remember the losses — and the win.

The *win*. The Great Ocean Road Race last year.

My gaze snapped up to his. 'This is—' I couldn't finish the sentence. My jaw wobbled and I clutched the handlebars a little desperately.

'It is. Took a bit to find it, but you can thank Fergie and the team at headquarters for that.'

And Colin Gallagher, who'd been there that day, cheering me on, and I hadn't realised.

I took the handlebars gingerly when Fergie urged me to. 'My career was kind of lacklustre, you know,' I murmured, not minding the truth of that statement just now. 'Except for that day.'

His arms slipped around my waist and he rested his chin on my shoulder. Doug slipped away with an awkward smile.

Pressing a kiss to my temple, he spoke in my ear, his deep voice with this earnest tone growing familiar. 'It's not all about your results. When I watched you ride, there was so much life in you. You *glow* on a bike — as well as looking fucking hot.'

I elbowed him gently.

'Is this a fancy way to make sure I keep riding?'

'I'd like to ride together, but you don't have to. I can just come back to you. But something about a bike still calls to you, right? I just want you to be happy. I want you to see yourself the way I see you.'

'Well, I... think you're going to see me on this bike,' I joked to stave off the tears that were threatening in earnest. He'd just earned the white jersey, come fourth overall in the Tour de France, but he was still using his spare time to prepare surprises for me and insisted on moving to the States for the winter so I didn't have to choose between him and my career.

He could be impulsive and struggled with his feelings sometimes, but he'd earned my trust in so many ways and I'd never felt more *myself* with anyone.

'Uh, one more thing,' he continued, his voice low. 'Don't laugh.'

I opened my mouth to promise not to, but thought better of it. 'I'll try.'

With a roll of his eyes, he fetched a folded and sagging piece of cardboard from behind the bike, looking more uncertain than I'd ever witnessed. 'I thought you should see this.'

I recognised it before I even saw the rudimentary 'Go Leesa' scrawled in black permanent marker. Thinking back to that day in the hospital, in pain — physical and emotional — still brought a twinge of mixed feelings.

'I was such a dick that day — self-absorbed and insensitive.' I could hear how much the memory had haunted him in his tone.

'You've apologised in about a dozen ways,' I pointed out. 'And I'm still here.'

'I can't quite believe it,' he commented, brushing a thumb over my cheek. 'I screwed up badly back then, but you need to know why, even though it's fucking embarrassing.'

'Hmm?' I took the sign from him and studied it. I'd accused

him of playing a joke on me with this sign, imagining the other side had a picture of a hairy man-eating spider or maybe just a pair of googly eyes, since he'd gone through a period of sticking them onto all my stuff.

He swallowed heavily. 'Turn it over.'

My skin prickling, I did as he said to find the reverse side scribbled all over, with words written in all caps, some of them crossed out with vicious strokes of the pen. It was a clumsy attempt at meaning and I saw the struggle, the utter frustration expressed on a single piece of cardboard and if I hadn't already fallen in love with him, I would have done it then.

~~I like you.~~

~~You're beautiful.~~

~~I dream of you.~~

I'm going to <u>miss</u> you.

You're EVERYTHING to me.

~~Maybe I love you.~~

It was more than my brain could process, so I reacted on instinct, throwing my arms around his neck and holding on, the cardboard hanging from my fingers. I clutched at his hair with my other hand, wanting to shove him and yell at him, but squeezing him close instead.

After a rough kiss that felt like a sob, I sagged against him as my head spun and my heart expanded.

I felt the deep breath he took before he spoke. 'It's always been you, Leesa. For me. I didn't take it seriously in September – or all the years before – and I made everything worse and I'm still so fucking sorry. But I'm ready now – for this, for *us*. Whatever it takes. No maybes – I love you.'

Staring again at his mixed-up heart poured out onto the sign, I groped for his hand. 'I think I felt this, back in September – something of it anyway. I started seeing *you*.'

'It was almost too late.'

'It wasn't too late. You're right. I need passion in my life and my work and I need cycling – at least as a hobby. My brain has always been the dominant part of me, but it's not the only part.'

He slung his arms around me. 'Your brain and I get on just fine, but I do like all the other parts too.' There was the cheeky smile I knew well.

'I might request to stay on the PowerFuel account,' I said thoughtfully. 'I think I might be an *ass*-et.'

That earned me a playful swat on the backside, which I'd known it would.

'You're more than an asset. You're a genius.' He punctuated his sentence with a smacking kiss on my cheek. 'Whatever you want to do, we'll make it work.'

Amazingly, I believed him. 'We will.'

'We absolutely will,' he said, almost aggressively, 'or I'm quitting.'

'Do *not* let your dad hear that!'

I should have remembered that Tony Gallagher had sharp hearing for his team and an uncanny sense of timing. 'Let me hear what? Get over here, Colin! You're needed for the podium protocol.' He glanced at his watch. 'And quick smart. I have to drive down to the women's team tonight or Seb will skin me.'

'Go,' I said, giving him a push.

'I'll bring you back a bunch of white flowers,' he said, flashing his eyebrows at me as he gave me one last kiss.

'Beware Colin Gallagher bearing gifts. Are they going to spray water in my eye?'

I smiled after him. I wouldn't mind if they did. Every gift from Colin meant something. Googly eyes on a croissant, bugs in my breakfast, a mug with his face on it. A necklace. A bike. My spark. Stubbornness, pride. Himself.

He'd given me everything.

# Epilogue – two-and-a-half years later

## Leesa

Mud spatter caught me right in the face, tasting of rotted life forms, moss and iron. Visibility was 100 per cent crap. My body and mind were at maximum effort just staying up on the bike, sweat turning instantly to cold sludge.

It was glorious.

I'd discovered this adventure bike race my first year in LA. In the foothills of the Sierra Nevada I'd found a community of bike enthusiasts – with questionable sanity – who'd become friends. This event was the ultimate outlet for my constantly somewhat frustrated desire to be on a bike.

Winter in California wasn't as harsh as in Europe, but it was still damp enough out here that I had mud in my ears, inside my gloves and soaking through my winter jersey. My parents would be horrified as usual, but they were here. They were watching me race, along with two of my favourite people in the entire world: my *boyfriend* and his sister.

Making a third in the trio of people I'd grown to consider family was Seb, Lori's husband, who was somewhere behind me in the pack of daredevil cyclists currently careening down the mountain trails. It turned out they enjoyed visiting us in the States – and had sneaked off to Las Vegas last year to get married on a whim with an Obi-Wan Kenobi impersonator officiating.

As I reached the bumpy meadow with the finish line coming into view through the fog, I picked up speed on instinct, my natural reaction to the knowledge that Colin was waiting for me.

He was too chicken to race — understandable, given the cost of an injury for the whole team — but he'd be there at the finish.

He'd always be there. He'd told me every day, although not always in person or in words, and I'd started to believe him, got used to the idea that the love of my life, my *person* had turned out to be Colin Valerio Gallagher.

I'd even found my place in the sport I'd thought had killed something inside me. After two more successful Tour de France campaigns for PowerFuel, I was collecting cycling clients and trips to Europe for work, while Colin spent all his free time in California. I was beginning to receive offers for in-house marketing roles and getting closer to taking one, especially a particularly interesting opportunity with the Tour de France Femmes.

As usual, Colin hollered embarrassingly loudly when he saw me. He always made a cardboard sign for my races with amusing phrases like 'Tap here if you love me' and 'Kubicka for president'. Today I had to swipe the grime out of my eyes and still his sign wasn't quite in focus.

Hurtling over the finish line, I steered in his direction, not seeing Lori or my parents anywhere, but not minding because I was planning to smear mud all over him while I lured him into a public display of affection. But when I saw the words on the sign, I nearly fell off the bike.

Wobbling while I dismounted, I let the bike clatter to the ground, my knees turning to Jell-O as I stared at those words, which seemed to stare right back at me.

'Are you still with me, Mags? I didn't think this would come as such a surprise.'

I loved that wry tone in his deep voice. Three years ago, I would have been certain this was a prank. I knew how much earnestness he was capable of now that he'd ditched the testosterone show with me, but I still didn't trust myself to speak.

'I didn't mean to ambush you. No one's filming. I can just put this away.'

'No!' I forced out, the word sending alarm into his expression. 'I mean, don't put it away. I'm just processing.'

He approached slowly, brushing a thumb along my chin a whisper and sinking to his knees, holding the sign against his chest. He took a moment to gather himself, a moment I clung to, hoping I remembered every detail of this when I was old.

'I think,' I began lightly, 'it's customary to be on *one* knee.'

'Fuck that,' he said under his breath. 'I'm gonna beg.' I would have reassured him, but he continued before I could, his voice gravelly. 'Lees, I wanna do this… life – you know – with you. I love you so much I can't imagine not being together.' He seemed to run out of words.

'That was good. Do you wanna ask me now?'

Pointing at the sign, he said, 'Wanna marry me?' with a pout I found increasingly irresistible.

I pulled him slowly to his feet, my fingers drifting into his wavy hair. 'Yes, Colin. I want to marry you. And now can I kiss you?'

'Fucking oath, you can,' he whispered, allowing me to draw him down for a slow, searching kiss as the cardboard sign fluttered to the ground.

Perhaps it was the perfect proof of our relationship that I felt as though nothing had changed. We'd been soulmates before and we'd be married soulmates afterwards.

And he'd be nice and muddy in a minute.

Breaking off, I smeared my hands all over his face and neck, leaving a trail of muck. 'You're my "mud prize" for this race.'

'I certainly deserved that.' His arms tightened around my waist. 'But the joke's on you. We'll need a shower *together* now.'

'All right, guys, are you done with the soppy stuff?'

I looked up to see Lori approaching with my parents, Seb trailing behind with his bike. Mom made to throw her arms around me, but froze with a grimace at the state of me and settled for a squeeze of my arm.

'He was very sweet while we waited for you, telling us what he wanted to do like an excited little boy,' my dad told me as he pressed a smacking kiss to my forehead. 'He got lucky, that one.'

'He is very sweet,' I drawled.

'You were supposed to get engaged, not give yourself a heart attack,' Lori said gruffly, poking Colin with her elbow. She shoved a tablet into his hands and he peered at it, a perplexed smile turning into a grin as he flipped the tablet around so I could see it.

On the screen was an electrocardiogram graph open in the app that connected to our fitness trackers — both of our fitness trackers.

'I think this is the moment you saw the sign and all the blood drained from your face.' He pointed to a matching peak in both lines, his a gradual rise and mine a sudden spike. 'Look how long it took you to put me out of my misery.'

'You can get it framed,' Lori said drily.

But Colin caught my eye over her head and mouthed, 'A tattoo.'

I paused before following the others towards the car, heading back to retrieve the soggy cardboard sign with the words 'Marry me' scrawled in black marker. Thinking back to that 'Go Leesa' sign that had been the start of everything for me, I flipped this one over. With a chuckle and a warm glow inside, I admitted Colin Gallagher *was* sweet, as surprising as that was.

He'd drawn a picture of two jellyfish holding tentacles.

# Acknowledgements

This book was made possible through the hard work of my agent Saskia and my editor Rebecca — as well as the copy editor, proofreader, cover artist, designer and everyone at Bedford Square Publishers.

I'm especially grateful to Rachel Fitzjames for ensuring Leesa comes across as American (and doesn't say things like 'shopping trolley'). Thanks for the 'thats'! A special mention also to Katherine Dyson and Mama W for checking my Polish language and vibes. As always, thanks to the best test reader in the world, Tatiana.

I'd also like to mention this time all the kickass women cyclists on social media with a very special mention of Alison Jackson, who is an absolute legend.

My biggest thanks go to all the readers who picked up a copy of *Head Over Wheels* and took a chance on a sports romance with little guys and Lycra! It's a privilege to make up characters for you.

# About the Author

Photo credit © Tatiana Gimenez

After leaving Australia 'for a year', Leonie Mack never went home and now travels across Europe jotting down love stories wherever she goes. She has a degree in languages and is an expert at taking public transport and travelling under her own steam on foot or by bike. 'Home' is now in central Germany, in the vineyards along the Main river, where she spends her time writing happy endings in English and speaking German with bad grammar.

**leoniemack.com**

# Bedford Square Publishers

Bedford Square Publishers is an independent publisher of fiction and non-fiction, founded in 2022 in the historic streets of Bedford Square London and the sea mist shrouded green of Bedford Square Brighton.

Our goal is to discover irresistible stories and voices that illuminate our world.

We are passionate about connecting our authors to readers across the globe and our independence allows us to do this in original and nimble ways.

The team at Bedford Square Publishers has years of experience and we aim to use that knowledge and creative insight, alongside evolving technology, to reach the right readers for our books. From the ones who read a lot, to the ones who don't consider themselves readers, we aim to find those who will love our books and talk about them as much as we do.

We are hunting for vital new voices from all backgrounds — with books that take the reader to new places and transform perceptions of the world we live in.

**Follow us on social media for the latest Bedford Square Publishers news.**

**bedfordsquarepublishers.co.uk**